Praise for the Demon Underground series

"Love, betrayal, vampires, and a mystery. How much better can it get than that?"
—*That Teen Can Blog*

". . . fast paced, exciting storylines . . . The ending took me by surprise; I can't wait for the fourth book to come out!"
—*C.J. Harris, Vampire Librarian*

". . . big, shocking and intense."
—*Lara Taylor, Fresh Fiction*

Other books by Parker Blue

Demon Underground Series

Bite Me

Try Me

Fang Me

Make Me

Forget You (short story)

Dare Me

Specials

Wolf Rising (a novella) in Magick Rising

Dare Me

Demon Underground Series, Book Five

by

Parker Blue

Bell Bridge Books

Bell Bridge Books
PO BOX 300921
Memphis, TN 38130
Print ISBN: 978-1-61194-323-8

Bell Bridge Books is an Imprint of BelleBooks, Inc.

Printed and bound in the United States of America.

We at BelleBooks enjoy hearing from readers.
Visit our websites – www.BelleBooks.com and www.BellBridgeBooks.com.

10 9 8 7 6 5 4 3 2 1

Cover design: Debra Dixon
Interior design: Hank Smith
Photo/Art credits:
Cover Art © Christine Griffin
Back cover art © Unholyvault | Dreamstime.com

:Lmds:01:

Chapter One

Val

I GLANCED UP and down the dark, threatening road, lit only by an anemic flickering streetlight. "Why can you never find an evil bloodsucker when you really need one?" I muttered. Here I stood, female, a mere eighteen years old, alone but for a small dog in a scuzzy industrial area of San Antonio, looking like a prime victim. Why couldn't I get any action?

Fang, the small dog in question, poked me in the leg with his nose. HEY, YOU'RE NOT EXACTLY HELPLESS WITH ME BY YOUR SIDE.

Yeah, but they don't know that. Especially since we had the advantage of communicating telepathically. *And I'm not exactly without skills myself.*

Fang, part hellhound, part scruffy terrier mix, and all snark, snorted. YEAH, I KNOW. BUT VAL SHAPIRO WITHOUT MOJO IS KINDA LIKE . . . A REGULAR HUMAN.

As if I needed a reminder. A month and a half ago, on Christmas Eve, I'd had to use a spell in the *Encyclopedia Magicka* waaaay too many times to exorcise demons not only from my enemies, but friends and allies as well. Ever since, my own personal demon, Lola, had been weak and wimpy inside me. Hard to be part succubus when I couldn't even . . . suck.

That was the disadvantage of using the spells in the encyclopedia. The more I used a spell, the stronger it became, making any other spells or magickal abilities harder to access. Weird balancing act, especially since I hadn't been able to rebuild Lola's strength yet. After all those spells, my succubus was only at about ten percent power.

AND WHOSE FAULT IS THAT? my own Jiminy Cricket wannabe asked.

"Shade's," I muttered. Everything had been going along just fine until my supposed boyfriend, the totally hot shadow demon, turned cold and distant. No sucking any lusty male energy from *him*, not when he'd been in a mood since Christmas. And all I'd done was leave him with another succubus . . . because he *asked* me to. Men. I'd never understand them.

YOU COULD FEED ON AUSTIN, Fang suggested, waggling his eyebrows. HE'D BE MORE THAN HAPPY TO BE YOUR STUDPUPPY.

Yeah, that was the problem. The hunky cowboy vamp was only too willing, and it kinda bothered me. Especially since I enjoyed it a tad too much myself. It felt like cheating on Shade.

SO, IF YOU WON'T FEED ON AUSTIN, AND YOU CAN'T FEED ON SHADE, HOW ARE YOU GONNA BUILD LOLA BACK UP?

Well, if an evil bloodsucker would just show up, I'd feed on *him*. No guilt there. I walked down the street a ways, hunching my shoulders, letting my eyes dart around as if I were scared there was a boogeyman around every corner. *Hello, anyone there? Helpless victim here.*

Fang helped, trotting along beside me, his tongue lolling out for all the world like he was a brainless toy. SO, WITH LOLA DOWN FOR THE COUNT AND YOUR STRENGTH AND SPEED GONE, JUST HOW ARE YOU GOING TO FIGHT ANY VAMPS WHO MIGHT SHOW UP? I MEAN, I'M GOOD, BUT I DO LIKE SOME BACKUP.

I have the amulet, I reminded him, fingering the crystal teardrop hanging on a chain inside my shirt. Dina, the power-hungry succubus who tried and failed to rule the Demon Underground, had used the amulet to enhance her succubus abilities many fold, even controlling men after they left her presence. With the crystal, I could enhance Lola's abilities until I could get her back up to speed. I didn't really want to use it, but I had no choice.

I'M NOT SO SURE IT'S A GOOD IDEA TO RELY ON THAT THING, Fang said. YOU DON'T KNOW ANYTHING ABOUT IT.

I knew enough. I glared down at him. *Would you rather leave, go check on Princess? I'm sure she'd love that.* After all, the Cavalier King Charles Spaniel was heavily pregnant with Fang's puppies.

Fang shuddered. GIMME A BREAK. I JUST ESCAPED FROM HER FOR A FEW HOURS. DO YOU HAVE ANY IDEA WHAT IT'S LIKE DEALING WITH A PREGNANT HELLHOUND?

I suppressed a grin. I had a pretty good idea. Princess was demanding at the best of times. Pregnant, she must be a real bitch—pun intended. *Ah, poor Fang. You—*

But I didn't get to finish that thought as something big, strong, and incredibly fast slammed me up against a brick building. I felt a sharp pain as fangs pierced my neck. What? No foreplay?

Crap. I tried to fight back, but my strength was gone, and he had me pinned. And now that he was within Lola's field, he was enjoying it waaaaay too much.

Fang clamped his jaws on the guy's ankle, but he was wearing heavy boots, and Fang couldn't get a grip. Fear surged through me, and I shoved Lola into the vamp, yelling, "Stop," but Lola was too weak. It only made him pause for a moment.

He tried to control my mind, keep me quiet. Big mistake—his. That gave me access to his thoughts, and I realized what a cold killer Bruce here really was, how many defenseless people he'd murdered.

How could I stop him? The amulet! Concentrating, I called on it and tried harder. "Bruce, *stop*," I commanded, trying to control my panic.

That did it. He froze, fangs still at my neck, then cursed and jerked away, swatting at his rear. No wonder. Fang had jumped up and clamped his jaws on Bruce's butt.

"You can let go," I told Fang. "I got him."

YEAH, I KNOW. BUT HE PISSED ME OFF.

Fang gave one more shake then let go. The big bloodsucker stood there, awaiting my next order, my blood dripping from his fangs, and his blood dripping from his butt.

Anger surged through me, and I snatched a stake from my back waistband. Damn it, he'd almost killed me. I wanted to shove the pointy end through his heart but stopped myself. First, I'd drain every bit of energy I could out of him. I put my other hand on his chest and concentrated. Sinking Lola's energy tendrils into his chakras, I let lust for my succubus fill him then tried to pull his energy into me.

It was like sucking molasses through a straw. Lola couldn't draw hard enough, so I used the amulet to augment her puny strength. Oh, yeah, that was the ticket. The flow eased right up, and all that luscious energy surged into the empty wasteland my chakras had become. It was weirdly unsatisfying but more of a rush than usual. This could get addictive.

VAL, WATCH OUT, Fang yelled.

Another vamp was suddenly on me, yanking me away from Bruce.

"Leave him alone," she yelled.

She? Oh, crap. Lola wouldn't work on a woman. What weapons could I use on her?

Oh, yeah. Him.

"Stop her," I told Bruce.

He tried, and if I hadn't half drained him, he'd have had no problem. Instead, they were pretty evenly matched.

DON'T JUST STAND THERE, Fang said. STAKE THEM!

Yeah, I would, but they were moving too fast. If they'd just oblige by standing still for a *moment* . . .

Instead, their fight shoved them into me and knocked me off my feet. Crap. I hated being so helpless, without the strength I'd leaned on for so long.

Suddenly, a blur whizzed by me, yanking the stake out of my hand. Another vamp had joined the fray, staking first Bruce then the woman. I scrambled to my feet. What the heck . . .?

I reached out to control him before he could turn on me, too.

I'd barely sunk my energy tentacles into him when he turned and winked at me from under his Stetson. "You don't need to do that, darlin'."

Austin. I should have known. I felt a pull from the amulet, urging me to yank the annoying cowboy under my control, but I ignored it. Instead, I said, "Oh, yeah? Dare me." I yanked another stake out of my waistband and held it high in my fist.

He dropped his bloody stake by the vamps' bodies. As it clattered on the pavement, he sauntered toward me, hooking his thumbs in the loops of his jeans. He raised an eyebrow and grinned at me, daring me in return to take him on.

WHAT'S THE MATTER, VAL? HE JUST HELPED YOU.

That was the problem. I didn't want to be indebted to the sexy vampire, especially since he always seemed to be amused at my expense. When he was a couple of feet away, I said, "Stop right there. Have you been following me?"

He slowed. "Seems that way," he drawled.

"Why?"

He moved closer, not at all afraid of me or my weapon. "Because you need me."

Yeah, right. "I'm Val Shapiro, the Slayer, the Demon Underground's Paladin protector. Why would I need *you*?"

His gaze slid toward the bodies he'd staked then back to me, inviting me to make the connection myself. He didn't have to say a word.

Crap. He was right. I dropped my arm and tucked the stake back in my waistband. "Okay, so I lost some of my mojo. I'm trying to get it back."

He raised an eyebrow again, now even closer. "By getting yourself killed? What were you thinking?"

I was thinking I was bored out of my mind. My roommate, Gwen, recently turned vamp without her consent, had moved out of the townhouse to live with the good vamps in the New Blood Movement. Shade wasn't talking to me, Micah was busy rebuilding the Demon Underground, and even Fang spent more time with Princess than me.

POOR BABY, Fang crooned in my mind. SHE'S LONELY.

Oh, shut up. Out loud, I said, "Well, Micah hasn't really figured out how to use me yet, and I don't have anything else to do. Why do you care?"

"Because we—the Movement and the Underground—need you."

"So why have you appointed yourself my protector?"

"You need me. Until you're better able to defend yourself."

I touched the wound on my neck where the vamp had pierced my vein. It was still bleeding. That had been close. Too close. Maybe he was right. Damned if I'd admit it, though. "As soon as I'm at full strength, I'll be able to defend myself just fine." That snack on Bruce had only added a little to Lola's tank.

Austin moved even closer and looked down at me with a slow, sexy smile. "I can help with that."

Oh, jeez. "I'm not sure that's such a good idea," I murmured, taking a step back. Unfortunately, that put my back up against the wall.

"Why not? You need to rebuild your succubus powers so you can be the Slayer again." He placed his arms on both sides of my head and leaned into me, then licked my neck, slowly, sensuously.

Whoa. Sensations thrilled through me. Sensations I had no business feeling. Not with Austin. I jerked away. "What the hell do you think you're doing?"

"Using my saliva to stop the bleeding on your neck." He grinned and tried to look innocent. "What did you think I was doing?"

I gulped then glared at him. "Trying to make me uncomfortable."

TRYING? HECK, HE SUCCEEDED, Fang snarked.

Austin gazed down at me, his eyes hooded. "I'm here. I'm available. Use me, Val."

I swallowed hard and tried not to show how uncomfortable I felt. "No. You enjoy it too much," I snapped and shoved my hand into his chest to keep him at bay. Sharing lust with my boyfriend was okay, and making bloodthirsty killers drool over me so I could drain them of their sexual energy was only fair. But sharing lust with someone I didn't date and didn't stake . . . it just seemed wrong.

He backed off, and his expression went blank. "On the contrary. I don't enjoy it at all."

Huh? Lola plus male equaled lust. No exceptions to that equation. I let out a disbelieving snort.

He shrugged. "Oh, you can make my body enjoy it, but unless you're controlling me, my mind is my own."

Confused, I asked, "What does that mean?"

One side of his mouth quirked up. "My body might feel satisfied, but no real man enjoys . . . that . . . without pleasuring the woman who helped get him there."

Whoa. The sudden visual made my eyes widen. Oh, crap. I was in waaaaay over my head.

NOW THERE'S AN UNDERSTATEMENT, Fang said with a chuckle.

Austin reached out and fingered a strand of my hair. "Let go, Val. Live a little. Let me show you—"

But I didn't get to hear what he would have said, because my phone buzzed. I pulled it out of my pocket and answered it, turning away slightly so I wouldn't have to see his expression. "Hello?"

"Hi, Val, it's Micah."

"Hi, Micah," I said, letting Austin know this was probably an important phone call. A phone call I had to take which meant I couldn't possibly, thankfully, continue this disturbing conversation. "Is there a problem?"

"Yes," he said, surprising me. "Someone broke into Shade's apartment, looking for him."

"Is Shade okay?" I asked.

Fang's head popped up. PRINCESS? IS PRINCESS OKAY?

"And Princess?" I added.

"They're both fine," Micah said soothingly. "But Princess is a bit wound up. I need your help."

"My help? Why?" Shade wasn't much fun to be around lately, and neither was Princess. If they were both okay . . .

"Because you're my Paladin," Micah said. "Just come."

Fang walked toward my motorcycle, shooting a harried glance back over his shoulder. COME ON, LET'S GO.

"All right, I'll be there," I told Micah and hung up. Without meeting Austin's eyes, I said, "Micah needs me at Shade's apartment." As if he didn't already know, with his super vampire hearing and all.

"So I gathered."

I followed Fang, saying over my shoulder, "You don't need to follow me. I can take care of this myself."

"Sorry, Val," Austin said, not sounding at all regretful. "You just proved you do need help. Until you get your mojo back, you're stuck with me." Austin sauntered after me.

"Then who will take care of the bodies?" I no longer worked for the Special Crimes Unit, so couldn't call on one of their pickup units.

"I texted Alejandro while you were talking to Micah. He's sending Luis to take care of them."

Vampires texting . . . it just seemed wrong somehow.

Behind me, Austin drawled, "And now, if you're all out of excuses . . .?"

"Okay," I said, not at all graciously. "I guess I can't stop you. But don't get in my way."

"Wouldn't think of it," Austin said. Then deliberately added, ". . . darlin'."

My back stiffened, and he chuckled. "But don't think this conversation is over. We'll take it up again when we're alone."

Yeah, that's what I was afraid of.

Chapter Two

Val

I HEADED TOWARD Shade's apartment, trying to lose Austin on the way. After all, I was on my nimble Valkyrie while he had to follow in one of Alejandro's big ass luxury cars. It didn't work, though. Austin knew where Shade lived.

When I reached the apartment complex, Fang jumped off the motorcycle without even waiting for me to take off his goggles and ran to Shade's place. I caught up with him at the door and took them off.

He pawed at the door impatiently. MICAH, SHADE, LET US IN, he broadcast.

Micah opened the door, and Fang and I entered, Austin somehow right behind us. The place was trashed, Shade's beloved electronics tossed every which way. I tried to read Shade's face, to see not only how he felt about the destruction, but about having me here as well. Unfortunately, the shadow demon's expression was covered in swirling gray ribbons of light, like usual. Touching him would make him look like a normal human—a totally hot normal human—but he hadn't exactly encouraged my touch lately.

Besides, Princess, heavy with Fang's puppies, was broadcasting exactly how upset she was with the situation, the intruders messing up *her* space, treading on *her* delicate sensibilities, endangering *her* puppies. Fang tried to console her, but the pregnant hellhound was rather enjoying her whining diatribe.

I couldn't tell how much of it was true. "Was she really in danger?" I asked Micah quietly.

"Not really," he murmured as Austin helped Shade pick things up. "She hid under the bed when the two men burst in, but they weren't looking for her."

"What were they looking for, then?" I glanced around at the expensive games and computer components littering the floor. Thieves would have taken those, so they weren't common burglars. "Were they demons? Could she read their minds?"

"No," Micah said. "But Princess overheard them talking. They were looking for *el demonio de la sombra*—the shadow demon. Apparently, she picked up a bit of Spanish before we met her."

Princess had a skill? Who knew?

Micah continued, "Shade wasn't here at the time, so I guess they took out their frustration on his belongings."

"Is anything missing?" Austin asked, a battered keyboard in his hands.

Shade picked up an iPad with a smashed screen and sighed. "I haven't found anything missing yet. Just damaged." He tossed the broken tablet in the trash.

I glanced at Princess. Fang had one of his paws on hers and was nuzzling the spaniel's ear. "Did they say why they wanted Shade?" I asked her.

She cast me a mournful glance. THEY WANT TO KILL MY HUMAN, she declared.

Fear thrilled through me. Oh, crap. "Shade's in danger?" When Austin cast me a questioning glance, I told him what Princess said.

Princess let out a snort. HE CAN TAKE CARE OF HIMSELF.

Maybe, but if Shade lost his temper, bad things could happen, like popping the cork to another dimension and letting a whole bunch of rampaging evil demons into our world. "Why would they want to hurt Shade?" I asked.

I DON'T KNOW. THEY DIDN'T SAY. THEY GOT IMPATIENT AND LEFT, BUT THEY'RE PLANNING ON COMING BACK.

I wanted to question Shade, but he wasn't real communicative lately. In fact, he was doing his best to act like I wasn't there. I glanced at Micah, hoping he'd know the answer.

Micah asked for me. "Shade, do you know of any reason why someone would want to kill you?"

Austin raised an eyebrow at that, but I couldn't read Shade's expression since he was still all swirly.

"No," Shade said. "No idea."

Shade wasn't the type to piss anyone except me off, so I didn't have a clue either.

YOU MUST PROTECT US, Princess insisted, looking at Micah.

THAT'S MY JOB, Fang said. AND VAL'S. YOU CAN COME STAY WITH US.

What? Whoa. I wasn't sure I wanted to deal with Princess's whining and Shade's moods right now.

WHAT'S THE PROBLEM? GWEN IS STAYING AT ALEJANDRO'S, SO SHADE CAN USE HER ROOM.

We had the space, true, but . . . "Can't Shade stay with you?" I asked

Micah.

"I'll stay here," Shade said, biting the words out. "I can take care of myself *and* Princess."

Whoa, he sounded determined . . . and totally pissed. For some reason, that made Austin smile and quirk his eyebrow in disbelief. Annoying man.

Micah frowned. "But who will take care of that green cloud above your head?"

Oh crap, he was right. The gateway to the demon dimension was forming before our eyes.

"Stop," Micah ordered.

Instead, the cloud grew, snapping with a miniature lightning storm, and scaring the crap out of me. Once before, I'd stopped a portal from opening to the demon dimension by wrapping my body around Shade, using Lola to distract him before he killed himself. But he wouldn't welcome that now, and I wasn't up for rejection.

Use me, the crystal whispered.

Without consciously deciding to do so, I reached out with the amulet to touch Shade lightly, ready to use it to force him to control himself if necessary. It was so easy, effortless, as if the crystal had an affinity with the shadow demon. Maybe it did, since Dina had used it on him before.

Shocked, I realized I could see his expression, even with no one touching him. Did the amulet do that? He looked like a tortured angel, dark blond hair falling into his eyes, and his beautiful face clenched in a rictus of agony as he fought to control his anger and the portal.

"Lock it down," I said urgently.

"I'm . . . trying," he gritted out as he fumbled with his back pocket and pulled something out.

Fear spiked within me. A knife. I knew it, damn it. Shade would rather kill himself than let more demons into the world through his portal and was fully capable of slitting his own throat.

I wouldn't let that happen. "Drop the knife, Shade," I ordered. "There's no need to kill yourself. You can do this."

I was about to force him with the amulet, but there was no need. Austin was suddenly there, slamming Shade up against the wall.

"Let me go," Shade exclaimed, his eyes blazing at Austin. The cloud grew.

Austin shoved his forearm against Shade's throat and used his other hand to grab the wrist holding the knife. "You heard Val. Lock it down, *now*, or I'll kill you myself." The vamp's fangs descended, and his voice was so menacing, it scared the crap out of me.

But my outrage was even stronger. Was he *trying* to get us all killed? I leapt forward to yank the vamp away from Shade, but Fang's voice stopped me.

NO, VAL, LET IT BE. AUSTIN'S PLOY IS WORKING.

Ploy? Sure enough, I could see the struggle on Shade's face as he fought to control his anger. Evidently, though he was willing to kill himself, he wasn't willing to let Austin do it for him. Go figure.

The knife clattered to the floor, and slowly, the small green cloud dissipated.

Austin backed off, but Shade's haunting blue eyes were still blazing. He was obviously seething inside, though he managed to keep the cloud from reforming in the face of Austin's threat.

I gave Austin a nod of thanks. He just shrugged, smirked, and lounged against the wall, arms folded as if nothing had happened.

Remembering what we'd been talking about, I said, "See, there's no need for Shade to come with us. He has it together."

LIAR, LIAR, PANTS ON FIRE, Fang taunted.

Even Austin raised a disbelieving eyebrow in my direction. Didn't they get it? I didn't want to babysit Shade when he obviously didn't want me around.

Micah gave me a stern glance. "You accepted the position of Paladin, to protect members of the Underground, remember?"

How could I forget? "Yes, but—"

"This is the first time I've asked you to fulfill your promise. Are you turning me down?"

When I hesitated, Micah asked quietly, "Do we need to appoint a Lethe instead?"

I winced. No way would I condemn anyone to that sort of existence—part demon, part vampire, and all nut job. Especially since the soothsayers said the only one suitable for the position was Shade. He'd never forgive me. Shoot, I'd never forgive myself.

"You really think blackmail is the best way to motivate her?" Austin drawled.

Micah didn't take that well. "I'm simply reminding her of the consequences of her actions. What's important here is Shade's safety. I thought Val wanted that, too."

Crap. He really knew how to twist the knife. Austin was right. Micah was trying to blackmail me into doing what he wanted.

NO, Fang said flatly. HE'S JUST TRYING TO DO HIS JOB, TAKING CARE OF HIS PEOPLE. YOU'RE ONE OF THE BEST TOOLS HE HAS TO DO THAT. DON'T YOU WANT SHADE AND PRINCESS TO BE SAFE?

Now Fang was laying a guilt trip on me? *Yes, but—*

NO BUTS. YOU'RE THE BEST. WITH MY HELP, OF COURSE.

Shade muttered, "Don't I have a say in this?"

He sounded annoyed, but the anger—and the cloud—were totally gone. Then he glanced at me, and the pain and longing in his expression took my breath away.

Longing? My heart leapt in response.

Holy cow, it was like laying his soul bare without his knowledge—invading his privacy, since he had no clue I could see his expression now. Not knowing what to think, I released my light hold on him with the amulet. Sure enough, I could only see swirls again where his face was. Interesting.

"No, you don't have a say," Micah said. "Not when it means keeping the door to the demon dimension closed. Until we find and deal with the people trying to kill you, we need to keep you safe with Val."

Guess I didn't have a say, either.

LOOK ON THE BRIGHT SIDE, Fang said privately. MAYBE TIME TOGETHER WILL HELP YOU AND SHADE KISS AND MAKE UP.

Somehow, I doubted it. But one thing was for sure—*something* would come to a head. Maybe that was a good thing. Being in limbo sucked. Knowing one way or another if we had a future together would be better than not knowing at all.

I sighed, accepting the inevitable. Shade did, too, though he must dislike the idea as much as I did.

"Besides," Micah added, "Shade can use the time to digitize the *Encyclopedia Magicka.* We need the information in case the books are ever stolen again."

Was he serious? "You want to put the spells in a computer . . . where anyone can copy them to the World Wide Web and share them with the world?" What if evil mage demons surfed the Internet? The mind boggled.

"Not all of it," Micah explained. "I meant just the first book, the one that describes demons, vampires, and other nonhumans, and what we know about them. Digitizing it will give us more access—searchable access—to it, and we can add other things we've learned. And it wouldn't hurt to have Shade put together an index of the spells available to you in the other two books, either."

"I can do that," Shade confirmed.

Micah nodded. "We're not planning on sharing them on the Internet."

"That makes sense, but I'd rather not use the spells unless I have to," I protested. "They make Lola even weaker."

"No problem," Austin said. "I can hang around to help with

your . . . feeding needs."

I glared at him. Shade and Austin and me all cozy together in one place? Oh my. "Not a good idea," I said. "Tell him, Micah."

Micah looked surprised. "Why? I think it's an excellent idea. We'd be glad to have your help, Austin, if you think Alejandro can spare you."

Austin nodded. "I already told Val I'll protect her until she can rebuild Lola's strength."

"I don't need your help," I gritted through my teeth. "They're men, right? I can take care of them with the amulet."

Go ahead, show them, that small voice whispered. I stroked the crystal teardrop and called on its power, reaching out to Austin. The amulet made using Lola so easy, so pleasurable. All I had to do was slip my hooks into Austin's chakras and clamp, and he was all mine. "Tell him I don't need you," I commanded Austin.

"She doesn't need me," Austin parroted obediently.

Could Micah tell I'd used the amulet? He knew when I used Lola. But when he shot me a suspicious glance, I realized he couldn't.

NO, BUT I CAN READ IT IN YOUR MIND, Fang said. To everyone, he added, SHE USED THE AMULET TO FORCE AUSTIN TO AGREE.

Traitor. He was supposed to be helping me.

I AM, Fang insisted. BY CALLING YOU ON YOUR BAD DECISIONS.

"You used that thing?" Micah repeated incredulously and glanced at Austin.

Could they tell by looking at him that he was under my control? To me, Austin just looked more relaxed . . . and quiet. Just the way I liked him.

"That's crap, Val. That's what Dina did to me," Shade said, frowning.

Chalk up another reason Shade found to be angry with me. I allowed myself a mental shrug. What the heck—what was one more?

"Let him go," Micah said. "We don't control friends."

"I'm just proving a point," I said defensively. "I'm able to control him easily, like I would any other man who comes after Shade and Princess."

Fang snorted. ALL YOU'RE PROVING IS THAT THE AMULET IS BAD FOR YOU. I HEARD IT CALLING TO YOU, URGING YOU TO USE IT.

"So? Why shouldn't I use the amulet? Didn't you just say we should use any tools at our disposal? This is my best one."

Micah's mouth firmed. "That's probably what Dina thought, too. Maybe that's why she turned into a power-hungry dictator. Do you want to be like her?"

No, but I was no Dina. Where was the danger?

YOU DON'T NEED AN ARTIFICIAL AID TO PROTECT SHADE, Fang said. ALL YOU NEED IS LOLA. AND ME, OF COURSE. LET HIM GO.

Looked like they'd badger me until I gave in. "Okay, fine." Reluctantly, I released the vamp, but it was harder than I expected to give up that power. Having Austin around wouldn't be so bad if I could make him do what I wanted him to. "But I'm supposed to be able to protect the members of the Underground without the assistance of outsiders . . . vampires."

BUT YOU CAN'T, Fang reminded me unnecessarily. FORGET ABOUT YOUR STUPID PRIDE AND DO THE RIGHT THING.

Oh, all right. I glared at Austin. "Okay, but once I'm able to build Lola back up to full capacity, you're out of my way."

Austin rubbed his chin thoughtfully. "Agreed, if you give up the amulet."

"No way. I might need it."

Micah shook his head. "It's dangerous."

"Not to mention it's wrong," Shade added, his voice sounding tight and ticked.

YEAH. IT JUST MADE YOU WANT TO USE IT MORE.

"Forget it," I said flatly. "I'm not going to get rid of a weapon that might help me save Shade's life."

"I'd rather die than have you use that thing on me again," Shade bit out.

Whoa. "I didn't use it, Dina did," I said gently.

"You know what I meant," Shade said, not giving an inch.

Micah and Austin looked just as stubborn as Shade sounded. "Okay, what if I promise to use it only in an emergency?"

Micah and Austin exchanged uneasy glances.

"I can handle it. I swear." Sheesh. What did they think would happen?

"We'll try it," Micah said reluctantly. "But Fang will monitor you. If it gets too strong a hold on you, I'm taking it away."

Annoyance flared within me. He could try. Too bad the amulet wouldn't work on an incubus, or I'd force *him* to do what I wanted.

SEE? Fang said. THAT'S THE KIND OF THOUGHT YOU WOULDN'T HAVE HAD BEFORE. THAT AMULET'S DANGEROUS.

Was it? Maybe. Maybe not. "I said okay, didn't I? I just need to rebuild Lola's strength so I won't need it."

"Good," Micah said. My mulish expression must have tipped him off, because he added, "You'll accept Austin's help, Val. As the leader of the Demon Underground, I insist. It's your responsibility to protect Shade and Princess to the best of your ability. Using Austin is the best way to do that . . . unless you know of someone else who will volunteer to let you feed on them?"

I glanced at Shade, wanting to use the amulet on him, force him to step up. I resisted it . . . barely. With no verbal clue from him, I realized that I wasn't going to get any help from Mister Swirly Face, not even to save his own butt.

"Okay, fine," I muttered, then changed the subject. "Can the Special Crimes Unit help with finding out who did this?" Normally, the SCU only dealt with keeping the unaffiliated vampires from snacking on the tourists, but they might also be able to find a clue as to who was looking for Shade and why. Maybe even be there as back-up in case Shade's would-be captors showed up again.

Micah nodded. "I was just about to call Lieutenant Ramirez." While he was at it, Micah also called in a couple of his people to transport Shade and Princess along with their things to my townhouse.

"Looks like you'll have back-up for a while," Austin said. "I need to go back to the mansion, let Alejandro know what's going on. I'll meet you back at the townhouse."

Shade and Austin and me, all together and cozy-like? Oh, joy.

Unfortunately, there was nothing I could do to stop him.

Chapter Three

Austin

FOR THE SECOND time that day, Austin slammed a man up against the wall. This time it was Luis in the basement of the mansion. Austin wanted to rip the vamp's head off, but satisfied himself with shoving his face into Luis's instead. "What do you think you're doing?"

Luis didn't resist. He merely glared back. "Your job," the aristocratic Spaniard snapped back. "Someone has to train the new ones, and you haven't exactly been around, have you?"

For good reason, but Austin didn't owe Luis an explanation. Luis sure owed him one, though. Gwen and Elspeth cowered in the corner of the basement sparring room. Though the walls and floors were padded, and there were no furnishings to get in the way, the two still had cuts, scrapes, and bruises all over their bodies. They'd heal soon, but it still pissed Austin off, not least because he felt guilty for leaving them to suffer Luis's brutal training methods.

"Terrorizing is not training," Austin bit out. Frustrated, he gave Luis one last shove against the wall then backed off, clenching his fists and vowing to *not* let the man provoke him.

Luis straightened his shirt and brushed some nonexistent lint from his sleeve. "They need to learn how to handle themselves in a fight against hunters and rogue vamps. My methods may be harsh, but they work. You're too soft."

"Not soft. Effective. All you do is destroy their confidence, make them even easier prey."

Luis sneered. "That's your opinion."

"No, that's why I'm in charge of training, and *your* job is to work the political angles. How's that going for you, Luis?" Austin mocked.

He knew the answer—not well at all. Luis was supposed to lobby to pass legislation in Texas that would require all vampires to subscribe to the creed of the New Blood Movement and afford them protection under the law while outlawing the rogues. Doing so would make the climate right for the Movement to reveal itself, but that initiative had stalled.

"That's irrelevant," Luis said, scowling.

"Is it? I don't think so. I think that's why you're trying to horn in on my business, because yours is so badly screwed up."

Luis took a threatening step forward and shoved his face in Austin's. "Talk about screwed up. I'm trying to make sure they're trained, to save them and us. Someone has to."

"Look, bud—" Austin began.

"What's going on here?" Alejandro demanded from the doorway, Rosa right behind him.

Out of respect for Alejandro, Austin backed away from Luis but kept his mouth shut. This was between him and Luis.

"Just a little disagreement in training methods," Luis said, his expression bland.

Alejandro scowled. "We have enough problems without two of my lieutenants at each other's throats." Alejandro glanced at Gwen and Elspeth, who had regained their composure. "Are you all right?"

Elspeth lifted her chin and glared. "Yes. We know combat training is necessary in our new lives, and we don't object to it, but the manner in which we are being taught is most displeasing."

Alejandro nodded. "Luis, training is Austin's responsibility. Leave him to it," he said dismissively.

About time Alejandro put Luis in his place. Luis gave Alejandro a short, jerky bow then strode out of the room, his expression rigidly controlled.

Facing Gwen and Elspeth, Alejandro said, "Ladies, if you would excuse us?"

He gestured toward the door, and the two women took his hint and left. Only Rosa stayed behind. The beautiful Latina had her hand possessively on Alejandro's arm, but he didn't seem to notice. Or did he?

Austin didn't understand the relationship between these two. Rosa obviously yearned for Alejandro with all her heart, but if Alejandro realized it—and Austin didn't see how anyone could miss it—he never let it show in public. Nor had he ever taken advantage of what she offered, so far as Austin knew. In fact, Alejandro never dallied with anyone, female or male. Either that, or he was the most discreet person on the planet.

Alejandro played his cards, whatever they were, very close to his vest. So why did he let her touch him so possessively?

When Rosa saw Austin watching her, she snatched her hand away. And, as she obviously believed the best defense was a swift offense, she glared at Austin. "Where have you been? Alejandro has been looking for you."

Austin raised an eyebrow at her. They were equals, she and he. He didn't have to answer to her. And she probably didn't expect it, either. Undoubtedly, she was trying to cover her embarrassment. She glanced away, confirming his suspicion.

"May I talk to you alone?" he asked Alejandro.

"Of course," Alejandro said graciously. "Rosa, if you don't mind . . .?"

He glanced at her and smiled. It was a polite smile, as smiles go, but Rosa beamed as if he'd declared his undying love. "I do mind," she said, slanting an annoyed glance at Austin. "But if you wish it, I'll go and leave you two to your secrets."

Alejandro nodded. "Thank you." Rosa left, and as there was no seating in the sparring room, the two of them remained standing. "I have not seen much of you of late," Alejandro said.

Austin winced. Alejandro's tone wasn't disapproving, but Austin laid a guilt trip on himself anyway. If he hadn't shirked his responsibilities, Luis wouldn't have interfered. "I know. I've been protecting the Slayer."

"Oh?" Alejandro raised an eyebrow in inquiry. "And why is that?"

Austin refused to feel defensive. But he didn't have to tell the whole truth, either. "She's vulnerable now. You know that."

"And you feel it's your responsibility to watch over her?"

Annoyed, Austin said, "She exposed Lily as a traitor for us, got rid of mage demons who threatened both the Demon Underground *and* our Movement, became the keeper of the *Encyclopedia Magicka*, and took down a corrupt demon leader who would have caused us trouble. I think we owe her. Besides, didn't the soothsayer say that Val is key to getting what you want?"

"I'm not disputing that," Alejandro said. "I asked why you feel it's *your* responsibility to repay her."

"I'm one of your lieutenants. Who better?" Austin challenged.

"Again, I'm not arguing with your ability, merely your motives. Why?"

"Because I'm the one who saw the need." It was so plain to him, to Micah, to any right-thinking being that she needed that assistance. To everyone but Val and Shade, of course. They were thinking with their hearts, not their heads. Maybe it was to be expected from two so young, but Austin had come to expect a lot more—from Val, anyway. He didn't know Shade well enough to expect anything. Nor did he want to. Shade had taken advantage of Val's trust, caused her to lose her powers by making love with her, then acted like a lily-livered coward.

Well, maybe not a coward, Austin admitted, unable to lie to himself.

But Shade had put Val in danger with his actions, insisted she leave him with another succubus, then blamed her when it didn't turn out all sunshine and roses. Austin would make sure that didn't happen again.

"Could it be that you have feelings for Ms. Shapiro?" Alejandro asked.

He seemed more curious than challenging, but Austin wasn't sure he wanted to admit that quite yet. He snorted. "She's headstrong, stubborn, rebellious . . . and enamored of someone else." One who didn't deserve her. "Why would I have feelings for her?"

"Because she is also compassionate, honorable, and fierce in championing the innocent—qualities you possess and esteem in others."

Maybe, but Austin was reluctant to admit it. He shrugged. "She is a succubus. No man can resist her."

"You and I both know that her physical succubus allure does not linger beyond close proximity. Do you care for her?"

It appeared Alejandro was going to continue his polite insistence until Austin 'fessed up. He took a deep breath. "I am beginning to," he admitted at last, then glanced up to see Alejandro's reaction.

The leader of the New Blood Movement nodded thoughtfully. "I knew, of course. I wondered if you did."

Austin didn't know how to respond to that. Instead, he asked, "Is that a problem?" It had better not be. His feelings were none of Alejandro's business.

"It can be, if you let your feelings get in the way of your duty."

"They won't." When Alejandro looked thoughtful, Austin went on the offensive. "Is that why you don't show your feelings for Rosa?"

It was a stab in the dark, but apparently hit home. He surprised a look of pain on Alejandro's face, quickly wiped away and replaced by his accustomed mask of polite civility. "Yes," Alejandro said. "But I expect you to keep that to yourself."

Shocked by the admission, Austin blurted out, "Why? I mean, of course I'll keep it to myself, but why don't you act on it? No one will think less of you."

Alejandro sighed. "I cannot show favoritism. Rosa is extremely valuable to me as a lieutenant, especially with the women in the Movement. I fear elevating her to the status of consort would cause nothing but problems."

He was right. And though Alejandro probably wouldn't say it, he had to know the power might go to Rosa's head. Not to mention how she might purposely flaunt her victory and how the relationship could sow dissension among the women in the Movement, most of whom wanted nothing more than to be Alejandro's lover.

Alejandro was wise to stay unattached. But it had to be a lonely existence. Austin didn't envy him his position one bit. "That doesn't pertain to me, though." He'd had his share of liaisons with women in the house. It had never caused the sort of problems Alejandro worried about. "If I ever act on my feelings for Val, I won't let it get in the way of my duty."

"Perhaps not," Alejandro conceded. "But relationships with humans rarely work out."

"She's part demon," Austin reminded him.

"Only one-eighth. And all mortal—her lifespan is fleeting to one such as us. And she's in love with the shadow demon and sees you as nothing more than a bloodsucking monster."

Austin winced, and something twisted inside of him at that. "She's young and thinks she's fallen in love with the first man she slept with. It won't last."

Alejandro acknowledged that with a nod. "Very true. In fact, I believe she's come to value your friendship."

Austin snorted. "Hardly." She saw him as an annoyance, someone to avoid. Besides, he wanted more than friendship from Val Shapiro.

"Nevertheless, you have much to recommend you, and she will come to see that in time." Alejandro sighed. "But what you choose to do in your personal life is none of my concern, unless it affects your duty to me and the Movement."

About time he figured that out. "I won't let it," Austin insisted. His first loyalty was to Alejandro. The man had more than earned it. Not only had Alejandro given him his second life, he had provided meaning to what would otherwise be a challenging existence.

"And the training?" Alejandro said. "If you don't want Luis to—"

"I'll take care of it," Austin promised. Somehow. He owed it to Gwen and Elspeth as well.

"See that you do," Alejandro admonished him. "And you may assist Ms. Shapiro with my blessing, until she is able to protect herself, or until you become a liability to her and to us."

"Won't happen," Austin promised.

It wouldn't be easy, with Val fighting him all the way, but she couldn't think straight when she was around the shadow demon and his pretty face, so she was bound to made stupid mistakes. She needed someone to watch over her, and he'd elected himself for the job. He planned to be there for her whether she liked it or not.

Chapter Four

Val

WHEN THE WHOLE parade got to my townhouse, the number of demons seemed to have doubled.

Part demons, that is. Full demons are pretty much full evil, too. Cross them with humans, and the offspring were gifted with human compassion. Most of the time. In the case of the part demons in the Demon Underground, those offspring wanted nothing more than to fit in to the real world, to be treated like any other human and not like freaks. Ahem. Not that I have that problem, you understand.

And now the demons were all clustered around Princess, cooing over her, petting her, and generally brown-nosing the self-centered spaniel. Even Tessa, Micah's assistant, who I thought was more level-headed.

I wondered why, but doubted any of them would give me a straight answer. Who would? My gaze settled on Shade. I never realized how much I relied on nonverbal communication cues until I met the shadow demon. With the other dimensions swirling through his features, all I could get was words without context. I had no hints of true emotion revealed to me by the quirk of a lip or undisciplined eyebrows. Heck, I wasn't even getting words, lately.

Surreptitiously, I used the amulet to get a glimpse of his expression. Strange, he looked . . . amused.

Fang nudged me with his nose. HEY, HOW CAN YOU SUDDENLY SEE WHAT SHADE LOOKS LIKE WHEN NO ONE ELSE CAN?

I'm using the amulet the tiniest bit, I assured him. *Only so I can see Shade's expression.* When Fang gave me the cocked eyebrow look of disbelief, I added, *It's only fair. He can see us. This way, I can see him, too.* Tracking Shade's moods would be key to keeping him alive and safe. I reminded Fang of that fact.

OKAY, Fang said grudgingly.

"What's with the Princess love fest?" I asked Shade as if nothing was wrong between us. He could either choose to ignore me, or decide to be civil.

He grinned as if at a private joke, then explained, "They all want a puppy, a hellhound of their own."

Ah, good. He'd chosen civility.

Fang looked smug. WHO WOULDN'T WANT ONE OF MY KIDS?

Well, yeah, I got that, but I wondered . . . "Who decides who gets a puppy? Shade? Fang? Micah?" I hoped it wasn't Princess—the puppies would probably go to the people who spoiled her the most.

I HEARD THAT, Princess said with a mental sniff. AND I ONLY WANT WHAT IS BEST FOR MY BABIES.

Maybe motherhood would be good for her. "So who chooses?" I asked.

DUH, Fang said with a roll of his eyes. THE PUPPIES DO, ONCE THEY'RE OLD ENOUGH.

"Really? It seems like a pretty big decision for someone who's only six weeks old."

THEY DON'T HAVE TO CHOOSE THE MOMENT THEY'RE WEANED, Fang explained. THEY CHOOSE THEIR HUMAN PARTNER WHEN THEY FIND THE RIGHT PERSON, LIKE I CHOSE YOU, AND PRINCESS CHOSE SHADE. THEY CHOOSE THEIR OWN NAMES AS WELL.

I glanced at Shade. "Sounds like something we need to add to the encyclopedia."

He nodded. "I keep telling them the puppies will choose," Shade said, gesturing at the demons clustered around Princess. "But they seem to think that if they're here during the birth, they'll be able to get a puppy to imprint on them."

Like little baby ducks who toddled after the first moving creature they spotted? "So this is going to be Demon Central for a while?"

"Afraid so."

Too bad. This Demon Underground movement ought to be more *underground* in my opinion. Now there were way too many people in this small townhouse . . . and I'd worried about being lonely? Shade's tone led me to believe he wasn't crazy about so much company, either. And it wouldn't get any better after the puppies were born.

I clapped my hands to draw their attention. They all glanced at me. "Okay, people. My house, my rules. You can't be here at all hours of the day and night. We'll set up visiting hours, but for now, you need to go."

They looked mulish, so I added, "We all need to get some rest, especially Princess."

I AM A LITTLE TIRED, she admitted.

That did it. Heaven forbid Princess should get the least bit weary. Most of them left, though Micah and Tessa decided to stay until Austin returned, and cornered Shade in his room for a while. Fine. Let them have their secrets. At least it was quiet again.

When Austin arrived with his things, Micah and Tessa left, leaving the townhouse empty of all but Shade, Austin, the two hellhounds, and me. I glanced at the time. Most people were just getting up for work, but it was time for me to go to bed. I'd been out all night hunting, and Shade obviously hadn't gotten any rest either. I didn't know about Austin. But dawn was coming in about an hour, and my place wasn't vampire friendly.

I pulled the drapes against the sun that would soon rise and checked all of the windows and doors in the townhouse. "Shade, you'll take Gwen's room," I said unnecessarily, as Micah had already directed his things be taken there.

Shade glared at Austin, not knowing I could see his expression. "Where's *he* going to sleep?"

Childish much?

It didn't seem to bother Austin though—he just lounged against the wall, looking amused. "Well, darlin'," he drawled, "I do have a suggestion." He wiggled his eyebrows at me.

Lola was still weak, but Austin's offer made her perk up, urge me to live a little, and take what he offered. I, however, wasn't about to be ruled by the physical cravings of my succubus. I jerked my gaze away from him, feeling warmth creep up my face. "I don't want to hear it," I bit out.

"No one wants to hear it," Shade said, sounding pissed.

Annoyed by his jealousy when there was no reason for it, I thought about telling him I didn't need his help to handle Austin. But since it would only amuse Austin more, I decided not to.

I glanced around the place. Sheesh, the only options left for Austin to crash were my bedroom and the couch. Austin's long, lean length wouldn't fit very well there. And what about sunrise? "The drapes aren't exactly light-tight." All it would take was one twitch of the curtains or someone opening the front door to let the sun stream in, and we'd have toasted Austin in the living room.

I wasn't crazy about sleeping on the lumpy thing either, but it looked like I had no choice. "I guess Austin can take my room," I said reluctantly.

"You're letting him sleep in your bed?" Shade asked in disbelief.

Ignoring the mocking laughter in Austin's eyes, I snapped, "It's obvious he can't sleep in the living room. I'll take the couch, unless you want to share *your* bed with him?"

Shade scowled and kicked up his chin, looking stubborn. "No way. I'll sleep on the couch."

I assessed it from a security point of view. "I don't think so. If a demon hunter comes through the front door or back door, whoever sleeps on the couch will be the first person they see. I'll sleep there." They'd have to go through me to get to Shade. "It makes the most sense, right?"

"It does indeed," Austin agreed, though the amusement never left his eyes.

It just seemed to piss Shade off more. His mouth firmed into a straight line, but he had to admit I was right.

Sighing, I had a feeling it was going to be a long day. Knowing Shade was nearby and I couldn't cuddle with him, and that Austin was in the other room—in my bed—and wanted to cuddle with me . . . it was enough to make any self-respecting succubus a little crazy.

I DON'T CARE WHERE ANY OF YOU SLEEP, SO LONG AS YOU ACTUALLY LET US HIT THE SACK, TOO, Fang said. PRINCESS AND I ARE GOING TO BED IN GWEN'S ROOM. BE QUIET, WILLYA?

Whatever. "Come on," I said to Austin. "I'll show you where everything is." I led him to the bedroom and changed the sheets on the bed, then showed him where the towels were in my bathroom. I wasn't exactly a girly girl, but Austin made the rooms I'd had so much fun decorating seem ultra feminine and even a little fussy.

I accidentally brushed his arm with mine, and Lola leapt to attention, sending lust surging through my body. Reminding myself she'd react that way to any man, I pulled away, rubbing my arm where we'd touched. But why did she respond so much more easily and readily to Austin than anyone else? Maybe because she'd fed on him more than anyone else? Yes, that had to be it.

Annoyed by how self-conscious he made me feel, I asked curtly, "Need anything else?"

"No, I'm good." When I turned to go, he reached out for my arm and grinned. "Hey, remember, I'm only a scream away."

Lola urged me to scream right then and there, but I slapped her down. "Not gonna happen," I snapped and pulled free. Then, to push home the point, I said, "Good night."

I closed the bedroom door firmly in his face then sagged against the wooden frame, fighting to control Lola's disappointment. Sheesh. Why couldn't Lola have the hots for Shade instead of Austin?

Because Austin is interested and Shade isn't? a small voice said inside me.

Luckily, I made a habit of ignoring small irritating voices. I headed back toward the living room, expecting it to be deserted, but Shade was still sitting on the couch. "Val, we need to talk," he said quietly.

My heart leapt in my chest. This was what I wanted, wasn't it? So why did I have this sinking feeling?

Shade had never learned how to hide his feelings very well and probably didn't even try when he was all swirly. Since I needed some nonverbal cues for this conversation, I took a peek at his expression. Jaw and mouth firmed, no softness in his eyes. Crap. I wasn't sure I wanted to get into it with Shade.

IT'S OKAY, Fang assured me from the other room. YOU NEED TO HEAR THIS.

"All right," I said slowly.

Shade stood up to pace, looking a little sad now, yet frustrated at the same time.

Encouraged by his lack of anger, I whispered, "I'm glad you finally want to talk."

He nodded. "Micah and Tessa insisted. They said . . . you think I'm angry at you." He paused to spear me with an annoyed glance.

"Aren't you?" He sure acted like it.

"Not really. Not you, specifically." He made an abortive movement, like he wanted to punch something, but didn't want me to see it. "Just everything."

Sheesh. Looked as though I was going to have to pull it out of him. "Like what?" I ventured a guess. "Dina, you mean? Was it really bad?"

His ran a hand through his hair and grimaced. "It wasn't all that bad at the time. She forced me to enjoy everything she did to me. It wasn't until I was no longer under her control that I realized how I'd been made to dance to any tune she played." The bitterness in his voice and distaste in his expression showed far more of his feelings than his words did.

HE FELT USED, Fang added.

I cringed internally. Dina had possessed a great deal more experience than I had at being a succubus and had enjoyed it a whole heck of a lot more. I tried not to think about what she'd made him do, like something . . . deviant? I was so clueless about this stuff, I couldn't even imagine what that might be. "Do you want to talk about what she did to you?"

Shade shook his head and paced some more. "That's not important." But the tightness in his expression showed the lie. It did matter—he just didn't want to share it with me.

"I'm so sorry for leaving you with her. I didn't know about the amulet." Didn't know it would allow her to have control of him every minute of every day, even when she was sleeping.

He shrugged. "I don't blame you."

"Don't you?" I asked softly. Isn't that what this was all about?

He made a negating movement. "Not totally," he admitted. "I share some of the blame. After all, I told you to leave."

At least he finally understood that. "Then what's wrong?"

When he hesitated, Fang broadcast, HE WANTED TO DO HIS JOB, FIX THE PROBLEM, BE THE HERO. INSTEAD, DINA TOOK CONTROL OF HIM SO EASILY HE FEELS LIKE A FAILURE. ESPECIALLY SINCE YOU HAD TO RESCUE HIM.

Shade shot a murderous glance toward the bedroom where Fang and Princess had supposedly gone to bed. "Shut up, Fang. Let me tell this my way."

WHATEVER, DUDE. JUST GET ON WITH IT SO WE CAN ALL SLEEP.

"It's not your fault," I assured Shade. "No man could have resisted Dina, especially with the amulet. And we had no way of knowing she had that edge."

"I should have been able to do something," Shade said viciously. "Instead, I had to wait for someone—you—to rescue me."

But it would have been all right if he'd rescued me, I'm sure. A bit too twentieth-century macho dude for my taste. Then again, it was probably really frustrating for a demon with such a strong power to have to rely on anyone else.

AND HE'S A GUY, Fang reminded me unnecessarily. THAT MEANS IT WAS ALSO HUMILIATING.

I really didn't need the commentary, especially in a conversation that was supposed to be *private*. But Fang was right. Even if I didn't like it, guys did like to be the strong one in the relationship, the ones to be the protector and the savior . . . not the ones who had to be saved. Did he think I'd emasculated him or something?

Fang snorted mentally. DO YOU EVEN KNOW WHAT THAT MEANS?

Please, stay out of this, Fang, I said mentally. *Shade and I need to figure this out on our own.* To reassure Shade, I said, "You couldn't have done anything."

He grimaced. "Yeah, all I'm good for is bringing more evil into the world."

Did he really feel that way? "I didn't have enough strength to control the mage demon either," I reminded him. "Not until I used the amulet."

"That's my fault, too," Shade said, a strangely agonized expression on his face.

"Huh? How do you figure that?"

He ran a hand over his face and wouldn't look at me directly. "If we hadn't . . . made love, you wouldn't have lost your strength and speed. And when you had to use the spells, it weakened Lola even more."

"You can't take the blame for that," I said, exasperated. "Two of us made that decision." If anyone was to blame, it was Fang and Princess, for getting us caught up in their lovemaking when Princess went into heat.

HEY, Fang protested. I APOLOGIZED FOR THAT.

Butt out, Fang.

OKAY, OKAY. BUT DON'T STAY UP TOO LATE. YOUR THOUGHTS KEEP US AWAKE.

Whatever. Just leave us alone.

"I'm not blaming anyone," I told Shade firmly. "And I don't regret it, either. In fact, I kinda want to do it again."

Oh, crap. Had that really come out of my mouth? I must be more tired than I thought. And now my face must be flaming red. I wished *I* had the option of going swirly when I wanted to.

Shade looked startled, then gave me a tentative grin. "Do you?"

Duh. Well, crap. I'd already embarrassed myself. Why not go for broke? Carefully keeping Lola and the amulet in check so Shade wouldn't think I was trying to force him to feel something he didn't want to, I rose to my feet and leaned in to kiss him softly on the mouth. He was so surprised, he didn't respond much. But he didn't pull away, either.

"I do," I said. Then, because he looked so confused, I added teasingly, "Don't you know you're the espresso in my coffee, the chai in my tea, the marshmallows in my cocoa, the—"

"Okay, okay," he said, laughing as I'd hoped. "I get it."

I grinned. "Good, 'cause I was running out of hot drinks." His smile faded, and I could see him visibly compose himself to say something. Something I wasn't sure I wanted to hear. My heart sinking, I pulled back an inch and said it for him. "But you don't feel the same way." I meant that to sound matter of fact, but it came out sounding accusatory.

"Actually, I think I do feel the same way," Shade said.

He *thought* he did? Didn't he know? My hopes rose, but I sensed there was a "but" coming.

"But I need some space right now. I need to work through some things."

And there it was. "Like what?" Quickly, I added, "I'm not being nosy. I'm just trying to understand what you're going through." I wanted to see if there was any way I could help, but I wasn't sure I should say that part aloud.

"It's not about you," Shade said. "It's about me. About my past."

I didn't know much about Shade's history, before he joined the Demon Underground. He'd never said, and ashamed, I realized I'd never asked. "What about it?"

"I don't remember much and didn't realize that until after you saved me from Dina's clutches."

How weird. "But you're remembering now?"

"Sort of. It's mostly feelings, as opposed to real memories." He frowned. "I can't describe it, but I need some time to figure it out. That means I need all my wits about me." His mouth twisted in a wry grin. "And I'm pretty witless when I'm around you and Lola."

Well, that was something, anyway. "So, if Lola can't cozy up to you, that means I have to feed on other people." Like Austin. Though I'd avoid it as long as possible, for Shade's sake.

He grimaced. "I guess I'll have to live with it. But don't enjoy it too much, okay?"

"Never," I declared to make him smile. I just hoped it was the truth.

But I wanted him back to normal as soon as possible. "Have you asked Elspeth for help? She was the Memory Eater for so long, she might know something that might help you, even though she no longer has that power."

He nodded. "That's a good idea. Thanks for understanding." He leaned over to give me a hesitant kiss on the forehead, like I was his aunt or something. Whoopie. Not exactly what I wanted, but right now, I'd take what I could get.

He headed off to bed, and I stared bleakly down at the couch—my bed for the foreseeable future. Sighing, I headed toward my linen closet to get a pillow and a blanket.

Unfortunately, I came face to face with Austin. He leaned against the open door to my room with the strangest expression on his face.

"Were you eavesdropping?" I asked belligerently. I was used to it with Fang, but didn't care for it with other people.

He shrugged. "Not intentionally, but vampire hearing, you know." Grinning, he added, "Hey, you didn't hear *me* complain when you saved my life."

What was he trying to say? "That's because you saved mine right back."

"Exactly. Our relationship works both ways."

Was that a slam at Shade? "We don't *have* a relationship," I reminded him. My mouth firmed into a thin line, and I tried to push past him.

He blocked my way with his arm. "Maybe. But ask yourself, what is Shade not saying?"

I backed up to keep him out of Lola's energy field and glared up at him. "What do you mean?"

"Even though Lola is weakened, you're still the strongest person I know. Stronger, faster, smarter than the average demon . . . than *him*. That's a hard pill to swallow for any man. Ask yourself this—does he resent you for it?"

I jerked my arm out of Austin's hold. "Don't be ridiculous," I bit out and stomped off down the hallway. Unfortunately, I couldn't escape his words as easily.

Did Shade resent me? Subconsciously? It would sure explain some things.

I shook my head fiercely. No, that was just Austin trying to mess with my head. There was a future for Shade and me. Wasn't there?

Chapter Five

Shade

SHADE WOKE IN a sweat, his heart pounding. He'd had that nightmare again. The one he couldn't remember, the one that left only feelings behind, as if he'd lost everything important to him. Unlike his normal dreams, this one was more slippery. It packed a wallop of fear and pain, then bled away into formless mist when he woke. Though he struggled to remember what was so important about it, he could never recall anything but the emotion that hit him right in the gut.

He rubbed his hand over his face and realized he was in a strange bed in a strange room. As the reason came back to him, he shook off the elusive dream and fumbled until he found a bedside lamp and turned it on. Princess and Fang lay curled together at the foot of the bed like a furry yin yang symbol.

Fang opened one eye. YOU'RE IN GWEN'S ROOM AT VAL'S PLACE, he informed Shade.

Yeah, I got that. The bright flowery bedspread kind of gave it away. It was dark out again, so he must have slept through the daylight hours. Was he keeping vampire hours now?

Fang closed his eye and snuggled into Princess. YOU'RE KEEPING VAL HOURS, Fang told him. YOU SHOULD BE USED TO IT.

He hadn't been lately, but as Micah's watcher for so many years, he was used to lurking in the dark shadows of the night. Easier to hide the weird shifting dimensions of his appearance that way.

But what other people didn't realize was that it was even stranger on the inside. Unless he was grounded in someone from this world, bizarre images and feelings constantly flickered through him from other realities. Some even felt like *this* reality, fuzzy events that seemed as though they'd happened to him in his past, though he couldn't remember those things actually occurring.

Idly, he wondered if he was tapping into alternate realities in those other dimensions, with a million other Shades leading slightly different lives. Maybe in some of those places, he wasn't even part shadow demon. Too bad that wasn't *this* reality.

DON'T BE SILLY, Princess said, waking and stretching. IF YOU WEREN'T PART DEMON, WE WOULD HAVE NEVER FOUND EACH OTHER.

Shade grinned and rubbed the hellhound's long silky ears as she settled again beside him. Her view of the world never failed to amuse him. She never had to worry about right and wrong—it was all black and white and Princess-centric. *Not finding each other would have been a fate worse than death*, he assured her.

OF COURSE, she said serenely, never doubting he felt that way. I WOULD LIKE FOOD NOW.

Shade jumped out of bed and gave her a mock bow. "Your wish is my command, your highness."

Princess took it as her due.

Fang snorted, and said privately, YOU REALIZE SHE DOESN'T RECOGNIZE SARCASM.

I know. That's what makes it so fun. He helped the very pregnant spaniel down off the bed, pulled on some pants and a T-shirt, scrubbed his hands through his hair to get it out of his eyes, and headed for the kitchen. Surely there'd be something for the hellhounds to eat there. And maybe something for a shadow demon, too.

He passed through the living room, trying to be quiet, but Val's eyes were already open.

"I'm awake," she said, yawning and stretching. "Just waiting for you to get up."

She sat up and rubbed her eyes. Her unruly hair was flattened on one side, and she looked sleepy and a bit goofy. So why did he find her so hot?

Down, boy. She was a succubus, so the lust was a given, but he shouldn't be feeling the effects at this distance. He shook his head. What was he thinking? He didn't need Lola to make him feel that way toward Val. She did that all on her own. Not just because she was cute and sexy, in a not-even-trying kind of way. But despite all the crap she'd been through, she was compassionate, strong, and always did the right thing.

Unfortunately, he'd added to her problems when he made love to her. He didn't regret the act itself, but losing her virginity had made her lose the strength, speed, and healing abilities she needed. How could she forgive him for that? Heck, how could he forgive himself?

The fact that she still wanted *him* even now should make him feel like the luckiest guy in the world. So why was he so convinced it wouldn't last?

It all came back to Dina and that cursed amulet. The thought of getting caught up in another relationship that would leave him alone sickened him.

Another relationship? Where had that thought come from?

It didn't matter. The point was, he was too unsettled right now to be in a relationship with anyone. Until he got his act together, he couldn't let his problems affect anyone else in his life.

"You okay?" Val asked, blinking at him.

Shade rubbed a hand over his face, not realizing until now that he'd been staring at her, lost in thought. "I'm fine."

Princess pawed at his leg. FOOD NOW, she insisted.

"Okay, okay," he said, grateful for the distraction. "Let me see what there is."

Val got up off the couch, having slept in the clothes she wore yesterday, and padded into the kitchen after him. "Gwen left some chicken, rice, and yogurt meals for Princess. You just need to heat it up."

BLEH, Princess said, and he could hear her pout. I WANT REAL FOOD.

WELL, YOU'RE NOT GETTING IT, Fang said. YOU'RE EATING FOR OUR KIDS, AND I WANT THEM TO BE HEALTHY. He perked up when Shade opened the refrigerator. HEY, IS THAT LEFTOVER PIZZA?

Shade glanced down at Fang with a smile. "Maybe you should set a good example."

MAYBE YOU SHOULD MIND YOUR OWN BUSINESS, Fang retorted. PRINCESS IS THE ONE WHO'S KNOCKED UP, NOT ME.

Shade shrugged. "I don't care what you eat." A hellhound's metabolism was different than a normal dog's, and they could eat just about anything without it affecting their health. But no one wanted to take any chances with Princess while she was pregnant, just in case.

Val chuckled. "There's enough pizza for all three of us, if you want."

I WANT, Fang assured her.

"Sure," Shade said.

They heated up Princess's healthy meal and the pizza for the rest of them. Shade even gave Princess a couple of bites of his pizza so she wouldn't look so forlorn.

But he wasn't ready to talk with Val about what had happened last night, especially with vampire hearing being what it was. Apparently, neither was Val. They ate pretty much in awkward silence, until the hellhounds went outside and Shade finally asked, "Where's Austin?" at the same time Val said, "What's up for today?"

"You first," Shade said.

She picked at her pizza without looking at him. "To answer your question, Austin woke earlier and said he had to make some phone calls—arrange to take care of his responsibilities in the Movement so he can hang out here and be a pain in my butt."

She grimaced, and Shade felt a little better knowing she didn't want the bloodsucker around any more than he did.

Continuing, Val said, "I'm new at this Paladin thing and not sure what I'm supposed to do except watch you. You have anything planned?"

For some reason, the reminder that she was the Underground's Paladin annoyed him. He didn't need a babysitter. "Not really," he said curtly. "Thought I'd get started digitizing the encyclopedia. Don't think you'll need to protect me while I'm doing that, unless you suspect the laptop of nefarious intentions."

She shot him a hurt glance, and Shade cursed himself. Sheesh, was he trying to pick a fight? It was like he was trying to push her away first, before she could do it to him. Micah and Tessa were right—he needed to get his head together. Val didn't deserve his pissiness. "Or maybe I'll do as you suggested and talk to Elspeth," he said.

There, that made her face clear up. "Good idea. I'm sure Austin can reach her for you."

"Austin already did," the cowboy vamp said from the doorway as he tucked his phone into his jeans pocket. Before Shade could complain about his nerve, Austin added, "I've sponsored Gwen and Elspeth into the house, so it's my responsibility to ensure they integrate smoothly into their new lifestyles."

Val raised an eyebrow. "You mean they're coming here so you can give them lessons on how to be a vampire?" she translated.

"Something like that," Austin said, looking annoyed.

Shade shrugged. It was none of his business what they did. To have something to do, he helped Val clean the kitchen, then straightened the living room and made his bed while he waited for Elspeth to show. It didn't take long, and she and Gwen entered without knocking since this was, after all, Gwen's home. Former home, anyway. Now that she was a vampire, she was living in Alejandro's mansion.

Elspeth, the former Memory Eater, was just as creepy-looking as he remembered. But that wasn't her fault. One of the rare demons who could turn vampire without going insane, she'd still been more than half crazy. Micah had told him she'd starved herself deliberately—if she didn't drink blood, the vampire and the demon didn't war within her so much. But now that Val had exorcised the demon from her, there was no more war, and Elspeth looked better.

When he first saw her, she'd looked like an emaciated bundle of sticks with an animated death's head mask. But "eating" regularly had given the vampire a small layer of . . . he couldn't even call it fat, on her bones. Healthy skin, maybe. And her hair looked a lot better. Thicker, not lank and stringy. She'd even put it up in some complicated, old-fashioned twist on top of her head. It made her look almost human, less likely to frighten children on sight.

Once she'd regained her sanity, she was totally kind and professional, so Shade had no hesitation in approaching her. "Could I speak to you alone?" he asked.

She glanced at Austin, who said, "Go ahead. I can work with Gwen on some things you already know."

"We can use the bedroom," Shade said, then glanced at the others to ensure they didn't take that wrong.

They didn't. As Austin and Gwen went into the kitchen, Val looked bored. She flopped down on the couch and grabbed the remote. "I guess I'll just watch television," she said with a sigh. "Yell if the boogieman comes."

Glad that Val hadn't tried to push herself into this meeting, Shade showed Elspeth into his room. He offered her the chair by Gwen's desk while he sat on the bed and swiped his suddenly damp palms on his jeans.

"Do you mind if I touch you?" Elspeth asked. "I would see your face, if it pleases you."

"Uh, sure." He must look as creepy to her as she did to him.

She moved to sit on the bed beside him and touched his wrist lightly. As always when someone grounded him in this reality, he felt more human, more . . . together, somehow. The images and emotions from other dimensions stopped flowing through him uncontrollably. Now, they'd only come through if he wanted them to, such as when he deliberately called upon them to heal someone.

"How can I assist you?" she asked, her gaunt face softening into an expression of concern.

He wasn't quite sure how to ask her what was going on in his brain without sounding crazy. "Uh, you've known a lot of demons, lived a long time. I was wondering if you could help with the encyclopedia, flesh out the knowledge in there so future generations won't be so in the dark."

"Of course. But, I do not think that is the only thing you wanted to ask me, is it?"

Shade grimaced and figured he'd better just lay it out there. "No, I guess not. I'm having a few weird things going on with my memories, and since you were the Lethe for so long, Val thought you might be able to help."

"I may be able to," she said. "What seems to be the problem?"

"I'm not sure. I don't know if you're aware of what shadow demons are . . .?"

"I have some past experience," she said encouragingly.

"Well, I always have strange emotions running through me from other dimensions, but lately, it seems that I'm feeling things I shouldn't. Things people say or do that never bothered me before now make me react in ways I don't expect."

"How so?"

"Like earlier. Val mentioned that she was a Paladin, and it just ticked me off, for no reason."

"I see," Elspeth said thoughtfully.

"And I'm having weird dreams. Bad ones, that I can't remember but scare the heck out of me anyway." He felt foolish for admitting it, but she had lived so long, seen so many demons, maybe she knew more about shadow demons than he did. "Is it possible that the other dimensions are alternate realities and memories from other Shades are leaking into this world?"

"I've never heard of anything like that happening," she said, then cocked her head to give him a piercing look. "How is your memory?"

How was that relevant? "Fine, I guess. Why?"

"How much do you remember of your earlier years?"

He shrugged. "Not much, like everyone else." It was pretty much a big blur. Besides, it wasn't relevant, so why should he think about it?

"What is your earliest memory?" she persisted.

"I don't know." And for some reason, he didn't even want to think about that either.

"Do you know where you lived before you came to San Antonio?"

"Of course." He frowned. No, he *didn't* remember. "I mean, I've always lived here."

She looked at him thoughtfully, as if she didn't believe him. "I see. Do you have strange dreams, dreams that feel like memories? Dreams you have a hard time remembering upon awakening?"

"Yes, sometimes. Doesn't everyone?"

"No, not everyone."

Puzzled, he asked, "What does it mean, then?"

"It means your submerged memories are trying to come through."

Huh? "What submerged memories?"

She patted him on the hand. "Don't worry about it, and don't fight it. Shadow Boy will remember what he once knew in his own good time."

Shadow Boy . . . that sounded familiar. But who the heck was Shadow Boy, and what did he have to do with Shade?

Chapter Six

Austin

THE NEXT EVENING, Austin called Gwen and Elspeth to come to Val's so he could talk to them about their training. With Micah and the other demons holding a powwow in the living room about the Underground's response to Shade's attacker, Austin asked the two new vamps to join him in the kitchen at the table.

He regarded them thoughtfully. They'd healed from their "training" with Luis, but what a contrast. Gwen, a young, pretty redhead whose human life had been taken from her by her brother's ex-fiancée, looked bright as a new penny against Elspeth's gaunt, aged appearance. And though Elspeth had been turned hundreds of years ago with her full consent, she'd been living in isolation ever since in the Demon Underground. Now that Val had exorcised the demon and the madness from her, she was fully vamp and ready to take her place in the New Blood Movement alongside Gwen.

Two very different women, but with the same ignorance of their new existence.

Austin cleared his throat. "First of all, I apologize for shirking my duty in training you."

Gwen shook her head. "It's not your fault. We understand you have other duties, other commitments." She smiled. "Like saving San Antonio from mage demons and the like."

Gwen was trying to be nice, but he wouldn't let himself off the hook. "No excuses. You are my responsibility, and I should have been more proactive in helping you acclimate to your new life. How are you adjusting?" This sort of life after death could be challenging for new members.

"It is more difficult for Gwen than it is for me," Elspeth said. "Not only because she was turned against her will, but because she is not accustomed to drinking blood, and she is still becoming acclimated to the demands and changes in her body."

Gwen shrugged as if it were no big deal, but she wouldn't meet his eyes. "I'll adjust. It's just that . . . my whole life changed. I can't go back to work at the ER, and while most people at the mansion are kind and helpful, I really need something to do."

"I would appreciate some meaningful occupation as well," Elspeth said.

Austin could appreciate that. Boredom was one of the chief problems with a vampire's existence. Too many had turned rogue, killed themselves, or set themselves up as despots simply to alleviate the monotony. "I understand. I was giving you a chance to acclimate first, but I'm sure we can find something for you to do. Gwen, with your medical training, you'd be invaluable in assisting us at the blood banks, for medical assistance and research. Would you be interested in that?"

"I haven't done much research, but yes, I'd love to help in any way I can." She smiled as if he'd given her a present, and Austin kicked himself for not thinking of this earlier.

"Good. I'll get you in touch with Vincent." He glanced at Elspeth. "I'm sorry, I don't know your skills . . .?"

"I have none that translate well to this age except for holding house. I would be happy to assist Rosa in that area."

Well, that was a relief. Too many thought management of the household was beneath them, and Rosa could always use the help. "Excellent suggestion. I'll talk to her about it, and we can work around your training. Right now, with Val so vulnerable and unknown demons attacking, I need to spend more time here with Val and won't be able to do the physical training you need until this crisis is over." He hesitated, then added, "I'm sorry, I should never have left you vulnerable to Luis's training methods, but I'll rectify that as soon as possible." He tried not to let his anger at Luis's presumption show through, but wasn't sure he was successful.

Elspeth nodded. "We accept your apology. But is the battle training really necessary?"

"I'm afraid it is," Austin said with regret. "The fact that we are what we are paints a target on our backs, makes us vulnerable to the unaffiliated vampires who hate what we stand for, and to the occasional human zealot who doesn't understand the difference between us and the rogues.

"We need to teach you to be aware of your vulnerabilities and how to defend yourself and the other members of the Movement. Too often lately, we have been attacked for what we are, with no regard to how we truly interact with humans."

"Are humans really a threat?" Elspeth asked. "After all, we are so much stronger and faster than they are."

"We are, but we have a responsibility to the Movement. Our goal is to come out to the world, to pass legislation that will require every vampire to belong to the New Blood Movement. This would not only provide us protection under the law and allow us to live in harmony with humans, but any rogues who refuse to join and follow our precepts would not be afforded that protection."

They nodded their understanding, so Austin continued. "The Movement isn't just about providing blood banks to protect the humans, it's also about ensuring humans have no cause to fear us, no cause to enter into witch hunts. So, first and foremost, we must ensure we do not harm them."

"Not even if they attack us?" Elspeth asked, looking worried.

"That's what the training is for," Austin explained. "To learn how to defend yourself against them without hurting them." When Elspeth looked worried, he added, "It's not always possible, but it should be our primary aim."

Gwen and Elspeth exchanged uncertain looks. Gwen asked, "Does everyone have to follow that rule, even Alejandro's lieutenants?"

"Are you thinking of Lily?" Austin asked. Alejandro's former lieutenant had fooled them into believing she followed their creed, then went her own way. "She was an aberration, and we took care of that. We police our own," he added sternly. Not that he worried about these two going rogue.

"No, not Lily," Gwen said hesitantly and exchanged another glance with Elspeth.

"Then who?" Austin demanded. He knew it wasn't him, so that left only Rosa and Luis. "Did *Luis* do something?"

"We must tell him," Elspeth said, placing a hand atop Gwen's.

"Yes, tell me," Austin bit out. But he had a feeling he wasn't going to like what they had to say.

Gwen glanced down at the table where she'd twisted her hands into a knot. "Alejandro asked Luis to give us a tour of a blood bank last week," Gwen explained. "And he left us in the lobby while he, uh . . ."

Understanding her reluctance to finish that sentence, Austin said, "While he went to a private room and fed directly from the source?" Austin didn't agree at all with this option of the blood bank—it provided too many temptations.

"Yes," Elspeth said, and it was obvious she didn't approve either.

Gwen continued. "A man came in, upset that his wife was, er, donating, and attacked Elspeth. He stabbed her in the shoulder with a stake, and I grabbed him from behind to hold him off. We were defending ourselves all right—without hurting him—but it created a huge commotion in the lobby, and Luis came out, livid."

"And?" Austin prompted, trying to keep the anger from his voice at what he suspected was coming.

Gwen twisted her fingers even tighter. "He . . . he broke the man's neck."

Elspeth nodded. "It wasn't an accident. He did it deliberately."

Rage surged through Austin. Luis had always been arrogant, but he'd played by the rules. What possessed him to do this? "Why haven't I heard about this?"

"Because he removed the memories of every human present and staged an accident to look as though the man fell off a roof . . . in another part of town," Elspeth explained, sounding indignant. "We found the notice in the paper the next day."

"That's why he was training us," Gwen said. "He said we had to learn how to defend ourselves."

Austin wanted to hit something, wring Luis's neck. "Really? Or was he trying to punish you?"

"Both, I believe," Elspeth said quietly.

Austin fought to control his anger. "This is a total violation of everything we stand for. We can't let him stay in a position of power any longer. We have to tell Alejandro."

"No, you can't," Gwen said, reaching out a hand as if to stop him. "He said that if we ever told anyone, he'd . . . take care of us."

He dared? "Alejandro and I will protect you," Austin said. "And Alejandro will banish him." Maybe even eliminate him. Austin would gladly take on that responsibility himself.

"Will he?" Elspeth asked calmly. "Alejandro sees the best in everyone. Luis said it was an accident, that he didn't mean to do it. Alejandro will believe him and think Luis can be rehabilitated."

"You see?" Gwen said. "If you tell him, we'll still be in danger."

Austin shut his eyes in pain. They were right. He couldn't reveal Luis's perfidy without endangering these two women, who were supposed to be under his protection. He couldn't watch them every moment of every day and take care of Val at the same time.

"Perhaps we should leave, join a group in another city," Elspeth suggested.

For a brief moment, Austin entertained the idea, but when he saw the misery on Gwen's face, he said, "No. You're safest here." They had no idea how lucky they were here, and they might not be treated as well elsewhere, especially since they were so new, so vulnerable, so ripe for exploitation.

He sighed. "All right," he said. "I won't tell Alejandro." But if *Austin* caught Luis, there would be no need to keep his mouth shut. He'd have to keep an eye on the Spaniard. "But I want you to stay with me, or Rosa, or others we trust at all times until Luis is satisfied you're not going to reveal his secret."

Elspeth nodded uncertainly, and Gwen said, "Okay," in a fearful voice.

And for that alone, Austin could kill Luis. All he needed was for the so-called aristocrat to slip up just one time, and he'd have his head on a platter.

Chapter Seven

Val

HAD I REALLY complained about being lonely? The next days were jam-packed with part demons and vampires coming and going to see Shade and Princess. I felt more like a traffic cop than a Paladin. Now, Shade and three other demons chatted up the hellhounds in the living room, and, since it was after sunset, three vampires hung out in the kitchen.

Yep, the kitchen. My former roomie turned vampire, Gwen Sullivan, might not be able to eat human food, but she still enjoyed cooking for the demons in the Underground. I think she missed our townhouse, too. Austin and Elspeth were in the kitchen with her, as Austin gave them both pointers on how to be good little vampires.

My life was so weird.

I wanted to get away from them all, but the only places not occupied were the bathrooms and the two bedrooms. Being in Shade's room seemed like an invasion of privacy, and being in my room, where Austin had slept, felt too intimate somehow. I even tried lounging fully clothed in the tub just to be alone, but that seemed too strange even for me. Too bad I couldn't leave. I had to stay here to protect Shade, but sheesh, the only thing that seemed to threaten Shade right now was being talked to death. So, I wandered back and forth between the two groups.

Seeing Shade sitting somewhat apart from the others reminded me of his problem. I wandered into the kitchen where the three vamps chatted around the kitchen table.

Austin broke off what he'd been saying and grinned at me. "Ah, Slayer. How may I assist you?"

I squirmed inwardly, not caring for the intimate tone of his voice, especially when it hit Lola's buttons juuuuuust right. But I couldn't call him on it without looking like an idiot. What was I supposed to say? Don't be so nice because my succubus likes it too much? Instead, I asked, "Am I interrupting an important lesson?"

"Not at all," he assured me. "I live to serve."

Ignoring his attempt to get my goat, I asked Elspeth, "Can I talk to you for a few minutes?"

"Of course," the former Memory Eater said.

Relieved to be out of Austin's disturbing presence, I led her out onto the small back patio where I could still see what was going on in the living room, but have a bit of privacy. It was cool, but not too cold if I didn't stay out here too long. Gazing up at the crescent moon, I asked, "Elspeth, has Shade talked to you about anything?"

"He has talked to me of many things. I am helping him flesh out the entries on the demons and other creatures in the *Encyclopedia Magicka*."

Her perspective, having lived through hundreds of years of the Demon Underground, would be invaluable for that, but my question was more personal. "I mean about the memories that have been coming back to him."

"Yes, he has spoken of that. Why do you ask?"

"Is there something I should know about?"

She hesitated. "I don't think I should speak of that with you."

Crap. I'd hoped it might give me some insight to the mystery that was Shade.

Elspeth continued, "His memories are his alone, and he must rediscover them in his own good time. Though I believe it is time for him to remember what he forgot."

I glanced at her in surprise. "Do you know what his lost memories are?" Then, suddenly remembering what she'd been, I asked incredulously, "Did you eat his memories?"

She frowned. "You realize I did not actually eat memories, do you not?"

Embarrassed at using the politically incorrect term out loud, I said, "Sorry, you know me." Open mouth, insert tootsies. "I should say, as Lethe, did you remove his memories?"

She seemed mollified. "Anything I did, I did at his request and Micah's father's."

That was a yes. "Do you remember what they were? The memories, I mean."

"I remember everything. It is part of being Lethe."

What an awful curse. "If you took them, how can he rediscover them?"

She sighed and hesitated, as if reluctant to reveal anything. "In this particular case, I did not remove the memories—I hid them from him until he's able to deal with them."

"Is he ready now?" I asked.

"I believe he is. He is having dreams, flashes of memories trying to break through. But I cannot force it. It must happen naturally, or it may damage his psyche."

Holy crap. "What happened in Shade's past that made him want to forget everything?"

"I will not tell you that."

I figured she'd refuse, but it was worth a shot.

She placed her bony hand on mine. "Do not worry about that, Paladin. Let me worry about his past. Your job is to protect his future."

But the past always had a huge impact on the future. I sighed, knowing I wouldn't get anything more from her on this subject. "Being Paladin seems like an empty title. There's not a whole lot of smiting or shielding needed. Is that how it's always been?"

She smiled. "No, but times were different then."

"When?"

Her eyes took on a faraway look. "The Knights of the Round Table are believed to have been Paladins, as was the legendary Roland of Charlemagne's court. And, of course, Paladins were sorely needed during the Inquisition."

"And in your time?" I knew it was considered bad manners to ask the vamp how old she was, but she was a demon before she became a vamp.

"Of course they were needed, or I would not have been made Lethe."

Sheesh. Talking with Elspeth was a pain sometimes. With her ancient perspective, she didn't get that I was trying to weasel out how old she was. Either that, or she was deliberately misunderstanding.

Shade came outside, his face hooded from view in case of nosy neighbors, and said, "Don't you think it's time for everyone to leave? Princess doesn't feel very good."

I went inside and saw that Princess was panting and pacing, seeming restless. "What's wrong with her? Is she all right?"

SHE'S FINE, Fang reassured me, his head on his paws. SHE'S JUST READY TO GIVE BIRTH. Then his head jerked up. OH, CRAP. SHE'S READY TO GIVE BIRTH! He leapt to his feet, wide-eyed. Now? Oh, wow. And was that panic I heard in the hellhound's mind voice?

"Really?" Shade said. "How can we help?"

When a clamor of voices asked the same thing, they just increased Fang's anxiety and Princess's irritation. Making a shooing motion toward the door, I said, "Sorry, everyone, you'll have to leave. This show is very private." When they seemed reluctant to leave, I added, "At the parents' request."

That did it. Austin held a low-voiced, intense conversation with

Gwen and Elspeth, then everyone left except Shade, Austin and Fang. The four of us followed Princess as she wandered into Gwen's room and pawed at the blanket she'd insisted we prepare for her at the bottom of the dark closet.

Fang jittered in place, looking strangely indecisive. SHE'S NESTING, Fang said unnecessarily. THE PUPPIES ARE COMING. THE *PUPPIES* ARE *COMING*. QUICK, DO SOMETHING, he shot at Shade and me.

"Like what?" Shade asked, squatting down to soothe Princess.

I DON'T KNOW. BOIL WATER OR SOMETHING.

I couldn't help but grin at Fang's panic. "You really think that's gonna help?"

I DON'T KNOW. I'VE NEVER BEEN THROUGH THIS. WHAT DO YOU SUGGEST?

We gazed down at her, uncertain. "Doesn't she kind of do this on her own?" Shade asked with a quizzical grin. "It's instinct, right?"

I'LL TELL YOU WHAT YOU CAN DO. YOU CAN SHUT UP AND GO AWAY, Princess told all of us, including Austin who had come in to watch.

Fang suddenly realized the vamp was there and growled at him.

Looking surprised, Austin said, "What's up?"

"Princess is about to give birth," I explained. "And I don't think Fang wants you around when that happens."

DAMN STRAIGHT, Fang confirmed. WHAT IF THE BLOOD SETS HIM OFF OR SOMETHING?

Eww. Luckily, Shade repeated that so I wouldn't have to.

"No problem," Austin said, backing away with his hands up. "It won't 'set me off,' but I'll wait in the other room."

"Good." Fang was so anxious now, I was afraid he'd get into it with Austin just to have something to do.

"There's nothing you can do right now," Shade told the fretful father-to-be. "Let Princess do her thing, and you can . . . pass out cigars or something later."

VERY FUNNY, Fang said, obviously not amused. But that didn't stop him from pacing outside the closet.

OH, LOOK, he said excitedly, suddenly freezing in a quivering position that made him look like a hound on point. HERE COMES THE FIRST ONE.

Sure enough, Princess was heaving, and a puppy was slowly making its way into this world.

"Wow," Shade said, looking awed by the process of birth. "That's incredible."

Maybe. Looked kinda gross to me.

GO AWAY, Princess repeated. I'LL LET YOU KNOW WHEN IT'S DONE.

A remarkably self-possessed thing for the self-obsessed hellhound to say.

"Forget it," Shade said. "I'm not going anywhere."

YEAH, Fang agreed. I GOT YOU INTO THIS. THE LEAST I CAN DO IS WATCH.

The guys seemed totally fascinated by the whole gross process, but me . . . not so much.

The doorbell rang, and I went to answer it. Talk about saved by the bell. Or not. If this was another demon who'd found some lame excuse to be first in line to imprint on a hellhound pup, I was going to go all Paladin on his or her butt.

Austin came in from my bedroom, looking alert for trouble. I didn't expect any, but taking precautions wasn't a bad idea. He positioned himself next to the door so he'd be behind it when it opened, then nodded.

I opened the door, but I didn't recognize the two men—both Hispanic in their mid-twenties or so. From another Underground, maybe? The grapevine must be working overtime. "Sorry, guys," I told them. "Visiting hours are over."

They exchanged stone-faced glances, then one of them said with a slight accent, "We are here for the shadow demon."

Whoa. That changed things. Were these the thugs who'd trashed Shade's apartment? I called to Fang mentally. *Hey, Fang, can you check these guys out? See if they're demons?*

He snarled mentally from the other room. CAN'T YOU TELL I'M BUSY?

I stared at them, trying to read their expressions. They looked kind of determined and ready for action. *These guys are looking for Shade. You think they might be the ones who want to kill him?*

WHAT? Fang asked, startled. Then said, NOT DEMONS. I CAN'T READ THEM.

Weird. *Make sure Shade stays out of sight, okay?* I told Fang as I readied Lola for action. *I'm gonna try to get rid of these guys.*

YOU GOT IT.

Our mental exchange took only a fraction of a second. "Sorry, guys," I told them. "No shadow demon here. I don't even know what that is," I lied. "You'd better leave, or I'll call the police."

My threat didn't faze them one bit. I wished I could ask Princess if these were the guys who trashed Shade's place, but she was too busy birthing puppies to pick someone out of line-up right now.

"We want the shadow demon," the speaker said again.

Broken record, anyone?

"Too bad." Not wanting to deal with them while there was drama going on in the bedroom, I tried to shut the door in their faces.

It didn't work. One of them straight-armed the door. They bulled their way just inside and shut the door behind them. "Where is the shadow demon?"

Austin entered the conversation from behind them. "You heard the lady. Leave."

They whirled, looking surprised.

"Friends of yours?" I asked Austin.

"Nope," he said, coming to stand next to me.

Okay, if they weren't demon and they weren't vamp, they must be human. "Sorry, guys, wrong house," I said. Seriously, what could they do to me?

The silent one pulled a gun. Oh, they could do *that*. Crap. And it had a silencer, too. That didn't bode well . . .

Without even *trying* to negotiate, the gunman pointed the pistol at me and pulled the trigger.

Chapter Eight

Val

IN THE NANOSECOND between the time the round left the gun and would have hit me, Austin flashed in front of me, taking the bullet. It hit him somewhere in his shoulder, spinning him so he fell backward against me. We went down in a tangle of arms and legs against the couch and end table. I heard something shatter.

Austin was a vamp. He'd live. Angry now, I reached out from my sprawled position on the floor with Lola to grab hold of the two thugs and teach them a lesson before they could shoot again.

Nothing—it was like nailing water to a tree. Cursing, I grabbed the amulet and tried again. I certainly couldn't help Shade or anyone else if I was dead.

But the amulet didn't work either. Crap. They must already be controlled by someone else.

Austin and I both scrambled to our feet, and Fang was suddenly there, his eyes flashing purple. Austin used his superior strength and speed to wrench the gun away from one guy while Fang went for the other guy's 'nads.

"They're human," I yelled to Austin. Killing evil bloodsuckers was all in a day's work, along with nasty demons who couldn't get their powers under control. But full humans? Let the police handle them.

Austin must have had the same idea, so he pulled his punches. As the one guy crumpled in agony under Fang's attack, Austin tried to incapacitate the other guy. I stayed out of it, knowing I'd just be in the way, especially since the creep seemed to be a whole heck of a lot stronger and faster than he should be.

Finally, Austin managed to pin him, but the guy convulsed and lay still. "He's dead," Austin said in surprise.

"You killed a human?" I asked. Oh, crap. That could be trouble.

"No, I'm pretty sure he committed suicide. Look at his mouth."

Yeah, there was some kind of foamy spittle oozing out of his lips. "Poison?"

"Looks like."

VAL, A LITTLE HELP HERE, Fang called out.

The guy he'd disabled was rising unsteadily to his feet, clutching his crotch but reaching for the gun Austin had taken away from the other guy. I whirled, prepping my kick. Maybe Lola wouldn't work on him, but *savate* sure would. My foot connected with his head. He went down and out. That felt good.

"Check his mouth," I told Austin. "We don't want him killing himself, too." Not until we got answers, anyway.

Austin bent down to look in the guy's mouth, and Fang took off for the maternity ward again, snarling, I SHOULDA OFFED HIM FOR MAKING ME MISS THE BIRTH OF MY SONS AND DAUGHTERS.

Austin fished a capsule out of the guy's mouth. "Yep. He had one, too." He glanced around at the carnage. One man dead, one unconscious, and the living room looked like it had been whipped in a blender. "What do you want to do about them?"

"Call Lieutenant Ramirez. He'll figure it out."

"I already did," Shade said from the doorway, holding up his phone. "He's sending someone."

"Do you know these guys?" I asked.

Shade crossed the room to stand above the two and gaze down at them. "No. Never seen them before."

Austin methodically went through their pockets.

"You killed them?" Shade asked in disgust.

Austin glared back. "I don't kill humans. Only one of them is dead, and he killed himself. I'm just trying to find identification or something that will give us a clue as to who they are and what they want with you."

He fished a piece of paper out of the dead guy's pocket. "It has Val's address on it, but that's all they have. No ID."

The door suddenly flew open, and Dan Sullivan was there, peering around the door frame, his gun pointing inside. He didn't have far to look since the door had smacked the dead guy in the head and barely missed the other. The Special Crimes Unit cop—and my ex—lived in the same complex, so he must have run over immediately after he got the call. He stuck the gun in his back waistband and came in, closing the door behind him. He was dressed in jeans, a T-shirt, and socks, but nothing else.

"We've got it under control," I said.

He glanced down at the two men on the floor. "Dead?" he asked dispassionately.

"One dead, one unconscious," Austin responded.

"Vamps?"

Austin shook his head. "Human."

Amazing how men could communicate so much with so few words. "Stronger and faster than regular humans, though," I told Dan. "And I wasn't able to control either one of them, so they must be controlled by someone else."

"Vamp?" Dan asked again, looking at Austin.

Austin shrugged. "Maybe."

What was this? A contest about who could use the least amount of words to communicate? "Some mage demons can control people as well," I reminded them. "So we don't know who's doing it. And Austin didn't find any ID in their pockets."

Dan nodded. "I'll call Ramirez."

As Dan called the lieutenant to let him know the situation was under control but that we still needed help with a prisoner, Fang came trotting out.

IT'S A BOY! he announced. AND A GIRL! AND ANOTHER BOY AND ANOTHER GIRL.

I grinned. He sounded so proud and happy . . . and rather stunned at being a father. "Congratulations," I told him. When Austin and Dan gave me perplexed looks, I explained, "Princess just had her pups. Two boys and two girls." But that wasn't important right now. "Did you call Micah, too?" I asked Shade.

"I did, but there was no answer. I'll try again." He held a brief conversation with someone then hung up, looking grim. "We weren't the only ones to get visitors tonight. Two other men showed up at the club looking for me. Micah's bouncer managed to get rid of them."

Crap. If they showed up at Club Purgatory and my place, they knew more about the Demon Underground than I cared for.

"What's going on?" Dan asked.

I explained everything to him.

Dan glanced at Shade. "And you have no idea why these people want you dead or who they are?"

"No."

"So," Dan continued, "this place isn't safe for you, and neither is Club Purgatory. You need to find somewhere out of harm's way."

"I know a safe place," Austin said. "A penthouse at one of the blood banks. They won't know to find you there. And there's built-in security."

Yeah, they'd have to go through a whole lot of bloodsuckers to get to him. "That's a good idea," I said.

"This is ridiculous," Shade protested, his voice tight. "I don't need a babysitter."

"You need protection," Dan said firmly. "And you're going to get it whether you like it or not. I'd like to avoid as much collateral damage as possible."

"He's right," I told Shade. "And Micah will agree, too. You know he will." When Shade didn't say anything, I took a peek at his expression. He looked pissed and stubborn, so I added, "It's only temporary, until we determine who's behind this and take care of them."

YEAH, Fang interjected. AND I WOULDN'T MIND PRINCESS AND MY KIDS BEING OUT OF THE LINE OF FIRE WITH A FEW BLOODSUCKERS BETWEEN THEM AND DANGER.

I AGREE, Princess said. YOU MUST PROTECT MY PUPPIES.

Shade gave in, unable to resist his hellhound's wishes. "I'll get my stuff together," he muttered, and went back to his room.

"Do we have to wait for nightfall again?" Dan asked.

Good question. The sun was now rising, so it would be a while before it was dark again.

"No," Austin answered. "I can arrange for one of our human friends to take us in a darkened limo to the blood bank."

Dan glanced at Austin, and his eyes narrowed at the blood on his shirt. "Were you shot?"

"Yeah," I said. "He took a bullet meant for me. Thanks for that, by the way."

"What a gracious expression of gratitude," Austin drawled.

Okay, yeah, I could have been a little more thankful, but now I owed Austin, and it bothered me. Unfortunately, I didn't know how to respond to his mocking. "You okay?" I asked gruffly.

He might be able to heal fast, but it still had to hurt. Not that he'd shown any pain.

He tossed me another mocking glance. "I was happy to take a bullet for you. Any other little thing I can do for you tonight? Rob a train? Catch a falling star? Feed your succubus?"

My face warmed. He was just doing this to make me feel uncomfortable. Too bad he was succeeding. Uncertain how to respond, I said, "No, I'm good. Just glad you survived."

Austin squinted at the drapes. "With the sun rising, maybe I'd better do my surviving in the bedroom. I'll call from there."

Yeah, just in case someone else came barging through the door. Austin left for the bedroom and the security of the blackout curtains I'd had installed. A lot of the tension went out of the room when he left, and I felt a lot more grounded, more like myself.

A knock came at the door and when I answered it, Lieutenant Ramirez was there, along with a couple of other guys from the SCU.

We explained what had happened, and the SCU pick-up guys took away the body to do an autopsy and see what they could learn about him.

The other one—the live one on the floor—moaned and started to sit up. Ramirez handed Dan a pair of cuffs, and Dan restrained him, propping him up against the back of the couch. "What are we going to do with him?" he asked. "He's human, so we can incarcerate him and charge him, but he's being controlled by someone else, so there's something woo woo about the whole thing."

Woo woo? What was that? A new SCU technical term? "Yeah," I said. "Plus he's stronger and faster than the average human, which might cause waves if you put him in with the general populace in jail. I'd like to question him. Maybe you'd let us have him?"

Lieutenant Ramirez frowned. "And do what with him?"

"The Underground has some jail cells where we could hold him." I knew that all too well, having been held there myself not so long ago. "We can keep him out of sight, question him, find out what he knows." It was in the basement of Club Purgatory, but that was the Underground's secret, not mine to reveal.

Ramirez frowned. "It's not protocol."

No, but it would be convenient for them. The SCU usually dealt with vampires who either ended up dead or escaping. They didn't keep their catch.

Dan snorted. "We don't have protocol for something like this. The protocol for 'special' crimes is what you say it is, boss. And Val is right—we need to keep him away from other humans until we know more about him."

Ramirez nodded, looking reluctant. "All right, for now. We can transport him there for you."

"Uh, I'd better check first to see if it's okay with Micah."

"I'll do that," Ramirez said.

He called Micah, and they agreed to have Dan transport the prisoner to Micah's jail, since Dan was already familiar with the situation. He left to get some shoes and a jacket, and the lieutenant said, "I'll wait until he gets back, just in case someone else shows up."

I was supposed to be the Paladin, yet here everyone was trying to protect me. Shaking my head, I put the living room back to rights and left Ramirez watching the prisoner while I went into the other room to see the puppies.

Princess lay on her makeshift bed, four newborns lying in a pile next to her as Shade stroked her head. Fang lay close by, keeping an eye on his family. They all looked exhausted.

The puppies were so cute. Four fuzzy little creatures, looking almost hairless with bright pink noses, like fat little mice. "They're adorable," I said admiringly.

YES, Fang said. AND ALL HEALTHY.

"What shall we call them until they pick their own names?"

Shade leaned over to look at the pups. "How about Alpha, Bravo, Charlie, and Delta?" He pointed at one of the pups who looked just like Princess. "Call her Alpha, because she was born first. Then the boy who looks like Fang is Bravo, Charlie is the boy who looks like Princess, and Delta is the girl who looks like Fang."

"Works for me," I said. "Fang? Princess? Okay with you?"

THOSE ARE AS GOOD AS ANY, I GUESS, Fang said. ESPECIALLY SINCE THEY'LL CHOOSE THEIR OWN NAMES WHEN THEY'RE READY.

Yeah. A knowledge of English would be helpful first. I wondered when they'd start being telepathic.

I'M NOT SURE, Fang said. I'VE NEVER HAD KIDS BEFORE. BUT DON'T WISH THEIR BABY BABBLE ON US TOO SOON!

I grinned. Fang already sounded like a harried father, and he'd only been one for what? Twenty minutes?

JUST WAIT. YOU'LL SEE.

I stroked one of them with my finger. Soft. And much tinier than I expected, smaller than my hand. So helpless. No wonder Fang and Princess were so protective.

I sighed, wishing I could stay all day and just watch the puppies, but unfortunately, it was time to get back to the real world.

Chapter Nine

Austin

ONCE INSIDE VAL'S bedroom, Austin sat on the bed and allowed himself to clench his jaw against the agony in his shoulder. It felt as if someone had shoved a hot poker inside him and twisted. He needed to get that slug out—soon.

But first, he needed to take care of business. He pulled his phone from his pocket and dialed Alejandro. "We have a situation here," he told his boss. "Some men came looking for the shadow demon. They pushed their way into Val's house and tried to shoot her when she refused to tell them anything."

"Is she all right?" Alejandro asked.

"Yes, she's fine. They hit me instead."

Alejandro paused, evidently thinking about everything Austin didn't say. "It was good you were there to watch over her, then."

"Yeah." Even if she didn't know it or want it. "She wasn't able to control either one of them because they're already being controlled by someone else."

"You suspect one of us?" Alejandro asked, his tone sharp.

Austin paused, wondering if Luis . . . Naw. Austin was just trying to find any excuse to hang the guy. Luis had no reason to want Shade dead. And if he did, he didn't need to control humans to do it.

"No. Perhaps some of the unaffiliated with a grudge might come after the Slayer, but why would they come after a shadow demon? That doesn't make sense."

"Some?" Alejandro asked. "You suspect more than one?"

Austin eased his shoulder to a slightly less painful position. "There were two of them, so two controllers would have to work in concert. But I'm not convinced it's the unaffiliated, either. Just because it's possible doesn't mean I'm ready to believe it." He hesitated, then added, "There's something peculiar about the two men who attacked her. They're not demon, not vamp—human, but stronger and faster. It's possible they're being controlled by another mage demon." Or something else the Movement didn't know of.

"Then you definitely need to stay by Ms. Shapiro's side for longer than anticipated."

"I plan on it. But in order to keep Val safe, we have to protect Shade, too. I'd like to use the penthouse in the blood bank on the south side. Is anyone staying there now?"

"No, it's available for your use." Alejandro paused for a moment, then asked, "And you? Did the bullet incapacitate you?"

"No." Just hurt like mad. "But I need to get it out of my shoulder before I heal around it. I don't fancy carrying lead around inside me for the rest of my life." His very long life, if he was lucky.

"Of course. That would be interminable. Vincent is at the lab below the blood bank. He can help you."

"That'll work."

"Do you need a human driver or another car?"

Austin thought for a moment. "No, we only have Val, Shade, and the hellhounds to transport. Val can drive." He'd take the back seat, which Alejandro had outfitted so it was protected against the sun's rays.

"Excellent. I'll call Vincent and tell him to expect you."

"Good. Thanks." But since Alejandro was being so agreeable, there was one more item of business Austin had to take care of. "And Alejandro? Can you ask Luis to not go anywhere near Gwen and Elspeth?"

"Why?"

Because he'd listen to Alejandro and no one else. But, remembering his promise to his trainees, Austin told a partial truth. "Because they're terrified of him after that training session."

Alejandro paused, then said reluctantly, "Very well. I'll ask him to leave them alone."

Austin couldn't help it, he had to say something. "That man is a loose cannon waiting to explode," he warned harshly.

Alejandro's voice turned frosty. "That is my concern, not yours."

Austin knew the Movement's leader highly disapproved of dissension among his lieutenants, but Austin couldn't let this slide. "It'll be everyone's concern if he's not brought to heel."

"Drop it, lieutenant." Alejandro's tone brooked no refusal.

Well, Austin had said his piece and wouldn't get any further by setting Alejandro's back up. Besides, he'd gotten Alejandro's promise to keep Luis at a distance and warned him as much as he could. "All right. I'm heading for the penthouse now."

"Good. Keep me apprised of events as they transpire."

"Will do." Austin hung up and rose from the bed. No time to waste. He stood behind the door and opened it so he wouldn't be caught in stray rays of killer sun. "Val?" he called out. "I need to talk to you about the move."

She came immediately and closed the door behind her, then switched on the light. It might be light outside, but with her windows blocked against the sun, the room was dark. To her senses, anyway. He hadn't even noticed.

"What's up?" she asked.

"I've arranged with Alejandro to move all of us to the south side blood bank penthouse. We need to go right away, in case your attackers had back-up."

She nodded. "Yeah, but what about the sun?"

"Not a problem. You and Shade pack up what you need and put it in the trunk of the car. I can secure the back seat against the sun if you'll drive."

"And the dogs?"

"You can put them in the back seat, too."

"Okay." She nodded at the bed. "Take that blanket so you won't get fried. I'll go get everyone organized."

"Wait," Austin said. "You'll need the keys." He reached into his jeans pocket to pull them out, and the movement sent a red-hot lance of pain through him. He couldn't help but wince.

"You sure you're okay?" Val asked, looking concerned.

He hated showing weakness in front of anyone. "I'm fine," he said, his tone terse. "Here, take the keys."

She weighed the keys in her hand, hesitating. "Maybe Shade can help heal you."

Not gonna happen. "I'd just heal around the bullet. No, thanks."

"Then how are you going to get it out?"

"Someone's waiting at the blood bank to help. And then I'll heal just fine on my own. Vampire," he reminded her. He didn't need the shadow demon's help. Besides, it might not even work on his kind.

"Okay, then I'll make this fast," she promised.

And, true to her word, she got Shade and the hellhounds and all their stuff into the car in record time. She knocked on the bedroom door. "Ready?"

Austin pulled the blanket from the bed and wrapped it around his head and his hands. "Ready," he said. "You'll have to lead me since I won't be able to see without burning myself."

"No problem." Val grabbed his arm and hustled him out of the townhouse and into the car, closing the door as fast as she could.

The side and back windows were all tinted dark enough to block out the sun, and Austin hit the button that brought down a darkened sheet of glass between the front and back seats. Once he was safely in the dark again, he threw off the blanket.

The blanket landed on Fang, who sat on the seat beside him. The hellhound burrowed out from underneath it and growled at him.

"Sorry," Austin muttered, understanding Fang's protectiveness. "Don't mean any harm to you or your family." Princess and the puppies were on the floorboard, so it wasn't like he'd even touched them. He'd just been annoyed by the necessity of the damned blanket. It would have served him right if Val had twitted him about needing her help, but she was all business.

When they reached the hotel-turned-blood bank, he had her pull into the special garage built in the back, so he was able to get out of the car without going up in flames.

Vincent met them there. The short, bald guy handed Val the card key to the penthouse and showed her to the elevator, saying, "Make yourself at home. We'll ensure no one bothers you upstairs." He turned to Austin and said, "You're coming with me. Alejandro told me what you need."

Austin didn't argue. He wanted to get the slug out as soon as possible. They headed down to the lab in the basement where they tested all the blood that came into the bank. After some stock had been contaminated with demon blood and driven a few vampires mad, it had become an essential precaution.

They also had a couple of medical treatment rooms available, in case one of the donors became ill or something happened to a member of the New Blood Movement. It wasn't like they could go to a normal hospital. Luckily, the Movement had some members who had medical training, like Vincent.

Vincent led him to one of the treatment rooms where Gwen was waiting. "So you've started working with Vincent already?" Austin asked.

Gwen nodded. "Yes. Vincent is letting me help him when I'm not training with you." She gestured at the shiny, sharp medical instruments laid out on a tray.

Austin sighed in resignation at the sight. This was going to hurt.

"Lie down," Vincent said sternly, snapping on latex gloves.

Austin took off his shirt and laid down on the examination table. When Vincent probed at the entry wound, Gwen asked, "Aren't you going to give him something for the pain first?"

Vincent shook his head. "Painkillers and anesthesia don't work all that well on us. A quart of whiskey might help dull the pain. Unfortunately, we don't have any here." He raised an eyebrow at Austin.

"You want me to send someone out for some?"

"No." The longer it took to get it out, the more his flesh would heal around the bullet and make it even harder and more painful to remove. "Just do it."

Vincent nodded as if that's what he'd expected Austin to say, and handed him a piece of leather.

"What's that for?" Gwen asked, looking puzzled.

In answer, Austin put it in his mouth and bit down hard. He shut his eyes against Gwen's horrified expression and spent the next few minutes in agony as Vincent probed for the bullet. Red haze filled his vision, even behind his closed eyes, and he could think of nothing except the excruciating pain in his shoulder. He couldn't hold on . . . any . . . longer. The world faded.

When he regained consciousness, Vincent was gone, but Gwen was still there, staring at him, looking even paler than a new vamp ought to. "Are you okay?" Austin asked.

"Me?" she said incredulously. "I'm fine. How about *you*?"

"Just peachy," Austin said and closed his eyes. Actually, the pain had faded to a dull ache, and he could stand it now. "It'll heal faster with the bullet out."

"That's what Vincent said."

Austin opened his eyes and quirked a smile at her. "Not like the medicine you're used to, huh?"

"No! Remind me never to get shot, or to always keep some whiskey on hand." She shook her head. "I don't know how you do it," she said, sounding lost.

He didn't ask what "it" meant. He knew she was having a hard time dealing with her new life, though she tried hard to make sure her friends didn't suspect. "You'll get used to it in time," he said soothingly and sat up, swinging his legs to hang off the side of the table. "It's harder when you're turned against your will."

"Yes, I imagine it is," Gwen said. "Is that how you . . . were turned?"

Austin bristled for a moment, then realized he hadn't explained the protocol yet. "It's not considered polite in our circles to ask how and why you became one of us."

"Oh. Sorry." Gwen looked down at her clenched hands, her eyes blinking rapidly.

Austin took pity on her. "It's a dumb rule. But I've lived by it so long, I guess I never really questioned it. I don't mind sharing—it was so long ago, it almost seems like it happened to someone else." That wasn't exactly the truth, but right now, Gwen needed to believe it would get better for her, eventually. He shrugged. "I wasn't exactly turned against my will, though I didn't ask for it, either. It was . . . different for me."

"How so?" Gwen asked hopefully.

Austin studied his own hands for a moment. "I was living in a small town in West Texas during the days when outlaws and bandits ran roughshod over the pioneers who were trying to make a living in this new land." He shrugged. "The outlaws got out of hand, so the sheriff deputized me to help."

"How old were you?" Gwen asked softly.

"Twenty-three. But that was considered much older in those days." At her nod, he continued, "A couple of men got drunk and decided the Mexicans in town were to blame for their troubles, and took it upon themselves to teach them a lesson. They beat a man unconscious, and when I arrived, they were dragging off his wife." He didn't think he had to explain what they wanted with the woman.

"What did you do?"

"I tried to stop them, but when they pulled a gun on me, I shot them." He'd been terrified—of killing a man, of being killed himself, and most of all, of failing to save the poor woman who had done nothing to deserve the degradation they had planned for her. "What I didn't know was that there was a third man. He shot me in the back."

Gwen gasped. "He killed you?"

"Yes. Well, as close as you can get, anyway." Austin's mouth twisted into a wry grin. "Alejandro happened to be passing through town at the time, and he saw what happened. The sun set shortly after that, and he saved the woman and dragged me off the street and turned me before I could die, even though I was a total stranger."

"Why?"

"He said it was because I was so 'brave and noble' that he couldn't stand to see me die at the hand of a coward." Austin snorted. "But I was just a kid. I didn't know any better."

"So, you didn't agree to be turned?"

"No, I wasn't given a choice. I wasn't conscious."

"Did you regret it?"

"Not at the time," Austin admitted. "After all, I figured being undead was better than the alternative. But I don't remember the process at all." Not like Gwen. She'd had a demon occupying her body and had been forced to watch helplessly as she was turned into a vampire.

"Do you regret it now?"

"No. Most of the time." He smiled. "I've seen a lot of strange and wondrous things in my lifetime, and the fact of being virtually immortal is very appealing. But there are times when I'd give it all up to be fully human again."

"Like to be with Val?" Gwen asked.

He shot her a sharp look. "That isn't possible."

"Maybe if I put in a good word for you?"

"Now why would you do that?" he wondered out loud.

She shrugged and wouldn't meet his eyes. "Has it ever worked out? With a vampire and a human or part demon, I mean."

She sounded wistful, and Austin wondered what non-vamp she'd fallen for.

"It can," Austin admitted. "I've seen it work. But it creates great strain on a relationship when one party grows old and feeble while the other stays young. Stressful on both sides. Not everyone can handle it."

"It would be worth it, though, for as many years as you could squeeze in together, don't you think?"

"Yes," Austin admitted. "Yes, I do." But would Val ever give him the chance to find out?

Chapter Ten

Val

I'D BEEN TO THE vamp penthouse above the blood bank before. With its dramatic black, white, and steel high tech décor shot with slashes of crimson, it appeared cold and hard, reminiscent of blood splashed on a modern horror movie set. I'd never actually seen anyone living here, though. They must use it to impress—or scare the heck out of—guests.

But one thing I did have to say for it, it was well stocked with human food and lots of beds. No worry about who was going to sleep where, and a lavish buffet of vamp "food" downstairs for Austin.

I assumed he was being well taken care of by his own, and since Shade and I were pretty tired, we hit the sheets—separately—and didn't wake until the sun went down again. I wasn't sure I wanted to get out of bed, but the smell of bacon made my mouth water. I dressed and tamed my mop of unruly hair, then went into the kitchen, wondering who was cooking.

Gwen. I should have known.

"Hello," she said cheerfully, stirring a pan of gravy.

I checked her out, trying to be subtle. She didn't look too pale yet. Guess she hadn't been a vamp long enough. In any case, she was still Gwen. "Biscuits and gravy?" I said hopefully.

"Yes—Shade asked for them."

"Yum." Feeling suddenly grateful for a cheerful person this evening, I gave her a quick hug.

She looked surprised. "What was that for?"

I shrugged. "I miss you." Was it that unusual for me to hug someone?

PRETTY MUCH, Fang said from under the table. WHAT? YOU MISSING YOUR BOYFRIEND SO YOU'RE GOING FOR A LITTLE GIRL ON GIRL ACTION?

Don't be stupid. Gwen is like family. She'd been there when my family wasn't, when I needed someone the most.

YEAH, I KNOW. SORRY, I'M A BIT GRUMPY. PRINCESS KICKED ME

OUT OF BED HOURS AGO.

I grinned. I bet it was a bit crowded with all six of them now.

Fang's head perked up. THE PUPS ARE WAKING. I'M JUST GOING TO SEE HOW THEY ARE.

He trotted off into another room, and I smiled at his obvious paternal pride. "Where's Shade?" I asked Gwen.

"Elspeth is talking to him in the other room."

"Good. I'm hoping she'll be able to help him with his memory loss." I glanced at the kitchen. Gwen pretty much had all the food ready, except for the gravy which she was still stirring. "Can I help set the table?"

"Sure." She nodded to a set of cabinets. "You'll find everything there."

As I set the table, I noticed someone else conspicuously missing. "Where's Austin? Is he okay?"

"Yes, he's healing fast. Right now, he's downstairs, doing some things for Alejandro."

"Good. I wondered if Alejandro could spare him."

Gwen gave me a crooked smile. "Well, Luis and Rosa aren't happy he's playing your bodyguard, but Alejandro thinks you're special so he's agreed to assign Austin to you."

"Are you getting involved in vamp politics now?" I asked in surprise.

"Not really. But you can't avoid it if you live at the mansion. And since Austin is sponsoring Elspeth and me, we're moving in here, too, for a while."

"For vamp lessons . . . or to avoid politics?"

Gwen shrugged but wouldn't meet my eyes. "Both," she said, though I suspected there was more she wasn't saying. "Plus I'm helping out in the lab. Vincent said he could use someone with my medical skills."

I watched her for a few minutes. She seemed to be her old self, but there was a seriousness or melancholy or something underlying her normal cheerfulness. "Are you okay?" I asked softly. "I know you didn't ask for this life, and it's kind of my fault you ended up this way." After all, the mage demon who'd caused her to get turned had kidnapped her, thinking she was me.

"I'm fine," Gwen said firmly, but her attention was primarily on the bubbling white gravy. "And it's not your fault. Sheesh, you and Micah are all too willing to take on responsibility for the world."

"No, just our little demon piece of it." But if she didn't want to talk about it, I wouldn't press her.

"So, how about you and Shade?" she asked, giving me a look over her shoulder. "How's that going?"

"I'm not sure," I said honestly. "He's kind of moody and withdrawn, like he doesn't want to be around anyone. And he lost his temper yesterday pretty easily, which he's never done before."

"You're hoping Elspeth can help him deal with his past?"

"Yeah."

She glanced at the table where I had laid out only two place settings. "You'll need to set at least three more places," she said.

"I'm sorry. I assumed you, Elspeth, and Austin wouldn't be eating." Not human food, anyway.

"Not for us. We have more people coming." She glanced up as the doorbell rang. "Can you get that? It's probably them now."

I opened the door and saw Micah and Lieutenant Ramirez there. And, of all people, Mood was with them.

The Emo girl with the emotion-altering power sniffed appreciatively. "Oh good," she said. "Gwen's cooking." She sauntered past me toward the kitchen, not even bothering to say hello.

What? Did I suddenly become invisible?

"Good timing," Gwen said. "The food is ready." She fluttered her hands at the table. "Sit, eat."

All of a sudden, she seemed nervous and flustered. And I noticed she glanced at everyone but Micah, who she studiously avoided. He seemed a bit tense around her, too. Had they had a falling-out or something?

OR SOMETHING, Fang said, trotting in from the other room. MICAH HAS A THING FOR GWEN, AND I THINK SHE FEELS THE SAME WAY.

Whoa. Micah and Gwen? When had that happened?

OH, PROBABLY WHEN THEY SPENT SO MUCH TIME TOGETHER WHEN THEY WERE KIDNAPPED.

Really? I loved them both, but could a relationship between a demon and a vamp really work out?

Shade joined us then. After our talk, I wasn't sure how to behave around him. Should I flirt? Act normal? Keep my mouth shut? I took a peek at his expression. After his talk with Elspeth, he appeared thoughtful, inward-looking. Guess it didn't matter what I did—he wouldn't even notice right now.

Sighing, I chowed down on Gwen's scrumptious cooking. Princess took a break from her puppies to get some of Gwen's food, and Elspeth went to get Austin. We didn't discuss anything important until we were all stuffed with biscuits, gravy, and bacon. I noticed I was able to see Shade's face without using the amulet and checked under the table to see why. Sure enough, Fang and Princess were lying on his bare feet so everyone could see the shadow demon.

SHADE THOUGHT IT WOULD MAKE THE LIEUTENANT FEEL MORE COMFORTABLE, Fang explained.

He must have said that to the whole table, because Mood beamed at Shade, saying, "That's so thoughtful of you."

Shade shrugged. "No big deal."

Yeah, it was nice of him, though not enough for Mood to gush about. Strange. But I let it go as Elspeth and Austin came in and pulled chairs up to the table.

"How's your shoulder?" Gwen asked Austin.

Sheesh, I should have asked him that, especially since he took that bullet for me. I frowned inwardly. I really shouldn't take Austin for granted. But heck, I didn't want to take him for anything.

Austin rotated his shoulder. "No problem," he said. "Happy to take a bullet for the Slayer." He smirked at me, which I did my best to ignore.

Shade shot him an annoyed look. Was he ticked that Austin had saved both of us? I understood that—I wasn't crazy about being taken care of either. At least with Austin healed, I didn't have to feel guilty. Besides, I was so used to him being invincible that it was hard to picture him on the injured list.

"Shall we get started?" I asked.

Austin spoke up first, looking at Micah and the police lieutenant. "What did you learn about the two who attacked us?"

Micah made a gesture for Ramirez to go first. "Not a lot," the lieutenant said. "We're running prints on both of them and did an autopsy on the man who committed suicide. He had a lot of scars on his back, like he'd been whipped, and several tattoos with religious sayings."

The lieutenant pulled up some pictures on his phone and showed them to us. "These look familiar to any of you?"

Micah frowned. "The man in our custody has the same scars, and one of the tattoos is the same—the one with a cross shaped like a dagger."

Idly, I wondered how they knew.

THEY LET THE GUY TAKE A SPONGE BATH. THAT'S HOW HE SAW.

That made sense. "Were they fully human?" I asked. "They seemed stronger and faster than most humans—maybe they had some demon blood in them?"

"Everything we've looked at so far indicates the dead man was fully human," Ramirez said. "But we'll continue testing."

Gwen nodded. "I've been helping Vincent test the other man's blood, and we found the same thing."

Ramirez glanced at Micah. "Did you get anything out of the other man?"

Micah shook his head. "So far, he's not talking, and we've taken away everything he might use to kill himself. He spends most of his time praying."

"So they both have whip scars and the same tattoos," I said. "You think they might be part of a gang?"

"Not one that I'm aware of," Ramirez said, "but we're checking it out."

Austin held out his hand. "Can I see that picture again?"

Ramirez handed it to him, and Austin frowned down at it.

"What is it?" I asked. "Do you recognize something?"

"No, but there's something about those scars that's a little off."

"No kidding," Shade said. "They've been beaten."

"That's not it," Austin said, shaking his head and handing the phone back to Ramirez. "I've seen that pattern before."

"Seen what pattern?"

Austin shrugged. "I don't know. Maybe it'll come to me later."

I snorted. "It probably seems off because why bother whipping someone you control that strongly? I mean, Lola couldn't even get a toehold in his chakras, which means someone else was controlling him. If the controller could handle the two men's minds that easily, why bother whipping them?"

Ramirez frowned. "Some men are just cruel and don't need a reason."

Elspeth nodded. "It has ever been so."

"Okay, but who's doing the controlling? A vampire?" I addressed that last comment to Austin.

"It's possible," he said, shrugging, "but most of us are just able to control one person's actions at a time. Not two."

"Okay," I said. "So maybe there's more than one vamp, or some kind of über vampire who's learned how to control more."

"Or a mage demon," Shade said. "That seems more likely."

"Maybe," I conceded. "But why would a mage demon target shadow demons?"

"Why would vampires target shadow demons?" he countered.

Good question. Not having an answer, I shrugged.

"Well, there's a way to check to see if there are any mage demons nearby," Micah reminded me.

I winced. The *Encyclopedia Magicka.* "Yeah, but if I use the spell to locate a mage demon, it'll take even longer to bring Lola back up to speed."

Austin said, "Micah's right. Better to look for a mage demon now and take him off guard than have to deal with him later." He gave me an apologetic look. "It could save us a lot of time and pain."

I sighed. Looked like I wasn't going to win this argument. As Gwen cleared the table so we could lay the book on it, I felt for the spell inside me. There it was, residing in my gut. I'd managed to ignore it as long as I wasn't using it, but now it churned, ready for action. I found the activating words in the book and, resisting the urge to make it sound too dramatic, I said, "Beacon, show me the way." My stomach lurched, and my head started spinning like the rinse cycle on a washing machine. Urp.

I glanced around, but nothing happened. Duh. I couldn't exactly see the telltale column of rippling green light from indoors. I checked out the window, but no green light. "I can't see anything from here," I told them, "but that doesn't mean there isn't a sign. I can't see the whole city."

"There's a stairway to the roof," Austin said. "You can check it out there."

I followed him up to the roof and viewed the whole three-sixty, but still no column of green light, for as far as I could see.

Darn it, I'd used a spell for nothing. "Now Lola is weaker than ever." Less than ten percent of her normal capacity.

"I can help with that," Austin said. Strangely, his expression wasn't mocking or amused. He grasped my wrist in a light hold. "Feed on me, here, while we're alone," he urged quietly.

Yes! Lola cried from deep inside me. Alarmed at how good that sounded, I jerked my arm away. "I don't think so."

"Why not? Let me replenish what you lost with that spell, at least."

"Why?" I asked suspiciously.

He sighed. "Because the sooner you get back up to full speed as a succubus, the sooner I'll be able to leave you on your own. I've been neglecting my duties."

He *wanted* to leave? For some strange reason, that felt like a slap in the face.

Stupid. I wanted him to leave, didn't I? "Okay, but just a little. Micah will be able to tell if I take too much." And maybe the others would, too.

Austin nodded and moved deeper into the shadows until we were no longer silhouetted against the sky or revealed by streetlights. "What do we need to do?" he asked. "Like last time?"

I felt heat rising in my face. The last time I'd let Lola feed fully on Austin, I'd lost control, wrapped my legs around his waist in front of half the Demon Underground, and sucked face. It was necessary then to save

Micah, Gwen and Shade. Did that pertain here? This was to help keep Shade safe, too, right? Besides, if I could get back up to full speed, Austin wouldn't feel the necessity to act as my bodyguard anymore.

Well, that was incentive enough. Slowly, I placed my hand against his chest. His arms came around me, and I stiffened.

"Just trying to steady both of us," he murmured. "I'll try to contain myself," he added dryly.

If Lola had been at full strength, he wouldn't be able to, but she was so weak, this close proximity would probably only make him lust a little. I nodded and tried to relax as I leaned into him. He settled against me as if he belonged there, as if I was precious, as if it was the most natural thing in the world to hold me in his arms.

Trying not to admit to myself how good it felt to be cherished by *someone*, even Austin, I let Lola free. She quested greedily for the vampire's chakras. It was easier with Austin than it had been with the rogue vampire. Lola already knew Austin very well, and he wasn't fighting it. The energy flowing from him to me was still weak and sludgy, but definitely moving in the right direction. I resisted the urge to use the amulet. It had helped ease the flow last time, but hadn't seemed to actually increase the volume.

Lola took long, slow, leisurely sips of the lovely, lusty energy, and I felt it flow into my starved chakras. Boy, I really needed this. I shouldn't have waited so long. I'd been holding out for Shade, but if I'd gone much longer, I'm not sure I could have done this at all.

Austin, thankfully, let Lola feed without making any more comments or getting any more intimate. When I judged I was back up to about twenty percent again, I eased the flow and stopped.

When the flow ceased, I realized I was snuggled up to Austin, my head resting on his shoulder. And it felt really good.

Crap. I pushed away from him and brushed my hands against my pants, not wanting to see the knowing look in his eyes. "Thanks," I said shortly. Then, remembering I should be more gracious, I added, "That really helped."

"Good," Austin said, and I was grateful he didn't try to make a joke of it. "Shall we rejoin the others?"

"Sure."

We came back downstairs and I reported to the rest, "Okay, no mage demons nearby," hoping no one would ask why it had taken so long.

Micah frowned. "I'm sorry you had to had to use another spell and weaken your abilities even more."

"Hey, I can help with that," Austin said suggestively, wiggling his eyebrows at me.

Oh, crap. And now everyone was staring at us, wondering if we were going to go off in a corner and make out or something. I didn't know whether to be grateful that he didn't reveal I'd already had a little snack, or ticked that he'd made me feel like a fool once again. "I'll pass," I said, avoiding looking at Shade. I didn't want him getting jealous or thinking I was into Austin.

Micah frowned. "Are you sure? You do need to strengthen your gift."

"I'm sure," I said with finality.

All of a sudden, I felt a surge of liking for Austin, like he was totally hot and I was waaaay into him. I took a step toward him and smiled up at him like he was all that and a box of chocolates. Yum. I licked my lips, liking what I saw.

"Val!" Shade protested explosively.

That brought me back to my senses, sort of. Weird. I didn't want to feel this way. In fact, I *didn't* feel this way . . . did I? What the heck was going on? Then I saw Mood staring at me with a small quirk in her smile and her eyes all glowy violet. A dead giveaway.

"Damn it, Mood, cut it out," I said. She was forcing me to feel this way—her and her blasted mood-enhancing powers.

She cut her gaze toward Micah. "But he said—"

"I'm pretty sure he didn't tell you to force me to feel all girly and swoony over Austin."

Austin grinned. "Interesting. Can she do it again so I can see what that looks like?"

"No. Period. End of sentence," I enunciated clearly so he couldn't possibly misunderstand.

Shade looked mollified, though I suspected he was a little embarrassed by his outburst. "Not so fun when you're the one being controlled, is it?" he asked.

Okay, he had a point. Not that I'd admit he'd managed to make me feel guilty for trying to do the same to him.

Micah gave the demon girl a disappointed look. "I didn't tell Mood to control you. Mood is here only to help Shade with his anger issues."

Anger issues? Like the green cloud he was sporting over his head yesterday? Well, maybe that was necessary. "Just keep your mood-enhancing out of my chakras," I told Mood.

She shrugged. "Sorry, I was just trying to help. I know how much we need our Paladin strong and whole," she said, her tone full of sarcasm. "Why don't *you* know that?"

Whoa, where was this hostility coming from? We'd been okay

before. Not BFFs or anything, but certainly more than civil, especially since I knew how she felt about Josh. Had she changed her mind about him? Was she interested in *Shade* now?

COULD BE, BABE, Fang confirmed. JOSH FOUND OUT HOW SHE FELT ABOUT HIM AND GAVE HER A VERBAL DEAR JANE. SHADE COMFORTED HER.

And that's probably all it took for a chick like Mood. Give her a little pat on the shoulder, and she probably assumed the guy was in love with her. Well, she could go play patty-cake somewhere else. I wasn't ready to let Shade go.

But you aren't ready to keep him, not really, are you? Especially since there's another alternative.

No, I didn't even want to go there. Firmly shutting out the small voice inside me, I asked Micah, "You really think Mood is necessary? I think Shade can handle his problems on his own."

I glanced at Shade, but he didn't comment. Maybe he wasn't as sure as I wanted him to be.

"Perhaps," Elspeth said, "but Mood's presence assures we can help him calm down if he needs it."

Use me, the amulet whispered seductively.

"You also have me," I reminded them. "I can control Shade if necessary. We don't need someone else here."

Shade spoke up for himself. "I don't think so, Val. As you just pointed out, Lola is weakened, and the only way you could control me is with the amulet, which you promised not to do, right?" And when I didn't answer, he persisted. "Right?"

"I guess," I muttered. But Mood was going to make it hard to get close to Shade, especially since she'd just been given permission to make him feel all soft and gooey whenever she was around. What if she made him feel soft and gooey about *her*?

Crap. This was *not* a good idea.

Chapter Eleven

Shade

ANNOYED BY VAL'S reluctant agreement, Shade dumped his plates in the sink and headed for his room. He didn't want to start a fight in front of anyone. Heck, he didn't want to fight with Val at all.

What was the matter with him? Sometimes, he thought he really cared for her, which explained those surges of jealousy that erupted within him whenever she was around Austin. But at other times, he felt a deep distrust of Val and her motives, more than could be explained by the way the amulet seemed to control her. That was the problem with Val—she evoked strong emotions in him that led to feelings like jealousy and anger . . . feelings that could cause him to open a portal to the demon dimension.

And *that* would be catastrophic. He absolutely had to control his anger no matter what, so it was best to try to kill any feelings for Val at all.

He closed his eyes in pain. He didn't want to lose these feelings. She'd been the only good thing that had happened in his life. Did he really have to push her away?

Sheesh, he didn't know what to do.

He opened the door to his room, which irked him even more. Shade owed his safety and even the place he slept to Val and, worse, Austin.

DO YOU NEED ME? Princess asked from the living room. ARE MY CHILDREN OKAY?

I'm good, Shade said, not wanting Princess to catch his crappy mood. He glanced down at the puppies, all snuggled together in a pile. *And your kids are still sleeping. I'll call you if that changes.* She needed the break.

OKAY.

Shade couldn't help but smile. Val and the others only saw Princess as a self-centered egotist, but when the hellhound loved, she loved with her whole heart.

"Could I be of some help?" Elspeth asked from behind him. "I sense you have some conflict in your soul."

Well, that was one way of putting it. Shade thought about denying it, but what the heck. Maybe the key to figuring this out was learning more about his past. She knew more about that than he did, which was just plain weird, in anyone's book. "Sure," he mumbled, and gestured her into the room, closing the door behind her.

When Mood tried to follow her in, Shade balked. What was it with the women in his life always thinking he needed to be controlled? "I don't need you right now," he told her.

Her face fell, and Shade grimaced at his blunt words. "Sorry, but I just need help with my memories. I'll be fine."

Mood reluctantly turned away, and the former Memory Eater sat gingerly on a chair next to the bed. Sighing, Shade sat on the bed and offered her his wrist to touch so she could see his face. That way *he* wouldn't frighten *her*. "Why don't you just tell me about my past?" he asked impatiently. "You know it all, don't you?"

"I do," she acknowledged, "but it is better for you if your memory comes back slowly and gradually, so you can deal with it appropriately. And, with recent events, I sense the past has started to affect the present, regardless of whether you choose it or not."

"Huh?" What the heck did that mean?

She tried again. "You may not remember your past consciously, but the deeper you, your unconscious, recalls everything. So, events of the present may trigger emotions from your past, even if you don't consciously understand them."

That could explain a lot.

She cocked her head and looked at him curiously. "Have you remembered anything more, any of your dreams?"

"Not much," Shade said, trying to sort through the vague impressions. "I think you were right, earlier. I think I did live somewhere else before San Antonio. I remember adobe walls when I was younger." Thick walls that enclosed him, protected him from the world. Not that San Antonio lacked adobe homes, but he somehow knew the walls in his memory existed elsewhere.

"And were you alone inside those walls?"

He shrugged. "I don't know. I mean, logically, I probably lived with someone else, like parents, but I don't remember them."

"Nothing?" she asked gently.

"Just a few impressions, that they existed. And emotions."

She nodded. "Good emotions or bad?"

Fear and pain mostly, whenever he tried to think of that time. And something like betrayal, that he didn't understand. "Bad, mostly. And all mixed up."

"What about the good times? What did you enjoy most as a child?"

"Playing online computer games." That popped out of his mouth without him even thinking about it. "But I don't know if that's a memory, or simple logic." He shrugged. "After all, I like them now. Stands to reason I enjoyed them as a kid."

"Who was your best friend?"

"A girl," Shade said, surprising himself. If he'd thought about it, which he hadn't, he'd have assumed his best friend would have been a boy. Or, more likely, that he hadn't had any friends. What sane kid would hang out with a shadow demon? Unless the other kid was part demon, maybe. "Was I a member of another Demon Underground?" he asked.

Instant negation and disgust filled him at the thought.

It must have showed on his face, because Elspeth said, "That caused a strong emotion. What do you think?"

"I'm not sure." Did it mean he'd belonged to one and hated it? Or that he didn't belong because there was something wrong with them?

"Let's go back to the girl," Elspeth said. "Do you remember what she looked like?"

He thought for a moment. "No, I don't know that I ever saw her face. Maybe we never met. Maybe we just communicated online."

"What was her name?" Elspeth asked.

He opened his mouth to answer. He almost had it, but then it was gone, whisked away behind a door that slammed shut in his mind and refused to open. He shook his head. "I don't know. It's gone." But this girl, whoever she was, was evidently tied in to whatever it was he didn't want to remember. He winced. "And now I have a headache."

Elspeth patted his hand. "That is probably enough for today. We don't want to push you too hard."

This was stupid. "What if I change my mind? What if I decide not to remember?"

"That is your choice, but if you remain here, I fear you will eventually recall everything whether you want to or not. And you may not be able to control the emotions the memories engender."

"Yeah," he said bitterly. "And I have to learn to keep them under lock and key, or the entire world will suffer the consequences."

She nodded. "As long as you remain a shadow demon, yes."

He glanced at her sharply. "What does that mean? Are you saying I don't *have* to be a shadow demon?" Impossible.

"Perhaps."

"How? I was born this way. How could I possibly stop being part demon, short of death?"

"I was once part demon," she reminded him. "And I am no longer."

Holy crap, she was right. It *was* possible, with Val's help. She'd used the exorcism spell to release the demon from Elspeth and others. She could do the same for him.

To be completely human . . . joy filled him at the thought. To be able to walk in public without hiding every inch of his skin, to not cycle through strange dimensions and feelings all the time, to not have to worry that losing his emotions would create devastating havoc . . . to not have strange men hunting him because of his abilities.

Wow. Incredibly empowering. Mind-blowing.

But . . . if he chose to do this, would he regret it later? After all, being part demon had defined him his whole life.

He'd have to think about it. Hard.

Chapter Twelve

Val

AFTER WE ATE and Shade went off to his room, Gwen drew me off into my bedroom, saying she needed to speak to me about something. After seeing her reactions earlier, I had a feeling I knew what she wanted to talk about. "Did you want to talk about Micah?"

"No," she said, shaking her head. "Why?"

I shrugged. "I wondered if you two had something going on."

"No, no. Nothing going on." Her mouth might say no, but the embarrassment on her face said yes.

"Yeah, right. Hey, I love you both, but a demon and a vamp together . . . can that really work?"

"Why not?" she asked, sounding defensive. "It's not like we're different species or anything."

"Well, yeah, I know the plumbing matches up and all, but I mean . . ." Heck, what did I mean? "Uh, it's not like you can have children together."

Gwen winced. "I can't have children, ever, now," she said softly.

I cursed my stupid tongue. I just had to go and remind her that being a vampire was irreversible. "I'm sorry—"

"Well, different kinds of demons can't have children together either, can they? Like you and Shade?"

"No, I guess not. But two demons . . . that's different."

"How?"

Crap. She had to go and call me on it. "Well, we're both the same kind of woo woo creature. You and Micah are different."

"Like you and Austin?" she said with an arched eyebrow.

I flopped down on the bed. "Huh? What does that have to do with anything?"

She sat on the bed beside me. "That's what I wanted to talk to you about. I noticed how you reacted to Mood and Shade, not to mention Austin. I thought maybe you might want someone to talk to."

I'd never really had guy problems before Mom kicked me out, and I just wasn't used to having anyone to talk to. "Why are you asking about

Austin?" I asked defensively. "You know I'm into Shade."

She shrugged. "I just noticed Austin really seems to have a thing for you. I wondered if you noticed."

I snorted. "I don't really think he has 'a thing.' I think he thinks he ought to have a thing, so he does."

Gwen looked confused. Heck, I'd confused myself. "Never mind," I said. "Look, Austin is totally sexy and everything, but I'm not interested. Why are you pushing him on me, anyway?" A flash of brilliance suddenly assailed me. "Is it because you figure another vamp-demon couple would help you not feel guilty about playing footsie with Micah?"

"No, nothing like that," she said, but she wouldn't meet my eyes.

Bingo. Now that I understood where she was coming from, it was a little easier to take.

Gwen shrugged. "I just thought you should know what kind of man he is." She paused, then added, "He's one of Alejandro's lieutenants for a reason. He's very well respected in the Movement and is the primary PR liaison with the general public because of his charm."

"Charm? Ha!"

Gwen punched me in the arm.

"Ouch," I exclaimed. "Cool it with the vamp strength there, Gwen."

"I'm sorry," she said. "I still forget sometimes. And don't change the subject. You know Austin has a lot of charm. He just doesn't always see the need to use it around you."

I threw up my hands. "Enough with the Austin love fest. I'm into Shade. And I'm not planning on changing my mind."

Gwen looked at me thoughtfully. "Does Shade feel the same way?"

Ouch. Hit me where it hurts, why don't you? "I think so." But I wished he'd show it.

"Shade has some issues," Gwen said carefully. "I'm not sure he's good for you."

I couldn't believe my ears. "So you think dating a vampire is better than dating a guy my own age, with whom I share demonkind in common, and who is totally hot?"

"Are those the only reasons you like him?" she asked softly, one eyebrow raised.

"No, of course not. Those are just the superficial reasons. There's also his intelligence, his loyalty to the Underground, his geeky brain—" I stopped, annoyed. "Why do I have to justify this to you?"

"You don't," Gwen said. "Like I said, I just wanted to make sure you weren't letting your hormones—and Lola—overrule your head because of a pretty face. You shouldn't let anyone control your relationships."

"Isn't that what you're trying to do here? Control mine?"

"No, but I know we girls tend to romanticize the first time, the first guy we sleep with. For you, that was Shade."

I grinned. "It was almost your brother, you know."

She smiled back. "I know. I don't think you're right for each other, either."

"So Dan and Shade aren't right for me, but Austin is?" Becoming a vamp had obviously done something to her brain.

"I didn't say that," she reassured me. "Just think about it, okay? Being in a relationship can be a lot of work. Both sides have to work at it, or it won't last. All I'm saying is, don't let it be one-sided. If Shade won't come around, maybe you should look elsewhere. You can't avoid feeding Lola because it might upset Shade."

I sighed. She wasn't going to shut up until I agreed. "Okay, I'll think about it."

"Good. Shall we go back in the other room to see if they've learned anything more?"

"Okay." I wouldn't let the conversation bother me. She was probably just trying to justify her feelings for Micah.

When we returned to the living room decorated in the latest in slasher décor, Micah's face brightened when he saw Gwen.

And weirdly, Austin's face seemed to light up in a quieter way when he saw me. It made me feel all warm and fuzzy . . . until I regained my sanity.

Crap. Wrong guy. I wished Shade's face would do that when I entered the room. Unfortunately, I didn't know if it did or not. His expression was too often obscured by other-worldly swirls, and right now, he wasn't even in the room.

HE WENT WITH ELSPETH TO HIS ROOM TO WORK ON HIS MEMORY, Fang explained. SOME OF HIS MEMORIES ARE RETURNING.

Really? What memories? What are they about? I groped for anything that might help me understand the shadow demon a little better. And, darn it, I should be there with him.

THAT'S HIS BUSINESS, Princess reminded me sharply. IF HE WANTS YOU TO KNOW, HE'LL TELL YOU.

Well, excuuuuse me!

SHE'S RIGHT, Fang said, though his apologetic tone let me know he realized Princess could have been more diplomatic. SHADE NEEDS TO BE READY TO TELL YOU HIMSELF.

Okay, I said. But I didn't like it. I glanced around the main room.

Micah, Lieutenant Ramirez, and Austin were making plans around the coffee table. Mood sat sulking on the couch. Guess that meant Shade didn't need her right now, either. Good.

"I'm going to check on the puppies," Gwen said with a smile.

I couldn't blame her. Looking at adorable fuzzy pups sounded like a whole lot more fun than joining the testosterone fest. Sighing, I hitched up my estrogen and took a seat.

Lieutenant Ramirez hung up the phone. "Good, you're here," he said to me. "We got a hit on the fingerprints of the guy you have in custody. His name is Jorge Ortiz, and he's from New Mexico."

"New Mexico?" I repeated in surprise. "Why would someone from New Mexico want to assassinate a shadow demon in San Antonio?"

"That's what we need to find out," Micah said.

"How?"

"Well, let's go pay Mr. Ortiz a visit."

Fang declined to go with us, preferring to stay with his newly increased family. Ramirez didn't want to be seen condoning the existence of the Underground jail, so he decided not to go either.

So, it was just Micah and me. "Is Austin coming, too?" I asked.

He grinned. "Miss me, darlin'?"

"As if. I'm just not sure if Micah wants you to see where we keep the prisoner."

"If you're going, I'm going," Austin said firmly. He gave Micah the beady eye, as if to show he meant it. "Besides, Elspeth told us about the cell where she used to live."

Micah nodded. "If we are to be allies, we need to trust each other more. Come on, we'll take my car."

We took his Lexus to Club Purgatory, where booze was flowing, and the joint was hopping despite the fact that this was a week night. Micah took us through the front door and had to peel off a couple of groupies who pouted when they learned he wasn't scheduled to dance tonight. That's how Micah fed his incubus—by taking small amounts of lusty energy from the women he mesmerized while he was on stage. He'd never gotten involved with any of them, or so I'd heard. Probably because it was hard to tell how women felt about him when all they felt was lust when they got near him. Which made me wonder what had happened between him and Gwen when they were kidnapped together, and why neither of them seemed to want to pursue it openly.

Micah led us down to the room where he stored the wine and beyond, into the part of the cellar that held several jail cells. One had belonged to Elspeth before I took the demon out of her and rendered her sane, and I'd even occupied one of them for a little while. Not because Micah put me there, but because one of his people had been trying to get my attention—and my support. It wasn't my favorite place in the world, but at least this time I was on the outside of the bars.

On the other side was Jorge Ortiz, who knelt in prayer at the cot in the cell.

"Mr. Ortiz?" Micah said.

The man looked up. Surprise flickered in his eyes momentarily, then he said, "So you know my name. It doesn't matter."

"We also know you are from New Mexico," Micah said calmly. "What are you doing in San Antonio, besides shooting this man?" He indicated Austin.

Austin rubbed his shoulder. "It's nothing."

The man's eyes widened, and he crossed himself. "You are *vampiro*," he stated, looking more disgusted than frightened. "You should be dead."

"Thanks to my sire, I am undead instead," Austin said cheerfully. He sauntered up to the bars of the cell. "And you were looking for a shadow demon. Why? Do you want to make him dead, too?"

"All demons should be dead," Ortiz said flatly. "The good book says, 'Thou shalt not suffer a witch to live.'"

"We were talking about demons, not witches," Austin corrected him.

"It is all the same. The holy one protects me from such as you." And with that, Ortiz crossed himself again and turned his back on us to resume his prayers.

Micah glanced at me, one eyebrow raised. Obviously, he wanted me to use Lola to see what info I could squeeze out of him. Unfortunately, Lola was still weak, even after feeding on Austin, but I did as he asked. No go. Lola's energy tendrils slid off him like he was Teflon and she was a limp noodle. The amulet didn't work, either. I shook my head. Ortiz was still being controlled.

Micah motioned us out of the room and led us to his office upstairs. "If he's still being controlled, what's our next step?"

"Maybe we should go to New Mexico," I suggested.

Micah thought for a moment. "I have a better idea. Let me call the Albuquerque Underground."

I wasn't sure anyone would be there this time of night, but a woman by the name of Kathryn answered.

Micah put the phone on speaker. "I'm here with my Paladin, Val Shapiro, and another ally. We have a situation here I'm hoping you can help with." He explained what had been happening here, ending with, "Do you know of some sort of super vampire, or a mage demon in the area, or any other kind of creature that could control someone from afar? And would want to kill a shadow demon?"

"A super vampire?" The woman sounded scornful, and Micah looked embarrassed.

"We're just trying to come up with an explanation that makes sense," he said defensively.

"I heard from a friend there that someone is after shadow demons, but I don't know of a mage demon here or any other kind of demon that can control a man's mind. None of the ones we have here, anyway. Don't you have an encyclopedia that explains that?"

Micah grimaced. "Yes, and we are searching through it, but the entries are surprisingly incomplete. Could you keep an eye out for anything like that?"

"We have problems of our own," she said, sounding snappish and tired. "Someone is picking off our demons one by one, and my Paladin is missing when I need him the most."

"Do you think our situations might be related?" Austin asked.

"I doubt it," the woman said. "There doesn't seem to be any mind control going on here. Just someone singling demons from out of the herd and taking them down."

"Shadow demons?" I asked.

"No, we don't have a shadow demon in our membership," she said. "They're targeting demons randomly. Sorry I can't help you."

"Thank you," Micah said and hung up. He turned to Austin. "Do you have any contacts in Albuquerque who might know something?"

"Maybe." Austin got a number from Alejandro and called it, but didn't have any better luck. But the vampires, too, seemed to have people missing.

Micah frowned. "This seems too coincidental. We still might need to go to New Mexico to check this out."

"You think someone is methodically taking out demons and vamps?" I asked.

"Like a demon hunter? Or vampire hunter?" Austin asked.

Like me, he meant. "I only stake the evil ones," I reminded him. Giving him an innocent-looking smile, I asked, "What's the state of your soul right now?"

He grinned. "Pure as . . ."

"The driven snow?" I'd heard the expression used before but didn't even know what "driven" snow was.

"Pure as yours, anyway," he said with a wicked smile.

And once again, Lola stirred. I couldn't blame Mood for it this time, but I wasn't blaming myself either. Lola liked to be near any man, but since she'd already had a taste of Austin, she rather fancied a big slurp this time. Luckily, I only had a mild struggle with keeping her in check.

Micah frowned, apparently sensing Lola's weak reach. "Val, you need to feed. You're no good to me as Paladin with your primary weapon blunted."

"I still have the encyclopedia," I said. And the amulet, but it was best not to remind him of that. Besides, how could I tell Micah *now* that I'd already fed on Austin earlier?

"The book only has a limited number of spells—and they put your other skills in jeopardy," he said with a stern look. "As your leader, and an incubus who knows it's dangerous to let your succubus get so weak, I'm telling you to feed right away."

"I keep offering," Austin said with a shrug.

I cast him a dirty look, but it did no good.

"I know," Micah said. "Val, take him up on it. We all know it's business, not pleasure. For the sake of the organization, for the sake of Shade's safety, just suck it up and do it. Now."

Oh, crap. His tone and his expression brooked no argument. I had to get all up close and personal with Austin. Again.

Chapter Thirteen

Val

"YOU CAN USE my office," Micah said. "I'll tell Tessa not to let anyone else in. Just get it done."

And with that, he strode out and locked the door. I was left with Austin. Alone. I had kind of a sick feeling in my stomach.

He still had a crooked grin on his face, but this one was half sad, which I totally didn't get. Holding out his hand, he said, "Come, Slayer. Let's feed that succubus of yours some more. We need you at a hundred percent if at all possible, and I can help you get closer."

I hesitated. "But I already fed on you earlier. Are you sure you're strong enough for more?"

He laughed. "I can handle it. Besides, Shade isn't here, so we are the only ones who will know what happens. What happens in Club Purgatory stays in Club Purgatory."

I gave him a half-hearted smile at his lame attempt at humor.

"Besides," he added, "Micah will be able to sense if you fed or not, won't he?"

Crap, he was right. I eyed him warily, but the smart ass grin was gone, and so was the attitude. Maybe this would even be bearable. I sighed heavily. "Okay. Let's sit on the couch," I suggested.

We settled on the sofa Micah kept in his office, Austin propping one boot on the other knee and his arm across the back of the couch. I sat next to him, almost in the circle of his arm, feeling like I was a teenager at her first dance. Not that I'd ever had that experience, but I imagined it was similar.

"Do you need to touch me again?" he asked softly.

Not always, but given Lola's weakness, it was probably a good idea. I nodded and moved in next to him, reminding myself I was doing this for Shade. It was just another way of getting the sustenance I needed to maintain my existence. Nothing wrong with that . . . despite the fact that the sustenance in question was lust.

He dropped his arm lightly on my shoulder. I stiffened.

"Relax," he murmured into my ear. "I'm not going to hurt you. I'm just going to sit here and let you do whatever you want to me."

I hid my face in his neck, certain it was flaming red by now. Sheesh, I was a succubus. Talk of doing the deed, or even sucking up wayward lustful energy shouldn't make me embarrassed. Unfortunately, it did.

"What do you want me to do?" he asked.

"I want you to shut up," I muttered. If I didn't have to look at his face, didn't have to remember this was Austin I was feeding on, maybe it would go better.

He chuckled but obediently zipped his lips. I placed one hand in the middle of his chest and closed my eyes. Lord, he smelled good. Like crisp autumn leaves, a smoky bonfire, and the wild scent of musk. I let his scent fill my nostrils and felt something tingle deep inside. Lola.

Oh, yes. Lola liked.

I urged her toward the cowboy smorgasbord waiting patiently for her to fill her plate, and her thin tendrils reached for him, sinking into his chakras. He let out a soft "ah" as if that's what he'd been waiting for.

Lola tried to draw hard on that energy, but her suction was too weak, and Austin's chakras weren't as full as they were earlier. I moved closer to the man feast, putting both hands on his chest and straddling his lap so our energy fields meshed together.

There. That was easier. I melted into him and let Lola do her thing. Austin's arms came around me, and it was as if he held me in a cocoon, transforming this plain caterpillar into the beautiful butterfly that was Lola. Warmth rose within me, and tingling spread throughout my body, especially where I was sprawled against Austin. I drew more energy, and it was heady stuff, making me light-headed and a little giddy. Wow, I didn't expect it to feel this good, especially when things were tingling that I really didn't want tingling.

Reluctantly, I pulled away. That was enough for now. Lola was maybe at forty percent now, but too much, and I'd probably have a lust hangover. Better take it a little at a time.

"Are you good?" Austin asked, his husky voice vibrating along my nerves. "You can take more if you need to."

"I'm okay for now," I assured him. "Thank you."

Suddenly realizing we were in each other's arms, and Austin's lips were only a kiss away, I froze, wondering how to get out of this with dignity and my ego intact. "Uh, can you—"

But I didn't get a chance to finish as Tessa knocked on the door, saying, "Val? Can you come out? Micah needs you."

I jumped away from Austin, stupidly feeling guilty. Not that I had any reason to. After all, everyone out there knew what we were doing in here. Heck, Micah had practically forced us to do it. So why now was he having Tessa interrupt us?

Then again, maybe he could sense when Lola was done. After all, I'd been able to sense him using his incubus energy. "For what?" I asked, straightening my clothes and hair.

"It's important," she said.

I opened the door, and her elfin eyes were wide and surprised-looking. She gestured at a woman in the outer office waiting area. "He has a visitor, and he needs you."

For what? I glanced around the door and saw a blonde, a girl about my age, standing there wearing something cute and perky and carrying a tiny dog—a teacup Chihuahua—in her huge purse. She looked vaguely familiar, but it was probably just because I'd seen her type before. A Paris Hilton wannabe?

She didn't look dangerous, but Micah's face was tight, as if he was trying to hold his expression in.

As Tessa left the stranger with us, I asked Micah, "You want your office back?" I was trying to get a sense of what was wrong, and wishing Fang was there to pass on some intel for me.

Micah smiled tightly. "Sure. Let's go inside." The two of them joined the two of us, and Micah said, "This is Val, my Paladin, and Austin, an ally from the New Blood Movement. Val, Austin, this is Sharra. She's from the Denver Underground, looking for shadow demons."

Whoa. Alarm thrilled through me. "What do you want with shadow demons?" I demanded.

"That's my business, Paladin," she said, saying the title as if it were a dirty word. "As I was just telling the leader of your Underground here."

"My business, too," I said. "And as Paladin, I need to know why you're hunting shadow demons."

Her mouth parted in surprise. "Hunting? I'm not hunting demons."

"Then what are you doing?"

"I'm looking for my brother, Shawn."

"And what does that have to with us and shadow demons?"

"Because my brother—my twin brother—is a shadow demon. After he moved here, I believe he took the name Shade."

And with that, she raised her hand from the little toy dog and went into total swirl mode, just like Shade. Only, with her, the swirls were bright, like sunlight, not dark and moody like Shade's.

Shocked, I could only stare for a moment. "You—you're Shade's sister?"

"Yes," she said. "I'm his twin."

Well, butter my butt and call me a biscuit. Shade didn't even remember his own twin? Or did he just not trust me with the information?

While I gaped at her, Micah recovered sooner. "Sharra, we didn't know Shade had a sister."

She grimaced. "I know. That's my fault."

"Why?" I asked. "How?" I was too flabbergasted to form more than monosyllables.

She put her hand back on the dog, and her face reappeared. Now that I was looking for it, I could definitely see the resemblance. She was just as good-looking as he was. And my opinion of her revised. It was pretty clever of her to carry a toy dog with her so she could stay looking human most of the time. I wondered how she'd found a non-hellhound dog who would come near a demon, though.

"Kathryn from the Albuquerque Underground called to warn me that someone was looking for shadow demons," Sharra told us.

"She knows what you are?" I asked, having regained my ability to utter more than one syllable.

"Yes, of course. We used to live in New Mexico."

Yet another thing I didn't know about Shade. Again, I felt like an idiot.

"So why did you come to San Antonio?" Austin asked.

Sharra looked surprised, as if it should be obvious. "To join forces with my brother and stay safe."

"Does Shade know you're here?" Micah asked.

"No, that's why I've come to you first. Things didn't go well when I last saw him, and we parted on a bad note. I learned a couple of weeks ago that your Lethe removed all his memories of me. I've come to get them back for him."

A gasp sounded at the door, and I turned in surprise to see Shade standing there next to Mood and Elspeth, the vampire's hand on his arm.

He looked positively stunned. "Sunshine Girl?" he whispered.

Sharra beamed and held out her arms. "You remembered!"

Shade clutched his head and fell to his knees, his expression momentarily filled with agony until Elspeth lost her hold on him, and he blipped out of focus.

Panic filled me, and I froze. What the heck?

Chapter Fourteen

Shade

THE DAM HOLDING back Shade's memories burst loose, and a flood of remembrances crashed through him. He huddled on the floor against the onslaught, helpless against them.

Images, emotions, snatches of conversation flitted through his head, too fast to process. He tried to grasp onto one or more, but they flew by too fast to make sense of them.

His human mother, laughing . . .

His shadow demon father lecturing him . . .

Sharra whooping as she beat him at some game . . .

The gut-wrenching verdict of his father's judgment ritual…

But the emotions were the worst—love, anger, joy, fear, betrayal—they all flashed through him, leaving him sick to his stomach.

"Stop," he heard Elspeth say fiercely. "He is having a memory cascade. Leave him be for a moment."

Cascade? Heck, it felt more like a tsunami. But though he could hear everything going on around him, he wasn't capable of responding to anything yet.

"Here," Micah said. "Bring him here."

Elspeth helped Shade stumble to the couch where it was at least a little more comfortable. He sank into the soft cushions and clutched his head in his hands, willing it all to *stop*.

It didn't help. He had absolutely no control over this process.

"What's wrong?" Val asked as memories pounded him. He felt her kneel beside him, sounding as helpless as he felt. She brushed his hair from his brow. "What's a memory cascade?"

"He is remembering his past all at once, instead of in bits and pieces," Elspeth said. "It will feel as though everything crashed down upon him like a bomb exploding in a confined space."

She had that right. Memories flipped past like pages in a rapidly-fanning book, too fast to understand, to absorb.

Elspeth continued, "Mood, can you help him, please?"

Mood took his hand, and Shade soon felt soothing waves of calm emanate from her and wash through him. It didn't slow the gushing memories much, but it did make them seem a bit more remote, easier to deal with—gave him a bit of relief. He fought to get his body back under his own control.

"I'm so sorry," someone said.

Shade realized it was his sister. He had a *sister*, a twin . . . wasn't that a kick in the head? He wasn't alone. He tried to isolate the memories surrounding her and got nothing but sadness and pain.

Sharra added brokenly, "I didn't . . . didn't realize this would happen."

"You should have," Elspeth snapped. "You knew he wanted to forget you and what you did to him."

Yes, that felt right. Everyone had left him, including the one person he thought never would—his twin, his best friend. It had hurt so much, he'd chosen to forget rather than remember the pain. Unfortunately, now he was reliving it all over again, fresh as the day it happened. The day everyone had gone, and he'd been alone. God, would it never stop?

"Are you okay?" Val asked.

Did it *look* like he was okay? "Everyone, leave . . . me . . . alone," he managed to gasp out. He needed to deal with this by himself.

Somehow, he needed to get through this without shattering into tiny pieces.

Chapter Fifteen

Val

I FELT SO HELPLESS, watching Shade go through all of this. He sat on the couch, clutching his head in his hands as if he had the mother of all headaches and could get rid of it by sheer force of will.

How could I help against something going on inside his head? Especially when he didn't want me anywhere near him?

"Give him some space," Micah ordered. "Everyone, back away."

Shade clutched at Mood's hand. "Stay," he said, his expression still tortured.

Mood shot me a triumphant glance, and her eyes glowed violet. Crap. Why could she help him when I couldn't?

Despite myself, I cast a glance at Austin, wondering what he thought. He nodded encouragingly then joined Micah on the opposite side of the room and gestured for Elspeth and me to join him. It didn't look like I had a choice. Unfortunately, Sharra followed us, though she stayed several paces away, petting her dog, as if unsure of her welcome. Smart girl.

"What happened?" I asked Elspeth. "What did he remember?" And, most importantly, what had his twin done to him?

Sharra, who was stroking her small dog again, looked sulky. "You tell them," she said, pointing her chin at Elspeth. "After all, I hear you're the one who ate his memories."

At Micah's nod, Elspeth inclined her head. "I will keep this brief. Their father, who was one-fourth shadow demon, accidentally brought a full demon into this world. When the Albuquerque Paladin caught him, their father elected to commit suicide rather than have his abilities removed. Sharra blamed her brother and told him she never wanted to see him again." Elspeth gave Sharra a disappointed look. "So your brother Shawn came here, changed his name to Shade, and asked for the boon of forgetfulness. Micah's father granted it to him, and I performed the procedure."

Holy cow. My gaze darted between Elspeth, Shade, and Sharra, looking for . . . I don't know what. Confirmation? I didn't know what to say to that.

Elspeth added, "He was beginning to remember, but it was coming slowly. Your appearance, young woman, made it crash upon him like Thor's hammer."

"So what does this mysterious shadow demon hunter want with you two?" I asked Sharra.

"I don't know," she said. "But I intend to find out and take care of it."

"All by your lonesome?" Austin asked with a raised eyebrow.

I suppressed a grin. Go, Austin!

"With my brother's help," she corrected.

"And mine," I declared.

She gave me a dismissive glance. "We've had enough so-called help from Paladins."

Enough of that crap. "I didn't have anything to do with your father's capture. And you sure need help from *someone*."

Austin sneered at her. "You shouldn't disdain help from the one person most qualified to give it."

He was defending me now? Well, I had to admit it felt good for a change.

She pointedly ignored us.

"Neither of you need to go to New Mexico," Micah pointed out. "Whoever is looking for you has come here. We know this area. That should make it easier to find him."

"Shawn and I can do it together," Sharra insisted. "Right, Shawn?" she called toward the couch.

I glanced at Shade. He didn't look quite so tortured and pale now, but either he didn't hear his sister or chose not to answer.

Mood frowned at Sharra. "You've upset Shade. Go away."

Shade's sister looked annoyed. "Don't be ridiculous. We're family."

Elspeth stepped forward, and Sharra recoiled a bit. I'd gotten used to her, but she was still pretty creepy looking.

"His memories are fresh and raw," Elspeth explained. "His mind is busy processing them. It's difficult for him to think of anything right now except for what's going on inside his head."

Sharra frowned, and her tough demeanor cracked a bit as she looked longingly at Shade. "So, when can I get my brother back?"

I stepped forward, my hands clenched into fists. "I'm not sure you can. That's up to him," I said, not sure I liked her attitude at all. Or what she'd done to Shade.

Sharra bit her lip. "Yes, but I need to apologize. I know now that I was wrong to blame him. I screwed up five years ago. I was just a child and didn't know any better. I do now, and I want to make up for it."

Shade raised his head from his hands, looking as if war had broken loose on his face. "Why now?" he croaked.

"Because I'm here now."

"Or is it because you need help?" Austin asked, saying what I had been thinking.

Shade shook his head, rejecting both answers, but didn't seem to be able to say more.

Elspeth spoke for him, her hand on his shoulder. "I believe what he is asking is, why did you wait so long to seek him out to make your apology?"

Sharra glanced around at the office full of demons and vamps. "That's between him and me. None of your business."

"On the contrary, it is our business," Micah corrected her. "The shadow demon hunters have come after Shade here in our territory. They have attacked people in our homes and place of business. If we are to keep Shade safe, we need to know everything about him and his past."

"Yeah," Mood said challengingly. "How do we know you're not the one trying to destroy him?"

Sharra rolled her eyes. "Don't be ridiculous. I'm a shadow demon myself. Why would I be hunting other shadow demons?"

"So you can be the only game in town?" Austin suggested.

I hated to admit it, but both Mood and Austin had plausible scenarios.

"What?" she said incredulously. "No." She glanced around at our faces and saw the same thing I did—suspicion. "Look, the reason I'm here is because Kathryn called me from New Mexico and told me someone was looking for shadow demons. My brother is the only other one I know of, so I thought we should join forces."

Yeah, right. "So answer the question. If you're so concerned about your brother, why did you wait so long to get in touch with him? You didn't have your memories taken away, did you?"

"No, but—"

"And you knew where he was all this time, right?" I persisted.

She looked uncomfortable. "Yes, but I didn't know at the time that he'd had his memories removed. I kept expecting him to come find me."

"Why would he do that?" Mood asked bitingly. "Especially after you blamed him for your father's death."

Sharra made a helpless gesture. "Because he had to know I didn't mean it." She wiped a tear from her eye. "We used to be so close. Inseparable. I thought . . ."

"What?" Mood demanded.

"I thought he hated me for saying that, that when he finally decided to forgive me for wanting to be separated from him, he'd come find me."

"How would he know where to go?" I asked, confused.

She glanced at me as if surprised by the question. "The same way I found him. I asked the Albuquerque Underground. I didn't know he'd removed his memories and had forgotten all about me and them. The longer I stayed away, the harder it was to believe he'd come after me. So when the Underground finally gave me an excuse to find him, I jumped at it, hoping to find he was still alive."

"Wait," I said, some pieces finally starting to drop into place in this puzzle. "You're from Albuquerque?"

"From a small town not too far from there," she confirmed. "But I've been living in Denver since . . . since we were separated."

Shade raised his head again. "I believe her." He spoke slowly, as if he believed that if he spoke too fast, something would fall out of his noggin. "I don't think she's involved in this."

Was he a bit biased, perhaps? I glanced at Micah, wondering if he wanted to take over the interrogation, but he nodded at me to continue. Gladly. "Are you aware that the men who are trying to kill shadow demons are also from New Mexico?" I asked Sharra.

"I wasn't before, but I gathered that from the conversation."

"Do you know who there would want to kill you and your brother?"

She shook her head. "Not a clue. We were just kids when we left and didn't hurt anyone. How could we? Our father kept us confined to the house. Plus we haven't lived there for years. Why would they want to come after us now?"

That's what I'd been wondering.

"What about your father?" Austin asked. "Did he do something that someone might want to seek revenge for?"

"I doubt it," Sharra said. "He kept a pretty low profile. The only major problem I know of is when he accidentally brought two full demons into the world. But he paid for that—twice over."

"Twice?" I asked.

Her face clouded, and she shook her head sharply, not answering.

Elspeth explained. "One demon he brought through killed their mother."

Sharra's chin tilted up. "Yes, and then he killed himself rather than submit to a Paladin's judgment," she said, with a resentful look at me.

Good grief—no wonder Shade wanted to forget his horrible childhood. No wonder becoming Paladin had driven a wedge between him and me. Sounded like Sharra wasn't quite reconciled with their childhood, either.

"Did the demon kill anyone else?" I asked. "Maybe someone's family wants revenge?"

"Not that I know of," Sharra said, her lips tight with annoyance. "But I think the Underground would've blamed him for that, too, if they knew of any. They didn't."

I wasn't sure I trusted her, so I pressed some more. "Kathryn said Diesel, their Paladin, is missing, and some demons and vamps have been attacked. Do you know anything about that?"

"No," she yelled, looking totally pissed off. "Don't you get it? I don't know anything about any of this. That's why I came to find Shawn, so we could figure it out."

"She doesn't know," Shade/Shawn said, his brow still creased with agony. "Stop badgering her."

I bit my lip. I didn't want to cause Shade any more pain, but we needed to get to the bottom of this, find out who was hunting them.

"Shadow Boy?" Sharra said, her lips trembling and her eyes pleading with Shade to notice her.

He sighed, looking his normal self again. "Hello, Sunshine Girl. What took you so long?"

With a smothered cry, she flew into his arms. That meant she let go of the little dog, and her enthusiasm knocked Shade out of Mood's grasp, so it was the weirdest thing watching the dark and light ribbons of interdimensional energy wind through them . . . like some sort of weird video game.

Surreptitiously, I used the amulet to read Shade's face. A softer emotion filled Shade's expression. He obviously loved his sister. The sister he knew years ago, anyway.

Well, Shade might be willing to trust her, but I wasn't sure I did. "Shade, can I speak to you . . . alone?" I asked. When everyone stared at me, I added, "As your Paladin, I have a few questions to ensure your safety."

"We don't need Paladins," Sharra spat out. "Tell her, Shadow Boy."

"Call me Shade," Shade said with a wry grin. "Shawn doesn't fit me anymore, and I'm no longer a boy."

Yeah, I could vouch for that.

"Look, Sharra, I understand why you feel that way about Val," Shade said. "But Val is more than just a Paladin. She's my friend, too."

Just his friend? Pain stabbed somewhere in the region of my heart.

"Where would you like to talk?" Shade asked.

I glanced at Micah. This was one of the quietest places in the noisy club. "Where can we go where it won't be too noisy?" I asked.

Micah glanced around uncertainly. "Well, if you don't mind the bathroom . . ."

Close quarters, but it would work. "Okay. Shade, if you don't mind?"

"Of course," he said. He was all swirls and obviously thought no one could see him. But I could. The amulet showed his tight expression. Pain still flickered across his face, probably from the memory cascade.

I glanced around at the people watching us and waggled my fingers at them. "Talk amongst yourselves." With any luck, their chatter would make it difficult for Austin to overhear my conversation with Shade. We didn't have enough privacy as it was.

Austin looked amused, as if he knew what I was doing. I didn't care, so long as it worked.

We closed the door behind us. Since the bathroom had a shower as well as a toilet and sink, it wasn't too tight a fit. I didn't touch him. Let him think I couldn't see his expression.

"Are you sure you trust her?" I asked.

His eyes seemed troubled. "I think so. The Sharra I used to know, yes. She was very much a people pleaser. But I haven't seen her in five years, though it feels like yesterday." He shook his head. "I'd like to tell you 'heck yes, I trust her,' but I don't know my sister anymore. A lot could change in five years."

"Do you believe her? Do you think she's behind these attacks?"

Irritation flashed across his features. "I don't know why she would be. What would she have to gain?"

"Maybe so she'd be the only shadow demon, as Austin suggested."

He huffed in disbelief. "Like that's an advantage? It doesn't make sense. I'm inclined to believe her."

"And what about me being a Paladin? I'm not this Diesel. Do you have something against me, too, because of my position?"

He thought for a moment. "I'd like to say no, but I don't know." He rubbed his forehead, looking very tired. "To tell you the truth, everything I think and feel and remember is all mixed up. I need to sort it out. It'll take time."

You can help, the amulet whispered. Yeah, better me than Mood. "Time . . . and Mood?" I asked.

"No, I don't need Mood for that. In fact, she would be a hindrance, unless I get angry. I need to learn to deal with this without her help."

Yay. "If you don't want Mood in your face, I can help with that."

"How?"

"Well, if I use the amulet to help you, she won't be able to force you to feel any way you don't want to." At least, that's how I assumed it would work.

Yes. Use me.

Only if I had to, I promised myself. But it was looking more and more like that was the case.

"No, but *you* could force me." Revulsion flashed across his face, though he didn't know I could see it.

Crap. He was repulsed? Maybe this sneak peek of his expression wasn't all that great after all. "I *could* force you," I conceded. "But I won't. If you need to heal in your own time, I'm good with that."

"Are you sure you don't just want an excuse to use the amulet?" he asked suspiciously.

Well, maybe. But what I really wanted was to be close to Shade. "I could use Lola. Only if you want, of course. Instead of having Mood tell you how to feel, Lola could." The reasoning was a bit convoluted, but I hoped it made sense to him.

He shook his head. "You mean you want Lola to feed on me?"

"No, that's not what I meant at all," I protested. "I don't need—" I broke off before I stuck my foot totally in my mouth.

"You don't need what, Val?" His eyes narrowed. "You don't need me because you've already fed elsewhere? Come to think of it, I do feel Lola's pull more now than I did earlier this evening. She's stronger." He glanced at the door as if he could see through it. "You fed on Austin, didn't you?"

"I had to," I said defensively. "You wouldn't let Lola feed on you, and Micah *ordered* me to tank up."

Shade looked pained and a little ticked. "But did it have to be Austin?"

"He volunteered," I said weakly. Was that jealousy I saw on his face? That could be a good thing.

His mouth twisted. "And you accepted because he's totally hot, and you have a thing for the bloodsucker, right?"

"No!" Okay, maybe I enjoyed it more than I wanted to, but that wasn't the reason I did it. Was it? "Micah told me to," I repeated lamely.

Shade just gave me a disbelieving look.

A little ticked off myself now, I said, "What do you want from me, Shade? You don't want me, but you don't want me to feed on anyone else, when you know I have no choice—I have to feed, or I might as well paint a target on my back and stand in a deserted alley."

"Maybe if I didn't suspect you enjoyed it too much," he said, frowning.

Crap. That's almost exactly what I said to Austin. "Let's be real, here," I said, fuming. "When Lola sucks up lustful energy, it feels good, yes. It feels *reeeeeal* good. That's the nature of being a succubus. I can't help it, any more than you can help being a shadow demon."

"I know that—"

"Yeah, you know that, but you still push me away, push me into the lustful field of other men because you can't figure out if you love me or hate me."

He looked taken aback, not to mention bewildered. "I don't hate you, Val."

"Don't you?"

"No, of course not."

I decided to lay it all on the line. "Well, I don't know much about psychology, but even I can see you have abandonment issues." Thanks to his lovely family, though I didn't say that part out loud.

"What does that mean?"

"That means that when I left you with Dina, you thought I abandoned you like everyone else. You can't handle it, so you're pushing me away. You can't accept me. You don't trust me. So you push."

"You think that?" he asked, looking surprised.

"Think about it. You may not have realized it consciously, but subconsciously, you were blaming your father, your sister, and me for leaving you. You can't stand for it to happen again."

"And my mother," he murmured.

"What?"

"Never mind," he said and wiped a hand across his face, looking weary. "Maybe you're right."

"I am," I insisted. "And maybe you need to get some real help—not just Mood to alter how you feel or Elspeth to help with sorting out your memories. You need therapy to sort through your issues." More gently, I added, "Until then, you're not going to trust me, or your sister, or anyone else not to abandon you again." I shrugged. "And, quite frankly, you're still going to blame me for being a succubus. I can't deny my nature, you know. It has nothing to do with you, except for the fact that you choose not to let me feed on you. You choose not to let me get close. You choose the very things that make you feel abandoned."

He thought for a few moments. "Okay, maybe you're right. Where does that leave us?"

"Waiting for you to get your act together, I guess." Suddenly, I felt weary of constantly being the one to fight for this relationship. "But don't take too long." I stared straight into his eyes to ensure the next part sank in. "Because I'm not promising to wait for you."

My eyes stung after that. To keep Shade from noticing, I walked past him to grab the doorknob. "So, you won't disappoint Micah, will you? You're going to let me do my job and protect you?"

"Yes, I'll do that," Shade said behind me. I couldn't decipher the tone of his voice. Accepting? Tight? Annoyed? I didn't know, and right now, I didn't care. "Good," I said shortly and walked out the door.

"Okay, everyone," I said. "Shade and I have an understanding. He's going to let me protect him, and I'm going to do that to the best of my ability." I glared at everyone. "But you are all going to give him the time he needs to deal with his newly acquired memories, is that understood?"

General agreement from the room, though Mood and Sharra looked mulish.

Austin was his normal amused self. "Yes, ma'am," he said crisply.

"And you," I said, staring at Mood, "are not going to alter his emotions unless he becomes angry and a threat to the rest of us. Is that understood?"

Mood folded her arms across her chest. "You can't tell me what to do."

"Actually, she can," Micah said. "It's the Paladin's place to protect us by whatever means she sees fit. I trust her. You should, too."

Yay, me. Maybe this Paladin gig wasn't so bad after all.

"Yes," Elspeth said. "The soothsayers do not make mistakes when it comes to choosing a Paladin. You must do as she says."

Mood looked pissed, but didn't talk back any more.

Well, it was nice to have back-up. Surprising, but nice. Maybe I should have asserted myself earlier.

"So, Slayer . . . Paladin," Austin drawled. "What's next?"

Heck if I knew.

Chapter Sixteen

Shade

SHADE INVITED Sharra to join him at the penthouse, wanting to get reacquainted with his newly-remembered sister. How could he have forgotten someone who had been such an important part of his life? Austin and Val sat in the front seat of Austin's car while Shade rode in the back with Sharra. He didn't want to talk to Sharra with anyone listening in, so he mentally replayed the argument he and Val had just had.

Was Val right? Had the memories of the past left him unwilling to care for someone else, to care for *Val*, for fear she'd abandon him, too? There might be something to that, he acknowledged, and was probably the reason he'd been pushing her away after she left him with Dina. But was it relevant now?

She'd basically given him an ultimatum—put up or shut up. His first instinct had been to fight for her, fight for their relationship. But that was selfish. He wanted her, he wanted to *be* with her, but wasn't sure they were good for each other. Val had lost part of her mojo because of him and their lovemaking, and in turn, he wasn't sure he could handle his emotions around her. Especially since she still shared Lola with Austin.

Shade closed his eyes against the thought. Val and Austin together, sharing lust . . . and what else? Angry jealousy surged through him. And *that*—that emotion—was why he'd ignored his first instinct. Maybe keeping Val at arm's-length was the best thing for both of them.

Staying calm and centered was the key to keeping his act together, to ensure he didn't provide an opening for more demons to come into this dimension. The thought terrified him, had always terrified him, and he realized he'd always taken his belief for granted: Portal, bad. No emotions, good.

But now that his memories were starting to integrate, he realized where that imperative came from—his father. Not only had his father belabored the need for the twins to control their anger whenever he had the chance, but his trial for accidentally opening a portal himself and his subsequent suicide really hammered it home. Portal bad. Definitely.

Shade sighed. When he and Val had made love that first time, he hadn't had to worry about any of this crap. He'd thought he could have a normal relationship, maybe even have a normal life like other people, despite his demon heritage. But that all went south in a hurry when he started getting angry and creating portals . . . just like his father.

He couldn't afford to let himself care for Val. Couldn't afford to let jealousy or anger control him and lead to the unthinkable. But he was also unwilling to give Val up entirely. Was it possible he could find some way to stay with her and keep an emotional even keel at the same time? If he couldn't, he'd have to give her up.

They arrived at the penthouse, and Austin waved in the direction of the bedrooms. "There are plenty of rooms," he told Sharra. "Pick one. You can use it as long as you like."

Sharra nodded. "Where's yours?" she asked Shade.

He nodded toward his, saying, "The one next to it is empty."

"Good," she said. "I'll take it." Giving Val and Austin a frown, she said to Shade, "Can we talk privately?"

"Sure." He gestured her into his room.

Fang looked up from where he lay next to the puppies. WHO'S THIS? he asked suspiciously.

"This is my twin sister, Sharra," Shade said. "Sharra, this is Fang, Val's hellhound. And my hellhound, Princess, with their puppies."

Fang's jaw dropped open. Whether in surprise or amusement, Shade wasn't sure. YOU HAVE A *SISTER*? the hellhound asked incredulously.

"Yes. I forgot about her until a little while ago, but now I remember. Show him, Sharra."

Sharra obediently raised her hand from the miniature dog and went all swirly as Shade let Fang and Princess read in his mind everything that had just happened.

GOOD, Princess pronounced. IT IS GOOD TO HAVE FAMILY.

"It is," Sharra agreed, and resumed petting her dog. She craned her neck for a look at the puppies, snuggled up warm and cozy next to their mother. "They're adorable."

THEY ARE, AREN'T THEY? Princess said smugly.

Shade grinned. "Good job, there." He closed the door and sat on the floor next to Princess so he could pet her and gestured Sharra toward the chair.

She sat, still touching her little dog, who had perked up for once and was staring with interest at the canine family on the floor.

"Thanks for that," Shade said, nodding toward her purse dog. "It's good to 'see' you."

She smiled. "I know what you mean. It's been so long since I've seen your face, I almost forgot what you looked like. You've changed."

Yeah, even when they still lived together, they hadn't seen each others' faces very often since they hadn't known anyone who could ground them in this world. It was great to be able to really see her. "Five years will do that to a person. You've changed, too." She was still pretty, though. "You look a lot like Mom."

Sadness flitted over her face and she grimaced. "I know. You do, too, in a masculine kind of way. It hurts sometimes, you know."

Shade nodded, though in reality, he didn't really know. Since he hadn't been able to remember his mother, it hadn't been an issue. And he didn't often catch his own reflection, either. "That was pretty smart of you, to find a dog you can carry around."

YOU CAN CARRY ME IF YOU WANT TO, Princess said. ONCE MY BABIES ARE WEANED.

Shade grinned down at his hellhound. "Thanks, but it would be a little more awkward to carry you than that little thing Sharra has."

HEY, WATCH IT, Fang said. DON'T HURT HER FEELINGS.

"I wasn't talking about her weight," Shade explained. "But I can't exactly carry a purse."

GOOD CATCH, Fang said privately.

No, it was the truth.

Sharra looked back and forth between them. "Is it always like this, having a hellhound?"

"Well, I don't usually have two around all the time, but these days, Fang goes where Princess goes. Isn't that right, buddy?"

YEAH, YEAH, Fang said. BUT ENOUGH WITH THE CHIT CHAT. YOU TWO HAVE AVOIDED THE IMPORTANT STUFF LONG ENOUGH. TALK TO EACH OTHER.

Sharra looked sheepish, and Shade imagined he did, too. Fang was right—he was trying very hard not to talk about the past . . . or the present, for that matter. Both were painful.

"I'm sorry," Sharra said, looking down at the puppies to avoid meeting his eyes.

"About what?"

"You know. About blaming you for everything. Right before Dad . . . died."

Pain bloomed within him as he relived that memory. The pain he hadn't been able to handle when he was sixteen was the reason he'd had the Lethe remove his memories. He opened his mouth to tell her it was okay, but it wasn't okay. He wouldn't lie. She was the only person he had left in his family, and she'd deserted him when he needed her most. The newly retrieved memory was too fresh in his mind to just let it slide.

YOU HURT MY HUMAN, Princess said, growling at Sharra.

Let me handle this, Shade told Princess.

Sharra stared at the hellhound in surprise. "I know. I'm so, so sorry. I screwed up."

"Yes, you did," Shade said. He wasn't going to let her off the hook too easily.

Her eyes filled with tears. "I was stupid, looking for someone to blame, and you were handy." She wiped away a tear. "But it wasn't your fault. It was that damned Paladin's fault, for bringing Dad in, making him face that judgment ritual."

Shade sighed. It would be easy to blame Diesel, easy to blame anyone else, except for the one person truly responsible. "No, my memories are so new, they're crystal clear. It wasn't Diesel's fault. It wasn't yours, either," he said, understanding Sharra probably felt guilty herself. "It was Dad's."

Sharra shook her head. "No—"

"Yes," he insisted. "Dad is the one who lost his temper when Mom tried to leave him. Dad is the one who let a demon through into this world. Dad is the one to blame for what happened to him, no one else."

Sharra choked back a sob. "You can't say that," she whispered through her tears.

"I can," Shade said softly. "Because it's true. That's why he was always bugging us to control our emotions, remember? So we wouldn't lose it and do the same thing he did."

"I know. But I still blame the Paladin for bringing him in."

"Diesel yes, but all Paladins? Sharra, you know better," Shade said softly. He didn't want any artificial barriers between Val and Sharra.

She looked at him and sniffed. "You mean Val, don't you? What is she to you? She's more than a friend, isn't she?"

"Yes, she is. Or rather, she has been. Whether she is in the future remains to be seen."

GEE, CAN YOU BE ANY MORE WISHY-WASHY WUSSY? Fang asked.

Shut up, Shade snapped mentally. *You have no idea what I'm going through.*

ACTUALLY, DUDE, I DO, Fang said. I CAN READ YOUR MIND, REMEMBER? I FEEL FOR YOU, I REALLY DO. BUT YOU NEED TO POOP OR GET OFF THE POT. YOU'RE KILLING VAL WITH YOUR INDECISION.

I know, I know. Sighing, Shade told Sharra, "You can't blame Val for the actions of another Paladin. And Diesel was only doing his job. It's not healthy to blame everyone else."

POT, MEET KETTLE, Fang taunted him.

Shade winced. Fang was right, and that was the key. *Shade* couldn't blame everyone else either. His reactions to what had happened to him in the past had colored how he felt in the present in a visceral way, even when he couldn't remember that past. Obviously, he couldn't change what had already happened, but he could change how he reacted to it. He could actually think about things instead of reacting instinctively. Starting now.

"Maybe," Sharra said. "But what are we going to do to find the shadow demon hunter?"

"All of us here at the penthouse are working on it."

"How can I help?"

"I'll talk to the others, see what they suggest."

"Okay, great." She came over to sit next to Shade and give him a hug. "I'm so glad the Dynamic Duo are back together. Shadow Boy and Sunshine Girl make an unbeatable team."

Shade smiled at her but made no comment. He still loved his sister, true, but could he trust her? That remained to be seen.

Chapter Seventeen

Val

AFTER SHADE AND Sharra disappeared into his bedroom, I worried over the argument we'd just had. Though it had burst out of me like a popped zit, I didn't regret a word of it. It had to be said, and I was glad I'd finally let it out.

When they finally emerged from Shade's room, I asked Fang privately, *Is his sister telling the truth about why she's here?*

YEP. SHE'S REALLY ANXIOUS TO DO THE FAMILY THING WITH SHADE.

Well, that was something I could understand. *And how does Shade feel about that?*

WHY DON'T YOU ASK HIM? Fang paused, then added, OH, RIGHT. BECAUSE YOU WANT ME TO READ HIS MIND AND BARE THE DEPTHS OF HIS SOUL FOR YOU. AIN'T GONNA HAPPEN, BABE. I HAVE SOME PRINCIPLES, Y'KNOW.

I sighed. *It's just that . . . we had a fight.* I let Fang read what had happened in my mind.

WELL, I'M GLAD YOU FINALLY LAID IT ON THE LINE AND I FEEL FOR YA, BUT YOU TWO HAVE TO WORK THIS OUT ON YOUR OWN.

Crap. No help there.

Getting back to the issue at hand, I somehow managed to muster a few ideas to put together the semblance of a plan as Shade read the encyclopedia, and we had Sharra researching the Internet to find out what was going on in New Mexico.

And as for Austin . . . I glanced at him.

He held up his phone. "Alejandro has been keeping me posted on what's going on in the Movement while I'm with you."

"Oh, if you need to go back and join them, I'll understand," I said hastily.

Fang snorted mentally. SUBTLE, YOU'RE NOT.

Austin gave me a half smile. "You can't get rid of me that easily. They're reporting acts of random violence on people in the Movement, somewhat similar to what Micah has been reporting."

"You think they're related?"

"Maybe. Two men tried attacking Rosa. Big mistake."

I grinned. Yeah, I wouldn't mess with that *chica* either. "What happened?"

"They got handed their heads."

"Literally?" I wouldn't put it past her.

"No, but she scared them off. She did get a good look at them, though."

"And?"

"They seem to meet the same description as the ones who attacked us. Male, Hispanic with religious tattoos."

"But the ones who attacked us were looking for shadow demons. What good does it do to kill vampires—or other demons, for that matter?"

Austin shrugged. "No idea. Religious mania, maybe?"

"You mean they think all paranormal beings are evil, no matter what the origin."

"Yes."

I thought for a moment. "I still don't see why they would look for one specific kind of demon at his home, then randomly target other demons and vamps. It doesn't make sense. Maybe they're not related."

"Maybe not," he said. "But there's one way to find out."

"You mean, become targets ourselves?"

"Exactly."

So, we checked Austin's intel, trying to figure out where the hunters would attack next. It wasn't real clear, but they seemed to be aiming for the most well-known spots where vamps and demons hung out.

"They weren't at Club Purgatory earlier, or we would have been attacked then," Austin said.

"That doesn't mean they're not there now," I said, feeling contrary.

"That's true. Where would you like to start, ma'am?"

That was the second time he'd called me that. "Stop calling me that," I snapped, more annoyed because he was throwing this on me than because of what he'd called me.

"All right, then. Where should we start . . . darlin'?"

Fang chuckled in my mind.

I winced. Me and my big mouth. Deciding that ignoring him and Fang was probably the wisest thing at this point, I said, "Let's check out all the blood banks. They're the most visible targets."

"Good idea."

It made me a little nervous to go with Austin, but he seemed to be behaving himself, for the most part. Maybe he was finally getting a clue.

OR MAYBE HE'S TRYING TO SOFTEN YOU UP, Fang said, CATCH YOU OFF GUARD, LOWER YOUR DEFENSES.

I glanced down at him. *Oh, thanks so much. I hadn't thought of that.*

I LIVE TO SERVE, the hellhound said humbly.

I snorted, and Austin raised an eyebrow.

"Something Fang said," I told him. I glanced down at the terrier. "You coming with us?"

YES, I THINK PRINCESS CAN DO WITHOUT ME FOR A WHILE, he said.

Besides, you're getting antsy, aren't you?

MAYBE A LITTLE, he said. But the bounce in his step and the gleam in his eyes betrayed his excitement as we took the elevator down to the ground floor of the blood bank.

"We're taking one of the fleet," Austin said, waving his hand at one of Alejandro's many black luxury sedans.

"No way. I want my bike." I felt more nimble on the Valkyrie, more in control and alive.

PLUS YOU DON'T HAVE TO TALK TO AUSTIN THAT WAY, Fang pointed out.

A huge bonus, I agreed.

"Don't be ridiculous," Austin began. "You—"

But he couldn't finish his sentence because a crossbow bolt suddenly sprouted from the side of his neck. What the heck?

THERE ARE TWO OF THEM, Fang yelled. His eyes flashed purple, and he took a running leap for the woman on the left who was reloading the crossbow. I charged for the guy on the right. His eyes widened when he saw me coming at him—why? because I was female?—but it didn't take him long to whip out a knife and wave it in my direction as a warning.

A knife? Like that would stop me. I ducked, whirled and used a *savate* kick to send it spinning out of his hand. He looked surprised only for a moment, then lunged forward, clearly intending to get his meaty hands on me. With him inside Lola's field, I hoped to be able to use her, still weak as she was, to call him off, but no go. He was being controlled, too, damn it. And if Lola wouldn't work, neither would the amulet.

He clamped his hands around my throat and squeezed. Crap. I tore at his hands, but he was too strong. Vampishly strong. Fast, too, if his reactions earlier were any judge. I tried to knee him in the 'nads, but he was too close. I couldn't breathe, and my vision was suddenly filled with giant, randomly sized polka dots.

Then suddenly, his hands let go, and Austin had *him* by the throat while Fang attacked his ankles. I leaned over, hands on my knees, and gasped for breath while the vampire and the hellhound saved me from the big bad vampire. Me, the Slayer, depending on other people to do my dirty work. Made me feel stupid, unnecessary . . . helpless.

Austin strangled him until his eyes bulged out, and he fell limp, then he dropped him.

TAKE THAT, YOU WORTHLESS PUPPY STEALERS, Fang said.

I glanced over at the woman. She was obviously dead, a crossbow bolt sticking out of her eye. Effective.

Austin pulled the bolt from his own neck with a grimace and dropped it to the ground. All kinds of vamps came pouring out of the blood bank then. A day late and a dollar short. The only one I knew was the bald vampire, Vincent.

As they fussed about the bodies, and Vincent promised to take care of them for us, I turned to Austin. "You okay?"

"I'll live," he said shortly. "I heal fast, and it didn't hit anything vital."

I nodded, glad to hear it. "Thanks for the assist."

ASSIST? Fang repeated. DON'T YOU MEAN THANKS FOR SAVING YOUR LIFE?

Ignoring him, I asked, "But since when did we graduate to killing them instead of questioning them?"

"When they put your life and the lives of all the people inside in danger," Austin said, his tone brooking no argument.

Oooookay.

"Your catch and release program isn't working," he bit out. "They aren't talking, and they aren't letting up. It's best to exterminate vermin like this."

Well, I couldn't argue with that, though I had hoped we could find at least one person who could be questioned. "You still think this place is safe?" I asked him.

"Yes. Safer than anywhere the Underground has, anyway. They won't be able to get past the blood bank employees without setting off an alarm, and won't be able to go up the elevator without access at all."

"No place is foolproof." I glanced at Fang and raised a questioning eyebrow.

TRUE, the hellhound said. BUT THIS COMES PRETTY CLOSE.

You feel safe leaving Princess and the pups here?

Fang nodded. I DO.

"Wait," Vincent said. "I know this guy. He's a new recruit." Vincent stared accusingly up at Austin. "It's Josef. You almost killed Josef."

"No, I didn't," Austin said. "He's one of us. He'll heal."

"Why did he attack me . . . and you?" I asked Austin.

"I don't know."

A woman let out a little screech when she saw the other body. "Cyndi!"

"Is she a vamp, too?" I asked.

"No," the woman said. "She's just a friend visiting me from Colorado." She glared up at Austin. "You killed her."

Stunned surprise filled Austin's expression. "Human?" he whispered disbelievingly. "I thought she was a new recruit, too. She was so strong, and she didn't fit the profile."

Yeah, not Hispanic, no visible tattoos, and definitely not male. Again, I repeated, "They attacked us. How were we to know who they are?"

"Why would they do that?" the woman cried. "Cyndi had no reason to hate anyone."

"Because she was probably being controlled by someone else," I said soothingly, though I kept an eye on Austin. He looked shell-shocked.

Josef stirred, and I said, "Maybe you can ask *him* why he tried to strangle me."

He stumbled to his feet and lurched for me again, murder in his eyes, but three vamps caught him and restrained them.

"Josef, what are you doing?" Vincent asked.

But the beefy bloodsucker acted as though he hadn't even seen or heard him. He was too focused on getting his hands on me.

"Get him down in the holding room, now," Austin barked.

And why was I not surprised they had such a thing on the property?

For once, I didn't argue. I really didn't want to know about any secret vamp basements in the blood bank, and I wasn't all that good at interrogation. I assumed Austin could torture the info out of the dude better if I wasn't there kibitzing.

"Okay," I said, rubbing my throat.

"Get Gwen to help you with that," Austin ordered, and herded all of us back inside.

What could she do? I ignored him and turned to Fang. *Let's call it a night.*

He hesitated for a moment, obviously disappointed, then he sighed. OKAY, BABE, BUT I GOTTA TELL YOU, YOU'RE RUINING MY FUN.

Yeah, well, mine's already ruined. I just need a good night's sleep.

After Austin used his mind mojo to make the humans from the blood bank forget all about the bloody fight in the street, I let him whisk me upstairs while he called Alejandro and Micah and warned them that this super vampire or puppet master or whatever you wanted to call him was controlling our own people and turning them against us.

Crap. It was a game changer. How could we trust anyone anymore?

Chapter Eighteen

Austin

STILL ANGRY WITH himself for killing a human, even accidentally, Austin tried to hide it by taking charge. He had Vincent and his helpers corral Josef in the special holding area downstairs. Alejandro had them installed in all the blood banks to hold members of the Movement who'd gone off the deep end after drinking demon blood.

After Austin made sure Val and the others were safe upstairs, he went downstairs as well. Someone had brought the woman in from off the street, too. She lay on an examining table while her friend sat in a corner, looking stunned. At least the friend was no longer hysterical—Vincent had probably taken care of that with his own special brand of mojo.

Now that the fight was over, and there was nothing left to do, Austin felt pain throbbing in his neck from where she'd shot him. No problem—he'd heal. But she wouldn't. He gazed down at the woman—the very human, very dead woman.

Agony stabbed through him, and it had nothing to with the hole in his neck. He hadn't wanted this—he hadn't wanted to kill anyone, let alone a human . . . a woman. He was responsible for her death, and he needed to ensure she was taken care of.

The Movement could take care of a vampire, and the Underground would know what to do about a dead demon, but he hadn't had to deal with a human dead by his own hand. There was only one person he knew who could help. He called Lieutenant Ramirez. "We have a situation here I'm not sure how to handle," Austin told him.

"What's that?"

"Val and I were attacked outside a blood bank a little while ago, and someone was killed—a human."

The lieutenant's voice sharpened. "Vampire kill?"

Yes, but not in the way he meant. "No, she and a member of the Movement attacked us, and she was killed in the scuffle. We think they were being controlled like the others."

"You mean she's Hispanic, with scars and tattoos like the others?"

"No," Austin admitted. "But she did have the incredible strength and single-minded ferocity of the others. It isn't quite like the rest of the pattern, but it's similar." He hesitated, then added, "She shot me with a crossbow bolt. When I tried to take it away from her, another bolt discharged into her eye."

"So it was an accident?"

"Yes." That was true as far as it went, but Austin knew he was still responsible. He should have been more careful, should have realized she wasn't a vamp. "Do you need an investigation?"

The lieutenant paused, then asked, "Val was there? She witnessed this?"

"Yes."

"Then I'll talk to her. We can't afford to let the paranormal nature surrounding this death make the news—it'll panic the population. I'll take care of it and send someone to pick her up. Where is she?"

Austin gave him the address, then hung up and looked down sadly at the woman. Her death would be glossed over, a story concocted, and her family and friends forced to believe it was true. Such a waste.

Vincent appeared in the doorway. "We have Josef contained," he said. He glanced at the woman on the table. "What do we do with her?"

"Lieutenant Ramirez is picking her up. He'll take care of everything."

"Good," Vincent said.

Austin gazed at the poor woman on the table and asked her friend, "What's her name?"

"Cyndi. Cyndi Krupa," the woman said, sounding as if she was zoned out. The mojo did that to some people. At least it was better than being in shock.

Vincent gave him an odd look. "Does it matter?"

"Yes. Yes, it does," Austin said, his anger heating. "It matters because I caused the death of a human, something I swore never to do when I joined the Movement." How could he condemn Luis when he'd just done the same thing? He couldn't. "I should at least know her name."

"But it was an accident," Vincent protested. "And she attacked you. Not your fault. If she was as strong as one of us, how could you know she was human?"

That made him a little better than Luis, but Austin was still at fault for stupidly assuming anyone that strong couldn't be human. He'd screwed up, and there was no way to make it right.

"Besides," Vincent added, "the real person at fault is the one who controlled her and sent her after you, unprotected."

True. Maybe there was a way he could atone, at least in some small measure. Austin's jaw clenched, and he gazed down at the lifeless body on the table. "I will find the person who caused this and make him pay," he promised Cyndi. Even if it was the last thing he ever did.

Chapter Nineteen

Val

AFTER AUSTIN WENT down to the secret bat cave, I walked back into the living room of the penthouse, hoping to get some rest. Unfortunately, the slasher movie décor was anything but restful. And Mood had turned up again and was looking awfully chummy, sitting on the couch next to Shade, reading one of the encyclopedias.

Alarm thrilled through me. "What are you doing?" I demanded, wincing as the harsh words hurt my throat.

She looked up in surprise. "Well, since *you* aren't looking to see if there are any spells that can help us with this, I decided someone needed to."

"*You* decided?" I croaked, then asked Fang, *Can you relay my thoughts to them?*

SURE.

I snatched the book away from her.

Fang broadcast to all three of us. DON'T YOU REALIZE HOW DANGEROUS THOSE BOOKS ARE IN THE HANDS OF ANYONE BUT THE KEEPER?

"No." She looked like she didn't believe it, either.

I didn't ask him to relay this next part, but he added it on his own. WHERE HAVE YOU BEEN FOR THE PAST TWO MONTHS? SIBERIA? OR IN SOME STUPID SELF-CENTERED EMO WORLD? YOU KNOW WHAT THOSE BOOKS DID TO JOSH. YOU THINK YOU'RE IMMUNE?

She looked uncertain. "But, Shade . . ."

SHADE IS ONLY READING THE ENCYCLOPEDIA PORTION OF THE BOOKS, NOT THE MAGICKAL PART, Fang explained for me. HOW LONG DID YOU HAVE IT OPEN?

"Not long," she said.

Probably true. We hadn't been gone all that long.

GOOD, Fang said for me. DON'T TOUCH, UNDERSTAND? OR THE PALADIN WILL BEAT YOUR EMO BUTT BACK TO THE STONE AGE.

Shade looked surprised and narrowed his gaze at me. "Didn't say that," I croaked.

"I didn't think you did," Shade said. He gave Mood an annoyed glance. "I'm sorry, I didn't realize what she was doing, or I would've stopped her."

Mood scowled, and I wondered if she'd been able somehow to make sure he didn't notice. I didn't totally understand her gift, but I wouldn't put it past her to use it for her own benefit.

KIND OF LIKE YOU DO WITH LOLA OR THE AMULET? Fang snarked.

It's not the same, I insisted.

UH-HUH. JUST KEEP TELLING YOURSELF THAT.

"So why haven't *you* been looking up spells?" Mood challenged me.

For one thing, I hated using them. Hated messing with the balance of power inside myself, worrying how much the spells would take away from Lola or other important things. But that was none of her business.

SHE'S TOO BUSY WITH PALADIN BUSINESS, Fang told Mood in haughty tones worthy of Princess.

Thanks, Fang. Appreciate the support.

NO PROBLEM. BUT SHE DOES HAVE A POINT.

I know. I picked up the third book from the coffee table and sat down in another chair to take a look.

SHE'LL LOOK NOW, Fang reported.

Shade looked puzzled. "Why is Fang talking for you?"

Sighing, I parted the collar on my shirt, figuring bruises were probably starting to show up. I knew the swelling was.

Mood gasped.

Fang said, SHE NEARLY GOT STRANGLED BY A CONTROLLED VAMP.

"Do you need me to heal you?" Shade asked in concern.

It was tempting, but the only other person here right now was Mood, and since Shade's form of interdimensional healing meant the two participants also shared memories and emotions . . . uh, no. I shook my head.

MASOCHIST, Fang said privately.

No, just private.

Shade gave me an odd look. "Your throat wouldn't require much healing. I doubt you and Mood would share much."

I gave Fang the beady eye. *Did you tell Shade what I was thinking?*

The hellhound studiously ignored me. That meant yes. *Busy body.*

"Do it," Mood said. "Can't afford to let our Paladin not be at her best."

I gritted my teeth, but couldn't find a way to refuse gracefully when Fang knew exactly why I didn't want to.

Shade told me to sit next to Mood on the sofa, then stood behind us and placed one hand on my throat and one on Mood's. A thrill went through me—it had been a long time since he'd touched me, for any reason.

But I tried to ignore my hormones and Lola's interest as the healing waves began. I got a sharp slap of awareness of Mood's irritation, then the healing was done. Thank goodness, Shade was right—I didn't have to share my mind with Mood.

"Thanks," I said, and was happy to see my voice was much better and the pain was gone. "Much better."

Shade nodded and came around to sit across from us. "How did this happen?"

I explained, and just as I finished, Austin returned to the suite, his face set in rigid lines. Was he pissed, or just trying to hold his emotions in so no one could sense them?

I'LL ASK MOOD, Fang said. Then, shortly after, he said, SHE SAID AUSTIN IS VERY UPSET. PROBABLY BECAUSE HE ACCIDENTALLY KILLED A HUMAN. WANT HER TO MELLOW HIM OUT A BIT?

Ask him, not me.

Fang apparently had a brief conversation with Mood on the subject. They both looked at Austin, but Mood shook her head, evidently deciding not to.

"You killed a human?" Shade asked incredulously.

Austin cast me an annoyed glance.

I held up my hands in defense. "I didn't say anything." I gestured at Fang, who didn't even look guilty. "It was an accident," I told Shade.

"You shouldn't be talking," Austin said. "Have you done anything for your throat?"

"Yes, Shade healed me, just now."

"Good."

No jealousy? Nothing?

INTERESTING HOW AUSTIN SEEMS ONLY CONCERNED FOR YOUR WELFARE, Fang mused. UNLIKE CERTAIN SHADOW DEMONS I COULD NAME.

I shot him a dirty look. *You're pushing Austin on me now?*

I'M JUST SAYING.

But Shade was talking now, so I could ignore Fang's disturbing insight.

"Val and Fang explained what happened," Shade said.

I glanced at Mood who was listening avidly. This was really none of her business. She wasn't exactly in the higher ranks of the Demon

Underground. *Why don't you ask her to check on Princess and the puppies?* I suggested to Fang.

He must have, because Mood brightened and said, "Princess needs some attention, I think," and headed for the hellhounds' room.

Austin was obviously trying to keep it together. He was much better at hiding his emotions than Shade, but even he let some things slip. Now, for instance, I saw grief and anguish cross his face.

"Not your fault," I reiterated.

YOU'RE RIGHT. HE COULDN'T HELP IT. I SAW IT ALL.

I repeated what Fang said for Austin and Shade's benefit.

"What exactly did you see?" Shade asked. He glanced at Austin. "Fang can help us relive the experience from his eyes. Remember when he did it before? Will you do that, Fang?"

SURE, Fang said. HERE GOES.

WE WERE EXITING THE HOTEL, Fang said, and I felt a little disoriented seeing myself from his eyes at knee level. I wondered if his neck ever got sore, looking up at everyone.

I DON'T LOOK UP TO ANYONE, Fang snarked to me alone.

I rolled my eyes. "Go on."

And suddenly, I was in Fang's head and thoughts once more.

I heard Val and Austin arguing, again. I wasn't about to get in the middle of that conversation, and I wished they'd just chill. All of a sudden, a bolt sprouted from Austin's neck. Crossbow! I spun and leapt heroically onto the most dangerous assailant—the chick with the crossbow—so she couldn't get off another shot. I couldn't read her mind, so she wasn't demon, and she didn't smell like vamp. Must be one of those shadow demon hunters. Unfortunately, she'd already reloaded the crossbow.

I bounced off her chest and landed nimbly on the ground. Austin was already on her, trying to take the crossbow away from her, but Ms. Charm snarled at him and attacked like a maniac. I set my teeth into the meaty part of her calf, but it was like the chick was on meth or something—she didn't even feel it.

Austin could have laid some serious hurt on her, but it looked like he was pulling his punches, not wanting to hurt a woman. Bad move. The crazy woman was just as fast and strong as the vamp.

He tried to use the crossbow in his hand as a club, but it was already reloaded and accidentally fired, right into the woman's eye and smashed into her brainpan. Down she went.

Austin glanced at Val, and his eyes widened. I whirled. She was in trouble! I leapt to help her, and Austin looked frantic. No time to waste. We had Val to save. We charged to the rescue, and Austin treated the guy to what it felt like to be strangled. Have to say, I cheered him on the whole way.

AND THAT'S HOW IT WENT, Fang said.

I blinked, suddenly back in my own head.

Shade blinked, too. He glanced at Austin. "Yeah, it wasn't deliberate. It was an accident, part of the fight. Don't worry about it."

It was generous of him to say so, especially since he obviously considered Austin a competitor. And it was better coming from him than me. Maybe Austin would actually believe him.

Austin looked like he wanted to, but wasn't quite there yet. He shrugged as if it was no big deal and gestured at the books in my lap. "Find anything there?"

Big tough Austin was strung out about killing a human? I had no idea he cared so much about the sanctity of human life. I stared at him for a moment, wanting to explore this new side of Austin some more, but let it go. He obviously wouldn't thank me for it. "I was just about to look," I said.

"Good," he said. "Oh, and Micah is calling a meeting with all demons later this evening at the club to talk about what happened here and what it means."

"Okay." Austin excused himself to go check on Josef, and I flipped through the pages of the second volume while Shade explored the first one that listed vampires, demons, and other paranormal creatures.

This wasn't a whole lot of fun, especially since I wasn't quite sure what some of the entries were about. There was one that showed how to call down the lightning to kill someone. That might be useful, but the warning made it sound very dangerous for me, too. Another detailed how to call a wolverine to your side, though I had no idea why you would want to do such a thing. Unless we were talking Hugh Jackman, of course.

Then there were some other things I just didn't get. Like, what was a boil, and why would you want to use magic to remove it? And there was a spell to clean your jerkin. What the heck was a jerkin? Some kind of pickle, wasn't it? Or was that a euphemism? In that case, I could see why you'd want a clean pickle.

Fang chuckled. REMEMBER, THIS BOOK WAS WRITTEN A LONG TIME AGO. SOME THINGS MAY NO LONGER APPLY. AND THE PICKLE IS A GHERKIN, NOT A JERKIN.

So what's a jerkin?

WHAT DO I LOOK LIKE, A DICTIONARY? He trotted off to see to his kids.

I shrugged and turned back to the book. There were other spells for causing major disasters like earthquakes, tidal waves, and volcanic explosions. None of them helpful in this situation. Worse, reading the magick words was difficult. I'd never had a problem with my eyes or reading before, but after about an hour of reading the spells, my vision began to blur, and the letters jumped around. That was new. And not at all helpful. Was it the magick?

Finally, I closed the book and rested my eyes. "Find anything?" I asked Shade.

"Not yet," he said, his head buried in the list of demons and other supernatural creatures. "There's a demon or two that can control someone for a short time, like the mage demons, but they don't make the person stronger and faster."

"Maybe we're on the wrong track," I said, frustrated. "Maybe they're being controlled by some kind of drug, or a talisman like Dina's teardrop."

"It could be," Shade said. "But I don't know how we'd go about learning about those—I haven't seen anything about objects in these books, just supernatural creatures."

I sighed. "The Internet? After all, some people on there do know what they're talking about when it comes to demons and vampires." Luckily, no one believed them.

Shade nodded. "It's worth a try, though it'll be a real pain working through all the crap to find anything useful."

"Then I'm glad computers are much more up your alley." My alley held monsters that I killed to keep San Antonio safe.

"I know." He glanced toward Sharra's room. "Sharra has my laptop, researching stuff in New Mexico. Shall we check on her?"

"Sure."

He looked a little reluctant, but probably felt I'd be a good buffer between them. I didn't know if the twins would be able to regain their former closeness, but hey, if it helped with Shade's abandonment issues, I was all for it.

I followed him into the room where Sharra swirled with interdimensional energy as she tapped rapidly at the keyboard.

"Any luck finding out what's going on in New Mexico?" I asked.

"Not on the Internet," Sharra reported. "But I have a friend who has a friend . . ."

"And what do these friends know?" Shade asked.

"Not a lot. Yet. But give them time. They'll put out some feelers and see what they can find out."

So, was Sharra as big a geek as Shade was? Surely not. Suddenly realizing there was someone missing, I asked, "Where's your little dog?"

"Tiny Tim? He's sleeping in his bed," she said, pointing toward a corner of the room where the small ball of fur was curled up, trembling. "He tried to get a look at Princess's puppies. She didn't care for that, and now he's a bit traumatized."

I grinned. "How do you get a real dog to be so calm around demons? They were all terrified of me."

"Well, little Timmy isn't the brightest pup in the pack," she said with a twist of her mouth. "I kept searching until I found one. Eliminates a lot of problems, you know."

"I imagine."

"I never would have thought of it," Shade said.

"Well, I think he has some hellhound strain in him, far back in his lineage," Sharra said.

REALLY, REALLY FAAAAAAAR BACK, Fang said from the other room. ONLY A DROP OR TWO. JUST AS WELL—WITH THAT TINY BODY, HE COULDN'T DO ANYTHING HELLISH IF HE WANTED TO.

I don't know, I sent to him privately. *You seem to do pretty good, and you're not exactly huge.*

I'M NOT THAT SMALL OR THAT STUPID.

Ooookay. I'd better drop the subject. "I take it Princess and the pups are okay?" I said aloud. "She didn't let Tim get close enough to accidentally hurt them?"

Sharra said, "No, she did not. She's fine. The pups are fine."

Fang snorted. HECK, THAT LITTLE RUNT IS ALMOST AS SMALL AS MY PUPS. WHAT COULD HE DO TO PRINCESS?

He could annoy her. And none of us want that.

VERY TRUE, Fang conceded.

"I'd like to do a little more research on the 'net," Shade told Sharra. He explained what we were looking for.

"Okay," she said. "Sounds like a wild goose chase to me, but it's your computer." She relinquished the laptop to Shade.

Austin showed up at the door, looking more serious than I'd seen him in a long time.

"Everything okay downstairs?" I asked. "Learn anything?"

"Maybe. Micah wants us to attend a meeting at the club to tell everyone what we've found out. You ready to go?"

I checked my watch. No rest for the weary. Micah was taking his job of protecting his people seriously now. But I could see why he'd want to hold it tonight—these hunters were dangerous. Best to warn everyone as soon as possible and all at the same time then let them ask questions.

I glanced at Shade and Sharra. "Should they stay or go with us?" I asked Austin.

"I think we can decide that for ourselves," Sharra said.

"It might be safer here," Austin suggested.

Shade snorted. "Or not. After all, you were attacked downstairs. They might try again, and if you're not here to stop them, they might be more successful this time."

"I doubt it," Austin said drily. "Alejandro amped security to the max after this incident. You'll be safe here."

"Maybe," Shade said reluctantly, "but I think we should be there to answer questions. After all, we're the primary reason for the trouble that has been brought to San Antonio."

"We don't know that for sure," Sharra said.

"I'm sure," Shade said with a tone of finality. "We're going."

Austin shrugged as if he didn't care. "We're taking one of the town cars," he said, staring at me to make a point. "Safer that way."

Probably true. This time I decided to concede.

There was enough room for Austin, Fang, and the three of us demons in one car, so Austin drove us to Club Purgatory. Micah had closed one section for the night, marking it as a "private party," and the demons all filed in there.

Word must have traveled fast, 'cause a gut-load of people had showed up. A few minutes after the appointed time, Micah got everyone's attention. "I wanted to inform you of something that is happening in our midst. In the interest of keeping everyone safe, which I promised when you did me the honor of choosing me as leader again, I want to tell you of a serious threat to each and every one of you."

Mutters and surprised looks exchanged in the crowd.

Micah continued. "But first, I need to introduce someone. Shade's sister, Sharra, has come to visit."

"Sister?" people murmured in surprise. Like me, no one else knew he had a twin either. Heck, Shade didn't know, so how could they?

Sharra waved, and when people looked doubtful, she took her hand off the teacup Chihuahua and revealed herself in all her swirly glory.

"That's nice," someone said. "But what does it have to do with us?"

Micah raised his arms to quiet the crowd. "Someone—we don't know who—is trying to capture and kill shadow demons. They've made three attempts on Shade's life already."

"Why?" Ludwig, the mountain-sized water demon asked.

"We don't know that either."

"What *do* you know?" some brave soul called from his hidden position in the back.

"We know they will stop at nothing to kill him," Micah said sternly.

"So you've put us in danger by bringing him here," someone accused.

"I hope not," Micah said, "but there's another danger you need to be aware of." He paused for quiet, then said, "Tonight, things have changed. We had an attack here at the club, and there was one at a blood bank as well. The targets were both demons and vamps."

"Who's doing this?" Ludwig asked. "The same guys who are trying to kill Shade?"

"We don't know that either," Micah said. "But what we do know is that they are controlling our own people to use them against us, and we are being attacked by vampire and human. They probably won't hesitate at using demons either." He waited for the uproar to subside, then added, "To solve this as quickly as possible, we have joined forces with the New Blood Movement." He nodded at Austin who was just finishing a phone conversation. "Tell them what you learned."

Austin tugged the brim of his Stetson as if saying hello to everyone in the room. "Val Shapiro and I were attacked this evening at one of our blood banks. The perpetrators were crazed, stronger and faster than normal, and completely devoid of any sort of free will, so we neutralized them and inspected them."

Neutralized . . . an interesting word choice.

BETTER THAN MURDERED.

No kidding.

"I just learned what they found," Austin continued. "A puncture on both—an injection site. We believe they were given a drug and commanded to attack us."

Interesting. They'd been busy.

"Why?" someone asked.

Another person shouted, "What drug?"

Austin raised his hands for quiet. "We don't know why, and we're in the process of trying to find out what drug they used. We'll—"

"Wait," Tessa said, interrupting him, which was unusual for her. "How do you know who is controlled and who isn't?"

"We don't," Micah said.

"So, anyone in this room could be an assassin, and we wouldn't know it," Tessa continued, glancing nervously around at the crowd.

Oh, crap.

I'M ON IT, Fang said.

He whirled, his eyes darting to everyone in the place. THERE, he said to the room at large, his nose pointing past Micah. ANDREW. I CAN'T READ HIS MIND.

Andrew tried to make a run for it, but two of the brawny bartenders caught him.

"Don't hurt him," Micah said. "He's doing this against his will."

"Yeah, but *what* is he doing?" I asked.

It was a rhetorical question, but Tessa answered. "Maybe I can find out." The soothsayer demon darted forward and laid a hand on his arm. For once, her prophecy was crystal clear.

"The bomb under the bar will kill everyone present if not defused within sixty seconds."

Chapter Twenty

Val

SEVERAL PEOPLE screamed, like that would do any good. "Where is it?" I demanded. I didn't know what I could do about it, but I had to try something.

It was chaos as most people ran away from the bar, and others of us ran toward it, including Micah, Austin, Shade, and, of all people, Sharra.

Austin, with his superior vision, saw it first. "There." He pointed urgently. "Next to the beer tap."

I leaned forward, but Micah pulled me back. "Don't. You might set it off."

"So what? It's going to *go* off in less than a minute. We might be able to figure out how to disarm it." Rapidly, I mentally ran through the demon powers of the people in the room. What would help defuse this thing?

"Don't need to," Sharra said urgently and pushed me aside. "Let me."

She held out her hands, and a green sphere sparking with interdimensional energies coalesced between her palms. "Shawn, help me guide it," she said.

"I don't know how," Shade said.

"Like this."

I don't know what the two of them did or how they did it, but they floated that green sphere until it completely encompassed the crudely-made bomb. Then, as we all held our breaths, the bomb exploded. Or at least, that's what I assumed happened, because the green cloud seemed to implode, then expanded rapidly outward to about five feet and dissipated.

Some of the people who had been stampeding for the exit stopped and slowed. I suspected Mood had something to do with that, but I wasn't complaining.

"Where'd it go?" Ludwig asked in awe.

"Into another dimension," I said. Then louder, so other people could hear, "The shadow demons saved our lives."

"I didn't know a portal could be that small and compact," Shade said thoughtfully. "How'd you do it?"

Sharra shrugged. "Practice. Remember, we learned—" She broke off. "No, I guess you don't."

"No, but I'm glad you did," Shade said. "More is coming back to me every day. You'll have to remind me."

Sharra, who was trying to avoid being hugged to death by Ludwig, grinned. "Glad to." Most people were long gone by now, fled to safety. I glanced at Andrew, the fire demon who had caused me so much trouble before. He was still being restrained by the bartenders, but he looked a little more with it now, shaking and jerking, as if he were reasserting control over himself.

"We need to get his blood tested for drugs too," I said.

Austin strolled over to the bartenders. "We have a lab that's processing the other samples. It'll be good to have a fresh one. I called Vincent to come pick him up."

Andrew blinked up at him, shrinking back. "Wha—?" he said, sounding dopey. "What'd I do now?"

Austin shook his head at the fire demon who'd stolen the encyclopedia, come under the influence of a rogue mage demon, and damned near burned down Austin's home. He'd worked off his debt to the vamps, but who could blame Austin for still being a bit miffed? The cowboy vamp's smile was a little evil. "I'll tell you when we have you under our control."

Bad Austin. I stifled a chuckle.

Andrew's eyes widened, and he tried to push Austin away.

I took pity on Andrew. "It's okay," I said. "You weren't responsible for your actions—this time. Vincent is just taking you to see what kind of drug you were given. And, if I were you, I'd think long and hard about exactly how that drug got into your system."

"I—I don't remember."

"You'd better start remembering. Val's right," Micah said sternly. "We need all the information you can give us. Do you understand?"

Andrew nodded, but looked like he was about to crap his pants at any moment.

Fang chuckled in my mind. YEAH, I IMAGINE AUSTIN HAS PUT THE FEAR OF . . . AUSTIN INTO HIM.

"Maybe we should get a sample of our 'guest's' blood as well," Micah suggested with a raised eyebrow at me.

Huh?

YOU KNOW, Fang reminded me. THE GUY DOWNSTAIRS.

Oh yeah, his *guest.* In the cell. Micah called Gwen and asked her to bring the necessary medical stuff—she was doing a good job of putting her skills to work in the vampire lab.

"The drug might have worn off already," Austin said.

"True," I said. "And there's a good way to test that. Shall we go downstairs?"

Tessa nodded. "I'll watch over Andrew until Vincent arrives."

Though more people knew about the cells in the basement of the club now, Micah still kept them as secret as he could. I think he was embarrassed that he had such a thing in his cellar, even if his father had built it. Since Austin already knew about it, he accompanied us.

We approached the cell, but Jorge didn't look as if he'd moved much. He still knelt beside the cot, his hands together, and his head bowed in prayer.

Lola was stronger now, but was she stronger than the drug? Or maybe it had been absorbed into his bloodstream now. Well, there was one way to find out.

I moved as close as I could to the bars of the cell. "Jorge Ortiz?" I said softly.

He ignored me.

Well, he wouldn't be able to ignore Lola. Slowly, I unfurled the energy tendrils from my chakras and let her reach for him. Thanks to Austin, Lola was at about forty percent power, so I didn't have to push quite as hard as I would've earlier. When the tendrils touched him, he stiffened. Oh yeah, he felt that all right. And I know it felt pretty darned good.

I intensified her hold on him. "Jorge," I crooned. "You're going to be a good little boy and tell us everything we want to know, aren't you?"

He stood and faced us, his face slack with desire. "*Si.*"

Yay, Lola finally worked on someone. I wanted to do a fist pump, but restrained myself, given the audience.

WELL, HERE'S A WOO FROM ME, Fang said. AND A HOO, TOO. WOO HOO, VAL.

Sarcasm or truth? Either way, I was taking it as a compliment.

"Can you read him now?" I asked Fang.

NOPE. DEFINITELY HUMAN, AS I SAID BEFORE.

I wondered if Jorge was an innocent victim, too, then realized I could ask him. "Were you forced to hunt down the shadow demon and kill him? Answer in English."

"No," Jorge answered.

"Then why did you do it?" I asked in exasperation.

"I am a soldier of the Lord," he said.

Uh-huh. "And who told you to do this? The Lord?"

"It is Emmanuel's will."

"Who is Emmanuel?"

"Our Lord's right hand."

"And he told you to kill shadow demons?" I asked.

"Yes."

His answers were short, but not sweet. "Elaborate on your answers as necessary," I said, annoyed. "Why were you told to kill shadow demons?"

"Because Emmanuel wanted it so."

I rolled my eyes, and Austin stepped forward. "Let me question him?"

Fine with me—this guy was doing nothing but ticking me off. I made a "be my guest" gesture and told Jorge, "Answer this man's questions thoroughly and completely."

Austin peered at him. "Explain why Emmanuel wants shadow demons dead."

"They are evil."

"Evil?" Austin repeated. "How do you know they are evil?"

"Emmanuel said so."

"And how does Emmanuel know?"

"Emmanuel knows all things."

My eyebrows rose. Seriously?

Austin continued, "What drug did he use on you?"

"He didn't use any drug."

Yeah, right.

"What did he use to make you stronger and faster than normal humans?" Austin persisted.

Jorge hesitated for a moment, and I realized I'd let Lola slip because I was too interested in the answers. I reinforced my control over his body. "Answer the question," I told him.

"He used his blood," Jorge answered.

Really? Ick.

"How?" Austin asked.

"The sacrament of Emmanuel's blood is given to the brotherhood by injection or drinking."

Again, ick. Sounded like a vampire to me. "So how did he control Andrew, the fire demon?"

"He used his blood."

I didn't get it. "Why would he give this 'sacrament' to people outside the brotherhood?"

"To convince them to do as they should."

Compel was more like it. "What does that mean?" I asked him.

"Demons, vampires, and other unnatural creatures must be purged from this Earth. It is our holy duty."

"Wait," I said. "Doesn't the Bible say 'thou shalt not kill'?"

"Yes, but Emmanuel explained that refers to humans only."

Convenient, if you planned on genocide. Exasperated, I asked, "Why do you believe anything this guy says? He beats you and tattoos you, and you just act like his own little kamikaze demon hunters?"

"No."

Baffled, I looked at Austin. Jorge didn't exactly answer the question.

"What do you mean, no?" Austin asked.

"He does not beat us or force us to get tattoos."

"Who does?" I asked.

"No one."

Ooookay. Confused, I asked, "Then who whipped you?"

"I did."

"What?" I looked at Austin, unable to believe my ears.

"That's why the scars looked different," he murmured. "They were all concentrated over his shoulders. The whipping was self-inflicted."

"But why?" I asked the hunter. "Why would you do such a thing?"

"As penance."

"Did Emmanuel tell you to?"

"No."

Austin looked as though a light bulb dawned over his head. "Do you belong to the Penitentes, *Los Hermanos*?"

"Yes."

"What's that?" I asked Austin.

"A Hispanic religious sect in New Mexico who believe in self-flagellation to do penance for their sins."

"Why have I never heard of them?"

"They are low-key, secretive. Especially since they reenact the crucifixion at Easter with a volunteer. They consider it a great honor to be chosen, even though the volunteer sometimes dies."

Yikes. It all fit. The scars, the religious tattoos, the fact that all the fanatics were Hispanic. Going back to an earlier question, I asked, "So, if you are one of the chosen few of the brotherhood, why did he inject others?"

"It makes nonbelievers compliant and renders them subject to Emmanuel's will."

"And what is Emmanuel's will?"

"To kill all demons, vampires, and unnatural creatures. Especially shadow demons."

Humph. If you asked me, this slavish adoration was unnatural. And we were talking in circles here.

"What can you tell us about Emmanuel?" Micah asked.

"Answer him, too," I ordered Jorge.

"Nothing."

My eyebrows rose. "Tell us everything you know about him," I ordered. Then, seeing that it sent him into a tailspin of confusion, I said, "Never mind. Austin, you ask him."

"Where did Emmanuel come from?" he asked.

"Heaven."

I snorted. Highly unlikely.

"What does he look like?" Austin asked.

"Like Jesus."

Huh? "Describe him," I ordered.

"Tall, long brown hair, bearded, with intense eyes and stigmata."

"What?" I turned to Austin.

"Describe the stigmata."

"Blood flows from the palms of his hands, just like our Lord."

Oh, crap. This Emmanuel guy must have studied old pictures of Jesus to play on their superstitions.

"You realize this man is not Jesus, don't you?" I asked.

"He is Emmanuel," Jorge answered.

Like that was any help at all.

"Has Emmanuel given you a reason to kill these creatures besides the fact that they're evil?" Austin asked.

Jorge said, "No. It is enough."

Yeah, that and mind control.

"Where is he now?" Micah asked.

"I don't know."

"Is he in New Mexico?" Micah probed.

"I don't know."

Helpful. *Not.*

"How long has Emmanuel been leading you?" Austin asked.

"About eight years." Jorge swayed on his feet and looked as though he was about to pass out.

"What's wrong with him?" I asked Micah.

"He has refused all food and drink." He shrugged. "He must be pretty weak. His way of committing suicide, I guess."

Why were they all so intent on killing themselves?

MAYBE IT'S ANOTHER FORM OF PENANCE FOR GETTING CAUGHT, Fang suggested.

That made a weird kind of sense. Annoyed, I said, "Jorge, sit down."

He sat down on the mattress but didn't look any better. I saw now that he had a full plate of food sitting, probably untouched, on the floor next to the bed, next to a glass of water. "Eat and drink," I told him. "Eat everything on your plate." I didn't want another demon hunter killing himself on our watch.

As Jorge ate, Micah asked Austin, "Do you know of any vampires who can control people from a distance with their blood?"

"No."

Micah sighed. "Maybe there's something about this sort of thing in the encyclopedia," he suggested. "After all, it has information about vampires and hellhounds. It might mention this, too, whatever it is."

"Good point. I'll put Shade on it."

"Okay. I'll question Jorge later."

That wouldn't work—he was only answering now because Lola forced him to.

Use me, Dina's crystal whispered.

Why not? "You can't compel him to respond, but I can. If I use the amulet, I can tell him to answer any questions for you in the future."

"Not a good idea," Austin said.

And Micah just flat said, "No." Then he added, "If we need to question him more, we'll bring you back."

"Sounds inconvenient," I muttered. The amulet would be far easier.

AND A HECK OF A LOT MORE TROUBLE, Fang said. YOU REALLY OUGHT TO GET RID OF THAT THING.

Nope. Not while it might still help.

Ignore them. Use me anyway. They'll never know.

I was seriously tempted, but Fang, at least, would know I'd done it. I fought against the temptation and won, but my frustration was more to do with them not recognizing that we were abandoning a perfectly good tool than because they had some sort of irrational phobia about it.

Fang muttered something too low for me to hear, and I didn't ask him to repeat it.

With the help of the bartenders, we got Andrew and the shadow demons back to the penthouse without incident. Luckily, we'd lost Mood somewhere along the way. I don't know if it was because Micah didn't think Shade needed her babysitting his attitude anymore, or if Mood herself had gotten sulky and gone walkabout. Whichever one it was, I was glad of it.

JEALOUS MUCH?

No—just annoyed by her attitude, I told the smart-aleck hellhound.

YEAH, BABE. JUST KEEP TELLING YOURSELF THAT.

Ignoring him, I told Shade and Sharra what we'd learned from

Jorge. "Apparently, he started this cult or whatever it is eight years ago. You were in New Mexico then, weren't you?"

"Yes," Sharra said, petting her little dog. "But I don't remember anything like this. Then again, we were pretty remote and not really dialed in to what was happening in the Underground then. You could ask Kathryn."

"It would help if we knew what he was," I said.

"I vaguely remember something from the encyclopedia," Shade said. "Hold on and I'll look it up."

It only took him a few moments of rapidly turning the pages until he found what he was looking for. "Here it is. A blood demon."

A demon? Crap. I really didn't like messing with politics or religion, and this had holy water stamped all over it. "What's a blood demon?"

"According to the book, a blood demon can heal others who ingest his blood. Unfortunately, he can control them with it as well. The stronger he is, the longer the control will last. Their adoration makes him stronger. He . . . feeds on it," Shade said in disgust.

Tailor-made to rope in a group like the Penitentes. "Does it say anything there about making them stronger and faster?" I asked.

"No, but that doesn't mean that *isn't* one of his abilities. The encyclopedia is sketchy in many places. But, depending on how much demon blood he has in him, he might be able to pass on some of his own abilities."

So a half or a quarter demon would be able to do it easier than someone like me who was only one-eighth demon.

I asked Austin, "If Emmanuel is part demon, and someone injected Josef with his blood, why didn't that make Josef go crazy like the others who drank it? Because it was injected instead?"

Austin frowned. "I doubt it. That shouldn't make a difference."

Fang, who was now sitting on Shade's foot, said, SHADE HAS A THOUGHT ABOUT WHY THAT MIGHT BE.

I looked at Shade, but he looked annoyed and didn't really seem to appreciate Fang's "help." "What's your thought?" I asked him.

"According to what I've read, it's the combination of the human, demon, and vampire blood that causes insanity. Take the human out of the equation and you have—"

He broke off and glanced at Sharra, who looked horrified.

"You have what?" I demanded.

"A full demon," Sharra whispered.

Okay, I got why that was bad, but not as bad as the expression on the twins' faces made it look. What was up with that?

DON'T YOU GET IT? Fang said.

Evidently not.

THIS DEMON STARTED HIS CULT EIGHT YEARS AGO. THAT'S WHEN THEIR FATHER ACCIDENTALLY BROUGHT A FULL DEMON INTO THIS WORLD.

Stunned, I asked, "You think this is the full demon your father brought from the other dimension?"

Sharra looked away. "Dad said he looked for the demon, but never found him." She covered her mouth. "Has this nightmare come back to haunt us?"

I'M AFRAID SO.

There was a lot I still didn't understand. "So, your father brought him through. So what? Why does Emmanuel want to kill you for that? I thought demons *wanted* to be in this dimension."

"They do," Austin confirmed. "But think about it. Shadow demons are also the only ones who can send him back."

WELL, YEAH, Fang quipped. I SEE WHY HE'S AFTER THEIR BUTTS NOW. HE DOESN'T WANT TO GO HOME. EVER.

Chapter Twenty-One

Val

UNFORTUNATELY, I think Fang had hit the reason right on the nose. "But why has Emmanuel waited so long to search for shadow demons? Why now? Why not eight years ago?" I asked.

"Yeah," Sharra said. "The Denver Demon Underground said there have been some suspicious characters looking for me there the past few days, too. Why now?"

"Probably because he just learned of your existence," Austin drawled. "And most likely from someone in New Mexico. Who there knew?"

Sharra shrugged. "Everyone who was at the judgment ritual that condemned our father. And everyone they told. Could be a lot of people."

"Yes," Shade said. "But not everyone knew where we went. Kathryn did."

Sharra frowned. "I can't believe she'd reveal that. Not unless she was coerced."

"We just talked to her," I reminded them. "I think she would have mentioned it if she'd given up your location, even accidentally."

"Did anyone else know where you'd gone?" Austin asked.

Shade and Sharra looked at each other and, in unison, said, "Diesel."

"Diesel?" I repeated. "The Paladin? I know you don't like him, but do you really think he'd do this to you?" Paladins were chosen precisely because they wouldn't do this sort of thing.

"Not intentionally," Austin said. "Remember, they said he was missing?"

Oh, that's right. Didn't bode well for the Albuquerque Paladin.

"Yes," Shade said. "And I bet a full demon would be able to control even a Paladin."

I'd never fought a full demon before. They had to be far more powerful than anyone I'd ever messed with. What the heck was I supposed to do? "Oh, crap. I just realized . . . Emmanuel must be here in San Antonio."

"How do you figure?"

"Well, Andrew, Josef and Cyndi must have been injected here. And I doubt Emmanuel's followers could force him to do what Emmanuel wants. *He's* the blood demon, not them."

"That's right," Austin mused. "We really need to find out what Andrew knows. And Josef."

"They're both still in the lab," Austin said. "I'll ask Vincent to bring them up."

It wasn't long before Vincent had Josef and Andrew in the living room.

"Vincent heads up our lab downstairs," Austin explained. "Tell us what you've learned, Vincent."

I'd met the Jason Alexander lookalike before, but didn't realize he was a scientist. He didn't look like one.

WHAT? Fang asked. YOU THINK HE SHOULD BE WEARING A WHITE LAB COAT, OVERSIZED GOGGLES, AND RUBBER GLOVES AND BOOTS, LIKE THE MAD SCIENTIST IN *DR. HORRIBLE'S SINGALONG BLOG*?

Not really. He looked nothing at all like Neil Patrick Harris's character Dr. Horrible. *I don't know what I expected*, I said. I knew I sounded sulky, but I didn't care. My assumptions were stupid, I know, but did he always have to call me on them like some politically correct Jiminy Cricket?

SOMEONE HAS TO.

I felt like sticking my tongue out at him, but that seemed a tad childish.

"We don't know a lot," Vincent said. "But we did find injection sites on both of them." He nodded at Josef and Andrew. "The effects have worn off now."

"What do you remember?" Austin asked Josef.

The vamp frowned. "The last thing I remember is someone requesting a private room to donate blood." He slanted a glance at me. "We always accommodate such requests."

Of course they did. It meant they could get their blood "donation" directly from the source, instead of having to drink it out of a plastic bag. And, in return, they could give the donor one heck of a warm, fuzzy memory.

I nodded to let him know I understood. I tried not to judge. After all, the New Blood Movement made all donations voluntary, instead of the forced fang to neck kind the unaffiliated bloodsuckers were fond of.

Josef grimaced. "But the donor caught me off guard and stabbed a needle into me."

"What did the donor look like?" I asked. "Bearded? Intense eyes? Long hair?"

"No. He was an older man, Hispanic. Short, dark hair."

Not Emmanuel himself then.

"What happened after that?" Austin asked.

Josef frowned. "It isn't very clear, but I vaguely remember another man in the room, whispering to me, making my blood bubble through my veins."

"Was *he* bearded?" Shade asked.

"Maybe. Yes. I don't know. It's not really clear."

"What do you remember?" I asked.

Josef shook his head. "I remember wanting to do anything he asked of me, believing anything he told me." He paused, then frowned and added, "It was very disturbing, yet at the time it seemed completely reasonable."

"How long ago was that?" Austin asked.

"About three or four hours ago, maybe more."

Shade bumped Andrew with his shoulder. "Did you have the same experience?"

The red-headed fire demon shrugged. "Kind of. They grabbed me on my way into the club. I was on my way to meet Tessa. Some guys grabbed me, shot me with something, and told me what to do. I-I don't really remember much, except coming to and Tessa saying I'd planted a bomb." He folded his arms across his chest. "I don't remember doing it. And if I did, it's 'cause they forced me to."

"We know," I soothed. "It wasn't your fault."

Vincent added, "Andrew's fugue seemed to last about five or six hours, almost twice as long as Josef's."

"Why the difference?" Shade asked. "They're both about the same weight."

Vincent nodded. "The dosage could have been different, but I believe it's because Josef is fully vampire and will metabolize the magical component faster while Andrew is only part demon. The effects will probably last even longer for a full human."

That explained why the guy in the cell had taken longer to recover.

"What about Diesel?" Shade asked. "Shouldn't his have worn off, too?"

"Yes," Vincent said. "Unless they keep repeating the dosage."

"Or he's dead," Austin said.

Whoa. Trust Austin to cut to the heart of the matter. His conversational bomb silenced everyone as they stared at him in dawning horror.

Austin's phone rang in the quiet and he answered it, then held a low-voiced conversation on the far side of the room. He looked grim, so we pretty much all tried to eavesdrop. I don't know about the others, but I wasn't successful. And I wasn't too proud to ask after he hung up. "What was that about?"

"We sent out a warning to all the blood banks, and one of them caught a donor with a syringe. He tried to commit suicide, but they knew what to look for, so stopped him." He glanced at me. "Alejandro is asking if you can come interrogate him."

"Sure," I said. "But if he's being controlled by Emmanuel's blood, it won't work until that wears off."

"Let's try it anyway."

"Okay."

We left Vincent to follow up on the blood to see what they could learn, and Shade and Sharra stayed to see what they could find out about Emmanuel. I even let Austin drive. Not because I was getting mellow, but because it was raining outside, and getting soaked in January on my Valkyrie was not my idea of fun. Fang elected to stay out of the rain and spend time with his kids.

We endured the ride in silence. Austin seemed lost in his own dark little world, and I didn't want to disturb his thoughts. Besides, I didn't know what to say to him. Fang's comment had set me to thinking, and I found myself mentally comparing Austin against Shade . . . with Shade coming up wanting.

Disturbing. Then again, Shade was under a lot of stress, what with being hunted, his sister reappearing and regaining his lost memories. Once things settled down, maybe he'd get back to his old self. I hoped so, anyway.

Austin is under a lot of stress, too, and look how he handles it.

No, I didn't want to think about that. Luckily, we'd arrived at the blood bank. Austin thoughtfully popped open an umbrella for me, and we splashed through the puddles from the luxury sedan to the hotel-turned-blood-bank.

Tessa let us in to see the prisoner, who was held in a locked room that was devoid of anything he could use to kill himself.

Another Hispanic male, but this one looked surly and was restrained by zip ties and had a black eye. I bet he had scars on his back and a dagger/cross tattoo, too. Another Penitente, no doubt.

Austin and I entered alone. "Can you reach him?" Austin asked.

Lola was able to enter the man's chakras easily. "Yes," I said. Then, using Lola, I surged into the man, and he was mine. I thought about what I wanted to ask him. But first, I needed to make sure he gave us what we needed. "Answer our questions fully and completely—and in English. Do you work for Emmanuel?"

"It is my privilege to serve Emmanuel."

Ooookay. At least, this one seemed a little more talkative. "Where is he now?"

"I don't know."

"Is he in San Antonio?"

"Yes."

"But you don't know where?" I asked incredulously. "Why not?"

"He comes to me when he needs me. It is not for me to question the actions of the holy one. And if I don't know, I can't tell."

Well, that made sense. What else did we need to know? "Why is he targeting vamps, demons, and shadow demons in particular?"

"Because they are evil and must be purged from this world."

I'd hoped I might get a different answer this time, but no such luck. At least this one's English seemed to be better.

"May I ask a question?" Austin said.

"Sure."

"Once Emmanuel gets rid of all the 'evil' ones, what are his plans?"

The questioning went on for several loooong minutes, slow and painful as pulling a vampire's fangs, but we questioned him until a picture emerged. Emmanuel had placed people all around the Southwest to inject his blood into key religious leaders to make them believe Emmanuel was holy. He was building his following one city at a time, in hopes of eventually controlling the entire world.

"Why do you follow this megalomaniac?" I asked.

"His blood makes us strong, powerful, healed of all disease. He is a saint."

"But when the blood wears off, don't the people he's controlled change their minds?"

"No, they have seen the light and are converted."

Austin interpreted. "If they want to believe, they will, especially after a 'holy' experience."

Yeah, his insight was probably valid. There must be some hypnotic component in the blood as well. "But why does he want to rule the world?"

"Just as he provides us with healing and strength, our worship provides him with the sustenance he needs. The more who worship him, the more good he can do."

Yeah, right. But it confirmed what the encyclopedia said about him feeding on adoration. "How many cities is he in?"

"I don't know. Some in New Mexico, and now San Antonio."

"Seems like a slow way to do it, to me." Then again, he only had a limited supply of his own blood. Maybe he could only take one city at a time. Still, that was one city too many . . . and too close for comfort.

"That's why he's killing vamps and demons," Austin said.

"What do you mean?"

"To minimize his opposition. He fears us and knows that we know what he really is. So, his plan is to eliminate us first."

Yeah, I got that. But it made me think. "Did you know that Emmanuel is a demon, too?" I asked the prisoner.

"No, he is Emmanuel, a saint. He is not evil."

"Actually, he is. He's using his demonic powers—his blood—to make you believe he's holy, when he's really just another demon."

"You are lying. He is our savior, come in answer to our prayers."

Hmm. "Even with Lola, I can't make him disbelieve something he holds strongly," I told Austin. I could make him do what I wanted while he was under her influence, or tell me whatever I wanted to know, but I couldn't change his belief system.

"Too bad," Austin said.

There is a way . . . the amulet called to me.

"Well, maybe there's one way I could do it . . . ."

Austin frowned. "Not the crystal again."

"Yes, the crystal," I said and couldn't keep the irritation out of my voice. "It isn't all bad, you know."

"You don't know that," Austin said. "You don't know what it'll do to you, if it will turn you into another power-hungry damn-the-consequences succubus like Dina."

"Then what do you suggest?" I asked, annoyed. "If I use the amulet, I can control him beyond the time he's in my presence. I could send him to spy for us, learn more about Emmanuel, and find out where he's hiding out." At Austin's stubborn look, I added, "If I don't, what are we going to do with all of his minions we keep collecting? You don't like the catch and release idea, we can't kill them, and we can't continue incarcerating them. We don't have the space."

"The Movement will take care of it," Austin snapped back. "You'll use the amulet only as a last resort. It's too dangerous."

Stupid. When were any of them going to see that it was the only possible solution? "I'll use it just this once," I promised. "Face it, we really need the intel, and it's not like we've been successful getting it any other way." Exasperated, I added, "You all want me to be the Paladin, to make these tough decisions, but when I do, you second guess me."

Austin scowled, but apparently realized there really was no other choice, because he said, "All right, but if you use it again without checking with someone, I'll smash the blasted thing."

Finally. I grasped the tear-shaped crystal and concentrated. It was like endorphins flooded my system, making me feel wonderful, powerful. Concentrating on the hunter, I said, "You will find Emmanuel's location and report back to me immediately when you know where he'll be and when." I gave him my phone number and the address of the penthouse. "You will not tell Emmanuel or anyone else that you are under my control, and you will continue to act normally in all other respects. Do you understand?"

"Yes," the man said, deeply under the influence of not only Lola but the amulet as well.

Slowly, reluctantly, I withdrew the amulet's influence, and Lola's. It was harder than I expected to tear my will away from the amulet. I'd have to be careful of that. Have to be stronger than Dina.

The prisoner glared at us and spat. "Evil spawn. I will kill you next."

Hmm, maybe I should have told him not to attack me, either. "No, you won't," I said, reinforcing the order with the amulet. "You will not even try."

I let go of him again, so he was no longer under Lola's influence, but hopefully still the amulet's. Now, to test it. "Where is Emmanuel?"

"I don't know."

"But you're going to tell us as soon as you find out, right?"

"Yes," the man said, seeming at war with himself.

Well, I didn't care what kind of battle he had with himself, so long as I won the war.

The next step was to release him, but I didn't want to do that until I topped off Lola's tank. After all, he was handy and available. Though he deserved to be sucked dry, I'd leave enough for him to function as I'd ordered.

Unfortunately, it wasn't as satisfying as it could be, and Lola still wouldn't get anywhere near her former strength—only about forty-five percent. The amulet wanted to get in on the act, urging me to use it, to make the feeding more enjoyable, but I resisted its lure.

It was harder than I expected, though. Could Austin and Fang be right?

No, I'd just have to feed Lola more often so I wouldn't need the crystal. And be a lot more careful in the future.

Chapter Twenty-Two

Shade

AFTER VAL LEFT with her bloodsucking friends, Shade went back to his room to see what he could learn about this Emmanuel. He'd been more disturbed by the demon's existence than he'd let Val see, and now had to do whatever he could to counter this threat.

"You really think this is the demon Dad brought in to our dimension?" Sharra asked.

"Yes," Shade said curtly as he booted up the laptop. "It makes too much sense. And now he's after us."

"To kill us?" she asked, sounding worried.

"Probably," Shade said. "Or he might want us to open a portal and let some of his buddies in from the other side." He started an online search for the name Emmanuel in New Mexico.

She looked horrified. "We can't let either one of those things happen," she whispered.

"Exactly."

DON'T WORRY ABOUT IT, Fang said to them from his place by Princess's side. VAL WILL TAKE CARE OF IT.

"I fight my own battles," Sharra said. "I don't need a Pala—" She broke off with a guilty look at Shade, then finished with, "We don't need anyone else to help us. This is our problem. We'll solve it. Right, Shawn?"

"Shade," he insisted. Shawn was a surly teenager who didn't even exist anymore.

"Sorry, I keep forgetting."

He nodded as he continued to search online. "But Sharra's right. This is our responsibility."

WHAT CAN YOU DO THAT VAL CAN'T? Fang challenged.

"We can create portals into other worlds," Shade said. Obviously. "Sharra saved everyone in the Demon Underground with one, remember?"

"Yeah," Sharra said. "Val couldn't do that."

Unfortunately, Shade wasn't sure if he would have been able to do it either.

Princess nipped at Fang. MY HUMAN IS JUST AS GOOD AS YOUR HUMAN. BETTER.

MAYBE, Fang said, nosing her affectionately.

Did the hellhound really believe it, or was he just placating Princess?

WHAT DO YOU THINK? Fang snarked privately.

It didn't matter what Fang and Princess believed. All that mattered was putting this blood demon back where he belonged before he caused any more damage. Unfortunately, the Internet wasn't proving much help. There were a few mentions of Emmanuel in New Mexico, but most of them talked about furtive religious meetings with superstitious people in the backward small towns near where Shade used to live, and rumors of healing that couldn't be corroborated. The reports hadn't put much stock into rumors of a new Messiah, and hadn't investigated his background any further.

Shade glanced up at Sharra. "We need to do some more digging. He seems to concentrate around Albuquerque and Santa Fe, but we need more info."

Sharra nodded. "I can do that. What about the *Encyclopedia Magicka*? You think it might have something to help?"

"There wasn't much about blood demons in it," Shade said with a shrug.

"Maybe one of the spells? Could there be something there?"

"Maybe. There's a spell to locate mage demons, but that's because the books are terrified of them. I don't know if they can locate other demons."

"It wouldn't hurt to try."

"We'll have to wait for Val. She's really the only who can access the spells part of the encyclopedia."

"Are you sure about that?" Sharra challenged. "Have you tried?"

"No," Shade admitted.

"Then let's try it. Where are they?"

Val was keeping them here in the penthouse to keep them safe. "In her room, I think."

HEY, YOU DON'T WANT TO MESS WITH THOSE, Fang said. REMEMBER WHAT HAPPENED TO JOSH AND ANDREW?

"Yes," Shade admitted. "But that's primarily because of the mage demon speaking through them, and the books' paranoid desire to hide. The books are safe now, and the mage demon is in another dimension." Shade had put him there. "I'm not like Mood. I know the dangers, and I'll be careful."

SEE THAT YOU DO, Fang said. I DON'T WANT TO HAVE TO TELL VAL WHY SHE HAS TO SCRAPE GRISLY BITS OF YOU AND YOUR SISTER FROM THE WALLS.

Sharra looked appalled. "You think that could happen?"

"No," Shade said dismissively. "Fang just thinks no one but Val can do anything right."

I DO NOT—Fang began, but was stopped by a nip from Princess.

YOU DO, TOO. LEAVE THEM ALONE.

And wonder of wonders, Fang listened to her.

"You can keep watch on us, Fang. If anything seems a bit off, you have my permission to stop us by any means necessary."

Fang seemed mollified by that so Shade went into Val's room. Being there smacked too much of invading her privacy, so he took the two books that held the spells into the living room.

"I'll take one, and you take the other," Sharra suggested.

THERE MIGHT BE AN EASIER WAY, Fang said.

"What's that?"

VAL TALKS TO THE BOOKS AND ASKS FOR THEIR HELP.

"Really?" Sharra asked with a raised eyebrow, then stared at the books. "Hey, you have any advice on how to capture a blood demon?"

Nothing.

"You try it," Sharra told Shade. "Since you're her friend and you've been handling them a lot, maybe they'll talk to you."

"They don't actually talk," Shade said. "It's more like they show her where the spells are in the books." But it wouldn't hurt to try, and approach them with more respect than Sharra had.

First, though, he'd find out if they'd even respond to him. Feeling strange talking to inanimate objects, he said, "Uh, we are looking for assistance in combating a threat. Can you give us advice?"

Surprisingly, one of the books glowed.

"Whoa," Sharra said. "Something worked. What does that glow mean?"

Shade opened the book, and it fell open at the glowing spot. "It's a spell." He skimmed it quickly. "It will allow the books to communicate with us." And the communication spell lasted for weeks, unless someone else used it in the interim.

"Cool! Do it," his sister urged.

"I'm not sure," Shade said. "The more you use the spells in the books, the less you're able to use your other abilities."

"Well, maybe that's a good thing. You think maybe it would make you a little less swirly, more human?"

"I don't know." But it was worth a try. It wasn't like he *wanted* to be at the mercy of his anger and accidentally create portals.

Shade whispered the words of the spell, and magick rushed through him like a shot of wild static electricity, leaving the hairs on his arms standing on end. It didn't feel at all like the dimensions he cycled through. This was far more visceral, as if the spell took up space in the very cells of his body.

A blank space appeared on the page, and letters appeared one at a time, in glowing script. *Speak to me.*

Ooookay. "Do I look any different?" Shade asked Sharra. He certainly didn't feel changed—he still cycled through dimensions.

She peered at his swirls for a moment. "No, I can't tell a difference." Turning to the book, she asked, "Do you have any spells that will help us locate this blood demon?"

Nothing happened. Sharra poked Shade. "You try it."

Shade repeated the question, and this time the response was immediate. The previous words disappeared, and a single word took their place. *No.*

"Do you have any additional information about blood demons?" he asked.

No. All available information is written herein.

"Well, that was a bust," Sharra said, sounding disappointed.

"Maybe if we asked a more open-ended question," Shade suggested. "Is there anything you want to tell us?"

Yes.

He waited for the book to elaborate, but realized he might have to be more specific. "What else do you want to tell us?"

The keeper is in danger.

"Val?" Shade said, not really surprised. Her life pretty much put her in jeopardy all the time. "How is she in danger?"

The amulet wishes to control the keeper.

Shade's mouth thinned. He knew that damned crystal was trouble. "Please give us as much information as possible. Tell us how the amulet is bad for Val."

The keeper must not be controlled or she can no longer be the keeper.

Sharra stared at him. "What is this amulet, and why is it dangerous?"

Shade explained it, and Sharra looked appalled. "You mean she can control *you* with this thing? Even when you're not within her field, not near her?"

"Yes, it allows her to control any man, forever."

"That's dangerous."

Shade nodded. "Especially since it seems to have more power over her each time she uses it."

"We have to get that thing away from her," Sharra exclaimed.

Oh, great. Another reason for Sharra to distrust Val.

Shade stared at the books, their last communication still glowing on the page. "You mean that if she's controlled by the amulet, she can no longer use the spells in these books?"

Yes.

"But I just used a spell. Does that mean anyone can?"

No. Only a potential keeper can use this spell.

He was a potential keeper? What exactly did that mean? Shade shook his head. It didn't matter. He'd ensure Val remained the keeper. "How can we keep her from using the crystal?"

Bring the succubus to full power. Use the vampire.

Tell Val to feed on Austin all she wanted? Shade didn't care for that solution at all. Maybe there was another way. "How can we get rid of it?" he asked. He didn't have much experience with magickal objects, but he suspected that getting rid of them wasn't as easy as tossing them in the trash. Besides, Val's connection with the damned thing might lead her to it no matter where he put it.

Through a portal.

That made sense. She couldn't enter other dimensions on her own. "Can I use other spells in this book?" he asked, hoping there was something Val had missed, something he could do to help.

Not until you become keeper.

Well, that wasn't going to happen.

"What else do we need to know?"

Do not let the keeper know you can use this spell until the amulet is gone.

Damn. That was his best argument—give up the amulet because the books wouldn't like it. "Why?"

If she uses the communication spell, you will no longer be able to communicate with me unless you use it again. Each time you use it, you will lose more of your abilities and may not be able to open the portal.

Sharra poked him. "It's right. We have to keep this secret."

Shade nodded. Yes, the books could be a wealth of information, but only if he was able to use the spell. "Okay, I won't tell her," he agreed, feeling odd about making promises to a book. But now he had to figure out how to get that crystal away from her . . . for her own good.

Chapter Twenty-Three

Val

WE RETURNED TO the penthouse to let Shade and Sharra know what we'd learned about Emmanuel, which wasn't much. I insisted they both touch Tiny Tim so everyone could see their expressions.

"This is *our* problem," Sharra said. "Our father caused the problem in the first place, and Emmanuel is after us because of it. We'll take care of it. Right, Shade?"

He nodded. "She's right. We need to fix this."

Tired of suddenly being the bad guy in their eyes, I asked, "How do you plan to do that? Or do you actually have a plan?"

Austin raised his eyebrows in surprise, probably because I was becoming rather annoyed with Shade.

"Micah has watchers out looking for this Emmanuel," Shade said.

"And what are you going to do when you find him?"

"We'll think of something," Shade said curtly.

"That's what I thought," I said, not caring how cold it sounded. "You don't have a plan. And you don't know anything about this guy except what Austin and I have found out for you. You need us."

Sharra shook her head. "We don't need your help."

I didn't let her finish. "Forget your stupid pride. This is about a heck of a lot more than you and your brother. This Emmanuel dude wants to take over the world, one person, one city at a time. He's a full demon, eight times stronger than any of us. Literally eight times stronger than me. What kind of idiot wouldn't accept help to save the world when we're so clearly out of our depth?"

WHOA, HARSH, Fang said.

Just trying to beat some sense into her head. I sure wished I could use the amulet on her.

YOU USED IT AGAIN, DIDN'T YOU? Fang asked suspiciously.

That's not important.

YOU DID. YOU USED IT AGAIN. TALK ABOUT IDIOTS.

Austin said it was okay. Sort of. I didn't tell him Austin had promised to smash it if I ever used it again.

Fang could read the truth in my mind. He didn't like it, but he didn't have to.

"That's enough, Val," Shade said, frowning. "You've made your point. And though we may need you to help find this blood demon, you also need us to send him back to his dimension when you do find him."

"Granted," I said grudgingly. "We need each other. Now, can we please come up with a strategy without arguing about who isn't going to do what with despised Paladins?"

I glared at Sharra when I said that. She looked sulky, but nodded. "What's *your* plan?"

I glanced at Austin, and he shrugged, obviously wanting to stay out of the line of fire.

Guess it was up to me. "Well, the first thing is to find Emmanuel. I sent the demon hunter back to him with instructions to report back his location."

"And you think he'll just do as you ask?" Sharra asked, looking dubious.

"I reinforced it with the amulet," I said, and dared them silently to condemn me for it.

Shade took up the gauntlet. "You did what? Are you crazy?"

"No, desperate. We need to find this guy before he kills more demons and vamps. This is the best way to do it."

Shade shook his head, looking annoyed. "That thing's dangerous, Val. You shouldn't be using it at all."

"It's done," I said. "Over. Let's move on."

There was so much tension in the air, you could stab it with a stake.

Austin broke the silence. "If we find him, can the two of you send him back to another dimension? I know Shade did it with a part demon, but this guy is four times stronger."

Finally, someone proposed something that actually sounded like a plan.

Sharra nodded confidently. "Working together, we can. I've been helping Shawn, er, Shade, learn how to control his powers like I do. The problem will be getting Emmanuel alone and away from his followers. They won't be too happy about losing their saint and will try to stop us."

I nodded. "We'll need to go in force to control them. Between the demons and the vamps, we should have enough firepower. And I can use Lola to help."

"Unless they're all hopped up on Emmanuel's blood," Shade reminded me. "That makes them extra strong and invulnerable to Lola, putting you in danger, Val."

I nodded. He had a good point. "The amulet—"

But I didn't get to finish what I planned to say, because Shade and Austin said, "No," in unison.

Crap. "Okay, how about we finalize a plan once we get more information?"

"Why don't you check the encyclopedia to see if it has any spells that will help find a blood demon?" Austin suggested.

"You know the problem with those spells," I reminded all of them. "I'd hate to use them and lose what little ground I've gained with Lola."

Shade looked like he wanted to object, but Austin said, "Better that than the amulet." On that one thing, they were united.

I sighed. "Okay, I'll check."

Remembering the books could hear and understand me, I concentrated on them where they lay on the coffee table and said, "Please show me a spell that might help locate or subdue a blood demon and his minions."

The third book quivered, then glowed. I opened the book at the glowy spot and read the spell. "It's a spell to gain the strength of ten men," I said in surprise. Sure wished I'd known that earlier. Then again, if I had, I might not have used it because of the trade-off problem.

"What are the limitations?" Shade asked.

I read the fine print at the bottom. "It only lasts for twenty-four hours."

"Still," Austin said, "it might be worth it to have it handy."

"Yeah." I read the spell out loud. Like before, as I read each word, it vanished from the page and resided within me like an unexploded grenade. When I needed it, I'd just have to recite the activating words, and I'd be Super Val again. It might even be better than the amulet.

"Let's go looking for him," Austin suggested.

Shade's lips thinned, and his eyes narrowed as he glanced between us, looking suspicious.

Sheesh, this was getting ridiculous. "Uh, can I have a few minutes alone to talk to Shade and Sharra first?"

Austin raised one eyebrow, then said, "Sure. I'll be downstairs in the lab. Come when you need me."

HEY, BABE, ARE YOU SURE YOU WANT TO DO THIS? Fang asked.

I'm sure. I'm tired of being treated like I have cooties.

Once Austin was gone, I faced the twins. "Okay, what's up with this 'Val is the bad guy' crap?"

Fang was obliging enough to stand between them, touching them both so I could see their expressions.

Shade frowned, but Sharra, who had apparently had a lot more practice in hiding her feelings, tossed her head. "I don't know what you mean."

"Yes, you do. You can't lie to me, you know. Not with a hellhound who can read your every thought."

Sharra glanced down at Fang in horror. "Can he really—?"

HE CAN, Fang said with a canine smile. AND HE WILL. C'MON, SPILL.

"Is this really necessary?" Shade asked, squeezing Sharra's hand.

Why couldn't he hold *my* hand? Weird. I even felt jealous of the attention he paid his sister. "Yes, it is. We need to work together for a common purpose—catching Emmanuel and sending him back to the hell dimension he came from. It's difficult to do that when you're obviously hating on me. What gives?"

"I don't hate you," Shade said.

TRUE, Fang confirmed.

"Can your sister say the same?"

Sharra wouldn't look me in the eyes. "I don't hate you."

KINDA SORTA THE TRUTH, Fang said to the room.

Belligerent now, Sharra said, "All right, the truth is, I don't trust you."

"Why not?" What had I done to earn her mistrust?

She avoided my gaze. "Because you're a Paladin."

"You realize that doesn't even make sense," I said. "Paladins are chosen to defend demons in the Underground, chosen in a ritual with the consensus of the membership. If they trust me, why can't you?"

She compressed her lips and refused to answer. Shade put his arm around her. "You have to understand, Val. It was a Paladin who captured our father, a Paladin who brought him back to the Underground for judgment. If it hadn't been for him, our father might still be alive."

AND IF YOUR FATHER HADN'T LOST CONTROL AND BROUGHT FULL DEMONS INTO THIS WORLD, HE WOULDN'T HAVE NEEDED JUDGMENT, Fang reminded him. And the snarky hellhound's tone was remarkably gentle for a change.

HEY, I CAN BE NICE WHEN I NEED TO, he said privately.

Yeah, he just didn't often feel the need. No matter. I was glad he'd said it so I didn't have to.

Sharra winced, so I guess Fang nailed the issue.

"Give her a break," Shade said. "We've talked about this, and she's trying, but it's an understandable phobia."

From his viewpoint, maybe. Especially since I suspected he kind of felt the same way.

HE DOES, A BIT, Fang confirmed.

I sighed. Diesel had just been doing his job, but I knew that wouldn't work as an argument. "Look, I understand the emotional knee-jerk reflex, but let's look at this logically." That should appeal to Shade, anyway. "You're shadow demons like your father. Does that mean you'll bring demons through into this world like he did?"

WHOA, WRONG ANGLE OF ATTACK, Fang cautioned me.

"It was an accident," Shade said tightly. "He didn't mean to do it. He lost control of his emotions."

"And he paid the ultimate price for that mistake," Sharra added. "You think we don't know that? You think we don't worry that we'll be just like him?"

Oh, crap. That's not what I meant at all. And, given Shade's willingness to kill himself rather than let demons into this dimension, it was obvious it had always been on his mind, even if he hadn't consciously remembered why. I spread my hands in a placating gesture. "Sorry, bad example. Look at it this way instead. There are some demons who are bad and some who are good. Just because you run across one, uh, fire demon who is an arsonist, that doesn't mean every fire demon is a firebug, right?"

Sharra didn't look convinced. "No, but—"

"So why do you assume all Paladins are bad?"

"It's the position, not the person," Sharra said stubbornly.

Shade looked exasperated. "It's not the same thing at all, Val."

"Why isn't it? Because it's personal? Because it happened to you?"

"Well, yeah," Sharra said.

"So because a vampire enthralled my sister and threatened to kill her and my stepfather, I should assume all vampires are bad?"

"Aren't they?" Sharra asked with lift of her eyebrow.

I stared at her in disbelief. "Where have you been? Haven't you seen how Austin and Alejandro have been helping us?"

"Because you have them under your sway, and Austin has a thing for you," Sharra said.

I snorted. "Under my sway? Not hardly. Shade, didn't you tell her about the New Blood Movement?" I ignored the second part.

He shook his head. "Sharra, she's right. Not all vampires are bad."

"Yeah," I said. "And besides, you've met Gwen and Elspeth. I can't hold *them* under my sway," I added triumphantly.

"No, but Micah could," she shot back.

"Okay, that's true," I conceded. "He could, but he doesn't. The New Blood Movement is a vein of vampires dedicated to living in harmony with humans, accepting blood donations through blood banks like the one down below. Kinder, gentler vampires."

Sharra snorted.

IT'S TRUE, Fang assured her. ONCE A BLOODSUCKER IS TURNED, HE BECOMES MORE OF WHAT HE WAS IN LIFE. SO, IF HE'S EVIL, HE BECOMES MORE EVIL. IF HE'S NOBLE, HE BECOMES MORE NOBLE. IF HE'S BRAVE, WELL, YOU GET THE IDEA.

Sharra cast an uncertain glance at Shade.

He nodded. "It's true. They're friends, Sharra."

We'd gotten way off the main point. "The point is, you shouldn't judge all of a group simply because of your bad experience with one of them." To be more clear, I added, "And you shouldn't judge me because of one bad experience with a Paladin. I'm not Diesel."

Sharra still looked uncertain.

YOU'RE MAKING HEADWAY, THOUGH, Fang assured me. AND SHE PROMISED SHADE SHE'D TRY.

To bring it even further home, I said, "Shade, have you ever known me to be as callous and uncaring as you obviously think Diesel is? Deliberately?"

Shade hesitated, and it felt like a slap in the face.

"No," Shade said finally. "Misguided, maybe, but you always do what you think is right, even if it hurts you or someone else in the process."

Sharra's lips firmed, and I had a good idea I knew why. Evidently, she didn't like sharing her newfound brother with anyone else.

BULL'S-EYE, Fang said.

I sighed, knowing I was going to have to address this, too, but really didn't want to go there. "Look, forget that I'm a Paladin. Forget that you're jealous I had a relationship with your brother when you didn't."

"I am not—"

"You are," I said firmly.

CAN'T LIE TO ME, Fang told her cheerfully.

That shut her up.

"Forget that crap. What else do you have against me?" It wasn't like I was a great beauty or incredibly intelligent or rich or anything like that.

"Nothing, I guess," she admitted with a shrug, but wouldn't meet my eyes.

"Then how about you get to know me first before you judge me?"

She finally met my eyes. "Okay, deal. But you have to do the same."

I nodded. Good enough. I'd much rather make friends with Shade's sister than have her as an enemy.

OH, GOODIE, Fang said. ARE YOU GOING TO GO PLAY BARBIES NOW AND CURL EACH OTHER'S HAIR?

I gave that comment the attention it deserved—silence. Sharra and

I glanced at each other and rolled our eyes in unison. Well, at least we had that in common—a disdain for stupid sexist comments.

YOU'RE WELCOME, Fang said.

Yeah, right. Like he'd done that on purpose.

"How about you, Shade? Are you willing to give me another chance? Put aside your distrust of Paladins and your abandonment issues to give me a chance to prove myself?"

He nodded. "Yeah, I get it. I can deal. And I never distrusted you."

"Okay, good. Let's—"

Two quick raps sounded on the penthouse door, and Austin stuck his head in. "Sorry to bother you, but I have news."

"It's okay," I told him. "What did you find out?"

"It's on all the news channels." He used some kind of fancy remote, and the humongous flat screen television came to life. He flipped channels until he found what he was looking for.

The announcer said, "Earlier this evening, Mission Concepcion was the site of what some are calling a healing miracle." They cut to the mission, and the pretty blond on-scene reporter added, "This evening, a man came to the evening service and offered to heal the parishioners. One man in a wheelchair accepted his offer and is claiming to be fully healed."

She pointed the mic at an older, fragile-looking gentleman who told how he was offered a healing elixir—with Emmanuel's blood in it, no doubt—and after he took it, he was able to get out of his wheelchair and walk. He was still a bit shaky after not having stood for so long, but he said he had feeling in his legs for the first time in twenty-four years.

Another man on the street, when asked for his comment, said, "It's some kind of hoax. They probably had it set up ahead of time."

Then they cut back to the older man again who raised his liver-spotted hands to the heavens and beamed. "It's a miracle!"

Back to the reporter. "Hoax or miracle?" she asked. "You decide."

They returned to the camera in the studio where the anchor was grinning. "Well, he'll be there all this week. Think I should get my hangnail fixed?"

They laughed and went on to the next news story, and Austin switched off the television.

"Emmanuel?" I asked.

Austin shrugged. "Another news story had a blurry shot of the healer and remarked on his resemblance to iconic Jesus paintings. And since he had the healed ones drink something . . . yeah, I'm pretty sure it's Emmanuel."

"Does the healing last?" I asked. "Or will it wear off as well?" If it was temporary, that news ought to squash his bid for power.

"According to the book, the healing is permanent," Shade said. "And now we know exactly where he'll be tomorrow night. What are we going to do about it?"

"We need more information," Austin said. "Need to confirm it's him."

I nodded. "I bet there will be a big crowd tomorrow. Why don't we join them, gather as much info as possible, then come back and decide how to proceed?"

They all made agreeable noises, so I called Micah and Lieutenant Ramirez to let them know what our plans were. With any luck, we'd catch a break and the bad guy at the same time.

YOU REALLY THINK IT'LL BE THAT EASY? Fang asked.

I can hope, can't I?

Chapter Twenty-Four

Val

MY NEWLY ACQUIRED and well-behaved mole in Emmanuel's organization called to confirm that his boss was going to be at the mission the next night—not that I needed the info now. When the time arrived, we left the two shadow demons at home where they'd be safe. No sense risking them until we really needed them—this was just a reconnaissance mission.

Shade and Sharra argued, but we pointed out that it might be difficult to keep their swirly demonosity hidden in a crowd. Besides, Emmanuel probably knew what they looked like when they weren't all swirly and would have people watching for them. Best for them to stay at the penthouse where the vamps downstairs, plus Gwen and Elspeth upstairs, could keep them safe.

They didn't like it, but they agreed. Fang elected to stay in and protect them as well, along with his puppies and Princess.

Austin and I joined up with Micah, Ramirez, and Alejandro outside the centuries-old gray stone church with its twin bell towers. Though I'd lived here all my life, I really hadn't spent much time at the city's famous missions. Mission Concepcion claimed to be the oldest unrestored church in America, and it looked it—crumbling and ancient. But they still held services here every Sunday.

The only thing that surprised me was how small it seemed. Maybe it was the huge crowd that made it appear that way—they couldn't all fit inside the chapel. I'd never seen so many sick-looking people in my life.

Good thing Fang had decided not to come. He might have been trampled.

"Let's split up," Ramirez suggested. "We might be able to get more info that way."

We all agreed, and wonder of wonders, Austin even agreed to leave me on my own for once. Strange, the only time I felt truly alone was now that I was in a crowd.

So many people tried to force their way into the church that it created a bottleneck at the door, with people shoving and cursing, desperate to get in and get their own personal miracle. Crap. Where was Mood when you needed her? This crowd could use some attitude adjustment.

I started to use Lola to persuade men to move out of my way so I could get to the front door, but a man in uniform with a bullhorn stood at the door and announced, "Please, everyone, calm down. We are moving outside so everyone can attend. I repeat, please, stop pushing. Everyone inside is coming out, and you will all be able to participate in the ceremony."

Ceremony? There was a ceremony?

A wave of calm flowed over the crowd like a sigh, urging peace and brotherhood. Ah, Alejandro and Austin must have joined forces to send out their own particular brand of mood-alteration. Thank goodness they only used it for good.

Everyone grouped politely on the lawn, and the people who had been indoors streamed out. After fifteen minutes or so, a small knot of people made their way to the center of the courtyard. I couldn't see very well, but it was obvious from the way the crowd reacted that Emmanuel was in that group. A priest climbed up on the low stone wall of an old well and held up his hands. "My children, I am happy to present to you a truly holy man, who will no doubt be canonized as a saint. Please, welcome Emmanuel."

Whoa, mind-controlled much?

The priest made a theatrical gesture off to his right, and Emmanuel joined him on the well. As advertised, he looked a lot like the pictures of Jesus, with white robes, long brown hair, a beard, and piercing eyes. I bet they flashed purple, though, just like any other demon, when he was using his power. He stretched out his arms, palms out, so the crowd could see the blood flowing sluggishly on his palms.

I rolled my eyes. Sheesh. If I pushed him into the well, would he be able to walk on water?

Gasps and cries filled the night air. Many people crossed themselves, and some even fell to their knees or fainted.

I had to admit, the guy knew how to make an entrance. I pushed my way forward, using Lola when I had to, to get a closer look at Emmanuel and his minions, and to assess his security, but stayed back far enough so as not to be conspicuous.

The core of his followers, who surrounded him closely and frowned into the crowd, had the same intent, fanatical look about them as Jorge and the other Penitentes. I didn't see any weapons in sight, but they could be hidden. Besides, if they'd recently had some of the blood demon's elixir, they were probably weapons themselves.

Another man, tan, bald, wearing a black leather duster, stood off to the side. His gaze scanned the crowd, and he murmured into a headset. Head of security, no doubt. Every once in a while, he glanced down. I scooted forward until I could see what he was looking at—a bulldog.

Strange. I could see using a pit bull or Rottweiler for added security, but a bulldog? Must be some mean doggie. Or could it be a hellhound? Naw—Emmanuel surrounded himself with humans, not demons.

But that was irrelevant. Emmanuel was obviously sucking up all that lovely adoration. I saw his eyes glow with pleasure. He lowered his arms, and the crowd quieted. "My children," he intoned, and his voice was deep and resonant, perfect for a false religious leader. "God has blessed me with the ability to heal the afflicted."

Sheesh. If I were God, I'd strike him dead for that blasphemy.

Cheers rose from the crowd, and he silenced them by raising his hands again. "However, I fear my stamina is not good, and I am unable to heal more than a dozen each day."

Only a dozen? I doubted it had anything to do with his stamina. More like that's all the blood he could give up per day. Or maybe it was an artificial limitation he set so he didn't have to come amongst the unwashed masses any more than he had to, or even to keep the demand high. The reason didn't matter, though. I was determined to ensure he wouldn't "share" any more than we could help. Not telling what would happen to the ones he'd healed. Were they permanently subject to his control? The idea nauseated me.

Arms waved in the air, and people yelled, "Pick me," plus what I figured was the equivalent in Spanish.

Emmanuel made shushing motions with his hands, and they quieted once again. "But first, I have a message for you."

Uh-oh. This didn't bode well.

"I have been given this magnificent gift, but it comes with a caveat." He glared. "I must warn you of a plague infesting this world. Among you roam unnatural creatures. Creatures who pass as men, yet have evil in their souls."

Murmurs rose around me, and I could almost feel fear spike in the entity that was the crowd. He was talking about us, and he had it all wrong—*he* was the evil one. Annoyed, I fingered the teardrop-shaped crystal, wondering if I should try to use it on him, wondering if it would even work on a full-blooded demon.

The amulet urged me to try, but I beat down the urge. There were too many people, too many minions around to try an experiment of that nature right now.

"They live among you, work among you, go to school with your children," he thundered. "But they are nothing but abominations."

It sounded so hokey, I kind of expected someone to laugh. But no one did. They desperately wanted to believe in the promise of healing, so they chose to believe in him.

Emmanuel continued, "They would steal the very blood from your veins, force your children into illicit carnal pleasures against their will."

Oh, crap. He was talking about vampires . . . and succubi and incubi. Us. Here, now. Did he know we were here?

I tuned out what he was saying. It was all in the same vein anyway, and I glanced around quickly, trying to locate my allies in the crowd. I didn't spot any of them, but when I glanced back up front, I saw that security guy in the black duster staring straight at me and frowning. He was talking into his headset, too, probably whispering directly into Emmanuel's ear.

Busted. I'd better get out of here before Emmanuel decided to point me out and have the crowd rip me to shreds.

I raised my hands in surrender to the guy in black to show I meant no harm, then disappeared back into the crowd. I didn't need to watch the healing anyway. I knew how it was done.

I made it back to the car and saw Alejandro waiting there. Austin strolled up a moment later. "He made us," I said unnecessarily.

"Yes, indeed," Alejandro said thoughtfully. "I wonder how."

"I don't know, but can we talk about it back at the penthouse?" I asked. Emmanuel and this whole situation gave me the creeps. I'd join up with Micah and Ramirez later to compare notes.

"Of course."

Everyone was quiet on the way back, no doubt digesting what we'd just seen and heard. When we got back to the penthouse, Alejandro said, "I'll be up in a moment. I wish to see first what progress they've made in the lab, if any."

I nodded and rode up in the elevator with Austin. "Quite a show, huh?" I asked.

He ignored me, like I didn't even exist. What was wrong with him now? Sheesh, I was sick and tired of everyone's moods. Couldn't everyone just be nice and pleasant for a change?

Austin remained silent. Guess not.

We entered the living room. It didn't look quite as cold and forbidding or slasher-like as it had before. Someone had added bright cheery pillows and a few colorful afghans that warmed the place up a bit. I'd bet anything it was Gwen's hand at work.

Shade and Sharra sat in front of the television, on opposite ends of the black leather couch.

All of a sudden, Austin snarled and shot toward Shade, moving so fast he was almost a blur. With the speed of a striking snake, he clamped Shade's head in his hands and sank his fangs into Shade's neck.

What the heck? Fear slammed through me.

Sharra screamed. Real helpful.

SAVE HIM, Princess yelled from the bedroom.

I flew over and tried to yank Austin off. No go. He had Shade trapped on the sofa where he couldn't even roll free. "Let go, asshole. What do you think you're doing?"

But Austin was ignoring me, intent on draining Shade of all his blood. Shade fought back, his eyes wide and fists and feet scoring quite a few hits, but he was no match for the much stronger vampire. Shade grew weaker with each sucking gulp.

Using Lola, I yelled, "Stop!" It did no good. Neither did the amulet.

Crap, he was controlled. As I tried unsuccessfully to peel Austin away from Shade, I yelled at Sharra, "Get help!"

She took off just as Fang came running in. USE THE SPELL, Fang said urgently.

Crap, I had to. What were the words for that strength spell again? I was so jazzed I couldn't remember for a moment, then did. I yelled the words and felt a surge of energy punch through my body, setting my nerve endings on fire and making me feel like Supergirl.

I grabbed Austin's jaws and pulled them away from Shade's neck. He fought me, but this time I was as strong as he. I also had the advantage of a valiant little hellhound biting at Austin's hands, forcing him to move them away from Shade's head or be bitten.

Finally, I got the vampire leech loose and jerked him away from Shade who fell limply back on the couch. I slammed Austin down on the ground, face first, and twisted his arms up on his back. Then I sat on him, pinning him.

Austin wouldn't stay still like a good little vampire, though. He kept squirming and bucking, trying to get me off him. Crap. I wasn't going to be able to hold him for the many hours this control lasted. And in the meantime, Shade needed help.

"How's Shade?" I asked Fang.

NOT GOOD. BUT THE CAVALRY'S COMING.

Elspeth and Gwen hurried in from the other room, their eyes wide.

"Austin is being controlled—he attacked Shade," I explained quickly while still wrestling with the cowboy on the ground. "He needs help." I nodded toward the couch, and they both dashed over to Shade.

Sharra came running back in then, Alejandro and Vincent right behind her. She pointed at Austin. "See?"

"He's being controlled by Emmanuel," I explained again as Austin continued to struggle. "He attacked Shade, and I'm having a devil of a time keeping him down. A little help here, please?"

"We'll take care of this," Vincent said.

But when I eased up for just an instant, Austin leapt to his feet and, with murder in his eyes, headed for the other shadow demon—Sharra.

Vincent and Alejandro were faster. As Sharra screeched, they each took one shoulder and body-slammed him back down onto the carpet, holding him as immobile as the struggling vamp would allow.

I stood back, trying to catch my breath. "We can't do this for four hours," I protested. "Can you knock him out?"

"Not necessary," Vincent bit out. "Get the syringe from my right jacket pocket."

I did as he asked. "Now what? Inject Austin with it? And what is it?" I asked apprehensively. I didn't want them to poison him or kill him or anything, just knock him out until he came to his senses.

"Just do it," Vincent ordered.

Alejandro nodded. "It will be all right, Ms. Shapiro. It is merely some of my blood. Since I am his sire, we hope this will help counteract the blood demon's control."

Well, in that case . . . "Gwen?" I said uncertainly. I didn't want to screw it up, and she'd been an ER nurse when she was alive.

"Got it," she said and snatched the syringe out of my hand. She stabbed the needle into him and depressed the plunger.

Heck, I could have done that.

Austin bucked and yelled, but he was held fast by both Vincent and Alejandro while I sat on his legs.

"Is it working?" I asked anxiously.

"We'll know in a moment," Vincent said.

And sure enough, Austin's struggles let up until he was quiescent.

"How do you know he's not faking?" Vincent asked.

"I can tell," I said. Lola was responding to Austin's nearness, and this time I didn't stop her when she tried to sink her tentacles into him. It worked. "He's not being controlled by anyone else," I informed them.

"Excellent," Alejandro said, and he and Vincent let Austin go.

I heard sobbing and realized it was coming from the couch. Sharra.

I whirled. Crap. Was Shade okay?

I leapt up off Austin and dashed over to Shade. Gwen had her hand on the bloody shreds of his neck where it looked like Austin had chewed on him, and Sharra had his head in her lap, stroking his hair and crying like a baby.

"Is he . . .?" I couldn't say the word, didn't want to believe it was true.

DEAD? Fang asked. NO, BUT HE'S NOT EXACTLY IN THE PINK EITHER.

"He needs medical help, pronto," Gwen said. "Or he's going to bleed out."

"And where do you think he's going to get it?" I asked her. "Has your ER ever treated a shadow demon? Know of anyone who won't freak at the sight of him, or what his blood looks like?"

"Then what do you suggest?" Elspeth asked calmly.

Princess came running out, leaving her children at the need of her human. YOU MUST HEAL HIM, she insisted, staring at me.

I can't, I told her. Unless there was a healing spell in the books?

SHARRA CAN, Fang reminded me. IF SHADE WAS ABLE TO HEAL DAN AND JOSH, SHE SHOULD BE ABLE TO HEAL HER BROTHER.

Crap, I was an idiot. Why didn't I think of that? I whirled on Sharra. "Can you?" I demanded. "Can you heal Shade?"

"I . . . I don't know. I never tried."

"Then you'd better damn well try now," I said, desperate. "Or your Shadow Boy is going to die."

Chapter Twenty-Five

Shade

SHADE OPENED HIS eyes, feeling weak and drained—literally. "You can do this," he told his sister. His voice came out more faint than he wanted, and the effort to say anything was enormous, not to mention painful whenever he moved his throat. But if she didn't, he wasn't going to make it.

DO IT, Princess insisted. DO IT NOW.

Sharra dithered. "I've never done it before—all I know is theory."

"Then use it to help Shade," Val insisted. "What are you waiting for?"

Val sounded frantic, and Shade supposed he ought to feel the same way, but all he felt was an increasing lethargy.

"I need a healthy person, someone to act as template so the destroyed tissues and ligaments in his neck have a template to emulate," Sharra said, sounding a little more confident now, but still with a bit of panic in her voice.

"Me, of course." Val's tone was final.

"No," Shade said. He wasn't sure where he'd found the energy to protest, but even though his mind was sluggish, he knew that wasn't a good idea.

"Why not?" Val demanded.

Shade didn't have the energy to explain or to find a way to say it that wouldn't hurt Val's feelings.

Princess did it for him, in her own blunt way. HE DOESN'T WANT TO SHARE HIS MIND WITH YOU.

That's not how Shade would have said it, but it got the message across. He closed his eyes briefly, trying to block out the view of Val's hurt expression.

"He's not going to want anyone here to share his mind," Val protested.

"Elspeth," Shade whispered. The former Memory Eater already knew everything there was about his past. Trusting her with his current thoughts was just one tiny baby step of trust forward.

"A vampire?" Val said in disbelief. "Will that even work? I mean, no blood flow."

"I—I don't know," Sharra admitted. "But if Shade thinks it will . . ."

Shade *wasn't* sure, but sharing with Elspeth was better than Val knowing every iota of what he felt.

He felt himself fading, then Elspeth gripped his hand. "If it will help, I would be willing to try."

"But you'll share *her* memories, too," Val reminded him. "Are you sure you both really want that?"

"It matters not to me," Elspeth said, "if it doesn't trouble him."

Share eons of the bad memories she'd eaten? Why not, after what she'd done for him? Besides, it was better than the alternative.

HE SAYS OKAY, Fang translated.

"All right, then," Sharra said. "Let's do this."

"He needs to replace his blood loss, too," Gwen reminded us. "Will the healing do that, too?"

Damn. Good point. It wouldn't.

"I don't know," Sharra admitted. "Shade?"

He didn't have the energy to explain, so Fang did it for him. HE DOESN'T THINK IT WILL WORK. IT HEALS TISSUES, MUSCLES, AND BONE, BUT HE DOESN'T THINK IT'LL REPLACE BLOOD LOSS. On his own, Fang added, HE'S VERY WEAK. HE'LL NEED THE TRANSFUSION.

Gwen nodded. "Do you know what your blood type is?"

No, he'd never had it tested. Demons tended to avoid doctors and medical labs, unwilling to let them see the peculiarities in their blood.

HE DOESN'T, Fang informed them.

"It's O positive," Austin said from somewhere on the other side of the room.

Shade couldn't help but cringe at his attacker's voice, and the bite on his neck throbbed. Intellectually, he knew the vampire had been controlled and was now neutralized, but his body still insisted on fight or flight.

"You can tell by the *taste*?" Val said, sounding appalled.

"Yes," Austin said, short and succinct.

"Good," Gwen said. "Alejandro, can we use some of your supply downstairs?"

Downstairs? Oh, yeah. The blood they kept on tap that the donors had supplied. Well, if he had to be drained, he guessed doing it at a blood bank was the best possible place.

THAT'S IT, BUDDY, Fang encouraged him. KEEP THAT SENSE OF HUMOR. KEEP AWAKE.

"Of course," Alejandro said. "Vincent will help you."

"It would be better if we could take him downstairs where we have the proper equipment," the other vampire said. "Is that possible?"

"Sharra, heal his wound first," Gwen said decisively. "We'll replace the blood afterward. Vincent, if you could get everything ready?"

Thank goodness someone took charge.

"Of course," Vincent said, and Shade heard a door shut on the far side of the room.

HURRY, Princess urged.

"Okay," Sharra said. "Let's do this."

Sharra knelt beside him, and Elspeth sat beside the couch on the floor. Princess laid with her nose on his leg, as if she could help him by her sheer presence.

"What do you need me to do?" Elspeth asked, putting her hand on Sharra's arm.

His sister looked frozen in indecision. He didn't have the strength to deal with this and was losing more with each moment that passed.

DO SOMETHING, Princess insisted, sounding frantic.

Fang's fuzzy face appeared in his vision. The hellhound looked intense. TELL ME WHAT TO TELL HER.

Gratefully, Shade closed his eyes and let the thoughts of what needed to be done fill his head.

SHARRA, PUT ONE HAND ON SHADE'S NECK AND THE OTHER ON ELSPETH'S, Fang directed.

Shade felt Sharra's cool hand on his neck.

NOW, FIND THE HEALING DIMENSION.

"I don't know where that is," Sharra said, sounding frantic.

YES, YOU DO, Fang said, continuing to relay Shade's thoughts. YOUR FATHER SHOWED IT TO YOU. REMEMBER, THE ONE YOU GUYS SAID FEELS PINK AND FLUFFY?

Then, privately to Shade, REALLY, DUDE? HOW CAN SOMETHING *FEEL* PINK?

It just does, Shade thought defensively. *Sharra will understand.*

"Oh, okay," Sharra said.

"I've been through this before," Val said. "You need to draw healing energies from that dimension."

"I'm trying," Sharra snapped.

TRY HARDER, Princess insisted.

LEAVE SHARRA ALONE, Fang told them all. DON'T DISTRACT HER—UNLESS YOU *WANT* SHADE TO DIE.

Luckily, that shut them all up.

Then, slowly, Shade felt the familiar ebb and flow. The healing energies swept through Elspeth, then Shade, then back again. Undulating like a wave, consistent as a metronome, it grew stronger and more powerful with each sweep.

But . . . the energies felt strange, wrong in some indefinable way. Was it because he was used to being on the other side? Maybe.

No, wait. His neck felt dead somehow. It wasn't supposed to do that, was it? Suddenly, a blast of memories assaulted him. Elspeth's, his own, a myriad of other people whose memories she'd eaten. Thoughts, feelings, snatches of sight and sound . . . they slammed into him, painfully ravaging his psyche.

Dear Lord, this was worse than the memory cascade. He stiffened against the onslaught and almost passed out.

STOP, Fang yelled.

Shade felt the energies pause as Sharra faltered.

"Why?" Val demanded. "What's wrong?"

THIS ISN'T RIGHT. SOMETHING'S WRONG.

I can handle the pain, Shade assured him. *It's part of the healing process.*

BUT YOU'RE SUPPOSED TO FEEL IT IN YOUR BODY, NOT YOUR MIND. I KNOW—I'VE WATCHED THIS BEFORE, REMEMBER? THIS IS WRONG.

"How?" Val demanded.

HIS NECK SHOULD FEEL PAIN, HEALING, GROWTH, NOT LIKE A DEAD PART OF HIM.

"Your neck feels dead?" Val repeated in disbelief.

Elspeth jerked away from Sharra's hand. "We must stop. It appears that a vampire's tissues are incompatible with a demon's." Her skeletal hand closed on Shade's arm. "You must allow Val to act as template."

No. *Someone else from the blood bank?* he suggested to Fang. Or maybe Micah could get someone here from the Demon Underground.

Fang repeated what he said.

"No," Sharra said. "No time. It must be Val."

"About time," Val muttered, and knelt next to the couch where Shade lay, offering Sharra her neck. "Let's heal him."

Crap. He didn't want to do this.

WOULD YOU RATHER DIE? Fang asked belligerently.

Maybe.

NO, Princess said. YOU DON'T MEAN THAT.

Okay, maybe he didn't. But he didn't look forward to it either.

Without asking for his consent, Sharra resumed the healing with Val as template, far more confident this time. Shade winced as the healing energies swept through him, but had to acknowledge this felt more like he expected. His neck no longer felt dead—it felt alive, too much so. Excruciating pain, physical instead of mental, filled him as damaged tissues began to heal. He gave himself to the pain, hoping it would overpower the feelings and memories.

No such luck. It was like trying not to think about blue polka dots. The more you tried, the more round blue balls appeared in your mind.

And so Val experienced everything he'd felt about her. Crap.

Chapter Twenty-Six

Val

"IT'S WORKING," Sharra said with a gasp.

Good. The now-familiar sensations swept through me. Soon, Shade and I would feel each other's emotions, live each other's memories. Some part of me wanted it, wanted to know how he really felt about me. But another part of me dreaded it, too. Because maybe I didn't want to know . . . and I sure as heck didn't want him knowing how I felt about him.

But I gritted my teeth against the pain, knowing it had to be much worse for him. I relived the agony of his mother's abandonment, his father's suicide, and his sister blaming him for the events that were not his fault. I didn't realize how deeply he felt, how passionately he cared about people, and how much it devastated him when they betrayed him, person after person after person. Including me.

He relived my leaving him with that slut, Dina. His hurt that someone else had left him, the closing off of his feelings, and holding back so he wouldn't be hurt again. The sheer pain of it made me reel, wishing I could take back everything I had ever done to make him feel this way, wanting to assure him he was loved by Sharra, by Princess, by the whole freakin' Demon Underground. And, of course, by me.

Princess's love resonated through him. In his mind, hers was the only true, undemanding love in his life. It broke my heart.

That knowledge swept through him as well, and to my embarrassment, he experienced every emotion I'd ever had about him. Every heartfelt, humiliating, drooling episode. Desperately, I tried to stop the gushing flow of emotion, but the healing process laid my soul bare. I wanted to pull away, hide my schoolgirlish crush that couldn't stand up to Princess's standards, but I couldn't until Shade was healed.

And I realized that Shade felt guilty for me losing my strength. Damn it. He thought he was bad for me, when clearly, I was bad for him. Humiliating.

At the height of my embarrassment, the final healing started. He closed his eyes as the agonizing pain hit him, and all emotion and thought ceased except for the crashing, swelling pain as tissues healed, the wound closed, and tendons knit back together. Shade's suffering continued nonstop until Sharra was finally satisfied.

Then, she let go, and Shade slumped back to the couch, unconscious.

"It worked," Elspeth said in wonder as she stroked the scars on his neck. They looked as though they had been formed a month ago.

Strangely, I didn't feel as wiped out as I had when I'd been Dan's template. Maybe because the strength spell was still in place. I nodded. "There are some benefits to having a shadow demon around."

HE IS WELL, Princess said, sounding relieved and satisfied. She licked his face, then Sharra's hand and said, THANK YOU. And with that, she returned to her puppies, who were crying out for her in the other room.

Of all of us, Princess was the only purely unselfish love he'd ever experienced. Yes, Princess. It boggled the mind.

WHEN SHE LOVES, SHE LOVES WITH HER WHOLE HEART, Fang agreed.

Gwen and Vincent came back in then. "We're ready for him downstairs," she said.

"Good," Alejandro said. And he leaned down to pick Shade up as if the shadow demon weighed nothing.

"Boss, please," Vincent said, looking horrified that the leader of the New Blood Movement had actually stooped to help a demon. "I can do that."

"And so can I," Alejandro said calmly, his long hair sweeping into his face. "If you wouldn't mind opening the way?"

"Of course," Vincent said.

Princess stayed upstairs with the puppies, but ordered Fang to keep an eye on her human. So, the rest of us trooped downstairs, following the leader of the New Blood Movement who carried Shade as if he were light as a pillow.

Vincent hurried to open the doors and operate the elevators. Once we were downstairs, Vincent hesitated. "Should they really be in here?" he asked, glancing at Sharra and me.

"They are our allies," Alejandro said, frowning.

Vincent looked taken aback, but he couldn't argue with his boss. Instead, he opened the door and hurried ahead to show Alejandro where to put Shade. Strange, it looked a lot like the hospital rooms I'd seen on TV. Why did he think we shouldn't see that?

Alejandro laid Shade gently down on the bed. He was already barefoot, which made him look even more vulnerable. Vincent and

Gwen busied themselves with IV poles and plasma to get good, whole blood into him.

Gwen glanced up. "We have this now. Maybe you could leave us to it?"

A polite way to say, "Get the heck out, you're bugging me."

"Of course," Alejandro said smoothly. He gestured us to enter the room next door, which looked like the one we'd just left.

Sharra, Austin, Elspeth and I followed him inside. Sharra accidentally bumped into Austin, whose face was an unaccustomed stone-like mask.

When she saw who it was, she shrieked, "Get him out of here."

"Calm down," I said, unwilling to put up with her hysterics. "Austin was being controlled by Emmanuel. It could have happened to any one of us who was there. It just happens that he was the one who was caught."

"No," Sharra said, shaking her head vehemently. "It's just an excuse. He hates Shade."

"No, he doesn't," I protested.

But Austin stayed rigid and unyielding, not even backing me up. I glared at him, wishing he could read my mind right now so I could tell him to reassure Shade's sister.

Alejandro glanced at Austin. "Perhaps as proof, you could show us the injection site?"

His mouth hard, Austin nodded and unbuckled his belt.

My face heated. I really didn't want to watch as Austin dropped trou. "That's not necessary," I protested.

For once, Austin didn't tease me. He just turned his back, unbuttoned his jeans, and used his thumb to yank down his pants about six inches, exposing a good portion of his butt.

Sharra looked appalled at the sight of tight male buns, and I wasn't about to move any closer.

COWARD, Fang said privately.

Yep. And I wasn't too proud to admit it.

BUT YOU WANNA TAKE A PEEK, DON'T YOU?

My face warmed even more. *Shut up.*

Elspeth was the only one brave enough to check out his ass. Peering at his exposed skin, she said, "There is indeed a recent injection site here."

Alejandro nodded. "As I suspected. They 'made us,' as Ms. Shapiro said earlier and took advantage of our being separated."

"How?" Sharra asked.

"Obviously they caught him by surprise from behind," I said.

Injection site in buttocks, no duh?

"No," Sharra said. "I mean, how did they know who you were?"

Relieved that Austin had yanked up his jeans and was now rezipping them, I said. "I'm not sure, but they had one person there who didn't fit the profile of the Penitente followers. He was talking into a mic, probably in Emmanuel's ear." I described the tan, bald man with the duster, adding, "And it was weird, but he had a bulldog with him."

Sharra gasped. "That's sounds like Diesel . . . and his hellhound, Max."

And I'd stupidly assumed Emmanuel wouldn't want any demons with hellhounds around him. "No wonder they were able to spot us."

YEAH, Fang said. MAX WOULD BE ABLE TO SPOT ANY DEMONS AND VAMPIRES IN THE AUDIENCE.

"And they *helped* Emmanuel?" Sharra said incredulously.

Well, that wouldn't help her opinion of Paladins. "I don't think Diesel had a choice, either," I told her. "Not if he was under the influence of Emmanuel's blood."

"But the hellhound?" she asked.

"The blood probably works on hellhounds, too," I said doubtfully.

IT WOULDN'T NEED TO, Fang said. ALL EMMANUEL WOULD HAVE TO DO IS THREATEN DIESEL, AND MAX WOULD DO ANYTHING TO KEEP HIM SAFE.

I stared at Fang. *You'd do that for me?*

OF COURSE, he said, seeming surprised I would even doubt it. BUT DON'T LET IT GO TO YOUR HEAD, BABE.

No chance of that—he wouldn't allow it. But I had to admit the capacity of these hellhounds to love was humbling.

I told Alejandro and Austin what Fang had said about Max. "Maybe we can use that," I said. "If Fang talks to Max, tells him our plan, explains we don't want to hurt Diesel."

MAYBE, Fang said. IF WE ACTUALLY HAD A WORKABLE PLAN. IF NOT, HE MIGHT TURN ON ME.

I repeated that to the others.

"Good idea," Austin said. "But first we need sleep. We can plan tomorrow."

"What about Shade?" I didn't want to leave him alone, with only vampires to keep him company.

"Shade is resting comfortably," Gwen said from the doorway. "I'll keep an eye on him."

Elspeth nodded. "As will I."

Okay, that I could live with—Shade trusted these two. "How long will it take?" I asked.

"A few hours," she said. "He lost a lot of blood."

Sharra shot Austin a dirty look, as if she wanted to blame him again. "I'll stay," she said. "He's my brother."

"He'll be fine," Gwen said. "And he won't even know you're here, so it's no use for you to stay. Why don't you get some rest, too? It's been a busy day, and you'll need all your wits about you to make that plan."

"An excellent idea," Alejandro said.

Sharra looked reluctant, but they slowly but surely guided us out of the underground lab. Austin personally steered Sharra into the elevator and made sure she rode up with us.

I headed for bed, wanting to be alone with my thoughts and what I'd learned about Shade during the healing. It wasn't to be, though. Austin followed me in to my room.

I glanced at him wearily as I sat on the bed. "I'm really not up for this right now."

He held up his hands. "I just wanted to apologize again. You know I would never deliberately hurt Shade."

"I know," I assured him. It wasn't his way. "Everyone knows, Austin. It wasn't your fault."

"I'm not so sure Shade will see it that way," he said with a wry twist of his mouth.

Maybe. "We'll convince him. No worries. Now can I *please* go to sleep?"

He frowned. "You're weak because of being a template for healing Shade, right?"

"Right." And this conversation was making me even more tired. "So?"

"So, it's my fault Shade needed to be healed, and that you had to use the strength spell which depleted Lola. The least you can do is let me help heal you. Help you recharge your batteries. Help Lola."

I sighed, unsure if I wanted to deal with this right now, but Austin looked stubborn, and there was a haunted look in his eyes. Maybe I should do this to help him. Or, even better, shut him up.

Why not? After all, Shade still wasn't willing to feed Lola. He was too afraid of his own emotions and too stupid to realize that I didn't need him to leave me alone "for my own good." Dumb. I was a big girl, and if I was willing to take a chance on him, damn it, he should be willing to do the same.

I glanced at Austin. No strings, no drama, no problem. And Lola was all of a sudden very, very interested, not to mention hungry. "Okay," I said reluctantly and patted the bed. "Sit here."

He sat and took off his cowboy hat, his short hair sticking out in strange places.

"You have hat hair," I said with a grin.

He quickly scrubbed his head. "That better?"

"Not really." The mussed hair had been endearing, making him look softer, more vulnerable.

Sheesh, what was wrong with me? Why was I seeing Austin as *endearing* fergawdsake? Must be Lola's influence. Or I was really tired.

Sighing, I lay down on the bed, unable to muster the energy to do this sitting up. It was more of a mental than physical exhaustion, though the healing had taken its toll there, too.

Austin lay down next to me. "Take as much as you need," he said.

Martyr much? But, understanding his need to atone, I decided to go ahead and do it. He was right—it was his fault Lola was so weak again since I'd had to use the strength spell to pull him off Shade. I rolled to my side and placed my hand on his chest. Our fields interlaced, and Lola reached weakly for the sustenance she needed.

Responding to Lola's need, Austin put his arms around me and drew me close. I should have pushed him away, but it would help with the feeding. Or so I told myself. If I was honest, I'd have to admit it was more than that. It felt good to be held by a man again, good to feel wanted for a change, good to just be me.

Why not give in? No one would know. Austin was a gentleman—he'd proved he wouldn't kiss and tell. And I so needed some affection right now.

I sighed and let the lust rise within me, feeling an answering desire in him. I snuggled into his embrace, breathing in his musky male scent, and lowered my guard to let Lola take over. Gleeful, she swept into his chakras and gloried in the wonderful male essence she found there. Given free rein for a change, she pulsed her joy to all the cells of his body.

Austin stiffened with a gasp of pleasure. Smiling secretly, I let him enjoy it for a moment before I began pulling on all that lovely, seductive energy. Slowly, drawing out the enjoyment for both of us, I siphoned off as much as I thought he could spare.

When I finished, I tipped my head up to gaze into his eyes. "You okay?"

"Very much so," he said, his voice gruff. "Val—"

I didn't want to hear what he said to say, so I stopped my lips with his. Just a brief kiss, a mere brushing of the lips. So why did it feel as though Lola had just pulsed inside me?

"Shh," I said, placing my finger against his lips. "This never happened."

I rested my head on his chest again, and he cleared his throat, then asked, "Did you get enough?"

"Yes. For now." Lola felt stronger, back up to about forty-five percent again. Maybe if I did this every day, she could regain full power.

Is that really the reason? a small voice inside me asked. *Or is it because it feels reeeeeeally good to be with Austin?*

Little voices had no business confusing me. I thought about pulling away, but why should I? It felt good to be held, comforted, to have someone care about me, even if it was Austin.

"Good," he said, and kissed the top of my head. "Go to sleep now." With a swift series of movements, he shucked off his boots, crawled in beside me, and made room for me under the covers.

Sleepily, I mused that it was nice someone had finally made a place for me, someone who didn't have one foot out the door. I sighed. This was probably a really bad idea, but I didn't care. I fell asleep in Austin's arms.

Chapter Twenty-Seven

Austin

AUSTIN COULDN'T believe it—Val actually fell asleep in his arms. Was it because she finally trusted him, maybe even cared for him?

No. That couldn't be right. She was exhausted, vulnerable. He couldn't count on her having changed her mind. But he'd take whatever he could get.

Now that her succubus was happy and sated, the pull wasn't quite as strong. Oh, he still felt the lust he couldn't help every time he came within her field, but now, it was a lot easier to ignore. He could think rationally, feel truthfully. But how *did* he feel?

She made him feel protective, humbled by her generosity, floored by her strength of character. She couldn't see how special she was, and he wasn't sure the people around her even understood it fully. But he knew, and he knew he didn't deserve her.

Why did she seem to trust him *now*, of all times? Not only had he killed a human, but he'd attacked the man Val thought she loved.

Yes, he'd been controlled by Emmanuel's blood, but unlike the others, he remembered full well everything that had happened. Maybe because Alejandro's blood had cleared his head before his command to forget had kicked in.

He'd stupidly let his guard down at the mission, wanted to play the hero for Val, try out his own brand of mental control on the blood demon. Unfortunately, he'd gotten too close to Emmanuel's followers when they came out of the church.

He remembered seeing the blood demon only a few feet away and maneuvered close enough to capture Emmanuel's intense gaze with his own. *Obey me,* he'd commanded the demon silently.

But his mental hooks had fallen limp and slid right out of the blood demon's mind. Damn. It wouldn't work on him.

Emmanuel's eyes narrowed. "No, *you* will obey *me*," he said, eyes glowing with satisfaction.

Austin felt a sting on his right buttock. Cold fire shot through his veins, bringing with it a kind of ecstasy. He wanted to move, to run away, but he was caught in Emmanuel's gaze.

The blood demon grabbed him with a savage grip at the back of the neck and pulled him close. "Kill the shadow demon," he whispered fiercely. "Then forget this ever happened." He pushed him away abruptly and kept on walking as if nothing had happened.

Austin raged inwardly at his own stupidity, but there was nothing he could do about it. Every ounce of his being was concentrated on that one imperative: *Kill the shadow demon.*

He froze for a moment as the crowed surged around him, following the Pied Piper that was Emmanuel. Austin tried to fight the compulsion that had been planted in him, but there was nothing he could do. He had to kill Shade.

Some hidden part of him, deep inside, reveled in the idea of eliminating his rival. Another, more rational, part knew it was wrong, but that part wasn't in control. Emmanuel's dictate was.

And so Austin had gone back to the penthouse, his purpose burning inside him until he'd spotted the shadow demon. With a dark satisfaction, he'd sunk his fangs into Shade's throat, giving him an illicit thrill that was both powerful and soul-satisfying, yet incredibly disturbing at the same time.

It shouldn't have mattered that Austin had been forced to this. It shouldn't have mattered that it wasn't his choice. What should have mattered was his promise to Alejandro to never take blood from an unwilling donor.

Instead, he'd *enjoyed* it.

What kind of sick bastard was he?

Val moved in her sleep and cuddled up close to him, bringing him back to the present.

She didn't deserve someone like him. But Shade wasn't totally pure either, and if it came to a choice between the two of them, Austin opted for himself over the shadow demon.

He glanced down at Val and realized there was one other thing he could do for her, even if she'd hate him for it. Slowly, gently, he removed the crystal from around her neck and went out into the hall, debating what to do with it.

Fang met him there and stared at him intently. Did the hellhound know what he'd done? Silently, he showed Fang the necklace. "Do you know what to do with this?" he asked softly.

Fang nodded and put his front paws on Austin's thighs, taking the crystal gently from his hands. Good. If Austin didn't know where it was, he couldn't tell her.

He glanced back at Val, looking oddly vulnerable in her sleep. He ought to go to his own bed now and leave her the heck alone. Forever.

He ought to, but he was weak. And this might be the last time he could be with her. Sighing, he lay back on the bed and drew her close. Just this once . . .

Chapter Twenty-Eight

Val

I WOKE, FEELING all warm and snuggly. I was on my side, spooning with Austin. He lay with his arm around me and one jeaned leg thrown over mine, snoring softly.

Memories of the night before came flooding back. Crap. I'd been so shameless the night before, and with Austin of all people. Worse, I'd enjoyed it.

I tensed, and his snoring stopped, though he snuggled up, nestling closer to my back. How could I get out of this without embarrassing both of us?

Then again, did I want to? It had been a long time since I'd felt the comfort of a man's arms like this—a couple of months at least. And though I felt like a traitor to Shade, it felt really good in Austin's arms. I closed my eyes again, pretending it was Shade cuddled up to me, Shade who, even in his sleep, wanted to be as close as possible. To me.

It didn't work, though. Austin's distinctive masculine scent made it far too obvious that it was the cowboy vamp whose embrace I enjoyed . . . the man I really wanted to be with in this moment.

Austin made yummy noises, and his hand headed north, into a very intimate zone. Something strange thrilled through me. Should I—?

"Well, isn't this cozy?" came a voice from the door. Sharra.

I jerked out of Austin's arms and sat up, patting my hair, trying to look appalled, as if I hadn't been awake for several moments enjoying his cuddle. "This isn't what it looks like," I assured Sharra.

"I know," she said dismissively. "Fang told me."

YEAH, Fang said from the other room. I LIED.

Oh, crap. I glanced at Austin, and he blinked sleepily at me with a wistful expression I really didn't want to see.

"Shade is awake and back up here in his room," she said. "I thought you'd like to know."

Good. I scrambled out of bed and followed her, slapping my cheeks to wake myself up. I must have been delirious. That hadn't really happened, had it?

IT DID, Fang confirmed.

Well, crap. Couldn't lie to myself with a snarky little hellhound around.

NO BIGGIE. JUST HUMAN NATURE. OR, IN YOUR CASE, SUCCUBUS DEMON NATURE. NOTHING TO BE EMBARRASSED ABOUT.

Yeah, right.

The snarkmeister in question kept his mouth shut as I entered Shade's room. I checked on the adorable puppies and their mom and dad, both sacked out beside them, Fang with his head on Princess's flank. Fang was obviously content to lie there and make rude remarks from the comfort of his bed. But before he could comment on my thoughts, I scratched his ears and kissed him on the nose. I actually missed having him in my bed since he'd been spending so much time with his new family.

I LOVE YOU, TOO, BABE. BUT THEY NEED ME MORE.

I know.

I turned my attention to Shade. "How are you doing?" I couldn't see him all that well, even with the amulet's help, since the room was still dark.

"Fine," he said. "But Sharra won't let me get up yet. Seems to think I'm a wuss or something."

"No," she said with obvious affection in her voice. "Just want to make sure I didn't screw up the healing."

"You didn't," he assured her. "You did it perfectly. Now, can I talk to Val alone?"

"Okay," she said and left the room.

Fang and Princess stayed, preoccupied with giving their pups tongue baths. I'LL TUNE OUT, Fang promised me. I'M BUSY, ANYWAY.

I hesitated for a moment, seeing Shade in a different light now that I'd spent the night with Austin. And the light wasn't exactly better. Still, I shouldn't have done that while I was trying to win Shade back. Was the mortification written all over my face? Would Shade be able to tell?

I sat on the edge of Shade's bed and reached out to turn on the bedside lamp on with one hand while I touched his wrist with the other.

He pulled away from me and said, "No, please."

I froze. So much for *him* lighting up when he saw me. And, apparently, he wasn't noticing anything but his own self at the moment. That was good, I told myself. I didn't want him to see too much.

Surreptitiously, I used my crystal-enhanced vision to see his face. "Okay," I said carefully. "How are you feeling?"

"Better. I'll be fine. Sharra really did do a good job."

"Yeah, I can tell." I paused then had to ask, "What do you want to talk about?"

He sat up, but remained silent for a moment, apparently searching for the right words.

I said, "You know Austin was being controlled by Emmanuel, right? He wouldn't have attacked you otherwise."

His mouth twisted as if he'd bitten into something sour. "Yes, I know. That's not what I wanted to talk about."

"Then what?"

"When Sharra healed me, you and I, we . . . shared a lot." He looked suddenly uncertain, vulnerable even. Maybe I should have felt guilty about spying on his facial expressions when he didn't know about it, but the heck with that. If it was the only way I could figure out what was going on in that swirly head of his, I was using it.

"Yep," I said, trying to sound casual. "That's the way it works. You warned me about that the first time I acted as template."

"So, you know about what happened in New Mexico."

Yes, and I ached for him, especially when I realized his mother had abandoned Shade and his sister when they started to manifest their shadow demon nature. Their father had tried to hide her horror of her own children from them, but they'd learned the truth anyway. "Yes, I know," I said softly.

He closed his eyes in what looked like regret. Why? Because I'd found out, maybe? Fang wasn't listening in to give me a clue this time.

"I'm so sorry," I said. "Sorry you had to go through losing your mother, father, and your sister when you were just a kid." And even sorrier that he'd felt it necessary to erase all memories of the traumatic time. "It must have been difficult to live through it again," I ventured.

Pain spasmed across his expression, as well as another strong emotion I couldn't identify. "It was," he said shortly. "I'm sorry you had to experience it, too."

"I'm not," I said softly. "It helps me know you better, to understand why you were so upset when I left you with Dina. Shade, I'm so sor—"

"Forget about it," he said, cutting my apology short. But from the pain in his expression, it was obvious he hadn't forgotten a thing. "That's not important."

Not important? Who was he trying to kid? Me? Or himself? "You know you have abandonment issues, right?"

Angry now, he said, "I don't need your pop psychology."

Ooookay. "Just trying to tell it like it is," I said defensively.

He glared at me, and it was all I could do to pretend I didn't notice his expression. "Then let's do that," he bit out. "Let's talk about Austin."

I sighed. "What about him?"

"That sharing feeling thing goes both ways. I know how you feel about him."

"Really, how?" 'Cause I wasn't so sure myself.

Shade's gaze narrowed as he searched my face. "You like him. You're attracted to him. A lot."

"No, I—"

"Don't lie, Val," Shade said, anger twisting his features.

"I'm not," I protested. "It's Lola who's attracted to him, not me."

Yeah, just keep telling yourself that. You might actually start believing it.

"Lola is a part of you. And, though you're not willing to admit it, what Lola feels, you feel. You have a thing for a vampire."

There might be some truth in that, but I didn't want to admit any of it. "You don't really get me, do you, Shade? If you read me at all, you know how I feel about you, too." Every last, humiliating moment of it.

His face softened, thank goodness. So he had gotten that. "I know you think you do, but you also can't stay away from the vampire who feeds your lust."

"Shade," I said helplessly, "someone has to, and you won't."

He closed his eyes in pain for a moment. "I can't do that. Not until I figure out . . ."

"What?" I asked when he didn't finish the sentence.

He shook his head and ran his hand over his face. "My life, myself. I'm still trying to piece my past back together, figure out what it means. The lust is too distracting."

"I totally get that. But . . . are you ever going to find room for me in your future?" Like Austin had obviously done?

He looked sad, lonely, and totally screwed up. "I'm not sure we're any good for each other."

Unfortunately, I'd learned how he felt about that, too. "That's dumb. I don't blame you at all for losing my . . . uh, my strength and healing. I participated in that, too, you know. Willingly." Very much so.

He shook his head. "It's more than that."

"I know. You're afraid that if we're together, you'll lose control of your emotions. I can help with that."

"No. I have to gain control myself, not have you using me like a puppet all the time." He sounded bitter.

"It wouldn't have to be all the time," I protested. "I'll back off once you learn to take charge of it yourself."

"No," he repeated. "I won't be under the control of that damned amulet again. In fact, you should give it up entirely—it's getting a hold on you I don't like."

I reached for the crystal teardrop, but it wasn't at my throat. In fact, it wasn't on me anywhere. "Where is it?" I asked. "Did you take it?"

"When have I been close enough to you to do that, Val?" he asked wearily.

True—and that was the root of our problem. But I'd just used it to see Shade's expression. It must be somewhere nearby. Did I drop it? I glanced around.

Here, the amulet whispered seductively. *I'm here.*

Strangely, the whisper was coming from the pile o' puppies on the floor. I leaned down to gently move one of them to the side, but Fang snapped at me.

I drew my hand back, fast. I'd expect that from Princess, but not Fang. "What the heck?"

LEAVE MY PUPPIES ALONE, Princess said.

"I don't want your puppies. I just want my amulet—one of your kids is lying on it."

NO, I AM, Princess informed me. AND YOU'RE NOT GETTING IT BACK.

What was this? Some kind of weird magpie nesting thing?

NO, Fang said. WE TOOK IT FOR YOUR OWN GOOD. AND WE'RE KEEPING IT.

MY HUMAN DOESN'T LIKE IT, Princess added for good measure.

Maybe I had been relying on it too much lately, but I needed it. "I can handle it," I assured him. "It's the best weapon I have to fight Emmanuel and his followers." Besides, it helped me see the emotions Shade tried to hide. Not that I was going to tell him *that.*

"Fang's right," Shade said. "It's dangerous."

"Come on. I have to keep any weapons that will give me an edge to protect the Underground. It's what I agreed to in the naming ritual. You know that."

Shade shook his head. "What about after we take care of Emmanuel? Would you be willing to give it up then—to Micah?"

"Why Micah? He could have the same problem, since he's an incubus."

"Okay," Shade said, his expression suspicious, like he didn't believe the reason for my objection. "Would you give it up to me, then?"

"What if I need it?" I protested, groping for time.

"If Micah and I agree you need it to protect the Underground, we'll let you have it."

"That only works if you're there when I'm in danger," I protested.

Distrust and something that looked like disgust joined the suspicion on his face. He opened his mouth, and I was absolutely certain I didn't want to hear what he was going to say next, so I preempted him. "Okay, I'll do it," I said. "I'll give it up *after* we get rid of Emmanuel."

He looked relieved. "Good."

"So what are you going to give me in return?"

"Huh?"

I'd surprised him there. "I'm giving up something very important to me, something that could protect the Underground and all the demons in it. What are *you* giving up?" I was hoping he'd offer to feed Lola. Maybe if we shared lust again, he'd remember how good we were together, remember how much he'd once cared for me. And maybe I wouldn't have to rely on disturbing cowboys with way too much sex appeal.

His mouth twisted in an expression I couldn't decipher. "I'm giving up . . . you."

"Huh?"

He shook his head. "I mean, after sharing memories and emotions with you, I realize that it's vital for you to get your mojo back with Lola. To do that, you have to feed often."

"Yes?" I prompted him, wondering where this was going.

"Austin is the best solution," Shade said stiffly. Pain and regret flickered through his expression, then he hardened his face as if he wanted it to spread to his heart. "I want you to feed on him as often as possible until Lola is at a hundred percent."

"What?" I couldn't believe my ears. Was he giving up on us?

No, Fang said. HE'S DOING WHAT HE THINKS IS RIGHT, EVEN THOUGH IT'S KILLING HIM. ACCEPT GRACIOUSLY, VAL.

I gulped, not least because it was exactly what I wanted to do. "I guess you haven't left me much choice."

YOU CALL THAT GRACIOUS?

Heck, it was the best I could do with the shock I felt.

Shade's answering smile was sad. "I do insist. Just . . . don't enjoy it too much, okay?"

I couldn't promise that and realized I didn't want to. I also realized I was tired of waiting for Shade to make up his mind. If he didn't commit to something soon, I was done with him.

I shook my head, not promising anything. "Is that what you wanted to talk to me about?"

"Yes, that and something else."

"Okay, what is it?"

"I want to talk about one of your spells."

"Huh?" That came out of left field. "Which one?"

"The demon exorcising spell."

"What about it?"

His mouth firmed, and he looked very, very serious. "I don't want to be a shadow demon anymore. I want you to take it out of me."

Chapter Twenty-Nine

Val

I JUMPED TO my feet, accidentally knocking over the lamp as I did so. I gaped at Shade, not caring if it made me look like an open-mouthed fish of a dork. "You've got to be kidding me. No way."

That came out a whole lot louder than I intended. The breaking lamp and the tone of my voice got the attention of the hellhounds in the room. The adult ones, anyway. The only thing the puppies could think about at this age was Mama and milk.

Sharra showed up in the doorway, too, all golden swirly. "What's going on?"

"Your idiot brother wants me to exorcise the demon in him."

NO WAY, DUDE, Fang said. He sounded shocked.

Shade looked stubborn, like he was totally resolved to do this stupid thing no matter what we planned to do. "Yes, Fang. Way."

"You can't," I protested. "You don't know what it'll do to you."

"You exorcised the demon from Elspeth," he said, still stubborn. "She seems all right."

"Yes, but the demon warring with the vampire inside her was driving her crazy. Removing her demon made her more sane, not less."

"And it'll do the same for me," Shade insisted.

"You're not insane," I practically shouted at him. "Or maybe you are, for even remotely thinking this is a good idea." I glanced at his sister, who was still standing in the doorway, hoping she'd back me up on this. Unfortunately, I couldn't read her expression with those whirling ribbons of light.

"We're not insane," Sharra said, her voice sounding strained. "But we are a danger to everyone around us."

"Huh? How do you figure?"

"If it wasn't for us, Emmanuel wouldn't be here looking for us, wouldn't be randomly killing demons and vampires in San Antonio."

"Wrong," I said. "He'd still be killing demons and vampires wherever he was. And he'd eventually get to San Antonio on his quest for world domination." Before they could respond, I added, "And we need you to get rid of problems like him."

"Problems which we caused in the first place," Shade reminded me.

"Your father did," I protested. "Not you."

"A shadow demon did it," Shade said. "And since shadow demons are a conduit to bring evil into this world, and we're the only known shadow demons, it only makes sense to get rid of that conduit forever."

Sharra crossed the room to grasp her brother's hand. "He's right. No shadow demons, no threat of new full-blooded dangerous demons entering into our world."

"But we have to get rid of Emmanuel first, and we need you two to build a portal for us."

Shade nodded. "Yes, we'll do that first, then you do the exorcism so we'll never risk demons crossing over again."

"But, but . . . you don't know what it will do to you. I used the spell on Gwen, only to get Lily out of her, and on the demons because they were unwillingly turned into vampires. And that was only to save their sanity." Mixing demon and vamp blood made anyone crazy, unless, it seemed, you were a full-blooded demon. "You don't know what will happen if I remove your demon."

"I know we'll be fully human," Shade said stubbornly. "And that's enough for me."

"Yeah," Sharra said wistfully. "Not have to worry about interdimensional energies covering our features . . ."

Shade nodded. "Not have to worry that losing my temper could bring about an apocalypse."

HE'S ALSO THINKING HE WON'T HAVE TO WORRY ABOUT KILLING HIMSELF TO KEEP THAT FROM HAPPENING, Fang let me know.

None of this had to happen. Couldn't Shade see that? Desperately, I said, "You can't do this without knowing exactly what it will do to you. You don't know how deep it goes into your psyche, how it might totally screw you up. You might really, really, regret it."

Sharra snorted. "Isn't that our decision?"

"No, it's mine. As keeper of the encyclopedia, I'm the one who would use the spell, and I think this is a really bad idea."

"As Paladin, you should be all over this, wanting to keep the Underground and the rest of San Antonio safe. What's the problem?" Sharra demanded.

Sorry, that was the wrong card to play. "Okay, let's look at it that way. As Paladin, defender of the Underground, why would I want to lose my greatest assets? A shadow demon can not only banish evil overlord types to another dimension, but can heal other demons in the organization without threatening exposure of their true nature to real humans. Why would we want to give that up?"

Shade frowned, concentrating, then his face smoothed out. "If you removed everyone's demon with your exorcism spell, there would be no need for a Demon Underground. Everyone would be normal, human, able to live in the human world without fear of discovery. Isn't that what we all want?"

Oh, crap. He had a point.

NO, Fang said, sounding appalled. IT'S NOT WHAT EVERYONE WANTS. THE DEMON PART OF THEM MAKES THEM SPECIAL, UNIQUE. A LOT OF THEM ENJOY THAT. AND IF YOU TAKE IT AWAY, THEY WOULDN'T BE SPECIAL ANYMORE.

"Being special is overrated," Shade said.

THAT'S YOUR OPINION, Fang countered. I, FOR ONE, WOULD *NOT* WANT TO BE A MERE DOG.

Heck, no. He wouldn't be Fang then.

Princess jumped up on the bed, ignoring the cries of her puppies, to lay her paw on Shade's hand and look at him imploringly. ME, EITHER, Princess said. AND IF YOU LOSE YOUR DEMON, YOU WON'T BE ABLE TO TALK TO ME ANYMORE. THAT WOULD BE HORRIBLE FOR YOU.

A brief flash of pain crossed Shade's face as he petted his dog's silky soft head. "Yes, that *would* be horrible and a steep price to pay. But I've been thinking about it for a while, and it's something I have to do."

"No, you don't," I said. "I'm the one who would have to do it, and I refuse. I won't be held responsible for such a stupid decision."

"Why, Val?" he asked, looking puzzled and a bit put out. "Don't you want me to be normal, to be like everyone else? The rest of you can pass easily. For Sharra and me, it's very difficult. Don't you want what's best for me?"

Was he implying I wanted to keep him a demon for my own special purposes, so I could keep him to myself?

PRETTY MUCH, Fang confirmed.

Well, that sucked. And could I even say it wasn't true? Yes, I liked the fact that Shade was part demon, just like me. It gave us something in common. If his demon was gone, would we still have that connection?

I shook my head. No. Regardless of what it would do to our relationship, or lack thereof, I couldn't do it. "Of course I want what's best for you, *and* the organization. I'm just not convinced this is the right thing to do."

"But if I didn't have to worry about my emotions getting loose and creating portals, we could be together," Shade said.

I closed my eyes. That was incredibly tempting, and I felt myself wavering for a moment, then realized my objections still held. What good was a live boyfriend if he had pudding for brains? "It's an unknown, too dangerous."

"What would convince you?" he asked.

I wasn't sure anything would, but I gave it some thought. "We just don't know enough about how it would really affect you," I protested.

"Well, there's one way to find out. Do it."

"Unfortunately, it's irreversible," I shot back. "Listen, I exorcised the demons from those guys in Austin who were turned into vampires. It's not exactly the same thing, but how about you talk to them, see how they've been coping with living without their demons?"

Sharra patted Shade's hand. "It's a good idea. We might get some idea of what we'd be getting into. We don't want to go from one bad situation into a worse one."

"Okay," Shade said. "But if it looks like a viable option, I want you to do it."

"I'll think about it," I hedged. "And I want to get Micah's opinion as well."

"Good," Shade said, as if the issue were settled.

DON'T WORRY, Fang said. PRINCESS IS GOING TO DO EVERYTHING SHE CAN TO TALK HIM OUT OF IT.

Well, that was good because I really didn't want to do this. I didn't want to examine my motives too closely, but the main thing was, I had a very bad feeling about it. "The former demons are now part of Lisette's branch of the New Blood Movement. I'll talk to Austin, see if we can arrange to meet with the vamps whose demons I exorcised. But I won't do anything until we've dealt with Emmanuel. We might need you to banish him to another dimension."

"Thank you," Shade said sincerely. "You'll see. This will be the best thing to do."

I sincerely doubted it, and I hoped to forestall any other attempts to make me do it. I shrugged and left the room, hoping to find Austin.

He wasn't in my room anymore, thank goodness, but he was in the living room, reading a book.

I felt a little shy, but decided to act as though nothing had happened between us. Briskly, I said, "There's been a new development."

Austin shrugged. "Yeah, I know. Vampire hearing."

"What do you think?"

"It doesn't really concern me, but I think you're right to get more information before you proceed with something so potentially dangerous."

I sank down onto the chair across from him. Now why couldn't Shade see that? And why did he want to do it, anyway? Curious, I asked,

"If you could have the vampire part of you removed, would you do it?"

"It's not an option, so I don't worry about it."

"Come on, you have to have an opinion."

He thought about it for a moment. "I do miss some things about being human . . . being warm, eating real food, feeling the sun on my face. But it's a trade-off. Losing those things gave me virtual immortality."

"So you wouldn't do it? What if you get tired of living?"

"I could always just walk into the sun. Growing old . . . doesn't look like much fun. But I don't know that I'll ever get tired of living. I've seen so many advances in my lifetime. The inventiveness of the human mind is endlessly fascinating. Who knew, a couple of hundred years ago, that we'd be able to travel in space, talk with people face to face in another part of the world with a small portable device, or exceed the speed of sound?" He gave me a half smile. "I'm always wondering what we'll invent next."

"Maybe a way to annihilate ourselves forever."

"Maybe. I'll wait and see."

That was an interesting perspective, one I'd never considered. And maybe I even envied him his immortality.

"What about you, Val? Would you give up Lola if you could?"

Hmm, must be time for philosophy. "Maybe. If you'd asked me a few months ago on my eighteenth birthday, there would have been no question. I would have said absolutely yes." Then, I'd longed for nothing more than to be a normal teenaged girl like my half-sister, Jen. "But now that using the spells weakens Lola, I see how much I rely on her. I'd really miss her if she was gone." Not to mention being unable to speak to Fang. Unthinkable.

I shrugged. "Besides, too many people know me as the Slayer, and I've created enemies. I'd hate to be without any ability to defend myself." I'd have to start over, in a new place, with no one who knew anything about me. I wasn't sure I could do it.

"So, why don't you want to remove Shade's demon? Because you think you'd lose him?"

"Boy, you don't have a very good opinion of me, do you?"

"On the contrary, I have a very good opinion of you. What I don't get is why you have such a good opinion of him." He shrugged. "Don't get me wrong, he's a good guy, but you have to admit he's a bit messed up." He slanted me a curious glance. "Is it some maternal instinct, wanting to nurture the broken boy back to health?"

I snorted. The last thing I felt for Shade was *maternal.* "Not hardly."

"Then what?"

I shrugged. All I had to offer him were cheesy greeting card sayings. "The heart wants what the heart wants."

"The heart can change," Austin reminded me. "Especially if it gets rejected or hurt often enough."

Boy, he hit the nail on the head there. "You speak from experience?" I asked curiously.

"No, observation."

Well, I still had hope. "I'm hanging in for the long haul."

"Good to know. I'm a long haul kind of guy myself. I can wait."

I shot him an alarmed glance. "I was talking about Shade."

"I know. But when are you going to stop loving people who can't love you back?"

Wham—that one really hit home, and I didn't have an answer for him. I just gaped at him.

He continued softly, "You'll eventually figure out that he's too broken for you to fix, or too caught up in his abandonment issues that he'll leave you rather than risk you leaving him again. When that happens, I'll be here for you, Val."

"So, what do you have to offer?" I asked incredulously. "The wonderful experience of watching you stay young forever while I grow old and die? How lovely for both of us."

"It could be. And I offer much more than that. Respect, an understanding of how special you are, and . . ."

"And what?" I asked, fascinated and flattered despite myself.

He leaned over and kissed me softly. "And love, Val. I'm falling for you."

Oh, crap.

Chapter Thirty

Val

I DIDN'T KNOW how to deal with an amorous vampire, except to ignore him, so that's what I did. I made myself so busy I didn't have time to talk or think about Austin, his offer, or his arrow-to-the-heart insights. It was too disturbing, especially since he made me feel all warm and fuzzy about being appreciated and loved for who I really was.

Forget that. Shade loved me, too. He had to. But could I wait until he got his act together so he could prove it?

Later, while it was still daylight, Micah, Lt. Ramirez, Austin and I gathered together in the darkened penthouse to lay out a plan to take Emmanuel down. After a good sleep, my brain was a little clearer, and I assumed everyone else's was, too.

I started. "We've identified Emmanuel's security as Diesel, the Albuquerque Paladin, and his hellhound, Max." Before anyone could ask, I added, "We assume he's being controlled by Emmanuel." I couldn't imagine a Paladin—or any demon—helping the blood demon otherwise. "And Max is going along with it only to keep Diesel from getting killed."

"Are you certain of that?" Ramirez asked.

"No, but Fang and I will find out for sure."

Micah frowned. "How are you going to do that?"

"Emmanuel has planned on a healing 'miracle' again tonight. I'll take Fang this time, see if he can talk to Max and find out what's really going on. And since we suspect the hellhound is the one feeding the info to Diesel and Emmanuel, maybe we can convince him to ignore us so we can fill the crowd with our people without Emmanuel knowing and take him down."

Ramirez frowned. "I don't care for a plan that hinges on the help of an unknown hellhound. What if he turns on us?"

"Then Fang should be able to figure that out right away and warn us. Right, Fang?"

PROBABLY, Fang said. BUT DIESEL WILL STILL BE CONTROLLED. WHAT IF EMMANUEL FORCES HIM TO TURN ON HIS HELLHOUND?

Good question. I thought for a moment, remembering what I'd learned in Shade's memories. I repeated the question for the non-demons in the group and added, "Diesel has some kind of telekinetic ability to move people and objects with his mind. That could be dangerous."

"Then we dose him with Perdo," Micah said, "so he won't be able to use his powers."

"Why can't you dose Emmanuel with Perdo?" Austin asked.

I glanced at him in surprise. I should have thought of that. "That should work," I conceded. "We know it works on part demons to remove their demonic abilities. It should work on a full demon, too."

"If you can get close enough to inject him with enough of the stuff," Ramirez reminded us.

"Maybe Max can help with that," I said.

"If he agrees," Micah reminded me. "If he doesn't, we're in trouble."

"Let's assume he'll agree," I said. "To get someone in close, they'll have to pretend to need healing."

"It would have to be a human," Austin said. "If Max doesn't agree, he'd be able to spot a demon or vamp. And Emmanuel might, anyway."

True. "But we're not sure it will even work," I said. "Would it remove his hold on everyone he's currently controlling if we did that?"

Austin frowned. "Speaking from experience, I'd say not. I was under his spell even when I wasn't in his presence."

Micah added, "I agree. Emmanuel's blood would still be in them and the orders he planted still in place. I think they would still be under his influence until the effects of the blood wore off. He just won't be able to issue new orders with the Perdo in him."

"What if it doesn't work?" I asked.

"It still might keep him from healing anyone new and expose him as a fraud," Austin said.

Good point. "Should we try it? Who could we get to do this?" Most of the people I knew were demon or vamp and would be spotted easily.

Ramirez shrugged. "I could do it."

Of course. I sometimes forgot he was totally human. "But you look really healthy. Won't he suspect something?"

The lieutenant grinned—the first time I think I ever saw him do that. "Don't worry about that. My wife is great with make-up."

"Good," Micah said. "If you'll arrange it, I'll provide the Perdo."

"Don't forget, his minions won't exactly be standing still and waiting for things to happen," I reminded everyone.

"That's where the rest of us come in," Micah said. "We'll be there in force to help subdue them and ensure no bystanders get hurt." He glanced at Ramirez and Austin. "Do you have people who can help as well?"

They both nodded.

"Good," Micah said. "Then, once they're incapacitated, Shade and Sharra can send the blood demon back to the dimension he came from."

"You mean they'll be on site?" I asked, frowning.

Micah nodded grimly. "They'll have to be, for this to work."

"But that puts them in danger," I protested. "What if Max doesn't cooperate? What if he tells Emmanuel that Shade and Sharra are there?"

Micah frowned in thought. "We won't bring them in until we're sure it's okay. And we'll be there in enough force that we should be able to protect them."

"I'll need the amulet," I said, raising my chin and daring them to argue with me. "I promise to give it up after we get rid of Emmanuel."

For once, they didn't argue. They could obviously see I was right.

Fang brought it in from the other room in his mouth and gave it to me. OKAY, BUT DON'T LET *IT* CONTROL *YOU*, VAL.

I won't.

Lt. Ramirez nodded. "It looks like we have a plan—"

The door crashed open, and three men stormed in, blood in their eyes.

VAMPIRES! Fang shouted.

We all leapt to our feet.

What the heck? They headed directly for those of us at the table.

"Give us the shadow demons. Now," one demanded.

Oh, crap. Emmanuel had enslaved more vampires. When Sharra and Shade came out of the bedroom to see what was happening, as one, we moved to place ourselves between the vamps and their targets.

"Get back in the room," I shouted, and saw Micah and Ramirez herding them back through the door.

They would be of no use in this fight, so it looked like it was up to Austin, Fang, and me. We each took on one of the bloodsuckers.

As I punched one in the face with my super strength and had the satisfaction of seeing him go down, I asked Austin, "Friends of yours?"

"No," he said, as he caught one of them in a headlock. "Independents. Bad guys."

"Good." I kicked the guy to keep him down and grabbed the one Fang was trying to hamstring. I threw him into the wall, just missing the window. That gave me an idea.

"Austin," I called, "find cover!"

He wrestled his opponent into the hallway near the bathroom, and I used a chair to break the window then shoved the room-darkening curtains aside. Sunlight streamed in, and the two vamps screamed and tried to roll out of the light.

No way. Grabbing one of them, I hauled him to the window and shoved him out. "Sparkle for me, baby."

And spark, he did. Otherworldly green flame ignited, and he was soon engulfed in fire and reduced to ash before he even hit the ground. All fight had left the second vamp—he was too busy trying to escape the deadly sunlight. I dealt with him the same way I had the first, and when I was done, I checked on Austin.

He had staked the third vampire with a towel bar he'd yanked from the bathroom wall. Hey, whatever worked. "Let me clean that up for you," I said, and grabbed the body. I hauled it into the living room and tossed it out the window with the others. Ash rained down on the sidewalk. Luckily, no one was outside the back of the hotel to witness it.

IT'S RAINING VAMPIRES, Fang quipped.

Micah glanced out the window. "Yeah, there's nothing but ash down there, with a bloody towel bar in the middle of it. Might want to get rid of it before someone else sees it." Then, over his shoulder, he called, "Lieutenant, it's safe now."

"Not so much out here," Austin added, looking down at something in the hallway outside the front door. "Looks like they brought us a present and left it here."

Huh? I went to see what he was talking about. A man lay crumpled between the penthouse front door and the elevator, covered in blood.

"He's dead," Austin said, and turned him over so we could see his face.

Shocked, I realized it was my mole in Emmanuel's organization. He'd had his throat cut and the word "traitor" was carved into his forehead. Appalled, I whispered, "He didn't even tell us anything we didn't already know. And I forced him to do that."

"It doesn't matter to a guy like Emmanuel," Austin said in disgust. "It's a warning. To us. He knew you'd controlled this guy and wanted to send a message."

Crap. I'd done this to the poor man. How had Emmanuel known? "What do we do with him?"

"I'll take care of it," Ramirez said, Sharra and Shade behind him.

I took a peek at Shade's expression with the amulet. He looked pissed. "How did Emmanuel know where we were?" he asked.

Micah grimaced. "Max probably read it in our minds when we attended the healing. We should have realized that before."

Ramirez nodded. "This safe house has been compromised. You

need to move them again."

"I can help with that," Austin said. "If someone would please dim the sunlight?"

Oh, yeah. The sun was on its way down, but still could be dangerous to one of Austin's persuasion. I crunched my way through the broken glass to close the drapes and ensure no ray of sunshine made its way inside. "It's safe now."

Austin came in and glanced down at the wreckage I'd created.

"Uh, sorry about the mess," I said. "You think Alejandro will be pissed?"

Austin shook his head. "It's nothing. Easily fixed. Better to break a window than a shadow demon."

"You got that right," Sharra said. "Where's a broom and dustpan? I'll clean this up—it's the least I can do."

Austin found them for her, and Sharra cleaned up the mess as the rest of us discussed where to move Shade and Sharra.

"Tell you what," Austin said. "I'll move them somewhere else safe and not tell you where. Max can't read my mind, and if you don't know where they are, he can't read their location in yours."

"But we'll need them to create the portal," I reminded him.

He nodded. "I'll bring them to the mission with back-up so they can be on hand to send Emmanuel back to his hell dimension."

"Good idea," I said, though I could see from Shade's expression that he didn't care for the idea of being beholden to Austin.

But his feelings didn't matter, not when his life was at stake. It was the only way to keep him safe.

Chapter Thirty-One

Shade

SHADE HATED THIS. He felt like a victim in one of those TV shows whose witness protection program location had been compromised—pushed around, clueless, and helpless to do anything about his own situation. Worse, they'd put him in the hands of someone he didn't like and wasn't sure he could trust.

If it had just been him, he would have refused the vampire's help, but he had to consider his sister, too. He didn't want to endanger her any more than he had to, so he agreed to go off with Austin. He dumped a few things in a duffel, hoping he'd be able to come back for the rest when it was safe.

WHAT ABOUT PRINCESS? Fang asked. AND THE PUPPIES?

Damn. Shade hesitated. He didn't want to leave them here and didn't want to take them with him to some unknown place the vampire considered suitable. "Why don't we take them back to Val's place? Emmanuel's goons will think we'd be stupid to return, so they won't check there. Princess should be out of harm's way."

"Good idea," Micah said. "I'll make arrangements to have my people watch over them. Mood can take them there."

OKAY, IT'S A PLAN, Fang said. PRINCESS IS ALL RIGHT WITH IT.

Well, that was one worry off Shade's shoulders. And now that the sun was going down, Austin sent his buddies downstairs out first to make sure it was safe. When no other madmen came out of the woodwork, he urged Shade and Sharra into the back seat of the darkened luxury car.

"Keep your heads down," Austin said. "Several cars will be leaving at the same time, to confuse anyone who might be watching."

Feeling like an idiot, Shade leaned over in his seat, out of sight. Sharra did the same, and Tiny Tim growled at the vampire, uncontrollable shivers wracking his small body.

As Sharra tried to comfort the Chihuahua, Shade asked, "Where are we going?"

"I won't tell you that while we're still in hellhound range," Austin said curtly.

Sharra clutched his arm, and though he couldn't see her face for the swirls, fear emanated from her. "Are you sure this is a good idea?" she whispered.

Not really. For all he knew, Austin was planning on taking them out to some remote alley, draining them, and dumping them. "Yes," he lied to calm her. Besides, he didn't really believe Austin would do that. At least, not until the shadow demons had gotten rid of the threat Emmanuel posed to the city. He didn't say any of that aloud, though, knowing the bloodsucker would hear him no matter how low he whispered.

Finally, about ten minutes later, Austin said, "You can sit up now. We weren't followed."

Good—Shade was getting a crick in his neck. He sat up and rubbed his neck, the raised scars from Austin's fangs surprising him anew. "Okay, we're out of hellhound range. Where are we going?"

"To Alejandro's mansion."

"What?" Straight into a whole vein of vampires?

"You know of any place safer?" Austin asked, his tone dry as the desert.

"What is it?" Sharra asked.

"The headquarters for the New Blood Movement," Shade said. And, for her sake, he added, "We'll be safe there." They'd better be.

Austin drove them around to the back of the mansion. "No sense advertising your presence in case anyone's watching. Alejandro knows you're coming."

He took them through the kitchen in the back and into a dining room, both devoid of any personality, unlike the other vampire properties he'd seen. They were obviously just for show since the bloodsuckers didn't need them. Unless they used the long, oval-shaped table for meetings or something.

Sharra plopped down in a dining room chair and looked around at the featureless room. "Oh, great. Now what do we do?"

Shade pulled out his laptop. "I guess we can do more research."

"Yeah, or we could call those people who had their demons removed." She glanced at Austin. "You know who to call?"

"Yes—Lisette will help you." He gave them the phone number, then left, saying, "Stay here. I'll let folks know you're here, find a place for you." He closed the door behind him.

"Good idea," Shade said. He pulled out his phone and dialed the number Austin had given them, then put it on speaker.

Lisette answered with a charming French accent, and Shade

explained what they wanted.

"Ah *oui*, but of course. If you will hold on *un moment*, I will fetch one of them for you."

Soon, someone came on the line. "Hello?" a male voice said. "Who is this?"

"Shade and Sharra, shadow demons." Shade hesitated. "And you?"

"Blaine Williamson, fire—*former* fire demon."

"Are you one of the ones Val Shapiro exorcised the demon from?" Shade asked, just to be sure.

"Yes. But the demon is gone. I'm fully vampire now, you know."

Unfortunately, Shade couldn't tell how the guy felt about it. He wondered how to phrase his questions, but Sharra jumped in without hesitation. "We're thinking of having our demon side exorcised, too. Would you recommend it?"

Blunt, but it did the trick.

Blaine hesitated for a moment, then said, "It's not the same thing at all. I was forced to become a vampire, and mixing that with my demon side sent me into loony land. Taking the demon out made me sane and saved my life, you know?"

Or rather, made him fully undead, he meant. "We understand that," Shade said, "but other than making you sane and a full vampire, how does it feel?"

"Weird, man."

"How so?"

"Well, I don't know what it's like for shadow demons, but for fire demons, there's always this spark deep down in your soul, you know?"

Shade didn't, but he made encouraging sounds.

Blaine continued, "The spark is what helped me create fire. Now, it's gone. Forever. I kinda miss it."

"How has it changed you?"

"I'm a vampire, dude."

Shade sighed. How could he pull the information he needed out of the inarticulate Blaine?

"We know," Sharra said, interrupting. "But surely, you and the other three who were exorcised have talked about the difference. Let's say you were fully human. No vampire, no demon, just mortal. How would that change things for you?"

"Well, it'd suck big time, you know?"

"How would it suck?" Sharra persisted.

"Well, we were kinda used to having these powers, you know? And now that they're gone, there's like this big hole where they used to be. Empty, you know?"

Shade wanted to yell that he knew, already, but didn't want to alienate the guy. "Okay," Shade said, encouragingly. "Tell us more."

"Well, it's not like we're Emo or want to do anything, you know, suicidal, but the drive is gone, man."

"Did it affect your intelligence at all?" Shade wanted to know.

"No, dude. We're all just as smart as we were before. Maybe smarter, you know?"

So he'd always been this way? Reassuring. "Okay, thank you," Shade said. "You've been very helpful."

He hung up and Sharra snorted. "Really helpful, 'you know'?"

Shade chuckled. "Well, he was annoying, but at least we know their intelligence didn't suffer. That is helpful, actually. And it's good to know that though they feel the absence of their powers, they're not zombies or suicidal."

"Yeah, they just have a hole somewhere in their psyche." Sharra thought for a moment. "I could handle that . . . to be fully human."

"Me, too." A dream come true.

She squeezed his hand. "Now we just have to convince your Paladin to help us get rid of this curse."

"Yes, but it won't be easy. And we have to take care of Emmanuel first."

Her mouth twisted in disgust. "Why do we have to wait for them? Can't we just take him out on our own?"

It was tempting, to be in the lead for once, instead of always being relegated to the rear. "No," Shade said regretfully. "Maybe if he was alone, but he has all those minions, and I don't think we could shove them all through a portal. Nor should we. They're misguided, misled by Emmanuel's trickery. They're not evil."

"Okay," Sharra said with a sigh. "But have you created a portal before? On purpose, I mean?"

He winced at the reminder that he was having a problem holding it together. "Yes, but it wasn't all that easy. Do you have a better way of doing it?"

"Maybe. Let me show you."

She demonstrated, then drilled him for about an hour until he could do it himself, then said abruptly, "I'm hungry." She glanced around the dining room. "Think they have any human food in the house?"

"I doubt it, but we could order in."

Shade started to stick his head out the dining room door, then remembered he might freak out any vampires who didn't know what he was. Freaked-out vampires—not a good thing. "You ask," he said, gesturing to Tiny Tim.

Sharra nodded and opened the door. Rosa was outside the door, filing her nails, but obviously guarding them. Keeping them from harm . . . or keeping them prisoner?

"Hi," Sharra said, her hand firmly on her Chihuahua. "We're hungry. You have anything to eat?"

Rosa shrugged. "Come. We will find something or order in."

Austin, coming down the hallway, gestured for Rosa to proceed. "Go on. I'll watch Shade."

Sharra raised her eyebrows at Shade, clearly asking if she should go with Rosa. "It's okay," he told Sharra. "I need to talk to Austin alone."

Now Austin raised his eyebrows, but nodded and closed the door behind him. Taking a seat at the table, he asked, "What do you want to talk about?"

"Val. We need to talk about Val." Shade wasn't looking forward to it, but there were some things that had to be said.

"Yes, we do," Austin agreed, his expression stern.

Surprised the vamp agreed, Shade said, "During the healing, Val and I shared a lot of memories and emotions. She loves me," he said bluntly. "Not you." *Never you.*

Austin smiled and leaned back in the chair. "She thinks she loves you . . . for now. And yet, she's not indifferent to me, is she?"

Unfortunately, that was true. "I just want what's best for Val."

"Do you?" Austin raised an eyebrow in clear disbelief.

"What the heck does that mean?"

"If you did, and you think you're best for her, why don't you tell her that? Why don't you *be* with her?"

Shade shook his head. "It's complicated." And he didn't want to get into his reasons with his rival.

"No, it's very simple. Either you're on her side, or you're not."

"Of course I'm on her side," Shade protested.

Austin tipped his chair forward and grabbed Shade's wrist—tight. Too tight. "No, you're on your own side." The cowboy's gaze bored into Shade's, as if by seeing into his eyes, he could see into his soul.

Let him look. He'd see nothing but the truth. Clenching the fist Austin held, Shade said, "I'm on hers *and* mine. I'm concerned about her, especially her use of the amulet."

"Yeah," Austin said. "That thing worries me." He loosened his grip, but still held on to Shade's wrist, no doubt so he could search for lies in his face.

He wouldn't find any—Shade was about to get very real and honest here. "It worries the books, too."

"The encyclopedia?" Austin asked in surprise.

Shade nodded and explained how he'd been able to communicate with them, how the books warned that the crystal was dangerous, that Val might lose her keeper status, and that they'd asked him to keep it a secret.

Austin frowned. "But how about when you shared memories with Val? Did she learn your secret?"

Startled by the question, Shade ran through the healing session in his mind. "No." He remembered everything from that healing session, and that hadn't come up. It was all about emotions—the more embarrassing, the more they came front and center. "She doesn't know. And we need to work together to get the amulet away from her so she can remain keeper."

"Okay, we're agreed," Austin said. "So how do we do that? I don't think staging an intervention would work with her."

Neither did Shade. She had too many excuses to keep it. "The book said we could get rid of it through a portal Sharra or I can create."

"What if we can't get it away from her?"

"The books did give me another suggestion," Shade said reluctantly, then sighed. He had to tell it all. "The next best thing is to build Lola back up, so she doesn't need the amulet. I can't help her there. Not yet." Not until the demon was exorcised from him, and he didn't have to worry about losing his temper. Shade took a deep breath, not believing he was actually going to say this, then spit it out before he could change his mind. "I give you permission to feed her as often as she needs to bring Lola up to full power."

Austin's mouth quirked in a smile that was anything but humorous. "I don't need your permission."

Shade knew that, but he had felt the need to give it, to be in control so the thought of Val sharing Austin's lust wouldn't send him off the deep end.

"Besides," Austin added with one of those infuriating smiles, "I believe she's more with me now than she is with you."

Exactly what Shade had been worried about. He stuck his face belligerently in Austin's. "That's what you think. But mark my words. As soon as I get rid of my demon, I'm getting Val back. And there's nothing you can do to stop me."

"I don't have to stop you. All I have to do is wait for Val to get tired of waiting for you to grow up. When she's tired . . . when that ship sails, I'm going to be on it. You can make book on that."

Chapter Thirty-Two

Val

WE FINALIZED OUR plans, then headed out separately. Fang and I took my Valkyrie to the mission where Emmanuel had promised another healing. We showed up about an hour before the promised time, hoping Max would be there with Diesel already.

We were in luck. As I suspected, Diesel was scoping out the security already. I glanced down at Fang. "Can you reach Max? Is he being controlled, too?"

YES, HE'S HERE, BUT HE DOESN'T KNOW YET THAT I'M LISTENING IN. SO FAR AS I CAN TELL, HE'S NOT BEING CONTROLLED.

"Will you—"

CAN IT, VAL. I KNOW WHAT TO DO. NOW HUSH SO I CAN DO IT.

I just want to know what's going on.

OKAY, he relented. I'LL KEEP YOU UPDATED. HOLD ON, LET ME CONTACT HIM.

There was silence for a while, and I grew antsy.

STOP FIDGETING, Fang said. I TALKED TO MAX, AND HE'S WILLING TO DO WHAT IT TAKES TO SAVE DIESEL FROM BEING CONTROLLED BY THE BLOOD DEMON.

Thank heavens.

Fang paused. HE SAYS HE JUST WANTS ONE THING IN RETURN FOR HIS HELP.

What?

Fang leapt to his feet, fur bristling. NO WAY!

What? What did he say?

HE WANTS TO DO THE DEED WITH PRINCESS. Fang sounded highly indignant.

Good grief, why?

BECAUSE HE WANTS STRONG HELLHOUND OFFSPRING, OF COURSE, Fang said.

I couldn't even imagine what the puppies of a bulldog and Cavalier mating would look like. "How does he even know about her?"

HE READ IT IN SOMEONE'S MIND YESTERDAY—SOMEONE WHO

WAS HOPING FOR A PUPPY.

That made sense. "Do you think Princess would go along with that?" I asked.

Fang's lip curled in a sneer. DOESN'T MATTER. *I* WON'T GO ALONG WITH IT. Then, saying so I could hear as well, he said, NO WAY, DUDE. FIND YOUR OWN BITCH.

"But Fang, if it will help save Shade . . .?"

He glared at me. WOULD YOU ASK SHADE TO BREED WITH ANOTHER SUCCUBUS TO SAVE ME?

Well, I'd kind of already done that—to save Micah, Gwen, and Princess. "Maybe."

WELL, I WON'T DO THAT TO PRINCESS. FORGET IT.

Max came around the side of the mission to take a leak, and incidentally, take a look at us. A deep gravelly voice joined Fang's in my head. I HAD TO TRY, the bulldog hellhound said to both of us. WHAT DO YOU WANT ME TO DO?

"We want to send Emmanuel back to his own dimension," I explained. "If you can refrain from telling him about the vamps and demons in the audience, we'll use Perdo to incapacitate him and find a way to get him apart from the humans so we can send him back to the hell he came from." Getting him away from the humans was going to be the hard part.

WHAT IF IT DOESN'T WORK? Max asked.

"Then we'll try something else. But this will work."

OKAY, THEN MY DEAL IS THIS—WHETHER IT WORKS ON HIM OR NOT, YOU GOTTA HELP ME GET DIESEL OUT FROM UNDER HIS INFLUENCE.

"No problem."

AND EMMANUEL WILL BE SUSPICIOUS IF I DON'T IDENTIFY ANY OF YOU, SO I MAY HAVE TO POINT OUT A FEW.

He had a point. I didn't like it, but had to admit it was the only option. "Okay, we'll let you know whose identity you can reveal."

ALL RIGHT, Max said, and trotted back around to the front of the church. KEEP ME POSTED.

When he was gone, I asked Fang, "Can we trust him?"

I THINK SO. I HOPE SO.

Me, too. The success of this operation was riding on an unknown hellhound whose primary loyalty was to a Paladin who was being controlled by a blood demon. Not exactly confidence-inspiring. But it was our best shot—we had to try it.

Fang kept me posted as people arrived. Austin brought Shade and Sharra in one of Alejandro's limos with a bunch of New Blood

Movement vampires to watch over them. He brought Gwen, too, which bothered me a bit. What was she doing here?

SHADE SAYS SHE INSISTED ON HELPING. AND NOW THAT MAX IS ON OUR SIDE, WE DON'T HAVE TO RELY ON JUST HUMANS TO GET CLOSE. THERE ARE THREE PEOPLE IN THE CROWD WITH SYRINGES FULL OF PERDO—GWEN, LUDWIG, AND RAMIREZ. HOPEFULLY, ONE OF THEM CAN GET THROUGH TO DIESEL AND EMMANUEL.

I frowned, really wishing Gwen could stay out of this.

SHE'S A VAMPIRE NOW, Fang reminded me. SHE'S MORE THAN CAPABLE OF TAKING CARE OF HERSELF. PLUS, THEY'RE LESS LIKELY TO SUSPECT HER. SHE LOOKS SO INNOCENT.

True, but that didn't mean I had to like it.

I spotted Lieutenant Ramirez in the crowd. His normal healthy skin looked grey and made him appear frail and sickly. Good make-up job.

We ensured everyone arrived in pairs, to make it less likely anyone else would be taken by surprise and turned into Emmanuel's blood slave. We also made sure at least one person of each pair was a demon so Fang could contact everyone. It was much better and more reliable than radios or cell phones. Plus, it was impossible for Emmanuel to overhear if Fang focused on only our people.

Fang told Max to identify the demons and vamps Diesel had already seen, like Austin and me. Hopefully, if he kept his eye on us, one of the three carrying Perdo would be more likely to get close to them.

The crowd tonight was even larger than the one the night before, and they didn't even try to hold it indoors. Word had obviously gotten around, and everyone wanted to be healed or at least take a peek at the guy who dominated the news. Unfortunately, news crews were everywhere, too. That might complicate things. I sure wished I had a flashy neuralizer thingy like the ones in *Men in Black* to make everyone forget anything strange that might happen here tonight.

"Where's Diesel?" I asked Fang softly.

UP BY THE FRONT OF THE MISSION. MAX SAYS EMMANUEL ISN'T HERE YET.

I frowned. It was fifteen minutes past the time when he'd promised to be here. Where was the guy? *Does Max know when he's going to be here?*

NOPE. EMMANUEL DOESN'T TRUST ANYONE ENOUGH TO GIVE THEM HIS SCHEDULE.

Paranoid much? Well, maybe he had good reason to be. And we couldn't take Diesel out of commission until after Emmanuel arrived since it would knock the Paladin out. Might make Emmanuel a tad suspicious.

The crowd was getting restless, and it was a good ten minutes later when the priest finally stood on the low wall again and raised his hands for silence. He got it. "Ladies and gentlemen, I give you . . . Emmanuel!" He made another one of those theatrical gestures, and Emmanuel rose to tower above the crowd on the old well.

He raised his hands so everyone could see the stigmata. The crowd gasped, and a few even fainted. Sheesh. It totally ticked me off that people were thinking of this creep as god-like.

As Emmanuel called for volunteers to come forward and be healed, I murmured to Fang, "Time to take Diesel out of the equation."

GOT IT, Fang confirmed. Then, to everyone in our group, he said, SHOWTIME, PEOPLE.

I'd been hanging at the back, but now I made my way toward the front, using Lola when I had to, to move men out of my way. At this range, she worked plenty well.

Ludwig, Gwen, and Ramirez moved toward the front as well, answering Emmanuel's call for those who needed to be healed. The plan was for them to get close to either Emmanuel or Diesel and try for one of them.

With any luck, as soon as we took him out, he'd lose control of his blood slaves, and we'd be able to denounce him and make everyone think him a fraud.

Diesel stood on an elevated platform where he could survey the crowd. He kept an eye on me and on the others Max had identified. Good—he didn't seem concerned about the people who had the Perdo. Max really was playing on our side.

I stopped well short of the front, so Diesel wouldn't be inclined to warn Emmanuel. As Emmanuel played healer and gave an old woman one of his snake oil elixirs, the man mountain that was Ludwig, the water demon, reached up to grasp Diesel's leg.

I don't know if the Paladin was suspicious of Ludwig's size or his demeanor, but whatever the reason, he resisted. Hard. With one sweep of his hand, he used his telekinetic power to propel Ludwig backward into the crowd, bowling over several people. But while he was distracted by that, Gwen darted forward and sank her hypodermic into Diesel's calf.

He scowled and made a gesture toward her, but couldn't complete it. He crumpled like a used tissue.

YAY. GO, GWEN! Fang exclaimed.

Max added, YOU PROMISED TO GET DIESEL OUT OF HERE SAFELY.

WE WILL, Fang assured him. WE ARE.

Austin was suddenly there, lifting Diesel like he weighed nothing. Some idiots in the crowd screamed, and, in the confusion that followed,

Ramirez managed to inject Emmanuel.

Yes!

But wait. The blood demon didn't crumble. In fact, it didn't seem to affect him much at all.

No!

Emmanuel lurched for a moment then leapt down from his perch, and his minions went nuts. One of them yelled, "Assassins," which was all it took to panic the crowd.

Crap. Now what? I lost sight of him in the crowd, so I reached for him with Lola, but she was too weak. I couldn't find him.

Luckily, Ramirez was paired with Mood, who immediately sent out waves of calm to the crowd. It slowed the minions down a bit, but didn't affect them enough. There were probably too many people for Mood's mojo to work effectively.

Use me, the crystal whispered urgently.

No. Not unless I had to. I'd promised.

You have to.

Maybe. Maybe not.

WATCH OUT, BUDDY, Fang said with a yelp as everyone in front of us tried immediately to get behind us. Afraid he'd be trampled, I picked the hellhound up and bulled my way forward. It wasn't as easy as I thought it'd be, with everyone pushing and shoving. Crap. There were a lot of sick people here. Someone was going to get hurt.

"Tell everyone to help the innocents," I told Fang.

He broadcast it to our group, but I wasn't sure how effective they'd be. Not when the Penitente followers were going berserk. I tried using Lola to reinforce Mood's calming mojo, but she wasn't strong enough to affect more than a few men at a time.

You have to use me now, the crystal insisted.

"I need to use the amulet," I said to Fang.

NO, YOU DON'T, he argued. WE CAN HANDLE THIS WITHOUT YOU GETTING SUCKED INTO ITS DARK NEEDS.

Crap. The only other useful ability I had at the moment was my super strength. I said the spell again and felt the power surge through me, hot and electric. I used it to shove my way to the front, where there were a lot fewer people. Only the minions and the good guys—us—stuck around to slug it out. Emmanuel had disappeared.

"Where's Emmanuel?" I asked Fang as I dropped him, ducked a punch, and used a *savate* kick to take the guy down.

DON'T KNOW, Fang said, leaping into the fray. HE'S GONE. AND MAX LEFT WITH DIESEL AND AUSTIN.

"Then why the heck are we fighting?" I asked, exasperated.

OH, I DON'T KNOW. MAYBE BECAUSE THEY'RE ATTACKING US? Fang snarked.

Okay, had to give him that. After having Fang transmit an order to get the shadow demons out of harm's way, I went Slayer on their asses. I knocked a few of them out before I heard the warning blat of a police siren and a bullhorn telling us to stand down.

Suddenly, the remaining minions took off as if they were allergic to police. Though we had Lieutenant Ramirez on our side, I didn't want to have to explain what was going on, so I told Fang, "Tell everyone to disperse. And make sure the vamps take care of the news crews' memories and film. We don't want this showing up on the six o'clock news." Having vampires on tap was even better than the *Men in Black*.

DONE. MICAH SAYS TO MEET HIM AT THE CLUB.

"Okay."

Fang and I leisurely made our way back to my Valkyrie, like good little law-abiding citizens, not wanting to give the police any reason to stop and detain us. Luckily, the motorcycle's small profile made it easy to weave through parked cars and get out into traffic without incident.

When I arrived at Club Purgatory, Tessa met us at the front door. "Micah wants you to wait in his office."

"Okay. Hey, was anyone injured or arrested?"

She shrugged. "Micah said there were some minor injuries—nothing serious. And the lieutenant ensured no one was arrested. He'll be here soon."

Ah, good news for a change. I was all for that. I smiled at Tessa and headed for Micah's office. It blocked out most of the noise from the club downstairs. Austin was already there, along with Max, strangely enough. Apparently, Micah hadn't been able to make it through the traffic yet.

"You brought Diesel back here?" I asked Austin. "To a cell downstairs?"

He nodded. "Yes, and the dog insisted on coming, too."

DAMN STRAIGHT, Max said. THOUGH IT TOOK ME A WHILE TO GET IT THROUGH HIS THICK HEAD THAT I WASN'T LEAVING DIESEL.

Amused, I wondered how he'd communicated that to a vampire who couldn't hear him.

Fang laughed in my mind. OH, WE HAVE OUR WAYS.

I could vouch for that.

Micah arrived then, just as I was asking Austin, "Did Shade and Sharra get away okay? And Gwen? And . . . your friends?" I wasn't quite sure how to refer to the rest of the bloodsuckers without offending him.

"Gwen's fine," Austin assured me. "And the shadow demons are safe. There were no serious injuries amongst the Movement."

"Good," Micah said and turned to Max. "Is Diesel still out of it?"

I DON'T KNOW. CAN'T READ HIM.

"Oh, that's right. He can't communicate with him because of the Perdo," I told Austin. "He'll be affected for a while, but we won't be able to get any intel out of him until Emmanuel's influence is gone." I looked down at Max again. "Any idea when that might be?"

Max harrumphed. SHOULD BE PRETTY SOON, I THINK. BUT YOU MIGHT WANNA MAKE SURE THE ASSHOLE'S CONTROL RUBS OFF BEFORE THE PERDO DOES. NO TELLING WHAT'LL HAPPEN OTHERWISE.

I had a sudden vision of the telekinetic Diesel bending steel bars, blasting through the door, and coming after us. Not good.

CAN HE ACTUALLY DO THAT? Fang asked Max. BEND BARS AND STUFF?

The bulldog managed a shrug. MAYBE, he said in his gravelly voice.

Real helpful. I wondered if he really didn't know, or if he just really didn't want to tell us. When neither hellhound clued me in, I repeated the exchange to Austin. "Maybe we should give him more Perdo," I suggested to Micah. "As insurance."

He nodded. "I have more downstairs. Let's check on him."

We trooped downstairs and found Diesel in the cell next to Jorge. They couldn't see each other, but Jorge was yelling at Diesel in Spanish.

The tan, bald dude in the leather duster didn't look so badass now. He was holding his head like it was a fragile thing about to pop. I knew how that felt, having been through it myself.

He winced when he saw us. "Can you shut him up, please?" he asked.

"Gladly," I said. Especially since Jorge had turned his curses against us. At least, I assumed that's what he was doing—I didn't understand much Spanish. Not that I really wanted to know.

Moron—if we let him go, Emmanuel would kill him like the other guy I'd controlled. Reaching out with Lola, I clutched him right in his chakras and said, "Sit down and shut up."

He obeyed.

Diesel glanced at me with one eye, the other still wincing. "Nice trick. How'd you do it?"

I shrugged. "My innate charm."

"Max!" Diesel cried when he caught sight of the hellhound. "I wondered what happened to you."

"Perdo," I explained.

I didn't have to say more. "Oh," Diesel said and waved his hand experimentally. "So that's why—"

When he broke off, I said, "Yes, that's why your telekinesis isn't working. And we know who you are. What we don't know is who owns your mind right now."

"I do," he said, sounding indignant.

"Does he?" Micah asked Max.

HOW WOULD I KNOW? the hellhound growled. I CAN'T READ HIM RIGHT NOW, REMEMBER?

Austin looked at me. "I take it Max can't tell. Having been in his situation myself, I don't think he's under control, but you can test it, can't you?"

"I was just about to do that." I hadn't been able to reach Jorge or the others with Lola when they were under Emmanuel's control. So, if Lola worked . . .

I reached for Diesel and let Lola's tentacles sink into him. Though she'd been weakened by the spell, she still had enough juice for this. And since I was able to feel his chakras, it appeared as if he was no longer under Emmanuel's influence. But, just to test it, I told him, "Stand up and tell us your real name."

He stood up abruptly and barked, "Hadley Percy Shelley."

Sheesh. No wonder he went by another name. I glanced at Max for confirmation.

YEP, the bulldog confirmed. BUT I ADVISE YOU TO FORGET IT REAL FAST.

I let go of Diesel. "Sorry about that. But we had to be sure of you before we let the Perdo wear off."

He glared at me. "Succubus, huh?"

I nodded. "And at Max's request, all of us will now forget we ever heard your real name."

He pointedly ignored that. "Well, now that you're sure of me," he said sarcastically, "can I get out of this damned cell?"

"Of course," Micah said, and hurried forward to unlock it. "Let's adjourn to my office. I have something for your headache there."

"Good," Diesel said and followed Micah out of the room.

When we got back to the office, the New Mexico Paladin still seemed a bit surly, but gulped down the painkillers and asked, "Who are you people?"

Micah leaned forward to shake his hand. "I'm Micah Blackburn, leader of the San Antonio Demon Underground, and this is my Paladin, Val Shapiro."

Diesel eyed me dubiously. "Paladin, huh? There must be more to you than can be seen with the naked eye."

"Yep, just like you."

Fang chuckled at that, and even Max let out a snort.

"And this is Fang, my hellhound, and Austin," I said as Austin shook his hand. "He's one of our liaisons to the New Blood Movement."

Diesel eyed him thoughtfully. "One of the good vamps, huh?"

"Yes," Micah said firmly.

"No problem here," Diesel said, holding up his hands. "But sometimes it's hard to tell the good guys from the bad without a scorecard."

I grimaced. "I know. And you were one of the bad guys yourself, not so long ago."

"Not by choice," he assured me.

"We're aware of that," Micah said. "But now that you're back to your senses, we can use your help to get rid of Emmanuel."

"Good," Diesel said with a curl of his lip. "I owe that bastard plenty."

"And you'll be able to help us give it to him," Micah assured him. "That is, if you remember everything that happened while you were being controlled. Some of our people were ordered to forget."

"He never expected me to escape his clutches, so I remember everything." Diesel's smile turned nasty. "And payback's a bitch. What do you need to know?"

Chapter Thirty-Three

Val

WITH DIESEL'S HELP, we learned where Emmanuel was hiding out and that he had twenty-five or so followers here in Texas. But the secretive blood demon didn't often reveal his whereabouts, so with any luck, there would be a lot fewer at his headquarters.

"We can't count on that," Diesel said. "I think he'll draw everyone in, just in case. He must know I'm compromised. He'll move as soon as he can."

"Then we need to go right away," I insisted. "Before he has a chance to regroup."

"Yes," Micah said. "I don't know who I'll be able to get on such short notice, but I'll send as many demons there to help as possible."

"Alejandro will send some people as well," Austin promised.

"I'll call in the SCU," Ramirez said.

I slanted him a worried look. "I'm not sure that's such a good idea. I know they're good, but they're all human and no match for his much stronger henchmen."

Ramirez nodded. "I don't intend for them to engage, but to guard the perimeter for you."

Thank goodness. "We'll need the shadow demons, too," I reminded Austin.

He nodded. "I'll have them there. Do you need Luis to bring you some weapons?"

"No, I have everything I need." Between Lola, the strength spell, and the amulet, I should be good to go.

Austin held his hand out. "Gimme."

I played dumb. "What?"

"Give me the amulet," he repeated. "You promised, Val. And don't worry, if we think it's necessary for you to use it, I'll give it back to you. But only if it's absolutely necessary."

Well, it wasn't ideal, but it would do. I handed it over and watched him put it in his back pocket. And, just in case they wouldn't let me use it, I changed my mind about weapons. I took my crossbow, sword, and a few stakes. I might not need any of them, but they made me feel better. "Okay," I said. "Let's go."

Diesel directed us to Emmanuel's hide-out, a high-faluting mansion not far from Alejandro's. Sheesh. Either being a blood demon paid really well, or he'd coerced some people into renting it to him. Heck, with his abilities, they might have just given it to him. We fanned out unobtrusively to surround the place. There were only a few each of the vamps and demons so far. Enough to tackle this place?

DOESN'T MATTER, Max said. WE NEED TO DO IT NOW. HE'S INSIDE, BUT WON'T STAY THERE LONG.

Good. "Do you know how many followers are in there with him?

NO, I CAN'T READ THEIR MINDS.

NO OTHER DEMONS, Fang explained. OR VAMPS. BUT MAX IS RIGHT—EMMANUEL IS GETTING READY TO LEAVE.

We'd just have to wing it, then, and catch him inside before he took off. "What's the best way to get inside?" I asked Diesel.

He shrugged. "There isn't one, not a quiet one anyway. He keeps all the doors and windows locked, so you'll have to break in. That'll give us away for sure."

"Put someone at each door and window," Ramirez said. "And all go in at the same time."

Swiftly, we assigned locations to everyone. I was going in the front door since Fang said Emmanuel was on the ground floor. Austin and Fang were going in with me. Couldn't shake them even if I wanted to, and frankly, didn't want to. "Okay, we need to go now." I glanced at Austin. "Are the shadow demons on their way?"

"Yes, they're here already, in a car guarded by some vamps. I'll have them brought in when we need them."

"Okay. Let's do this. And try not to kill any humans."

We took our positions, and, when Ramirez gave us the signal, Austin, Fang, and I all hit the front door simultaneously. The hinges gave way, and the door slammed straight down to the floor. It might have been solid oak, but it was no match for the combined strength of a vamp and my strength spell. Oh, and Fang, of course.

YEAH, AND DON'T YOU FORGET IT.

We leapt on top of the door, ready for action, the sound of glass breaking as others made their own dramatic entries. The door opened up into a large living area with a marble floor and a grand staircase going up the center and curving to both sides. Empty. Too bad no one caught our cool entrance.

But they soon came boiling out of the woodwork like cockroaches, about six of them, straight for us.

"A little help here," I called.

"Got it," Diesel yelled from the window on the right, his black leather duster flaring as he threw out his hand and used his telekinetic powers to sweep three of them into the wall.

"Go," Austin yelled as he blocked the charge of one guy who seemed intent on stopping us with his bare hands. "Find Emmanuel."

THIS WAY, Fang said, and took off running.

"Cover me," I yelled to Diesel and heard Max barking orders to the other demons in the room. I shoved one would-be attacker aside and dodged the others to charge after Fang who was acting as a furry beacon running straight to the blood demon.

Emmanuel was in a room at the back of the house that was probably intended to be used as a bedroom, but he had the walls shrouded in black, with an altar that held gleaming knives and a silver cup. For them to worship him? Yuck.

I took all this in an instant before I focused on the most important thing—Emmanuel. He knelt next to a man, cupping his head in one hand while holding his other palm to the man's mouth. Making him drink his blood? Ewwww.

When he saw us, he hissed, "Defend your savior."

The minion leapt to his feet, a fanatical gleam in his eyes, and snatched a knife from the altar, swiping it at me.

How could I stop him without killing him?

WE GOT THIS, Fang said, and he and Max hit the guy square in the crotch—Fang's signature move.

HEY, WHEN YOU'RE MY SIZE, YOU GOTTA STICK WITH WHAT WORKS.

The man went down, moaning, his eyes rolling back in his head. Max chomped down on the guy's hand. He released it, then Max picked up the hilt in his mouth and tossed the weapon in the corner.

Good hellhound.

Another follower tackled me, allowing Emmanuel to dart past us, yelling, "To me, to me." He ran out into the great room.

I scrambled away from the minion and left him to the dogs then followed hot on the blood demon's heels.

It was pandemonium out there. Vamps and minions fought hand to hand while Andrew fired out balls of flame to light their clothing on fire, Ludwig shot water torpedoes to bowl them down, and Diesel slammed them up against walls.

But the worst part of all, Shade and Sharra stood a few steps up on the staircase, looking like a couple of major swirl fests, cycling much faster than I'd ever seen before. A sickly green portal built between their outstretched arms, shot through with silent, creepy lightning. What the heck? Why were they here? It was too early.

THEIR IDEA, Fang said in disgust. THEY WANTED TO HELP.

"Use it, Val," Shade called out. "Send Emmanuel back."

Crap. Way to telegraph our plan. I leapt over a couple of fallen minions and raced toward the stairs.

Unfortunately, Emmanuel got there first, then grabbed Sharra by the throat. "Close it," he ordered Shade then pointed at me. "And you—don't come any closer or I'll kill her."

The portal faltered, and so did I, at the bottom of the stairs. I couldn't let either of the shadow demons get hurt. His minions dashed to defend him, eight of them intent holding the stairs against all comers. I couldn't get through without killing humans, or at least hurting them very badly. But at this point, I was willing to do just that.

NO, Fang said. YOU'D NEVER FORGIVE YOURSELF.

Crap, he was right.

Sharra fought, scratching for Emmanuel's eyes, and distracted him. That was my chance.

I knocked one guy out and turned around to find Austin. "Give me the amulet," I yelled at him. I had no choice—it was our only chance.

"No," he said as grappled with another minion.

"Damn it, I need it."

"No," Austin said, choking him until he passed out. "You're Val Shapiro, the Slayer. You don't need the help of a magickal object."

Use me now, the amulet called.

"Do something," Shade yelled. He was frantically trying to pull Sharra out of Emmanuel's hold, but the blood demon was too strong for him. Emmanuel held Sharra's head in a vise-like grip, shoving his bloody palm against her mouth. Gross.

Worse, the portal seemed to be growing without control, and I could see the flash of faces and body parts in the green cloud. Oh, crap. Demons trying to come through?

Well, if I couldn't use magick, I'd fall back on my Slayer skills. I backed up, then ran at the stairs full of angry followers grappling with demons and vamps. I took a flying leap, kicked one idiot in the face who tried to stop me, and bowled into the blood and shadow demons, ensuring the shadow demons rolled *away* from the cloud. They had to stay on this side of the portal.

We all went down in a chaotic mess of squirming arms and legs.

Sharra spit out blood. Emmanuel grinned evilly and grabbed her head and parted his lips. No! I had to stop him from ordering her to do something she'd always regret. I drew my sword and swung it at

Emmanuel's throat, desperate to stop him.

But I'd forgotten the strength spell, and the sword sliced through Emmanuel's neck like it was made of soft cheese. His head fell with a splat and bounced down the stairs.

Austin kicked it viciously. "That's for Cyndi Krupa."

It went flying into an open door.

AND HE SCORES! Fang cheered.

That took care of Emmanuel. Permanently. Who knew the mundane method would be the one that worked?

But if I'd hoped that would release his followers and make them all compliant, I was sorely disappointed. They screamed in rage and went berserk.

Chapter Thirty-Four

Val

ALL OF A SUDDEN, every single one of the minions seemed intent on murdering me. Just because I'd chopped off the head of their so-called savior? No sense of humor, obviously.

They left whoever they'd been fighting and all charged toward me.

Crap. There were about a dozen still standing. I couldn't fight them off by myself, and they might hurt Shade or Sharra. "Get upstairs," I yelled at the shadow demons. Catching a glimpse of bilious green out of the corner of my eye, I added, "And close that damned portal." We didn't need it anymore, and the thing was dangerous.

"Help Val," I heard Austin yell.

I backed up a step and held my sword horizontally in front of me, hoping that would deter some of the minions from wanting to get cut, but they didn't even care. Two of them sliced themselves on the sword to tackle me and knock it out of my hand, then the two of them and a third guy landed on top of me. They pinned me and took advantage of my surprise to pummel me. They'd been fed Emmanuel's blood recently, 'cause none of them were in the least affected by Lola, and their fists packed a heck of a punch. That hurt, damn it.

Austin, looking royally pissed, yanked one off of me. Fang and Max attacked another one's head, leaving me able to catch the third one in the stomach with both feet. I shoved, and he went flying down the stairs and hit his head on the newel post.

YOOOOOOU'RE OUT! Fang caroled with glee.

Another leapt up the stairs to grab me, but stopped short, bowed backward with his arms and legs jerking, then fell, wires attached to his back. Oh, good—Ramirez and his men had entered the fray, wielding Tasers. And now they were confining the tased followers with cuffs and zip ties.

I stood, chest heaving, as I surveyed the scene and tried to figure out where to join the fray again. My sword lay nearby, still, so I grabbed it, not wanting it to be used against me or anyone else I cared about.

"Val, above you," Austin yelled.

I spun and brought up the sword just in time to block the swing of a huge blond man who was just trying to sweep me out of his way. Where'd he come from?

THAT'S NOT A MAN, THAT'S A DEMON, Fang said as he ran by. A *FULL* DEMON.

What the heck? I glanced up and saw the roiling green cloud, now about six feet in diameter. An arm appeared, and I slashed at it. It disappeared.

"Close it," I yelled at Shade as the demon ran by me.

"I can't," he shouted back, arms splayed about a foot from the cloud, looking as though he was grappling with it.

Idiot—we couldn't let any more through and had to stop the one who had already made it. Where was Sharra? She ought to be helping him. I bellowed, "Stop that demon," pointing at him with the sword.

Ludwig, just as big as the demon who had come through, smashed the guy down with a Hulk-sized fist of water. The demon raised his arm to use some kind of unknown power, but he didn't get the chance. Diesel, bless him, shoved his arm forward with a mighty heave, and the demon went sailing back through the portal.

"Shut it down," I screamed at Shade again, worried that more demons would come through, or that he'd kill himself before he let that happen.

"Can't," Shade gasped out, hunched over at the base of the thing, his clawed hands pushing at the cloud as if he were suffering torture.

"Help him," Austin said. "We've got this."

He and Diesel and the two hellhounds acted as a living shield to keep the other demons off me as I whirled to see what was going on with Shade and the portal. He still knelt at the base of it as a demon arm and leg came through. I leapt up to cut at them, and they retreated. Why wouldn't he close it? Had he lost control of his emotions?

Well, crap. I'd have to help him. I tried Lola, but she was too weak.

Use me, the crystal called.

I couldn't take time for Mother-may-I when a horde of demons was waiting to come through into this world to rape and pillage. I knew exactly where the crystal was. I ran down to where Austin was and tried to grab it from his pocket.

"No," Austin said and shoved my hand away.

Damn it, no time to argue. I ripped off his pocket and snatched the amulet as it fell.

Yes, the crystal cried.

I used it to augment Lola's meager powers and slammed into Shade's chakras. No time to waste on delicate sensibilities. If he couldn't control his temper or the cloud, I'd do it for him. "Close the portal. Now!" I ordered him.

Under my control, Shade had no choice but to do just that. He straightened, face intent, and reached out to the boiling green cloud. He opened his arms wide, then brought them together slowly, painfully, as the portal shrunk until it was gone.

Once that threat disappeared, I was able to breathe easier. Especially once I noticed that all of Emmanuel's remaining followers—the ones who'd attacked us, anyway—had been incapacitated and rounded up for Ramirez to take care of. The poor great room, on the other hand, looked like a hurricane had swept through, scorched by fire, scourged by water, and shattered by burly men.

"Good job," Austin said, grinning at me.

"The hell it was," Shade said, charging down the stairs to yell in my face. "You broke your promise, Val. Now let me use my powers."

"What's wrong?"

He grabbed my shoulders. "Sharra's on the other side."

Oh, crap. What had I done? "What?" I asked incredulously. "How?"

"A demon snatched her up and hauled her through. *That's* why I didn't want to close it. Let me open it. Now."

He released me, then concentrated, and a small green ball of interdimensional energy formed in front of him.

"You can't do that," Austin protested. "There's a horde of demons waiting to come through."

HE'S RIGHT, Max said in his gravelly voice. I CAN SENSE DOZENS OF THEM THROUGH THERE, ALL WAITING TO LEAP INTO THIS WORLD.

Grimly, Diesel added, "We don't have the manpower to stop full demons. That would be a disaster."

"But, my sister's in danger," Shade protested. "They'll kill her!"

NO, Max said, sounding regretful. I'M SORRY, BOY. SHE'S ALREADY DEAD. THAT BIG DEMON BROKE HER NECK RIGHT BEFORE SHE WENT THROUGH THE PORTAL. I FELT HER GO.

Horror filled me. I felt so bad for Shade. And Sharra, too, of course. She didn't deserve to go this way.

"You don't know that for sure," Shade said, totally pissed now.

YES, I DO, Max answered. I CAN READ THE DEMONS THROUGH THE SMALL PORTAL YOU HAVE OPEN. SHE'S NOT THERE. SHE'S GONE, SON.

"No," Shade said. "Damn it, we can't just leave her there." He opened the portal wider.

STOP IT, Fang said. MAX IS RIGHT. SHE'S DEAD, SHADE. YOU CAN'T

HELP HER NOW.

Shade whirled on him. "I can bring her body back. That's the least I can do. Val, help me."

When I hesitated, Austin said, "No, Val, make him close it."

Trying to ignore Shade's pleading eyes, I reminded Austin, "I'd have to use the amulet."

Austin grimaced but said, "Do it." He frowned at Shade. "Think, man. You can't do this, or we'll all die."

"I don't care. I can't abandon her. Ever." Shade turned to me. "Come on, Val. You can't do this now, not when I need you the most. Who are you going to choose? Austin or me?"

He was strung so tight, he might just explode. But he was wrong. This wasn't a choice between two men. I shook my head. "It's not a matter of—"

"Forget it, Val. No time for mealy-mouthed platitudes. Choose. Choose *me* for a change," Shade challenged, looking defiant, hopeful, and resigned all at once.

I closed my eyes against the pain. Leave Sharra's body in a demon hell . . . or let evil demons infest San Antonio? There was only one possible choice.

I sighed and gave him a pleading glance. "I can't, Shade." Couldn't he see that? "I'm so sorry," I whispered.

His shocked look spoke volumes. I'd lost him now, forever. A great pressure rose in my chest, threatening . . . what? Tears, a meltdown, pure relief?

I wasn't sure, but whatever it was, I beat it back. I had to. I was the Paladin.

"Close it, Shade." Once more, I used the amulet to force Shade to bow to my will. And this time, no one tried to stop me.

With an agonized expression, Shade turned to the portal and made it shrink, leaving the body of his twin sister on the other side.

When it was done, Shade just stared at it, defeated.

"Can't you see?" I released him and pleaded with him to understand. "This is about far more than you and me and Austin. It's about the whole *world*."

YOU COULDN'T DO ANYTHING ELSE, Fang assured me.

"You don't get it, do you?" Shade sneered.

"Yes, I get it," I said softly. "What you don't get is *me*. Not if you think I'd ever do such a thing. What kind of a person would put their own selfish desires against the needs of the entire world?"

And the answer struck me—that's what Shade wanted to do.

Shade just shook his head. "We're through, Val. Completely and utterly through."

If he hadn't said it, I would have.

As he stormed off, I let my gaze slide to Austin. His answering glance was compassionate. "I had to," I said, feeling the need to defend myself.

"I know," he said softly.

He got it. He got me. I knew that, now.

Austin's gaze narrowed on Shade's retreating back. "Do you think he'll try opening the portal again?"

Crap, I hadn't thought of that.

NO, Fang answered. HE KNOWS HE CAN'T GO THROUGH IT HIMSELF. AND MICAH WILL ENSURE NO ONE TRIES TO HELP HIM.

Max grunted agreement. THE BOY WAS SPEAKING IN THE HEAT OF THE MOMENT. HE REGRETS ASKING YOU TO DO THIS THING.

Too little, too late.

I nodded and sighed, noticing I still held the amulet clutched in my fist. I was sick of it. Sick of having the thing talk to me, sick of trying to defend my use of it, and sick of forcing people to do my bidding with it. "Here," I said, thrusting it at Austin.

He weighed it in his hand and gave me a quizzical glance. "What do you want me to do with it?"

"I don't care. Just get it out of my sight." I put my hands on my hips. "We have clean-up to do."

Austin shook his head ruefully and tucked it in his jacket pocket. "Whatever you say . . . darlin'."

Epilogue

Val

TWO DAYS LATER, Fang and I were finally alone in my townhouse, crashed on the couch watching prime time television. We'd cleaned up the mess Emmanuel had made, and Shade had gone into hiding. Max must have been right about his change of heart, because we didn't hear anything about bilious green clouds or portals to another world.

Now that the field was clear, you'd think Austin would come by to see me. Yeah . . . not so much. He must be busy with those duties of his now that he didn't have to stay close to protect me.

I sighed, allowing myself a little pity party. No doubt everyone else was off somewhere with their significant others, celebrating Valentine's Day. All over the country, women were being gifted with flowers, chocolate, and teddy bears, while I didn't receive so much as a card to show someone cared about me. Ironic that I, the girl named Valentine, had never actually received a real valentine in my life. The ones from my mom, stepdad, and sister didn't count.

Fang jumped up on the couch and gave me a big slurpy kiss on the cheek. I LOVE YOU, VAL.

I grinned and rubbed his soft, fuzzy ears as I surreptitiously wiped the slime from my face. "I know you do, Fang. And you're the best thing that's ever happened to me. But—"

The door suddenly flew open behind me, and I leapt off the couch. What the—

It was Gwen, looking flustered and upset. "You have to come now," she said. "Hurry."

SADDLE UP, Fang said, and charged after Gwen.

I didn't know what the problem was, but if Gwen was in trouble, I had to help her. I paused only to grab my bag o' weapons from beside the door and ran after them.

"Come on," Gwen said, motioning me into her car where it sat idling by the curb. "Get in. There's no time to waste."

Fang and I jumped in, and I barely had time to fasten my seatbelt before she was peeling out of there like a mob of demons was nipping at her back tires.

"What's wrong?" I asked as she careened through the streets.

"Zombies," she bit out, keeping her eyes on the road.

"Zombies? Are you kidding me? Zombies don't exist." Did they?

I'VE HEARD OF STRANGER THINGS, Fang said. LIKE VAMPIRES AND DEMONS.

He had a point.

"That's what Micah said," Gwen told me. "He asked me to come get you."

"But—"

"Hush, please," Gwen said urgently. "I need to concentrate on my driving."

Well, crap. I wracked my brain, trying to remember what I knew about zombies. All I knew was that they were risen from the dead, couldn't feel pain, and craved brains. At least, that's how the movies portrayed them. Now I wished I'd grabbed the encyclopedia. But I didn't remember anything about the walking undead in there and had no idea how to make them really dead dead.

I still wasn't back up to full strength. Would Lola work on them? Would I need the strength spell? If the zombies moved as slowly as the ones in the movies, I might be okay.

YOU'LL HANDLE IT JUST FINE, Fang assured me. YOU ALWAYS DO.

"Just tell me this," I said to Gwen. "Where are we going?"

"Club Purgatory," she said, her gaze intense on the road ahead.

Micah's place? Worried, I called Micah to find out what was going on. No answer. Crap. That didn't bode well. Tessa didn't answer, either.

A few hair-raising minutes later, Gwen pulled up to Club Purgatory, and we all jumped out and ran to the front door where the doorman, dressed like Bela Lugosi, stood waiting.

"Where?" Gwen gasped out.

"The Ladies' Lounge," he said, and pointed in that direction.

That's where Micah danced. Was he onstage tonight? Was he in danger?

I flew through to the lounge and shoved open the door. It was dark and quiet—too quiet. Bodies lay strewn all over the stage, and the women in the audience were all slumped over the tables. Oh, crap. What had happened here?

I looked around for something to fight, but nothing was stirring.

"There," Gwen said, pointing.

My gaze followed her pointed finger to the stage where one body was moving feebly. I started to head for it, but Fang leapt in front of me. NO WAIT, THERE'S SOMETHING OFF HERE.

Ya think? Eerie music began to play offstage, then the body lurched to its feet, dressed in the rags of a man's suit, its face white and what looked like blood staining the bottom of its mouth. But the hair—I recognized the hair and eyes. "Is that Micah?" Oh, crap. What had happened to him?

More white-faced bodies rose jerkily from the stage, dressed in rags, and took shuffling steps toward the audience. I froze, not knowing how to handle any of this.

The music intensified, and the zombies stopped shuffling and started moving in unison . . . to the music.

What the heck?

Then it dawned on me—the music was Michael Jackson's "Thriller," and they were *dancing*. Was this a joke?

NOT A JOKE, Fang said, sounding amused. A FLASH MOB.

I took deep breaths, trying to calm the adrenaline that had surged inside me as I watched in stupefaction. Gradually, members of the audience joined the dance—even Gwen—until the only ones not dancing were Fang and me. What the heck?

THIS IS FOR YOU, VAL, Fang told me. A VALENTINE'S DAY GIFT.

For *me*? Something bloomed within me then, something wonderful and special. They had all given up their holiday to do this for me?

Emotion suffused my chest and threatened to swamp me. I covered my slack-jawed mouth as I watched in amazement, trying to pick out the dancers. Some, I knew, were the male strippers who performed at the club. But that big guy, was that Ludwig? And the red-haired one—that had to be Andrew. Surprised, I even saw some members of the Movement and the SCU dancing up there.

Vampires, demons and cops all dressed up as zombies? I couldn't help it—I giggled.

You were in on it? I asked Fang.

WE ALL WERE.

I watched in delight as the "zombies" continued their dance. *Who arranged all this?* I asked Fang.

YOU'LL SEE IN A MINUTE.

The music ended, and the zombies all froze. The lights went out on stage, and a spotlight suddenly hit me, blinding me. I heard one of the dancers jump down from the stage and come toward me.

I shaded my eyes, trying to see, but it was impossible until he was right in front of me. Ah, I got it. This zombie was wearing a cowboy hat.

Austin grinned at me, then removed his hat with a flourish and gave me a sweeping bow, presenting me with a huge bouquet of pink roses from behind his back. "Valentine Shapiro, will you be my valentine?" He lowered his voice. "At least for tonight?"

I couldn't stop grinning. "Best. Present. Ever," I whispered. *So* much better than chocolates and a teddy bear. This was a Valentine's Day worth waiting for.

"Is that a yes?"

I dipped my head to smell the sweet fragrance of the roses, stalling for time.

EVERYONE'S WAITING FOR YOUR ANSWER, Fang reminded me.

Austin *so* got me. Why not? "Yes."

Everyone cheered, the lights came back on, and the zombies headed for the bar. Austin linked my arm in his and led me to a table. "Think you could bring yourself to be mine for more than just one night?"

"Maybe," I hedged, not knowing how I really felt yet.

AH, COME ON, Val, Fang said. LET THE GUY OUT OF HIS MISERY.

Austin had more than proved himself.

"We'll see." I grinned at him. "But I gotta tell you, it's looking reeeeeal good."

Forget You

This story takes place five years before the events in Bite Me, *the first book in the Demon Underground series.*

SHAWN SAT HIDDEN in the shadows inside his adobe home and glared outside at the relentlessly sunny day, hating how it kept him trapped inside. Here, in the desert of New Mexico where people believed in aliens and UFOs, and the brotherhood of *Penitentes* still practiced their self-flagellation ecstasies in secret, *he* was considered weird.

The land of enchantment? Maybe for other people. Other teens. For him . . . not so much. The nice day kept him inside, for fear someone might pass by, even out here in the boonies, and catch a glimpse of the freakish demon boy. *Welcome to another episode of* As the World Spurns, he thought bitterly. Out loud, he muttered, "Being part shadow demon sucks."

Shawn said it more to lash out at his father than because it was true. When he got no reaction, he said it again, louder. Why did his father have to have children, anyway? Why couldn't Shawn have been born to fully human parents?

His father turned away from working on the computer and asked, "What's the problem now?"

Shawn's twin sister, Sharra, came over to rub his shoulders, trying to soothe him. "It's okay, Dad, he's just restless." Then, whispering so only Shawn could hear, she said, "What's wrong with you lately? You act as though you have a burr up your butt all the time. Come on, remember your promise. Don't get mad at Dad—don't let him get mad at you. Take it out on me instead."

Shawn shook his head mutely. It was a stupid promise, even if she did make him pinky swear. How could he take it out on her? Sharra was the only good thing in his life.

Louder, Sharra said, "Come play a game with me."

He glanced at her and scowled. His blond sister's pretty features were hidden by the curse of the shadow demon. Everywhere there should have been skin, all you could see were swirling energy ribbons of golden light. Unfortunately, he matched her, but the ribbons whirling through him weren't so pretty. They looked more like giant worms, dark and grey, endlessly moving through his skin. That's what came of being a shadow demon, existing partly in this dimension, partly in others.

The only time they didn't look like members of a freak show was when they were touching another living being—another non-shadow demon, anyway. That grounded them in this world, making them look and feel fully human. But it hadn't happened since Mom had deserted them, three years ago. Apparently, she couldn't take living with children who looked like monsters anymore. Who could blame her?

"No thanks, I'm not in the mood for games." Shawn knew he sounded sulky, but he didn't care.

"Come on," she wheedled. "Let's play Grand Theft Auto."

"Why? So I can beat the crap out of you again?"

"Don't be so sure about that, Shadow Boy. I've got moves you haven't seen yet."

"Big talk for a loser, Sunshine Girl." Though his father's dumb nicknames usually cheered him up, he wasn't in any mood to be teased into a good humor. Not even by his sister, his best friend, and the better half of their Dynamic Duo. Shawn asked, "Don't you ever get sick of this? Don't you ever wish we could have normal lives, like every other sixteen-year-old on the planet?"

She shrugged. "Of course, but it's not like we can change what we are. What good does it do to complain?"

"So sorry your own existence inconveniences you," his father said. Dark worms swirled through his features, too, so Shawn and Sharra couldn't gauge his feelings by facial expressions. Instead, they'd gotten very good at learning to judge his moods by the tone of his voice. For example, now, his voice was filled with sarcasm, with just a hint of anger.

Sounding horrified, Sharra protested, "I didn't mean it that way."

Of course she didn't. Sharra was the good twin. Shawn was the bad one, the one who always got into trouble. The Dynamic Duo usually balanced each other out—he made Sharra more bold, and she smoothed his rough edges. But not this time.

"I did," Shawn said. "I hate living trapped in this house. How come everyone else can live a normal life, and we have to live like . . . like . . . lepers?" It was bad enough dealing with a cracking voice and a changing body. But when puberty hit, life had turned to crap. He and his sister had started looking like Dad, their awareness constantly moving through other dimensions. It was weird, having strange images and feelings flicker through him from other realities. He still hadn't gotten used to it, though Dad said he would, eventually.

"Don't exaggerate," his father said. "Why don't you talk to some of your online friends?"

The computer was their only real link to the outside world. Through it, their father made a living doing research, and they ordered food, clothing, all the necessities of life. Shawn wanted to work with his father on the computer, to help bring in some cash, but his father wouldn't even let him do that, insisting that he be a kid as long as possible.

Shawn shook his head. "My friends aren't home." Sometimes, when he was online, chatting with friends he'd never be able to meet, Shawn could pretend he was as normal as everyone else. But today, that false sense of normality didn't hack it.

In fact, it really hacked him off. "Why can't we live somewhere else, like Albuquerque?" That's where his friends were right now, at a gaming convention he couldn't attend.

"You know why," his father said, his tone warning Shawn not to push it.

Shawn didn't care. "Yeah, but there's a Demon Underground there."

"I wish I'd never told you about that. As I said before, it's not for us."

"Why not?" Shawn persisted. "At least we'd be around others like us, instead of stuck here in Nowhere, New Mexico."

"No one else is like us." His father's voice had turned curt.

"Maybe not exactly like us, but they're all part demon, right? We could fit in better, maybe have something resembling a real life."

"No." This time, he sounded uncompromising.

But Shawn couldn't leave it alone. "No? Just . . . *no*?" he asked incredulously. "How about an explanation for once, Dad?"

"Don't, Shawn," Sharra whispered. "You *promised*."

Shawn had never broken a promise to his sister before, but this time he shrugged her off. Sharra was too nice, always trying to make peace between the two of them. Well, he didn't want peace.

"Shadow Boy, you're—" his father began.

"Don't call me that," Shawn yelled. He wasn't a baby anymore, to be cajoled by a stupid nickname. Shawn didn't want to be calmed down. He wanted an explanation. He wanted *change*.

Dad turned to Sharra. "Sunshine Girl, maybe you can talk some sense into him." His words were calm, but his tone of voice showed he was trying not to lose it.

"Why should she?" Shawn demanded. "She feels the same way I do. She's just too nice to say it."

"Calm down," Sharra said, shaking his shoulder. "Remember, Dad said it's not good to get angry. You're swirling faster."

Her attempt to soothe him ticked him off more. Damn it, even without a face, his emotions were on display for everyone to see. He shrugged her off. "I can't help it. Don't you hate this as much as I do?"

"Of course, dummy. But what good does it do to get ticked off? It just makes everything worse."

"How can it get worse? It won't change how we look. It won't bring Mom back." Shawn glared at his father, pissed off even more because his father couldn't see Shawn's expression and know how much he hated him at this moment. "Why'd you have children anyway when you knew they'd be freaks like you?"

Sounding like he was trying to rein in his anger, Dad said, "Your mother wanted you."

Shawn snorted in disbelief. "Oh yeah, she wanted us so much that she left as soon as we started changing and looking like a freak show."

"You know she loved you," Dad protested.

He'd heard that before, but actions spoke a whole hell of a lot louder than words. "Oh, yeah? Then why hasn't she come back? She can't even stand to look at us."

His father stood, then paced as if trying to control his temper. "That's her issue, not yours. You and your sister have to be strong to survive in this world."

"I'm *tired* of it," Shawn practically yelled. "Don't you get that? I'm tired of watching the world through the television and the Internet. I want to experience it first-hand like everyone else. Why can't we?"

"Damn it, you know why."

"Please, stop, both of you," Sharra begged.

Shawn ignored her. "Yeah, but we wouldn't be monsters in the Demon Underground," he said, trying to sound reasonable. "Why can't we at least try it out?"

"I have my reasons."

"Like what?"

"I don't like how they're run," his father bit out.

"So you condemn us to a life of eternal boredom?"

"Stop it," Dad said, almost yelling now. "You have no idea what the world is like, how cruel it can be."

"How can we ever learn if you keep us trapped here?" Shawn spat back. As soon as he turned eighteen, he was *so* out of here.

"Shawn, stop it now," Sharra said, grabbing his arm. "You shouldn't get so angry."

"Why?"

"You know why."

Yeah, their father insisted that anger made them lose control of the inter-dimensional energies. But Dad never said why that was bad. He mouthed vague warnings about something awful happening, then kept them constantly drilling, cycling through the dimensions to identify each one by how it felt, showing them which dimensions would allow them to pull different abilities to use. Too bad they never got to actually practice using those abilities.

"I don't care," Shawn said, pulling roughly away from his sister. "He's always warning us about some mythical, horrible thing that will happen, but it never does. Maybe he's lying to keep us quiet."

His father took a step toward him. "You fool, you don't know what you're talking about."

His sister grabbed his arm again. "Shawn, stop it. Can't you see what's happening?" She pointed to the space between him and his father where a bilious green cloud had formed.

"So what? A fluffy green cloud? Big whoop." He turned back to his father. "You say I don't know what I'm talking about? So tell me."

The green cloud grew larger. "You don't want to see me angry," his father warned, though it sounded like he was already way past that.

"Who do you think you are? The hulk?"

"Don't start with me, young man," his father bellowed as lightning flashed in the depths of the cloud.

Shocked, Shawn gulped and took a step back. Maybe he'd gone too far.

Sharra flew to their father, throwing her arms around him. "Daddy, don't. Please, calm down."

Their father took a deep, shuddering breath and the lightning disappeared. Thank heavens. Maybe—

The door suddenly burst open and a large man stood there, his tanned bald head gleaming in the sunlight. He wore jeans and a dusty leather jacket.

Dad shoved Sharra behind him to protect her, and the man thrust an open hand at Dad, then turned his palm sharply as if he were swatting something. Dad flew through the air and slammed up against the wall.

What the . . .? The guy hadn't even touched Dad.

"Shut it down, *now*," Baldy said. He gestured with his other hand and the door slammed shut behind him. "I saw the green glow from outside. Thanks for making it easy to find you."

Fear and shock spiked through Shawn. No one ever came into their home, especially not uninvited. And never anyone with powers like these. He must be some kind of demon.

The anger boiling in Shawn's stomach turned sour, wretched.

Sharra ran to their father again, whispering reassurances, calming him as only she could. As the green cloud faded and shrank, Baldy lowered his hand, and Dad was no longer pinned to the wall.

Something moved at Baldy's feet, and for the first time, Shawn realized he'd brought a dog in with him—an ugly bulldog mix who surprisingly didn't seem at all phased by facing three shadow demons.

WHO YOU CALLING UGLY? a gruff voice said in his head. YOU EVER TAKE A GANDER IN THE MIRROR, BUB?

What? Where had that thought come from?

The dog growled. FROM ME. AIN'T YOU EVER HEARD OF HELLHOUNDS?

The dog *talked*? Weirdly, his gravelly voice made him sound like he should have a cigar stuck in his mouth and a crumpled fedora on his head. *Uh, no,* Shawn thought at him. *I've never heard of hellhounds.*

WELL, NOW YOU HAVE, PAL, AND YOU BETTER ACT REAL NICE 'CAUSE YOUR PAPA HERE COULD BE IN REAL TROUBLE.

What the hell was going on?

Sharra asked the question for him. "What's going on, Dad? Who is this guy?"

"He's a filthy Paladin," their father spat out. "The Underground's executioner."

"Executioner?" Shawn repeated, his voice cracking. Fear pounded through him again, making him light-headed and sick to his stomach. Was this why Dad didn't want to go to the Underground?

"Protector," the man corrected their father. "The Paladin is the protector of the Demon Underground, son. They call me Diesel, and this here is Max."

Diesel . . . like Vin Diesel? And that was supposed to make him feel better?

CHILL, Max told him. HIS REAL NAME IS HADLEY AND THAT JUST DOESN'T INSPIRE THE KIND OF RESPECT A PALADIN NEEDS TO DO HIS JOB, Y'KNOW.

Like Shawn even knew what a Paladin *did*.

Diesel continued, "I know you kids haven't had much contact with the Demon Underground, but we're all part demon there, descendants of full demons. With each successive generation, the demon side gets weaker, the human stronger. We strive to blend in, to help others like ourselves, live normal lives."

"Yeah, we know," Sharra said. "Dad told us all that."

"Did he also tell you that part of our job is also to ensure no other full demons come into this world?"

"No," Shawn said, wishing like hell he could see his father's expression. "So what?"

His father interrupted. "Shawn, Sharra, I'll handle this. Go to your rooms."

No, his father was *not* going to treat them like little kids. "I'm staying," Shawn said belligerently.

"Me, too," Sharra said, coming to stand by his side. She was just as nosy as he was but usually more polite about it. And way more stubborn.

THE KIDS DON'T KNOW, Max said.

Don't know what? Shawn asked the hellhound, but it was obvious Max was talking to Diesel.

Diesel nodded at Max, then said, "Let them stay. Isn't it about time they learned the truth?"

Dad collapsed into a chair and put his head in his hands. "I didn't want them to know, ever."

His father sounded defeated. Sad, even. It scared the hell out of Shawn. Sharra, too, from the way she was clutching his hand so hard it hurt like hell. Maybe he didn't want to know. *Can I take it all back?*

SORRY, KID. IT DOESN'T WORK THAT WAY, Max said. He sounded regretful.

Though Shawn was pretty sure he wouldn't like the answer, he had to know. "Why are you here?" he asked Diesel. And why was his father in trouble?

Diesel didn't take his eyes off his father. "I've been searching for your dad for a long time. We want to talk to him about an incident that happened three years ago."

"What incident?" Sharra asked. Her body was as tense as his was. "What happened?"

Diesel sighed. "When a shadow demon loses control of his emotions, a green cloud forms like the one we saw when we came in here. And when it gets too big, it opens a portal between this world and another dimension."

"A portal?" Shawn asked in disbelief. "You mean like a door?"

"Yes, a door. Why do you think your consciousness shuttles between so many dimensions? You're gatekeepers between them." He gave them an apologetic look. "And one of those dimensions houses full demons like the ones we are descended from. Interbreeding with humans gives the demon's descendants humanity and compassion, but full demons don't have any. They want to get into this world where their powers make them almost god-like, so they can satisfy every base urge they've ever had."

Shawn glanced at his father for confirmation, but he said nothing.

Just sat there, a beaten man, with his head still in his hands.

Diesel continued, "Portals open when shadow demons lose control of their emotions. And the more demon blood you carry, the less control you have."

Shawn and his sister were only one-eighth demon, but Dad was one-fourth, making it twice as difficult for him. Did that mean . . .?

YES, Max confirmed. AND YOU HAD TO KEEP PUSHING HIM, DIDN'T YOU?

Horror rose within Shawn. *I didn't know . . .*

"Dad would never—" Sharra began.

Diesel interrupted her. "It's usually not intentional."

"Why do you think it was our father?" Shawn asked. "It could have been some other shadow demon." Not that he knew any, but if Dad existed, there were probably more somewhere.

"There are no other shadow demons in the US," Diesel said.

"Three years ago is when Mom left," Shawn said, grasping for straws. "Whatever Dad did, it's not his fault. It's hers, for deserting us."

When Diesel looked skeptical, Shawn added, "Ask Max. He can read my mind, he'll tell you."

Diesel shook his head, looking regretful. "Yes, Max can read any part demon's mind, including your father's."

"What does that mean?" Sharra asked, sounding worried.

"Your father accidentally opened a portal three years ago. We knew it was probably him but couldn't find him. I finally tracked him down today. Just in the nick of time, apparently."

"No!" Sharra screamed. "Dad, tell them you didn't."

I'M AFRAID HE DID, Max said. THE DEMON CAUSED A LOT OF DAMAGE, HURT A LOT OF PEOPLE BEFORE WE . . . STOPPED IT.

Killed it, they meant.

When Dad remained silent and didn't say a word, Shawn knew it was true. Fear raised its ugly head again. "So what are you going to do? Murder him, too?"

To Shawn's horror, Diesel didn't deny it. "That's not for me to decide," he said gravely. "We're taking him to face a judgment ritual in Albuquerque. The will of the Underground decides his fate. They might even find him innocent."

But Diesel didn't believe that—Shawn could see it in his face. So far, the dog was the only one they could count on to give them the full unvarnished truth. Shawn stared at the hellhound. "Max, you tell us. What will happen to my father?"

Max sighed. AS DIESEL SAID, THE RITUAL DECIDES.

"Don't give me that crap. Tell it to me straight."

Max glanced up at Diesel and the Paladin nodded, as if giving Max permission. "They deserve to know the truth."

THE UNDERGROUND CAN'T AFFORD TO HAVE A ROGUE SHADOW DEMON JEOPARDIZING THE WORLD. THE JUDGMENT RITUAL WILL PROBABLY SEND HIM TO THE MEMORY EATER.

"What's a Memory Eater?" Sharra asked, sounding horrified.

"The proper term is Lethe," Diesel said. "The Lethe . . . removes harmful memories. Or, in cases where the demon is a potential threat to good order, the Lethe might block his knowledge of how to use his demonic abilities."

"How would that help?" Sharra asked. "I mean, if the portal only forms when he gets mad, wouldn't blocking his memory of how to use his abilities make it harder for him to stop it?"

Diesel's gaze shifted away from them and was silent for a moment before he spoke again, reluctantly. "Since anger triggers the problem, the Lethe would remove his ability to get angry."

"What? Like an emotional lobotomy?" Shawn asked in disbelief.

YES, OR THE DEMON COULD CHOOSE DEATH, IF HE PREFERS, Max added helpfully.

Shawn gulped. Lobotomy or murder were the only choices? No. This wasn't right. He couldn't let this happen. Fear threatened to swamp his senses.

Sharra turned and slugged Shawn in the shoulder as hard as she could. "This is all your fault," she yelled. "You and your wanting to join the Underground."

Stunned by the way his normally meek sister turned on him, Shawn massaged his shoulder where she'd hit him. "I didn't want *this*." Not at the expense of his father's life. "Dad, tell them it isn't so," he pleaded.

"It's true," his father said heavily. "And you deserve to know the whole truth."

"We don't need to know," Sharra said. "Honest, we know you're a good person."

"No, Sunshine Girl, you need to know so you don't make the same mistake I did."

"What about us?" Sharra asked, her voice shaking. "We're shadow demons, too."

"But you've done nothing wrong," Diesel soothed. "The Demon Underground in Albuquerque will take you in, give you a good home, continue to train you to control your powers."

Diesel laid his hand on Dad's shoulder, and now that Dad was grounded in another being of this world, Shawn saw his father's face for the first time in three years. Careworn, looking as if he'd aged five years for each of the three that had passed, Dad looked like an old man, beaten down by life. Worse, scars crisscrossed his face and neck, healed scars Shawn had never seen before. He wanted to tell Diesel to remove his hand and let Dad have his privacy, but he couldn't. He had to know what happened, see his father's face to know it was true.

"What mistake?" Sharra asked in a small voice.

"When your mother left, I followed her, begged her to come back and be there for you children."

He paused, and Shawn had to know. "What did she say?"

"She loved you, she really did, but she wasn't strong enough to handle our life. She couldn't take living in secret anymore, and she'd met a man, a full human, who loved her and wanted to take care of her."

"Mom left us for another man?" Sharra wailed.

Dad nodded, looking sad. "She was going to, yes, so I . . . became angry."

NO WONDER, Max said in disgust. SHE CALLED HER OWN CHILDREN MONSTERS.

Dad shot the hellhound a dirty look. "They didn't need to know that," he said in a clipped tone.

"You read that in Dad's mind?" Sharra asked, sounding as stricken as Shawn felt.

YES. THAT'S WHEN YOUR FATHER GOT MAD.

"I'm sure she didn't mean it," Dad said, looking earnest. "But yes, I got angry. And the damned portal opened." He glared up at Diesel. "I tried to stop the demon that came through. How do you think I got these scars? But I couldn't. He killed your mother and knocked me unconscious."

Shawn gasped. Mom was *dead*? All this time, he thought she'd just left and never come back. He didn't realize . . . he'd never see her again. Tears filled his eyes, and for once, he was glad no one could see his face.

Dad turned to look at Shawn and Sharra, grief-stricken. "I'm sorry I kept it from you. I didn't want you to hurt more than you already do."

THERE'S MORE, ISN'T THERE? Max said.

"Yes." Dad looked at Diesel, remorse in his eyes. "What you don't know is that a second demon came through that day, one I've been trying to track down ever since."

Diesel looked shocked. "Did you find it?"

"No. I've followed every lead I could, but I haven't found any demonic happenings anywhere in the area." He paused. "I think it either went so far underground we can't find it, or it died shortly after it got here. Maybe the first demon killed it."

Diesel shook his head, his mouth a grim line as his hand tightened on Dad's shoulder. "You'd better hope so."

Shame rippled through Shawn. Dad had a good reason for keeping his secrets. All of a sudden, he wished he could time travel back to the events of this morning, back to when he was ignorant of all this, back to when his life hadn't been turned upside-down.

His stomach churned so much he wanted to throw up. Why had he pushed Dad so hard? Why hadn't he left well enough alone, damn it? Instead, he'd just turned everyone's lives into pure and utter crap.

DIESEL DIDN'T GIVE them time to pack much, saying the Underground would send someone back to get their belongings. They took just enough to last for a few days and headed toward Albuquerque in a van with heavily tinted windows. Sharra cuddled up next to Dad the whole way, pointedly ignoring her brother, as Shawn marinated in guilt.

IT'S NOT REALLY YOUR FAULT, YOU KNOW, Max said.

Shawn knew that intellectually, but it didn't *feel* that way, especially since Sharra was so pissed at him. *Tell Sharra that.*

I DID. SHE'S NOT LISTENING TO REASON RIGHT NOW.

Stubborn as always. But Shawn couldn't blame her. *Whose fault is it, then? Diesel's?* he asked the hellhound. After all, if the Paladin hadn't arrived, they wouldn't be on the way to his father's trial. Maybe Dad was right to hate Paladins.

YOU CAN'T BLAME DIESEL FOR DOING HIS JOB, Max said. IF ANYONE IS TO BLAME, IT'S YOUR FATHER, OR MAYBE YOUR MOTHER.

No way. They'd all been doing just fine until Diesel showed up. The Paladin was the one who'd ruined their lives. He brooded all the way to Albuquerque, worrying about what might happen to Dad, to him and his sister, praying with all his might that everything would turn out fine, that Dad would be found innocent of wrongdoing. After all, he hadn't done anything bad on purpose. That had to count for something, right?

They arrived at a bar in Albuquerque, where the Demon Underground had its headquarters, and were rushed down to the spacious basement where a bunch of people sat around in a circle. All conversation died as they came into the room and everyone gawked. Guess they'd never seen a shadow demon before, let alone three.

They practically had to pry Sharra from Dad's side as they seated her and Shawn outside the circle. Max settled himself between them, saying in what sounded like a gruff mental whisper, TOUCH ME AND SHOW THEM YOU'RE MOSTLY HUMAN. THAT MIGHT HELP.

Yeah, he had a point. Though Shawn didn't really want anyone to see how terrified he was right now, he didn't want them to be scared of him, either. He and Sharra grounded themselves by touching Max, and people stared even more at their human faces. He shifted uneasily under the scrutiny. Sheesh, what did it mean if other freaks thought they were weird?

A gray-haired woman came over and took his father's hand so everyone could see him, and led him to the center of the circle. "I'm Kathryn, Albuquerque's Underground leader. We have a quorum here today to form a judgment circle. Would you like to have the ritual now, or wait a few days?"

Please say you'll wait, Shawn begged silently. He had a feeling this was going to go horribly wrong, and he wanted to put it off as long as possible.

"I want it over with," his father said, his face set in hard lines. "I'd like to have the judgment now."

Crap. It was all moving too fast. He needed everything to slow down long enough for him to get a real grip on what was going on, find his options, *fix* this.

"Very well," the woman said. "Please, have a seat."

She led him to a chair at one end of the circle, then sat next to him, keeping her hand on his so everyone could see his face. The Paladin stood behind them, ready to take action in case Dad tried anything.

It wasn't like any trial Shawn had seen on television. Kathryn asked a bunch of questions about what happened, and Dad answered them honestly and completely, telling them the same story Shawn had heard earlier. He didn't even try to defend himself. And, when asked, Max confirmed he was telling the truth.

Horror warred with worry within Shawn. This whole thing was surreal. Shawn desperately wished this was all a dream and that he'd wake up soon because things didn't look so good for Dad right now.

Finally, Kathryn asked, "Does anyone else have anything to add?"

Shawn opened his mouth, but Sharra beat him by a millisecond. "I do," his sister said. "Can I speak?"

The look Kathryn gave them was compassionate but resolved. "Were you a witness to the portal opening?"

"No, but I am a witness to my father's character," Sharra said in a pleading tone. "Doesn't that count?"

Kathryn looked sad. "It isn't customary for non-members to speak unless they are witnesses, but I'll make an exception in your case. Please, say your piece."

Sharra stood and Max shifted to keep contact so everyone could see her face. She took a deep breath, then said, "He's a good father, kind and loving but gives us discipline when we need it. He's been teaching us how to use our powers, how to control them, and make sure that what happened to him will never happen to us. He bugs us all the time about keeping our anger in check and won't allow us to do anything that would jeopardize that. Doesn't that prove he won't allow himself to lose control again?" She looked around, and the faces looking back wore expressions from compassionate to unfeeling. "He only started to lose control this last time because my brother was being so nasty." Sharra shot Shawn a dirty look, and he couldn't help but wince at the truth in her statement.

Sounding more passionate now, Sharra added, "I was calming him down, I always do, but Diesel arrived before I could finish. I promise, if you let him go, I'll watch him and ensure this *never* happens again. Please, please, find him innocent." Her voice broke then, and tears started flowing. She sat down abruptly.

Shawn stood up, carefully keeping contact with Max. "I agree with everything my sister said. We love him . . . we need him. It was an accident—he didn't do it on purpose. You can't do this to him when he doesn't deserve to be punished." He didn't know what else to say, how to convince these indifferent strangers to believe them, so he sat down again, his eyes as watery as his sister's.

"Anyone else?" Kathryn asked. When no one said anything, she rose and said, "Then, we shall conduct the ritual. Soothsayer, if you will?"

As everyone put on dark blue robes and dimmed the lights, Shawn turned to Max. "What do we do?" he whispered.

YOU CAN STAY OUTSIDE THE CIRCLE AND OBSERVE, BUT DON'T TRY TO INTERFERE, OR IT WILL GO BADLY FOR YOUR FATHER.

Shawn glanced at Sharra to see her reaction, but she was still ignoring him. Suddenly, he felt all alone and vulnerable, as if something momentous was about to take place out of his control, and the only one who cared a hoot was the ugly dog at his feet.

The soothsayer—a short, thin guy who couldn't be much older than Shawn—had everyone but Sharra and Shawn sit in the circle, with Dad, Kathryn and the soothsayer on the inside.

The soothsayer, who was the only one wearing a white robe, lit a large candle in the center and asked for silence.

When it was totally silent, the three of them formed a triangle inside the circle, with the candle centered between them.

Kathryn turned to Dad and asked in a formal voice, "Will you accept the judgment of your peers and abide by any decision they make?"

Dad, who now looked swirly, maybe even scary to everyone else, said, "I will."

He sounded resigned, as if he already knew there would be a guilty verdict. Shawn's heart clenched and it hurt so bad he could hardly stand it.

Kathryn took a deep breath, then spoke, sounding solemn. "You have come before us today to be judged for your actions in opening a portal and letting full-blooded demons into our world. We have heard your testimony and are ready to pass judgment. If you would all join hands?"

There was a rustle of fabric around the circle as everyone clasped hands. They closed their eyes and concentrated, and the room seemed to heat up. Shawn desperately wished he could hold someone's hand, too, but Sharra was still angry at him, and he didn't want to try it. Instead, he gripped the rolls on the dog's neck, needing to hold onto something real. *What's going on?* he asked Max silently. *What are they doing?*

THEY ARE FOCUSING THEIR ENERGY ON THE SOOTHSAYER. HE WILL GO INTO A TRANCE AND READ THEIR WILL IN THIS MATTER.

His father's fate was in the hands of one puny little guy? It didn't seem fair.

NO, IT'S IN THE HANDS OF THE UNDERGROUND MEMBERS HERE TODAY, Max told him. SOOTHSAYERS DON'T MAKE MISTAKES.

The short guy raised his hands, palms up, and stared at the ceiling.

"Everyone, repeat after me," Kathryn said. "Demonkind come together to hide, to encourage, to flourish and thrive."

They repeated the words solemnly and warmth flowed across Shawn's skin, raising the hackles on the back of his neck. Some kind of magic?

"*Everyone is important, every one alive.*

"*Our rules are simple, our rules are true.*

"*Follow them faithfully, that you must do.*

"*But one amongst us has broken that trust.*

"*Truth we seek, only right, only just.*"

They repeated every line after Kathryn, and tension built until power, full of truth and foreboding, spiraled around the circle, ruffling hair and clothing, making the candle flame leap higher.

Kathryn looked up from the book to stare at the little guy. "Soothsayer, this shadow demon is accused of opening a portal and admitting full-blooded demons into this world. What is the circle's verdict?"

The soothsayer stared blankly at Kathryn, then said, "Guilty," in an eerie voice.

Oh, crap, no! Shawn let out a disbelieving whimper.

DON'T SAY ANYTHING, Max reminded them quickly.

Sharra gasped but clapped her hands over her mouth.

"And the circle's judgment?" Kathryn asked.

They paused, and Shawn held his breath for what seemed like forever as the soothsayer weighed the intentions of the people of the Underground.

Finally, he turned to Kathryn, his unfocused gaze implacable, and spoke. "There was no malice involved, no intent. The death penalty is not warranted."

Shawn continued holding his breath, growing dizzy, and hoping desperately that meant the sentence would be light.

The soothsayer continued, "But we cannot afford another such incident. Therefore, the shadow demon is sentenced to see the Lethe."

Oh, crap. How much of his father would remain if they did that?

Dad raised his head, pride in his voice. "I claim the right to meet my judgment at my own hand."

Shawn glanced frantically at Kathryn, hoping for a clue. Did that mean what he thought it did? Surely his father wouldn't—

"So be it," the soothsayer said. "Justice is done. So as it has been, so it shall always be."

The circle repeated the words after him. "So as it has been, so it shall always be."

The tension in the circle suddenly released, and the soothsayer seemed to come out of his trance. He blew out the candle.

"No!" Sharra screamed. "How can you do this to us?"

The members of the circle got up silently and filed out of the room, not looking at Dad or them. The only ones who stayed were Kathryn, Diesel, and Max. Kathryn laid a hand on Dad's so they could see his face.

Sharra wiped tears from her face. "What does that mean, Dad, what you said?"

Shawn had a feeling he knew all too well. "You can't," he protested.

"I can, Shadow Boy." His father turned to look at them, deep sorrow in his eyes. "I love you both, but if I met the Lethe, I would be left little more than a vegetable. I can't let them do that, can't allow you to see me like that. Better it all end now."

"No," Sharra sobbed. "Daddy, no!" She threw herself at him, and hugged him tight.

"Your father is right," Kathryn said. "This is a more humane way. I promise you, we'll help him find a way that is painless."

Shawn stared at her incredulously. Like that was supposed to make it better? "When?" he asked, his voice cracking. "When will you do it?"

"Your father will be allowed to put his affairs in order first."

That didn't answer his question, not really, but Shawn said, "Dad? How long?"

Dad didn't answer. Instead, he opened his arms and said, "Come here, Shadow Boy."

Shawn rushed into his arms, not caring that he might look like a baby. This was the last time he might see his father. They hugged each other tight, though Sharra studiously avoided all physical contact with her brother.

His father stroked Shawn's hair. "I'm so proud of both of you. You two are my pride and joy, the only reason I kept on living when your mother left. But you have to be brave for me. Promise me you'll be brave."

"No, Daddy," Sharra said in a thick voice. "I don't want to be brave. I want you."

"I want that, too," Dad said, "but it can't be. I need you to finish your schooling and practice your drills so that you never lose control like I did. I want you to live long, healthy lives. Be a credit to me and to the Underground. Promise?"

It was the only thing he had left to give his father. "I promise," Shawn said fiercely.

Dad let go of them both, holding them away.

"No, I don't want to lose you," Sharra exclaimed, then hauled off and slugged Shawn. "*Do* something."

What the heck did she think he could possibly do to stop this?

His father stilled and his voice changed. "Kathryn, will you find good homes for my children until they're ready to be on their own?"

"Of course," she said. "We'll make arrangements for the two of them to stay here—"

"You've *got* to be kidding," Shawn said, not caring how rude he sounded. Sharra was sobbing again, so Shawn spoke for both of them. "You want us to stay with the people who murdered my father? No way."

"You're right," Kathryn conceded, looking flustered. "I wasn't thinking. We can place you with another Demon Underground, in another state. I'll make arrangements."

"Wait," Sharra said, her voice thick with the effort of crying. "Not together. I don't want to be with my brother anymore. I hate him."

"What?" Shawn asked in disbelief. "You can't mean that. We're the Dynamic Duo, remember?"

"Not anymore," she said fiercely. "This is all your fault. You broke your promise and see what happened? I don't ever want to see you again. I don't even want you to know where I *am*."

Stunned into silence, Shawn could say no more. He could only feel, and what he felt was horrific—lost, betrayed, abandoned by everyone he had ever loved.

Does she really mean it? he asked Max.

SHE DOES NOW, BUT SHE'S UPSET. APPARENTLY, PROMISES ARE VERY IMPORTANT TO HER—SACROSANCT. MAYBE SHE'LL CHANGE HER MIND IN A DAY OR TWO.

But his stubborn twin didn't. For some reason, she'd latched onto Shawn as the scapegoat and blamed everything on him. That was the last he saw of his sister, or his father, since his father didn't want them to have to deal with any more goodbyes.

Shawn and Sharra's emotions were so out of control, the Underground feared they'd open portals accidentally, so they sedated them. And so Shawn stayed numb and foggy throughout the funeral and when they sent Sharra to some secret location. They respected her wishes and wouldn't tell him where.

When Diesel returned, he and Max took Shawn to San Antonio, Texas to meet an older man with dark hair and a smiling face.

"This is Lucas Blackburn, the leader of the Demon Underground here," Diesel said.

"You can live with me," the leader said, smiling down at him. "I have a son a bit older than you. His name's Micah. I'm sure the two of you will get along great."

"Whatever," Shawn said wearily. The man seemed nice enough, but everyone Shawn had ever loved had left him. He couldn't afford to get close to anyone else. It hurt too much now that he'd cut back on the happy pills.

Blackburn glanced down at Max and frowned. "Max tells me you're feeling down. Maybe even . . . suicidal?"

GEE, THANKS, PAL, Shawn shot at Max.

I DON'T WANT YOU TO HURT YOURSELF, Max said gruffly.

"So?" Shawn asked, not caring how surly he sounded. What did he care?

"Well, we might be able to help," Blackburn said.

"How?" Shawn asked. "Can you give me my father back? Can you force my sister to live with me?"

"No," Blackburn said softly, "but, with your permission, we can help you so it doesn't hurt so much."

"No more pills," Shawn said flatly. They made him feel dead inside.

"We have another way to help," the man said in a soothing tone.

Bitterly, Shawn said, "The only way you can do that is if it never happened."

Diesel put a hand on his shoulder. "His Lethe can help you forget what caused the pain."

Not feel this crushing sadness anymore? It was tempting, but he wasn't sure what they meant. "You want to wipe my brain?" Like they threatened to do to his father?

"No," Blackburn assured him. "The Lethe can be very selective about what memories to dull."

Shawn struggled to understand. "You mean I'll forget my family?"

"Not entirely. The memories will be there, but hidden. They'll seem like something that happened to someone else. But you can remember when you want to, when you're ready and willing to deal with the pain."

When Shawn still hesitated, Diesel added, "It won't be the lobotomy you feared for your father. It will help you learn to deal with the shadow side of yourself, keep your emotions in check so you won't have to use drugs."

And that was the best argument yet. If his only other options were to live in a foggy, drug-induced world or one that was depressing as hell, maybe he *should* forget. But wasn't that a bit cowardly?

NOT IF IT HELPS KEEP YOU SANE SO YOU DON'T END UP LIKE YOUR FATHER DID.

Yes, Dad wouldn't want that. And Shawn had promised he would try his best not to. The only problem was, every time Shawn heard his own name, he immediately thought of Sharra's, and he couldn't call himself Shadow Boy without thinking of Sunshine Girl. He doubted this memory loss thing would stick.

THEN CALL YOURSELF SOMETHING ELSE, Max suggested.

"Like what?"

LIKE . . . SHADE, MAYBE?

Shawn weighed it in his mind. Shade? He liked it. It was kind of a combination of shadow and sunshine, but it felt cool and gentle in his mind. "Okay, I'll do it. Bring on the Lethe. And you can call me Shade from now on."

Maybe someday he'd even have the courage to remember everything that had happened.

Acknowledgments

Many thanks to my writer friends who help keep me sane: Jodi Anderson, Donnell Bell, Karen Fox, Laura Hayden, Von Jocks, Sharon Silva, Angel Smits, and Jude Willhoff.

And special thanks to the canine companions who have given me so much love over the years: Princess, Scottie, Lady, Meagan, Caitlin, Bonnie, and Abby. Plus a big hug and smooch to those who share my home and my life today: Mo, Daisy, and Trixie. I don't know what I'd do without them.

Dear Reader

As you can tell from my acknowledgements page, I love dogs and have adopted several dogs from National Mill Dog Rescue, who re-homes dogs that have been used in puppy mills for breeding purposes. They had an auction recently to raise money, and I offered a set of my books plus the opportunity to name a character to be killed by a vampire in this book. Cyndi Krupa won the auction and chose to use her own name. So sorry, Cyndi, that Austin had to kill your namesake in such an awful manner!

Unfortunately, this book took much longer to write than I wanted. I didn't plan—or want—to go so long between books but sometimes, life gets in the way. However, in the interim, I did write a short story about Shade when he was young that's referenced in this book. If you purchased this as an ebook and are interested in reading that account, check out the short story *Forget You*, available in e-book for free as my gift to you. And, I've been busy on another project as well. In the recently released *Magick Rising* anthology, I have a novella set in a different world—*Wolf Rising*, in which a witch has to convince a werewolf to turn her into a lycanthrope before she dies of a deadly disease.

And, of course, there's another book coming to continue the adventures of Val and Fang, tentatively titled *Catch Me*. For more information on this and other stories, watch my website at:

http://www.parkerblue.net

or my Facebook page:

http://www.facebook.com/ParkerBlue

Thanks for joining Val and Fang in their world for another adventure!

—*Parker Blue*
Colorado Springs, CO

7569676R00143

Made in the USA
San Bernardino, CA
09 January 2014